The
MYSTERIOUS
BENEDICT SOCIETY
and the PRISONER'S DILEMMA

Written by Trenton Lee Stewart

illustrations by Diana Sudyka

Megan Tingley Books
LITTLE, BROWN AND COMPANY
New York   Boston

Copyright © 2009 by Trenton Lee Stewart
Illustrations copyright © 2009 by Diana Sudyka
Text in excerpt from *The Secret Keepers* copyright © 2016 by Trenton Lee Stewart
Illustration in excerpt from *The Secret Keepers* © 2016 by Diana Sudyka

Little, Brown and Company

Hachette Book Group
1290 Avenue of the Americas, New York, NY 10104
Visit us at lb-kids.com

Little, Brown and Company is a division of Hachette Book Group, Inc.
The Little, Brown name and logo are trademarks of Hachette Book Group, Inc.

The publisher is not responsible for websites (or their content) that are not owned by the publisher.

First Edition: October 2009

Library of Congress Cataloging-in-Publication Data

Stewart, Trenton Lee.
The mysterious Benedict Society and the prisoner's dilemma / by Trenton Lee Stewart ; illustrated by Diana Sudyka. — 1st ed.
p.   cm.
Summary: When an unexplained blackout engulfs Stonetown, Benedict Society members Reynie, Kate, Sticky, and Constance follow clues on an adventure that threatens to separate them from their families, friends, and even one another.
ISBN 978-0-316-04552-0
[1. Adventure and adventurers — Fiction.   2. Friendship — Fiction.
3. Schools — Fiction.   4. Science fiction.]   I. Sudyka, Diana, ill.   II. Title.
PZ7.S8513Myg 2009
[Fic] — dc22
2009025459

10 9

RRD-C

Printed in the United States of America

For Sam and Jake
—*T.L.S.*

Contents

The Prisoner's Dilemma

In a city called Stonetown, on the third floor of an old, gray-stoned house, a boy named Reynie Muldoon was considering his options. He was locked inside an uncomfortably warm room, and the only way out was to make an unpleasant decision. Worse, locked in the room with him — and none too happy about it — was a particularly outspoken four-year-old named Constance Contraire, who from the outset of their confinement had been reciting ill-tempered poems to express her displeasure. Reynie, though three times Constance's age and probably fifty times as patient, was beginning to feel ill-tempered himself. He had the hot room *and* the cranky girl to endure. Constance couldn't possibly want out more than he did. The problem was what it would cost.

"Can we just review our options?" Reynie said as patiently as he could. "We'll get out sooner, you know, if we come to a decision."

Constance lay on her back with her arms thrown out wide, as if she had collapsed in a desert. "I've already come to a decision," she said, swiveling her pale blue eyes toward Reynie. "You're the one who hasn't made up his mind." She brushed away a wisp of blond hair that clung to her damp forehead, then quickly flung her arm out again, the better to appear downcast and miserable. She panted dramatically.

"We're supposed to be in agreement," Reynie said, keeping his face impassive. Signs of annoyance only encouraged Constance, and she was always on the lookout for them. "You can't just tell me what to do and expect me to go along."

"But that's exactly what I did," said Constance, "and you're taking forever, and I'm roasting!"

"You might consider taking your cardigan off," said Reynie, who as usual had shed his own the moment they came upstairs. (The heating system in this old house was terribly inefficient; the first floor was an icebox, the third floor a furnace.) Constance gave a little start and fumbled at the buttons of her wool cardigan, muttering "better off" and "sweater off" as she did so. Already composing another poem, Reynie realized with chagrin. Her last one had featured a "dull goon" named "Muldoon."

Reynie turned away and began to pace. What should he

do? He knew that Rhonda Kazembe — the administrator of this disagreeable little exercise — would soon return to ask if they'd made up their minds. Evidently their friends Sticky and Kate, locked in a room down the hall, had settled on their own team's decision right away, and now were only waiting for Reynie and Constance. At least that's what Rhonda had said when she checked on them last. For all he knew, she might not have been telling the truth; that might be part of the exercise.

It certainly wouldn't have been their first lesson to contain a hidden twist. Under Rhonda's direction, the children had participated in many curious activities designed to engage their interest and their unusual gifts. Gone were the days of studying in actual classrooms — for security reasons they were unable to attend school — but any odd space in this rambling old house might serve as a classroom, and indeed many had. But this was the first time they had been locked up in the holding rooms, and it was the first exercise in which their choices could result in real — and really unpleasant — consequences.

The children's predicament was based, Rhonda had told them, on an intellectual game called the Prisoner's Dilemma. Sticky, naturally, had read all about it, and at Rhonda's prompting he had explained the premise to his friends.

"There are thousands of variations," Sticky had said (and no doubt he knew them all), "but it's often set up like this: Two criminals are arrested, but the police lack evidence for a major conviction, so they put the prisoners in separate rooms and offer each one the same deal. If one prisoner betrays his friend and testifies against him, while the other prisoner remains silent, the traitor goes free and his partner receives a ten-year prison sentence."

"So much for sticking together," Kate had observed.

"Well, they *can* stick together, right? They can both remain silent. But if they do that, then both are sentenced to six months in jail for a minor charge. So both get punished, although it's a relatively light punishment considering the alternatives."

"And what if each one betrays the other?" Reynie had asked.

"Then they both receive five-year sentences. Not good, obviously, but much better than ten. So the dilemma is that each prisoner must choose to betray the other one or remain silent — without knowing what the other one's going to do."

It was this last part that had gotten so complicated for Reynie, because the more he thought about it — pacing back and forth in this hot room — the more convinced he became that he *did* know. He glanced over at Constance, now making a show of letting her tongue loll out the way dogs do when they're overheated. "Constance, do you think Rhonda was lying about Sticky and Kate making up their minds so fast?"

"No, she was telling the truth," said Constance, who was even better than Reynie at sensing such things — if she was paying attention. You couldn't always count on that.

"That can only mean one thing, then."

Constance rolled her eyes. "To you, maybe."

"Yes, to me," Reynie sighed. Although in some respects he seemed the most average of boys — with average brown hair and eyes, an average fair complexion, and an average inability to keep his shirt tucked in — Reynie was anything but average when it came to figuring things out. That included people, especially such close friends as Sticky Washington and Kate Wetherall, whom he knew better than anyone. If Sticky and Kate had made their decision so quickly, then it was clear to Reynie what they had decided. Less clear was what to do about it.

Reynie continued his pacing. If only there weren't real consequences! But they were real enough, all right, even if they weren't actual prison sentences. Rhonda had carefully explained them all:

The children would be split into two teams of "prisoners." If both teams chose Option A — to remain silent — then both would receive extra kitchen duty for the rest of the day. (No small task, for including the children's families there were thirteen people residing in this house, and every meal produced a shocking quantity of dishes.) If, however, both teams chose Option B — to betray — then both would receive extra kitchen duty for the rest of the *week*. And of course the final possibility was the most diabolical of all: If one team chose silence while the other chose betrayal, then the traitors would get off scot free while the others did the entire week's dishes *by themselves.*

"Okay, so that's three meals a day," Sticky had said, "with an average of thirteen place settings per meal —"

"Not to mention pots and pans," Kate pointed out.

"And snacks," Reynie said.

Sticky's eyes were growing large with alarm. "And five days left in the week . . ."

As these daunting prospects were sinking in — and

before the children could make any private pacts — Rhonda had ushered them into their separate holding rooms to discuss the options. But discussion was impossible with Constance, who had insisted from the start that they choose Option B. Betrayal was the only sensible option, she argued, since Sticky and Kate would surely choose Option B as well. After all, neither team would care to risk all that kitchen duty without help.

But Reynie not only found this strategy distasteful (he could imagine sentencing enemies to the sink, but his friends?), he also knew what the other team had chosen — and it wasn't Option B. Sticky and Kate hadn't taken time to reflect. If they had, they might have considered that Reynie's confinement would be more miserable than theirs; that no one in the world was more stubborn than Constance; and that in Reynie's place they, too, would be sorely tempted to end the ordeal by yielding to her.

But Sticky and Kate had gone with their first impulse. The only decent choice, in their view, would be to remain silent, and they would expect Reynie to choose the decent thing too. Even if Constance rather predictably insisted on Option B — well, Reynie would just find a way to change her mind! Such was their confidence in him, Reynie knew. It made betraying them all the more painful to contemplate.

He couldn't help contemplating it, though. Rhonda had said the team must be in agreement, and Constance refused to budge. How long might they be stuck in here? Another hour? Another *two*? Reynie grimaced and quickened his pacing. He couldn't bear to imagine his friends' look of disappointment, but Constance was clearing her throat now — she was about to launch into another grating poem, and Reynie didn't know if he could bear *that*, either. Should he threaten to tell Rhonda about Constance's secret candy stash? No, Constance wasn't susceptible to threats, and she would make Reynie pay dearly for the attempt. The last time he had tried something like that, she'd peppered his toothbrush.

Constance drew a deep breath and sang out:

> *There once was a ninny called Reynie*
> *Who thought there was one choice too many*
> *Because he was wimpy*
> *He—*

"Enough!" Reynie cried, clutching his head. Maybe he could just apologize to Sticky and Kate and — yes, he would even offer to help them with the dishes. Anything but this.

"So we're going with Option B?" asked Constance brightly. She looked exceedingly pleased.

"Why on earth would you do that?" said a metallic voice out of nowhere.

Reynie and Constance jumped. They had thought themselves alone — and indeed they still appeared to be. Other than several crowded bookshelves and a few tall stacks of books on the floor, the room was empty. There was a big arched window, but it remained firmly closed, and nothing appeared beyond the glass except the gray January sky.

"Did you hear that?" Constance asked, her eyes wide. "Or was it, you know —?" She tapped her head.

"No, I heard it, too," Reynie assured her, casting about for the source. "Where are you, Kate?"

"In the heating duct, silly," replied Kate's voice. "Behind the register. There's a pile of books in front of it."

Reynie found the heat register behind a waist-high stack of science journals. Quickly moving the journals aside, he peered through the grille to find Kate's bright blue eyes peering back at him. She slipped her Swiss Army knife through the grille. "Let us out, will you? Sticky's feeling a bit claustrophobic."

Reynie hastened to find the screwdriver on the knife. The heat register was quite old and ornate, and slightly rusty, and it took him a while to get the register off — he was much less nimble with tools than Kate. This was nothing to be ashamed of (no one could compare to Kate when it came to physical ability), but Reynie was feeling ashamed, regardless, for having been about to betray her in the game, and he was grateful for her stream of friendly chatter as he worked.

"We kept wondering what was taking you so long," she was saying in her usual rapid-fire way, "and finally we decided we should come check. I thought maybe you'd had a heat stroke, but Sticky figured Constance was giving you serious trouble. And he was *right*, wasn't he? Shame on you, Constance! That was an awfully mean-spirited poem. Although, I have to admit I was curious to find out what sort of insult rhymes with 'wimpy.' "

"And now you'll never know," humphed Constance, crossing her arms.

At last Reynie pulled the register from the wall, and Kate sprang up out of the heating duct with a triumphant grin, raising her hand for a celebratory high five. Reynie lifted his own hand — and instantly regretted it. The slap couldn't have stung worse if it had been delivered by a passing motorcyclist. Cradling his palm against him like a wounded bird, he watched Kate reach back into the duct for Sticky, who was mumbling something about having melted. It took her a few tries — Sticky's hands were so sweaty she couldn't find a grip — but at last she caught him under the shoulders and slid him smoothly out of the duct like a loaf of bread from the oven.

Both of them appeared to have been baked, in fact. The heating duct must have been sweltering. Kate's cheeks were brightly flushed, and her blond ponytail was damp and limp as a wrung mop. Sticky looked to have suffered even worse. His sweat-soaked clothes clung like a wet suit to his skinny frame; his light brown skin had gone a sickly shade of gray; and behind his wire-rimmed spectacles, which sat askew on his nose, his eyes seemed dazed and glassy. Beads of perspiration glistened like dewdrops on his smoothly shaven head.

"Hot," Sticky said sluggishly. He blinked his eyes, trying to focus. "I am hot."

"Tell me about it," said Kate, already raising the window. "Why didn't you two open this? Oh, I see, it won't stay up. Well, we can just prop it with a book." She reached toward the nearest shelf.

"Please don't," said Reynie, who was very protective of books. (When he had lived at Stonetown Orphanage, they had often been his only companions.) "That won't be good for it — and if it fell out the window it'd be damaged for sure."

"Okay, you're right," said Kate, sweeping her eyes round the room, "and there's nothing else to use. Hang on, I'll be right back." And she disappeared into the heating duct as naturally as a seal slipping into water.

"She left her bucket in the other room," rasped Sticky, adjusting his spectacles with slippery fingers and smudging them in the process. He tugged a polishing cloth from his shirt pocket. It was as damp as a baby wipe.

Constance was incredulous. "Kate left her precious bucket behind?"

"The duct is a tight fit," Sticky said, resignedly poking the cloth back into his pocket. "The bucket would have made too much noise, and we didn't want Rhonda to hear."

Reynie smiled. He was reminded of their very first day in this house, almost a year and a half ago now. Kate had squeezed through a heating duct then, too. He remembered her telling him how she'd tied her bucket to her feet and dragged it behind her, and how amazed he'd been by her account. It was strange to think he'd ever been surprised by Kate's agility, or by the fact that she carried a red bucket with her wherever she went. Reynie had long since grown used to these things; they seemed perfectly normal to him now.

He was not at all startled, for instance, when Kate returned from her expedition in less time than it would have taken most people simply to walk down the hall. She emerged from the heating duct with a large horseshoe magnet — one of the several useful items she kept stored in her bucket —

and in no time had stood it upright and propped open the window with it.

"That should stay," Kate said with satisfaction, as wonderfully cool air drifted into the room, "but just to be sure . . ." From her pocket she produced a length of clear fishing twine, one end of which she tied to her magnet and the other to her wrist. "This way if the magnet slips I won't have to fetch it later."

All of this took Kate perhaps twenty seconds to accomplish. As soon as she'd finished, the children sat on the floor in a circle. It was pure habit. Anytime the four of them were alone they had a meeting. Together, privately, the children thought of themselves as the Mysterious Benedict Society, and as such they had held a great many meetings — some in extraordinarily dire circumstances.

"So what's your team called?" asked Kate, twisting her legs into a pretzel-like configuration. "Sticky and I are the Winmates!" When this declaration met with baffled stares, she frowned. "Don't you get it? It's a play on words — a portly man's toe, or . . . What did you say we call that, Sticky, when two words are kind of bundled together?"

"A portmanteau," said Sticky.

"Right! A portmanteau! See, we're called the Winmates because we're *inmates* — like prison inmates, get it? — who *win*." Kate looked back and forth at Reynie and Constance, searching their expressions for signs of delight.

"You gave yourselves a name?" asked Constance.

Now it was Kate's turn to be baffled. "You didn't? How can you have a team without a name?"

Reynie sneaked an amused glance at Sticky, who only shrugged. No need to point out whose idea this naming business had been.

"Anyway," said Kate, leveling a stern gaze at Constance, "we can *all* win, you know. You simply have to choose Option A, and so will we."

"Okay, okay," said Constance, heaving a dramatic sigh. "Go on back to your room and let's get this over with."

Sticky narrowed his eyes. "And you'll choose Option A?"

Constance pretended to notice something outside the window.

"That's what I thought," said Sticky. "Honestly, Constance, what's the point? If you insist on doing it this way, we'll have no choice but to choose Option B ourselves. Then we'll *all* have more work to do."

"It doesn't make any difference to Constance," Reynie pointed out. "She spends most of her kitchen duty coming up with irritating poems, anyway. She never actually cleans much."

Constance huffed indignantly at this, not least because Reynie was right.

Kate gazed longingly at the window. "I wish we really were prisoners. Then we could just skip the negotiations and try to escape."

"We *are* really prisoners," said Sticky in a weary tone, and there was a general murmur of agreement.

Everyone knew Sticky was referring not to the exercise but to their overall situation. For months now, they and their families had been the guests of Mr. Benedict, the man who had first brought them together and to whom this house belonged. Though perhaps a bit odd, Mr. Benedict was a brilliant, good-natured, and profoundly kind man, and staying with him would have been a pleasant arrangement if only his guests had been able to choose the circumstances. But in fact they had been given no choice.

Mr. Benedict was the guardian of an enormously powerful invention known as the Whisperer — a dangerous machine coveted by its equally dangerous inventor, Ledroptha Curtain, who happened to be Mr. Benedict's brother — and because of their close connection to Mr. Benedict, the children were thought to be at risk. The government authorities, therefore, had ordered that the children and their families be kept under close guard. (Actually, the original order had called for them to be separated and whisked away to secret locations — much to the children's dismay — but Mr. Benedict had not allowed this. His home was already well-guarded, he'd insisted, and room could be made for everyone there. In the end, the authorities had grudgingly relented; Mr. Benedict could be very persuasive.)

The children understood there was good reason for such precautions. Mr. Curtain was cunning and ruthless, with several vicious men in his employ, and the children and their families were obvious targets. No one doubted that they would be snatched up and used as bargaining chips if left unprotected, for Mr. Curtain would do anything to regain possession of his Whisperer. (And just the thought of such a reunion inspired dread in everyone, not least the children.) Still, after months of being forbidden to play outside alone, or ever to go anywhere in town, the young members of the Society were feeling more than a little oppressed.

"If we were *really* really prisoners, though," said Kate, "I could have us out of here in a heartbeat."

"Through the window?" Reynie asked, following her gaze. "Is your rope long enough?"

"Well, there'd be a bit of a drop at the bottom," she admitted, and her friends exchanged doubtful glances. Kate might be a perfect judge of distance, but her definition of "a bit of a drop" was much different from their own.

"Seeing as how I might break if we tried that," said Sticky, "how about this instead?" He gestured toward the door, which was locked from the outside with a dead bolt — but whose hinges were on the inside. "You could remove the hinges, right? With proper leverage we could pull that side open enough to squeeze through."

"Wait a minute," said Constance, aghast. "You mean the Executives could have broken out of here that easily? Just by taking the hinges off?"

She was referring to Jackson, Jillson, and Martina Crowe, three nasty individuals who had mistreated the children in the past (they were all former Executives of Mr. Curtain), and who had certainly not grown any more trustworthy since their capture. As part of the investigation surrounding Mr. Curtain, they had on a few occasions been brought to the house to be questioned. By themselves they presented no real threat — they were nothing like Mr. Curtain's wicked Ten Men — but the authorities, ever cautious, had insisted that dead bolts be installed on two rooms, and that anything that might be used for escape be removed from them.

"Those guys aren't like Kate, remember," said Sticky. "They don't carry tools around with them — they wouldn't be allowed, you know, even if they wanted to. Besides, even if they got the hinges off, they'd never get past the guards."

"Well, I hope they've stopped coming," Constance said. "I'm sick of seeing their stupid mean faces."

Kate snorted. "You *wouldn't* see them if you stayed away like you're supposed to. But you always manage to cross paths, don't you? So you can stick your tongue out at them."

"If they weren't in the house," Constance replied haughtily, "I wouldn't be tempted to do that."

"Anyway," said Kate, rolling her eyes, "back to Sticky's question, we could get through the door, but not very quietly — Rhonda would surely hear us." She drummed her fingers thoughtfully on her bucket. "She didn't say whether or not she was armed, did she? When she was explaining the exercise?"

"No, but she did say she was the only guard," said Sticky. "Remember? Constance demanded to speak to a different guard — someone who would give us better options — and Rhonda sighed and said for the purposes of this exercise we should assume she's the only one."

"It was a perfectly reasonable demand," Constance protested as the others tittered, remembering Rhonda's look of exasperation.

"I don't think she meant for the number of guards to matter," said Reynie, still chuckling. "After all, we can't *really* escape. I mean, it's not as if we're going to attack Rhonda, right? And we can't even set foot outside the house without permission."

Just then Constance stiffened and looked over her shoulder at the wall. "Uh-oh!" she hissed. "Here she comes!"

They all held their breath. When Constance made pronouncements of this kind, she was always right. Sure enough, a moment later footsteps sounded outside the door, followed by a knock. "Constance? Reynie? Everything all right in there? Have you decided yet?"

"We need more time!" Reynie called.

"Are you sure?" There was a note of concern in Rhonda's muted voice. They heard the dead bolt turning. "Do you need a drink of water or anything?"

"We're fine!" Reynie cried quickly. "Just a few more minutes, please!"

"Very well, but please hurry," Rhonda replied, and she locked the door again without entering. "We have more lessons to get through, you know."

"That was close," Kate whispered when Rhonda's footsteps had receded. "I thought about hiding behind the door, but my magnet would have given us away regardless."

"Not to mention *me*," Sticky pointed out. "I couldn't even have stood up in time, much less hidden behind the door."

"Sure you could have," said Kate. "I was going to help you."

Sticky stared at her, appalled. He had a vivid mental image of his arm being yanked out of its socket.

"And I was going to use the twine to jerk the magnet over to me," Kate said casually (as if accomplishing all this in the space of a second was the sort of thing anyone might do), "but then, of course, the window would slam shut, which is not exactly something Rhonda would fail to notice. So it was pointless to try."

"It's all pointless, anyway," Sticky said, thrusting his chin into his hands. "We're never going to change Constance's mind. I think we'll just have to betray each other and get on with it."

"I suppose you're right," said Kate. "Oh well, I don't mind washing if you boys will dry . . ." She trailed off, having noticed Reynie staring at the window with his brow furrowed. "Reynie, what's the matter?"

Constance's brow was furrowed, too. But she was staring at Reynie. "He's getting an idea!" she said, her face lighting up.

Reynie glanced at her absently and looked back toward the window. He was seldom caught off guard anymore by these flashes of perception. Neither were Sticky and Kate, who leaned eagerly toward him.

"Well?" said Kate. "What is it, Reynie? What do you have in mind?"

"Option C," Reynie replied, and gave them a sly smile.

When Rhonda Kazembe knocked on the door some minutes later, she received no reply. From inside the room, however, came a suspicious sound of frenzied movement. She knocked again, and this time heard a hushed voice saying "Hurry up!" and (even more disconcerting) "Don't look down!" These words were enough to make her scrabble at the dead bolt, especially since the voice had sounded like Kate's. How could Kate even *be* in this room? As she unlocked the door Rhonda heard the distinct sound of a window slamming shut, and in rising alarm she burst into the room. Her mouth fell open. The room was empty.

Rhonda, a graceful young woman with coal-black skin and lustrous braided hair, was every bit as intelligent as she was lovely. She instantly saw what had happened. In the far wall gaped an exposed heating duct; the register had been removed. That would explain how Kate had gotten into the room (and no doubt Sticky, too). "Oh, but surely!" she cried, flying to the window. "Surely they didn't!"

Raising the window with a bang, Rhonda held it open with one hand and leaned over the sill to look below. The children were nowhere to be seen. She looked up toward the eaves. Still nothing.

Much relieved yet equally puzzled, Rhonda frowned as she lowered the window. Had they fled through the heating duct, then? But those urgent words ("Don't look down!") and the slamming window had led her to believe . . .

Rhonda closed her eyes. The door. They had been behind the door.

Even before she turned, Rhonda knew what she would see. Sure enough, there they were, having already crept out of the room and now standing in the hallway. Reynie and Sticky were grinning and waving; Constance, like a pint-sized, pudgy princess, had raised her chin to demonstrate her smug superiority; and Kate was leaning in through the doorway, one hand on the doorknob, the other gripping a horseshoe magnet and a tangle of twine. With a wink and a half-apologetic smile, she pulled the door closed. The dead bolt turned with a click.

For a moment Rhonda stared at the locked door, slowly shaking her head. And then, with laughter bubbling up in her throat, she began to clap.

The Monster in the Basement

Mr. Benedict was amused. This was hardly unusual. Sometimes, in fact, Mr. Benedict's amusement sent him right off to sleep, for he had a condition called narcolepsy that caused him to nod off at unexpected moments. These episodes occurred most often when he experienced strong emotion, and especially when he was laughing. His assistants (who were also, as it happened, his adopted daughters) did what they could to protect him — he could hardly take two steps without Rhonda or Number Two shadowing him watchfully in case he should fall asleep and topple over —

and Mr. Benedict guarded against such incidents himself by always wearing a green plaid suit, which he had discovered long ago to have a calming effect.

Nevertheless, the occasional bout of sudden sleep was inevitable, and as a result Mr. Benedict's thick white hair was perpetually tousled, and his face, as often as not, was unevenly shaven and marked with razor nicks. (Unfortunately nothing was more comical, Mr. Benedict said, than the sight of himself in the shaving mirror, where his bright green eyes and long, lumpy nose — together with a false white beard of shaving lather — put him in mind of Santa Claus.) He also wore spectacles of the sturdiest variety, the better to protect against shattering in the event of a fall. But as the best kind of fall was one prevented, it was not uncommon to see an amused Mr. Benedict diligently suppressing his laughter. Such was the case now, as he sat at the dining room table with Rhonda and the children.

"The point of the exercise," said Mr. Benedict, the corners of his mouth twitching, "was more philosophical than strategic, you see. More than anything, it was meant to be an examination of the consequences of one's actions on others. Sticky, I am sure, could recite the aims of the original Prisoner's Dilemma, but Rhonda and I had thought to adapt the game for our own purposes." Here Mr. Benedict allowed himself a smile, adding, "Just as you did yourselves."

The children, thus far pleased by Mr. Benedict's response to their solution, began to feel uneasy. They sensed that they had overlooked something they ought not to have overlooked — a misgiving intensified by the appearance of Number Two, who just then came storming into the dining room. The young woman's normally yellowish complexion had darkened almost to the same hue as her rusty red hair; and her expression, stern to begin with, positively radiated disapproval now. If the children didn't know Number Two loved them, they might have thought she meant to put them on the curb and be done with them forever.

"With not one thought," said Number Two, pointing her finger at them, "not a single thought for how your trick might affect Rhonda, what do you do? You pretend to go outside without *protection*? You pretend to climb out the window *on the third floor*? You —" She interrupted herself to bite angrily into an apple, which she chewed with great ferocity, glowering all the while.

Reynie could hear her teeth crunching and grinding all the way from his seat at the other end of the table. He wished he were sitting even farther away than that — preferably somewhere in the distant past. Number Two's words had stung him like a slap. She was right. He had been so pleased with his idea that he hadn't really considered whether it was a decent thing to do. Rhonda gave no sign of being upset, but during those first few moments she must have been worried — indeed, he had counted on it — and looking back on his decision, Reynie was ashamed.

"We're sorry!" blurted Kate, who evidently felt the same way. "Oh, Rhonda, that was stupid of us! It seemed funny at the time, but —"

"It *was* funny," Constance interjected. "Just because you're sorry doesn't mean it wasn't funny."

"Constance has a point," said Rhonda with an easy smile. "But I do appreciate your apology, Kate, and I can see from the boys' faces that they're sorry as well. Really, it's all right."

"All right?" Number Two snarled. "When our only concern is for their safety? When our every thought and deed —"

"Number Two," said Mr. Benedict gently, "I quite concur. But as we are pressed for time, would you be so kind as to fetch the duty schedule? We need to reconfigure it."

Number Two swung about and stalked into the kitchen. Even from a distance they could hear her fierce attacks on the apple; each bite sounded like a spade being thrust into gravel. Reynie suspected Mr. Benedict was giving her an opportunity to calm down.

"Our original plan," Mr. Benedict told the children, "was to release you from kitchen duty next week, thereby offsetting any extra work you had to put in *this* week as a result of the exercise. We wanted the consequences to seem real, you see, to heighten the effect, but we didn't actually intend to work you like galley slaves. This way Rhonda could tell you the truth, if not the entire truth, and perhaps keep Constance from seeing through the ruse. Constance might have seen through it anyway, of course — we thought *that* worth investigating, too. Ah, thank you so much," he said as Number Two, somewhat calmer now, returned with the duty schedule.

"Why do we have to change the schedule?" asked Constance, who found the scheduling of duties even more insufferably tedious than the duties themselves. "Can't we just keep it as it is?"

"Today is errand day," Rhonda said. "That's why we chose it for this particular exercise. We needed to reschedule duties, anyway."

"I *thought* things were unusually quiet around here," Sticky said. "Errand day — well, that explains it."

Errand day was when all the adult houseguests went out to deal with shopping and business. These prized forays into Stonetown came but once every two or three weeks, always on a different day and never announced beforehand. The adults claimed this was for security reasons, and no doubt it was, but Reynie suspected they were also glad to avoid any begging and pleading, since the children were never allowed to go anywhere themselves.

Kate jumped to her feet. "Don't bother with the schedule, Mr. Benedict. Let me take extra duty today. It'll make me feel better."

"Me, too," said Reynie.

"Yeah . . . same here," said Sticky, trying to sound upbeat despite the sinking feeling in his belly. Kitchen duty with Kate was exhausting — you had to work madly to keep up — and he generally avoided it when he could.

"Count me in!" chirped Constance, and everyone turned to her in astonishment. She burst into laughter at this, for of course she had only been kidding.

The good thing about kitchen duty on errand day was the reduced quantity of lunch dishes. With the exception of Mr. Benedict, who claimed responsibility for Constance, all of the children's guardians were absent. Gone from the table were the Washingtons, Miss Perumal and her mother Mrs. Perumal, and Kate's father Milligan, whose own errand was to protect the other guardians as they ran theirs.

The *bad* thing about kitchen duty on errand day was the notable lack of wonderful aromas in the air, for their friend Moocho Brazos — a former circus strong man and, more to the point, a marvelous cook — was also out running errands, which meant soup and sandwiches for lunch, and nothing baking in the oven.

"I wonder where they are right now," said Kate, passing another well-scrubbed plate to Sticky, who had hardly started drying the last one.

"I hope they remember to bring us something," called Constance from the pantry, where she was pretending to be busy. "I meant to give them a list."

"They might have other priorities," said Sticky, drying frantically. "My mom needs to talk to someone about a job she can do from home. Or, you know, from here — she hasn't been able to work since September." He frowned at the plate in his hand. "Sorry, Kate, I got this one kind of sweaty."

Kate cheerfully scrubbed it again as Sticky (somewhat less cheerfully) mopped his brow with his sleeve. "Don't worry, Constance!" she called. "They always bring us *something*, don't they? They know it's our only consolation for being stuck here while they're out."

Reynie, bearing a stack of dry dishes, paused on his way to the cupboard. "I'll bet they had lunch on Stonetown Square," he reflected wistfully. "They can probably smell the saltwater from the harbor."

"And the dead fish," Constance called. "And the gasoline fumes."

Reynie shrugged. "At least dead fish and fumes would be something different."

"Speaking of different," said Kate with a grin, "I wonder how they look?"

The boys chuckled. They all knew the adults were compelled to wear disguises in public. For a secret agent like Milligan, disguises were run-of-the-mill — the children were rather used to seeing *him* transform into a stranger — but it was comical to imagine dear old Mrs. Perumal, for instance, or the burly, mustachioed Moocho Brazos, dressing up to conceal their identities.

The use of disguises and other security precautions were well-known to the children, who always pressed for every detail of the outings. They knew the routine by heart, and in lieu of actually getting to go out themselves they often went over it in their minds:

First Milligan would contact his personal sentries — a group of trusted agents posted throughout the neighborhood — to ensure they had seen nothing suspicious in the vicinity. Then he would distribute empty cardboard boxes and bags to the other adults, and with a casual word to the courtyard guard about "a project at Mr. Benedict's other property," he would escort his charges to a small house across the street. This house, with its narrow front yard and modest porch, looked as tidy and well-maintained as any in the neighborhood, but in reality its interior was in an awful state of disrepair. Mr. Benedict had purchased it years ago, not to be inhabited but to serve as a cover for the entrance to a secret tunnel.

Milligan would lift open the cellar doors at the side of the house. The doors were made of flimsy wood, set slant-wise to the ground and held closed with a simple, sliding metal bolt — the sort of cellar doors that suggest nothing more important lies beyond them than dusty fruit jars and discarded boots. In the cellar itself, however, was another door, this one made of steel, with a lock Milligan said could not be picked and to which only he possessed a key. This door opened onto the secret tunnel — a narrow, damp passageway that stretched several blocks and ended beneath the Monk Building, a typically drab and unremarkable office building downtown.

At the Monk Building the adults would mount several flights of a dark stairway (with Mr. Washington supporting Mrs. Washington and Moocho carrying her wheelchair) until they reached a hidden anteroom, where they caught their breath and donned their disguises. The anteroom opened by means of a secret door into an office that belonged to Mr. Benedict, and in its wall were tiny peepholes that allowed Milligan to ensure the office was empty. (He didn't want them stumbling unexpectedly upon an astonished custodian.) Finally, when he was sure the coast was clear, Milligan would lead the adults through the office, down the Monk Building's seldom-used public stairs, and at last out the building's front doors.

It was hard to imagine exactly how they felt as they stepped out onto the plaza in the heart of Stonetown's business district. Perhaps they broke into wide smiles at the prospect of a day's freedom. Or perhaps they were overcome with a sad nostalgia, remembering the days before they had ever heard of Mr. Curtain. But just as likely they would be glancing warily about and hoping not to draw attention. They must feel uncommonly strange in their disguises.

"Do you ever worry about them?" Sticky murmured after a pause, and Reynie and Kate returned his sober gaze. They could hear Constance rattling around in the pantry.

"Sometimes," Reynie admitted. "But I remind myself that the authorities are on high alert, and there's been no activity reported anywhere near Stonetown —"

"And Milligan can spot a Ten Man a mile away," Kate put in. "And he can do more than *spot* him, if it comes to that."

The boys nodded, even though the last time Milligan encountered Mr. Curtain's henchmen he'd needed several weeks to recover from the injuries. The circumstances had been different then — they knew because they'd been there — and they quite shared Kate's confidence in her father.

"You're right," Sticky said. "They couldn't be safer if they had a dozen guards."

"Yes, they're fine," Reynie said. "I'm sure they're fine."

"Of course they are," said Kate.

They spoke without real conviction, however, for though the adults were surely as safe as could be expected under the circumstances, the question remained: How safe *was* that, exactly?

Kate pulled the plug in the sink, and in troubled silence the friends watched the sudsy water drain away.

Constance emerged from the pantry with a half-empty sleeve of cheese crackers, her cheeks bulging like a chipmunk's. "What're you wooking at?" she said, spewing crumbs.

"Nothing," said the others at once, and Constance scowled. It infuriated her when they tried to protect her. They couldn't help themselves, though, nor were their reasons entirely selfless: Constance was always difficult, but when she grew anxious she was perfectly unbearable.

"Let's go outside," Reynie said, turning away before Constance could search his face. "We still have some time before afternoon lessons."

✌:~

The children enjoyed being outside, but getting there was a tiresome business. First they had to seek permission from an adult, who often had to check with someone else to verify the alarm code, for the code was changed almost daily and all the downstairs doors and windows were wired. (Mr. Benedict's first-floor maze had been renovated into makeshift apartments for the Washingtons and Perumals, and the alarm system — with its direct signal to the police station as well as Milligan's sentries — provided an important new defense.) Then they had to wait while the adult conferred with the outside guards, and only then could they venture into fresh air.

The children usually preferred the large backyard, where there was more room to run about, and in Kate's case to turn a few dozen handsprings and flips. The exception was when Mr. Bane was posted there. Mr. Bane was an unpleasant guard, a gruff and grizzled man who seemed to believe children should be kept in boxes until they were proper adults. When Mr. Bane was in the backyard, they went into the courtyard instead.

Today, as it happened, Mr. Bane was off duty altogether, and as soon as they had hustled into their coats and hats, and Reynie had helped Constance with her mittens (she was close to tears trying to get her thumbs in their places), they ran out the backdoor. They were greeted by Ms. Plugg, a tough, stocky guard who had been walking about on the frost-covered grass to keep warm.

"Afternoon, children," Ms. Plugg said, nodding as they came down the steps. She had an oddly large and rectangular head, rather like a cinder block, and when she nodded Reynie always had the disquieting impression that it was sliding off her shoulders. "Kate. Reynie. Constance. Um . . . Tacky? I'm sorry, I forget your name."

"Sticky."

"Right!" said Ms. Plugg, snapping her fingers. "Good afternoon, Sticky. I promise I won't forget again." Yielding the yard to the children, she took up a watchful position at the top of the steps, where Sticky, unfortunately, could hear her mumbling quietly to herself, "Sticky . . . Sticky . . . hmm. Always fiddles with his glasses . . . fiddlesticks! Okay, fiddlesticks. Good. I'll remember that."

Sticky's stomach fluttered disagreeably as he walked away from the steps. He had grown so used to being with his friends, he felt somehow caught off balance — and deeply embarrassed — overhearing a stranger's observations about him. Taking a deep breath to steady himself, watching it rise as vapor in the cold air, Sticky made a spontaneous, private decision.

Kate, meanwhile, had been about to put down her bucket, but Reynie caught her arm. "Don't start tumbling just yet," he murmured, and looking over at Sticky and Constance he said, "Let's walk a minute."

His look wasn't lost on any of them. Sticky and Constance glanced furtively over their shoulders, and Kate's eyes narrowed as she rebelted her bucket to her hip, opening the flip-top for quicker access to its contents. They all fell into step with Reynie as he set off around the yard.

No one spoke. The only sound was the crunch of their footsteps on the frozen grass. The yard was enclosed by a prickly hedge, behind which stood a tall iron fence with sharp points at the top of each paling. At the back of the yard Reynie stood on his tiptoes to see over the hedge, and through the fence, into the quiet lane beyond. Something had obviously spooked him.

"Guess what?" he muttered. "Mr. Bane wasn't here on the last errand day, either. Remember? First we moped around in the courtyard, and then we came back here to play kickball."

Constance shrugged. "So? Mr. Bane's never here on errand day."

Kate gasped in disbelief. "And you didn't see fit to mention that?"

"I never thought about it!" said Constance, her voice rising. "I never even —"

"Shh!" said Reynie, with a nervous glance toward Ms. Plugg. "It's okay, Constance. We all have a lot on our minds. But if what you say is true —"

"It's true, all right," said Sticky, already reaching for his polishing cloth. He caught himself, scratched his chest instead, then crossed his arms. "I should have noticed it myself. Mr. Bane's been off duty every single time."

"Like I said!" Constance snapped. "But what's the big deal?"

"The big deal is it can't be a coincidence," Reynie said. "The guards work on a rotating schedule, with different days off each week. It's not very likely errand day just happens to keep falling on Mr. Bane's day off."

"Highly improbable," said Sticky, doing the numbers in his head. "In fact —"

"What the boys mean to say," Kate interrupted, before Sticky could dive into an explanation of calculating odds, "is that something's going on. What do you think, Reynie? Mr. Benedict doesn't trust Mr. Bane? He doesn't want him to find out about errand day?"

"It's already being kept secret from the house guards," Sticky pointed out. "Why be extra careful with Mr. Bane?"

"Maybe because Mr. Bane is extra nosy," Constance suggested.

"Maybe," Reynie said. "But we should also consider the possibility that Mr. Bane *does* know about it. What if he's figuring out when errand day is going to be, then arranging the duty schedule so that he's off?"

"How could he find out?" Constance said. "And why would he do that?"

Reynie shook his head. "I don't know. But it makes me awfully uneasy."

It made all of them uneasy, and for a moment they stood in silence, contemplating what Mr. Bane might be up to. They had never liked the man, but until now no one had suspected he might be treacherous, mostly because they thought Mr. Benedict was too shrewd to allow someone untrustworthy to guard the premises.

"You know what?" said Kate, brightening. "If *we've* noticed this, you can bet Mr. Benedict has. He might even be the one behind it, right? So let's ask him later and stop worrying about it. We're wasting our fresh-air time!"

The others were less blithe than Kate, but she did have a point. So they agreed to drop the subject, and after some minutes of kicking a ball around they, too, began to shake off their misgivings. They even managed to feign enthusiasm when Kate whistled Madge down from the eaves and urged them to stroke her feathers.

Madge (whose full name was Her Majesty the Queen) was a talented bird, much attached to Kate and much smarter than most peregrine falcons, which Kate thought should endear her to everyone. The boys had pointed out — as gently as they could — that the raptor's cruelly sharp beak and cold, predatory expression made her somewhat less than cuddly, and that perhaps people could be forgiven for maintaining a respectful distance. But Kate had seemed hurt by this thought, so for her sake the boys tried to act fond of Madge (and Constance, perhaps not to be left out, did the same).

Today the three of them managed a few tentative feather-touches and false compliments before retreating to the steps, after which they felt remarkably better, for there is nothing like the fear of being raked by talons to take one's mind off other concerns. And as they watched Kate and Madge go through their training routines their spirits rose higher still — the routines were wonderfully entertaining.

Kate would puff on her whistle, producing different sequences of high-pitched notes, and depending on the sequence Madge would either alight on Kate's fist (now protected by a thick leather glove) or else circle above the yard, "hunting" for strips of meat, which Kate took from a sealed pouch in her bucket and flung into the air. Madge would stoop upon these tidbits with such astonishing speed and accuracy that her young spectators couldn't help but gasp and applaud (and once or twice Ms. Plugg couldn't help but join in), and Kate beamed happily and made comical, exaggerated bows, doing her best not to seem overly proud.

Sitting there on the bottom step, with the sun just breaking out from a cloud and his friends — even Constance — all smiling and chatting good-naturedly, Reynie was suddenly struck by the thought that this curious imprisonment of theirs, however they might grumble about it, could very well prove to be the best time in their lives. For who could say what would happen when all of this was over? Wasn't it possible, even probable, that their families would all go back to their former lives?

Reynie felt an old, familiar ache. He instantly recognized it as loneliness — or in this case anticipated loneliness — and not for the first time he lamented his too-vivid imagination. Too easily he imagined the pang he would feel the first hundred times he ate breakfast without his friends — without Kate chattering away much too energetically for that time of morning, without Sticky adjusting his spectacles and translating something from French, without Constance trying to sneak something from his plate. Too easily he imagined himself surrounded by strangers, trying to make new friends in some other place.

"You all right?" Sticky asked, nudging him. "Are you worrying about you know what?"

With a start, Reynie realized that he was staring off into the distance. He shook his head. "No, just . . . daydreaming. I'm fine, thanks." And he smiled to prove it, privately laughing at himself for being so gloomy. Wasn't he here with his friends right now? What good did worrying do? At this very moment Sticky was sitting beside him on the step, recounting a study he'd read on the "potentially salubrious effects of daydreams on mental health," and below them Constance was attempting to retie her shoe with her mittens still on, and Kate was there in the yard, spinning with her arms out wide and gazing up at her falcon in the sky.

Reynie took a mental picture, and saved it.

~:~

Watching quietly from the top of the steps, Ms. Plugg, like Reynie, was feeling a curious mix of emotions. She was impressed, charmed, and concerned all at once. In her two months at this job, she had never been on duty in the backyard when Kate worked with Madge. Like all of the guards, she'd been aware of a falcon nesting high in the eaves, and had known that it "belonged," more or less, to one of the children, but she'd had no notion of the bird's skill — or the girl's, for that matter — nor of the obviously strong bond of friendship between the two. And now from the bottom step she could hear the bespectacled boy (what was his name? Oh yes, fiddlesticks) — could hear *Sticky* speaking like a scholar about some study he'd read, and she observed his friend Reynie listening with actual interest and understanding as he tied the cranky little girl's shoe for her.

So charming was the scene that Ms. Plugg found it hard not to be distracted, which bothered her extremely, for Ms. Plugg was a dutiful guard, and her duty, as she understood it, was to look out for strangers (especially well-dressed men carrying briefcases) and for any activity that might be deemed suspicious. Her duty was not to gawk at this ponytailed girl training a bird of prey, or to eavesdrop on the brainy conversation of these two boys — all of which was certainly *unusual* activity, but none of it was suspicious.

Ms. Plugg was used to unusual. This house was an unusual house; this job an unusual job. For one thing, she had been told almost nothing about the house's residents. Their occupations and histories were a mystery to her, as well as to most — if not quite all — of the other guards. According to Ms. Plugg's superiors, the guards' job was not to ask questions. Questions would be a waste of time, for most of the answers were highly classified and would not, therefore, be given. Ms. Plugg and the other guards had been told only that the house's occupants were important, and that their importance was directly related to what was in the basement.

As all the guards knew, what lay in the basement was a bank of large computers. The computers hummed almost imperceptibly, and night and day, week in and week out, they continued in their mysterious activity. Ceaseless, rapid, extraordinarily complex activity. Although the guards (most of them, that is) had no way of knowing it, the computers were among the most powerful and complicated machines ever invented. They were unusual, in other words, and guarding them was part of Ms. Plugg's unusual job.

The climate-controlled basement in which the computers were situated was inaccessible except by way of a hidden stairway that originated inside the house. Once in a while, the guards had reason to descend briefly into the basement, but they were under strict orders never to touch the computers (or even to look at them too closely). These orders were hardly necessary. If an enormous monster had lain sleeping in that dimly lit basement, a creature far more powerful and intelligent than any of the guards, why, nothing on earth could have induced them to risk waking it, and their instinctive feeling about the computers was much the same. The only person who ever touched the computers was Mr. Benedict, whom Ms. Plugg, for her part, regarded as something like an amiable and perhaps half-foolish lion tamer entering the dreaded cage.

The guards understood nothing of the workings and secret purposes of these computers. All they knew was that the computers served yet another machine, one that had come dangerously close to wreaking terrible havoc in the world — and that in the hands of the wrong person it could do so again.

They had no notion of what this other machine looked like, or what it did, but more than a few of them (including Ms. Plugg) imagined it as something huge, spidery, and sinister, with gleaming eyes and countless whirring blades and a shrieking cry like the wail of a buzz saw brought to metal. Indeed, they suspected its appearance was even more beastly and frightening than that; they suspected their imaginations were incapable of evoking the true horror of this unknown machine. They knew only that these computers were its heart and brain (which must, for some unfathomable reason, be protected and preserved), and that in a locked and guarded chamber on the third floor, hidden behind a decorative screen, was a curious chair, and that this chair, too, was somehow linked to the terrible machine.

At least, this was what the guards thought they knew.

The truth was that the chair was the machine itself. The guards' imaginations had reached in the wrong direction — a reasonable error, for their imaginations had little to guide them. The chair appeared simply to sit there, quiet and still, behind the decorative screen in that cozy chamber. Doing nothing. Threatening nothing. With its curious red helmet attached to the seatback, the chair resembled an old-fashioned hair dryer — an eccentric piece of furniture, certainly, but a harmless one.

This was the Whisperer.

And for the moment, in the hands of Mr. Benedict, the Whisperer *was* harmless. Indeed, under Mr. Benedict's care the Whisperer had been made to seem as inoffensive as possible; it had even been made to do a certain amount of good.

Unfortunately, despite Mr. Benedict's best efforts and intentions, the Whisperer was soon to pass from his care. When it did, the fates of a great many people would once again be pulled along behind it, like leaves trailing in the wake of a speeding vehicle. And the very first to be so affected — and among the most important — were these four children now enjoying the fresh air under the watchful eye of Ms. Plugg.

REAL and OFFICIAL MATTERS

The rest of the winter passed more or less without incident: Sticky celebrated a housebound birthday, missing yet another optometrist appointment; the ever-exploring Kate discovered what she believed to be new nooks and crannies (she wasn't entirely sure she knew what a cranny was); Reynie learned a new chess opening and tried parting his hair on the opposite side; and Constance completed an epic poem about pig drool. But none of these events counted as news, exactly, at least not the sort the children so earnestly wished for.

There had been no word on Mr. Curtain's whereabouts,

no hint of progress in the authorities' search. Nor were there any developments on the home front, for when the children had approached Mr. Benedict about Mr. Bane's suspicious absences, he had said they were quite right to wonder about it but that he would be imprudent to speak of it further. And so they were left to speculate not only about Mr. Bane, but also about Mr. Benedict's reasons for maintaining silence on the matter.

Speculating grows wearisome eventually, however, and even secret society meetings lose appeal when there's nothing new to discuss (especially when the members have already spent too much time together). Time passed slowly for the children, therefore, with lessons every weekday, endless rounds of board games and cards, and never a foot set off the property. Until one day, just as spring was mustering itself for another appearance, something finally happened.

The day began normally enough, with newspapers after breakfast. As usual, Sticky blazed through all of them (Mr. Benedict subscribed to several) while Reynie and Kate traded sections of the *Stonetown Times.* Whenever they finished a section they would pass it to Constance, who glanced at the headlines and drew mustaches and devil horns on people in the photographs. The children were allowed to linger over the papers as long as they wished, but they seldom lingered long, for the older ones looked forward to their exercises and lessons, which offered a welcome change of pace, and Constance ran out of pictures to deface.

On this morning Sticky finished even more quickly than usual, then hustled off to find Number Two, who was letting him use her computer to access the Stonetown Library catalog. He was in the process of memorizing it, had already spent hours scrolling through the records, and today he hoped to finish. It had been tedious work, but it would make his future research more efficient, and Sticky was excited.

"I would have thought Mr. Benedict had every book in the world," Kate had said when Sticky first mentioned his project. "The whole house is crammed with them."

"I know," said Sticky with an eager, appreciative look, "and I still haven't read half of them, but whenever —"

"You've read *half* of them?" Kate cried, but Sticky was just gaining steam.

"— but whenever a bibliography mentions a book that Mr. Benedict doesn't have, there's nothing to do but request it from the library, right? And if the Stonetown Library system doesn't have it, then I have to ask for an inter-library loan, which means filling out a different form altogether. So think of how much faster the process will be when I can skip the catalog and go straight to the appropriate form! I'll still have to wait until errand day to get the books, of course, but it's much . . ."

"Naturally," said Kate, who hadn't really been listening. "But let me just be clear — you've read half the books in this *house*? This *whole* house?"

"Well, approximately half," Sticky said. "To be more accurate, I suppose I've read more like" — his eyes went up as he calculated — "three-sevenths? Yes, three-sevenths."

"Only three-sevenths?" said Kate, pretending to look disappointed. "And here I was prepared to be impressed."

After Sticky had gone out, Kate and Reynie discussed the newspaper articles they had read, almost all of which were about Stonetown having fallen on hard times. The city's government bureaucracy was terribly snarled, its budget a wreck. And what Kate and Reynie knew that most readers could *not* know — because the information was still classified — was that Ledroptha Curtain was much to blame.

"I used to think the Emergency was boring to read about," Kate observed. "But at least it was dramatic. This is just a tiresome mess. Sometimes I wonder if they'll *ever* get it straightened out."

Reynie had wondered this himself. After all, more than a year had passed since the Whisperer had stopped sending messages into the minds of the public — no longer was Mr. Curtain secretly creating the fearful, confused, desperate atmosphere known as the Emergency — and according to Mr. Benedict the mental effects of those messages had almost entirely disappeared. And yet Stonetown, one of the world's most important cities, was having difficulty paying its own bills and cleaning its own streets. Mental effects were one thing, Mr. Benedict had said, and practical effects quite another.

Reynie shrugged. "Mr. Benedict says it could take a long time. He says it's hard to fix a problem when so few people know the cause."

"That's what's irritating about it," Kate said. "The fact that it's classified. I mean, even most of the people in the *government* don't know the truth. Milligan says some officials insist on keeping it secret."

"It's because they're embarrassed," Constance put in, without glancing up from her work. (She was busy giving the mayor crossed eyes and insect antennae.) "They don't want people to know they were duped by Mr. Curtain just like everyone else."

Reynie and Kate looked at her in surprise. Constance rarely paid attention to these newspaper conversations, and when she did it was usually to complain that they'd said the same things a thousand times. (Which was true enough, but they found it impolite of her to mention.)

"I think you're probably right," Reynie said. "But I also think Mr. Curtain's spies might have something to do with it. They could be working to keep the information secret . . . but that's just a guess. I don't know what their motives would be, or even who any of them are, and Mr. Benedict won't ever talk to us about them."

"And why *is* that, Reynie?" Constance asked, propping her chin on her hand and affecting a look of serious interest.

Now Reynie was really suspicious. But before he could ask Constance what she was up to, Miss Perumal entered the room carrying a file folder. She and Rhonda were the children's primary instructors (though all the adults pitched in from time to time), and as she approached the table, her expression was so determined — and so resolutely cheerful — that Reynie knew she must be coming to work with Constance. Or try to, anyway. Yesterday it had been Rhonda's turn, and the day before that it had been Mrs. Washington's, and before that it had been Moocho's. None had had the slightest bit of luck. Constance might labor for hours on tasks of her own choosing, but she positively detested any work assigned to her.

"Oh, I'll do those exercises later, Miss Perumal," Constance said before Miss Perumal had even spoken. "Right now I'm discussing the newspaper with Reynie and Kate."

A look of understanding passed between Reynie and Kate. Constance must have known Miss Perumal was coming down the hallway.

"Is that so?" Miss Perumal said, carefully keeping any hint of disbelief out of her tone. "That's lovely, Constance. But why don't we get these exercises over with? Mr. Benedict designed them especially for you, you know."

Constance frowned. "I don't care. They're boring."

"But you haven't even looked at them," Miss Perumal said, passing a hand over her fine black hair as if to smooth it. Reynie recognized this as a sign of impatience; he'd often seen her do the same thing when disagreeing with her mother. "I think you'll be surprised —"

Constance made a gagging sound.

Miss Perumal pressed her lips together. "I thought we might do a craft project afterward," she said after a pause. "Once you've finished the exercises, I could show you how to make a sugar-cube igloo."

Constance looked at her out of the corners of her eyes. "You make the igloo out of . . . sugar cubes?"

"Why, yes," Miss Perumal said matter-of-factly. "And you use cake frosting to serve as a sort of glue. You don't *eat* any of it, of course — it's just for fun."

"No . . . no, of course," said Constance, suppressing a smile.

"Bribery," Reynie muttered to Kate, who rolled her eyes.

"Well, that sounds great!" Constance said, climbing down from her chair. "Let's do the igloo first!"

Miss Perumal shook her head firmly. "No, Constance. First the exercises, then —"

"Yes! It's igloo time, Miss Perumal! This'll be fun!" She was running for the door, speaking loudly so as not to hear Miss Perumal's protests. "I'll get the sugar cubes — I know where Moocho hides them!" And then she was gone, leaving Miss Perumal to stare bleakly after her.

"Nice try, Amma," said Reynie, grinning, and Kate laughed and patted Miss Perumal's arm sympathetically.

"I had so hoped that would work," Miss Perumal sighed, absently straightening Reynie's collar. "I admit it was a desperate trick." She forced a smile and moved toward the door. "Mrs. Washington will be in soon to work with you two. Rhonda is assisting Mr. Benedict this morning, and I'm with Constance until lunchtime."

"What's for lunch today, Miss Perumal, do you know?" Kate asked.

"I hope it's headache medicine," Miss Perumal replied, and went out.

⌣∶∾

Lunch was always an extravagant affair, in part because Moocho Brazos delighted in serving elaborate meals, and in part because lunch and dinner were the only times that all of the house's occupants were together. Even then Mr. Benedict was often absent, for his work spared few interruptions, and he and Number Two would only pass through, loading plates to carry away. Today, however, everyone was present but Milligan, and as usual there was much "clatter and chatter," as Constance had put it in one of her poems, "and tedious talk about what was the matter."

The real matter, today, was Constance herself, but it wasn't discussed until most of the dishes were cleared and Constance (having failed to grumble her way out of kitchen duty) had trudged out with Miss Perumal and Moocho.

"She's only four, of course," Mr. Benedict was saying, "and barely that. Her lack of interest in these exercises is perfectly understandable. By all rights she ought to be play-ing, and I've thought it best not to press her. Still, it seems important to be alert to developments in her abilities, the better to guide her through."

"You're quite right," said Mrs. Washington. She turned to her husband. "Haven't we often wished we'd had a better idea of Sticky's gifts when he was that age?"

Mr. Washington nodded, which for him constituted a lengthy response, as he was reticent by nature. A slender, bespectacled man, Mr. Washington resembled a taller ver-sion of his son — even more so lately, for he'd begun shaving his own head whenever he shaved Sticky's, just as something to do. (There were only so many improvement projects he could undertake with so many people in the house, and Mr. Washington, a skilled carpenter accustomed to hard work, was desperate for activity.)

"If we had done similar exercises with Sticky," Mrs. Washington continued, her tone suddenly regretful, "per-haps we'd have made fewer mistakes. Don't you think, dear?"

Mr. Washington considered this, then nodded.

"We learn from our mistakes, though," said Rhonda mildly. "And Sticky has turned out wonderfully well, hasn't he?"

Mrs. Washington's face lit up. "Oh yes, he has! Of course he has!" she cried (as Mr. Washington nodded), and both beamed fondly at their son.

Their son, meanwhile, squirmed in his seat. These days almost anything Sticky's parents said about him embarrassed him — they might have said "Sticky likes salt on his potatoes" and still he would have winced — but public adoration was more embarrassing by far. It was all he could do not to reach for his spectacles.

"We are none of us impervious to error," said Mr. Benedict. "I least of all. It was not so long ago, you'll recall, that I failed to perceive the character of my brother's plottings, to the great detriment of everyone here. So focused was I on protecting the Whisperer, I completely overlooked the possibility of Ledroptha's capturing *me* as a means of reclaiming it. A foolish mistake indeed, and I —"

"Mr. Benedict!" snapped Number Two, who in the midst of peeling an orange (she always followed lunch with a snack) slapped it down with such force that juice squirted across the table into Reynie's eye. "Sorry, sorry," she said as Mrs. Perumal handed Reynie a damp napkin, "but I simply cannot bear to hear such talk."

Pointing her finger accusingly at Mr. Benedict, Number Two said, "You spend so little time thinking of yourself that it was a natural mistake. You can't blame yourself for your brother's treachery!"

Everyone seconded Number Two's sentiment, but Mr. Benedict, acknowledging this with a grateful inclination of his head, persisted, "Nevertheless, I cannot say too often how deeply I regret the circumstances it has created for you all. I feel that —" Here his speech faltered, and his bright green eyes glistened all the more brightly with tears. (Kate discreetly took hold of his teacup, ready to slide it away if Mr. Benedict slumped forward.)

"But you *have* said it too often, Mr. Benedict!" said Mrs. Perumal in an imperious tone that was quite out of character. "And if you continue in this vein, I'm afraid we'll be compelled to cut our visit short. Surely there are other establishments that would host an entire troop of guests — indefinitely and without reward — and not feel obliged to apologize for it!"

For an instant only Reynie knew that his grandmother was joking; everyone else sat in startled silence. Then Mr. Benedict erupted into his high-spirited laugh (that peculiar, familiar laugh that sounded so much like a dolphin), and the whole table soon followed suit. Everyone laughed until their eyes watered, especially after Mrs. Perumal, who at first had succeeded in maintaining her haughty air, finally broke down into giggles herself. Mr. Benedict, having narrowly escaped falling asleep from regret, now came close to doing so from mirth.

At last the jollity subsided, and Mr. Benedict removed his spectacles to dab at his eyes with a napkin, saying, "Thank you, Mrs. Perumal, for lightening the mood. I daresay we all needed that." Resettling the spectacles on his nose, he took out his pocket watch, frowned, and grew businesslike again.

"I'm expecting visitors," Mr. Benedict said, "but before they arrive I must return to Constance a moment. As I said,

I do feel compelled to press her a bit, and toward this end I should like to enlist Reynie, Sticky, and Kate in an experiment. Provided you're willing, of course," he said to the children, "and only with your parents' permission."

When Miss Perumal had been sent for (she hurried in from the kitchen wearing sudsy gloves and a look of relief), Mr. Benedict explained his idea. After a brief discussion, the parents all granted their permission, and the children — somewhat reluctantly — agreed to help.

"I'll have to ask Milligan when he gets back," said Kate, whose father had been called away on a secret matter the day before.

"Actually, I've already secured his permission," said Mr. Benedict, "but you can discuss it with him later if you like. He's just returned."

"He has?" Kate cried, jumping up.

Sure enough, they could all hear Milligan whistling in the hallway (he was a supremely talented whistler), and the next moment he burst into the dining room, arms stretched wide in greeting. Kate flew to him happily — she was always relieved when he came home safe — and he laughed as she hugged him, taking a few steps backward to absorb her momentum and calling out a cheerful "Hello, hello!" to everyone else.

Milligan looked like himself for a change — no disguises, bandages, or casts — and his bright, buoyant aspect, so much like his daughter's, brought smiles to the faces of everyone in the room. A tall man with flaxen blond hair and ocean-blue eyes (the same color as Kate's), Milligan wore a shabby assemblage of boots, jacket, and hat that quite belied his position as a top secret agent. But agent he was, and no sooner had he greeted them than he drew Mr. Benedict, Rhonda, and Number Two aside to speak in private.

Reynie overheard the words "just as we thought" and "sooner than expected," and noting Mr. Benedict's expression — attentive and composed, yet also faintly troubled — he realized that here, at last, was some kind of important development. But whatever it was, it appeared to be an undesirable one.

"If you'll excuse us," Mr. Benedict said, turning to address the table, "my visitors have arrived. Mr. Bane is bringing them up presently. No, no," he said when the others made to leave, "please stay as long as you like. This is an official matter and must be dealt with in my study." He went out, accompanied by Rhonda, Milligan, and Number Two.

Mrs. Perumal murmured something to Mrs. Washington, who shared a questioning glance with her husband. Apparently Reynie wasn't the only one who had sensed this "official matter" was significant.

"You have half an hour before your afternoon lessons," Mrs. Washington said. "Wouldn't you three like to go outside?"

"Actually," said Kate, already moving to the door, "I need the boys' help with something. Don't worry, we'll keep out of everyone's way." She beckoned to Reynie and Sticky, who hurried after her so eagerly that the adults, had they not been intent on having a private discussion themselves, might have been suspicious.

The boys followed Kate down the long hallway past Mr. Benedict's study, thinking they were headed upstairs to talk. To their surprise, however, she turned at the stairs and darted down a seldom-used passage which, as far as Reynie knew, led to nothing but an overcrowded storage room and a utility closet.

"Wait, you really do want help with something?" Sticky asked as they hustled to catch up. "I assumed you wanted to talk about these mysterious visitors."

"We can talk later," said Kate. She opened her bucket and handed each of them an empty water glass that she'd smuggled from the dining room. "Right now we're going to listen."

"You mean eavesdrop?" said Reynie, raising his eyebrows. He knew this trick — by putting your ear to a glass and the glass to the wall, you could sometimes make out what was said in the next room. He felt his heartbeat quickening.

"But we'll be seen!" Sticky objected. "Eavesdropping on an official meeting won't go over very well, you know."

"Lower your voice," said Kate with a glance back down the passage. She drew the boys into the utility closet and shut the door. "Listen," she whispered as she groped for the light switch, "this meeting is obviously unusual. I mean, Mr. Benedict has countless meetings, but you can tell this one is different, can't you?"

The light came on. The boys, squinting, nodded.

"And chances are we won't be told anything about it, right? It's for our own protection, they'll say — and that's probably true — but aren't you curious? Don't you want to know?"

"Of course," Reynie said. "I'm just wondering how you plan to get away with it."

Kate looked at Sticky, who was trying not to fidget for fear of knocking over a broom or dust mop. They were rather tightly packed. Cautiously, he nodded. "Yes, how do we do it?"

"Like so," Kate said with a grin, scooting aside a mop bucket to reveal a large access panel in the wall. She quickly removed its screws, saying, "This old house has been through a lot over the years. Walls knocked down and relocated, plumbing replaced, sockets rewired, you name it. There are lots of what you'd call . . . eccentricities. Here we go now."

She lowered the panel to the floor, exposing a tangle of brightly colored, insulated wires draped before a dark empty space — like vines overhanging a cave entrance, Reynie thought, or a bead curtain in a doorway. Kate took out her flashlight, leaving her bucket on the floor nearby. "It's a tight fit," she explained. Sweeping the wires to one side, she shone her flashlight into the darkness, then looked back over her shoulder at the boys. "Don't worry about the wires, they're not connected anymore. Now listen, we need to be as quiet as mice. No, quieter than that. As quiet as . . . as . . . "

"Dead mice?" Reynie suggested.

"Perfect," said Kate with an approving nod. "As quiet as dead mice."

And with that, the boys followed Kate into the walls.

Through the Listening Glass

Having passed through the curtain of dangling wires, Reynie discovered that he could stand upright in the space between walls. It was narrow, with scarcely room to turn his head, but by edging sideways as if shuffling along a ledge he was able to move without bumping the walls. Once or twice Kate directed her flashlight at the floor, drawing his attention to a spot of uneven footing. Each time Reynie swiveled his eyes toward Sticky to be sure he had noticed, too. Then he nodded to Kate, and silently they moved on.

In this way they soon arrived at the wall of Mr. Benedict's study, beyond which they could hear the muffled tones of conversation. Ever so quietly and carefully, they raised their water glasses and pressed them to the wall.

Reynie heard Number Two's agitated voice as if from the bottom of a well: "...unannounced? If not for Milligan ..." Her words grew indistinct; Reynie pressed his ear to the glass so hard it hurt. "...the whole point being to catch you off guard, no? They want —"

Mr. Benedict's muted voice came in. "I know, Number Two, but at least we've had the experience of observing their methods. It's instructive, don't you think?"

A forceful knock sounded at the door. Through the listening glasses the banging came like a series of detonations. Reynie jumped, almost dropping his glass, and Kate (using her opposite ear and thus facing him) wrinkled her nose.

"One moment, please!" called Mr. Benedict, and then in a lower tone, barely audible to the eavesdroppers, he said, "Number Two, you and Milligan had better escort Mr. Bane back down to his post. We don't want — Why, hello!" — this in a louder, cheerful tone as the door was rudely opened — "Yes, please do come straight in! Take those two chairs. Just brush away the crumbs there — Number Two was enjoying a biscuit. Perhaps you'd care for something yourselves? No?"

A few more pleasantries (on the part of Mr. Benedict), a tense and hushed exchange the eavesdroppers couldn't make out, and the study door closed. Mr. Benedict and Rhonda had been left alone with the two visitors. One of them Reynie had deduced to be Ms. Argent, a highly placed official who often met with Mr. Benedict, and who was always present when the captured Executives were brought to the house for questioning. She was a key figure in the cases involving Mr. Curtain, and Reynie could easily picture her silver hair and pinched features.

The other visitor had been introduced as Mr. Covett S. Gaines, a man whose deep, gravelly voice, as perceived through the listening glasses, sounded like the rumblings of a tiger.

"Let us cut to the chase," rumbled Mr. Gaines when the door had closed.

"Certainly," said Mr. Benedict. "And who is to be chasing whom?"

"What? Is that a joke?"

"Perhaps not a very funny one. Please continue."

"Very well. Now let's see . . . you've thrown me off my track."

"I believe you were about to inform me that you are the head of a new committee assembled to deal with matters concerning the Whisperer, and that as such you have a few questions for me."

"How the devil did you know that?"

Ms. Argent said, "He often knows such things, Mr. Gaines. The best course is not to grow exercised."

The iciness in Mr. Gaines's tone was not lost even through the wall. "I thank you for recommending the best course, Ms. Argent. Perhaps you should lead the way, seeing as you know it so well."

Ms. Argent cleared her throat. "We're here to clarify certain things in Mr. Gaines's mind."

"Before you make your final decisions, you mean," said Mr. Benedict.

"No one said anything about decisions," growled Mr. Gaines. "Right now we're talking about facts — and I want all of them. I need to know how this Whisperer works, what powers it, what its connection is to you, everything. Start at the beginning, Benedict. Assume I know nothing."

"That won't be difficult," said Mr. Benedict, and Rhonda's spurt of laughter was surprisingly clear — she must be standing next to the wall — but she instantly disguised it as a coughing fit as Mr. Benedict pressed on. "I mean to say it won't be difficult to give you the facts. It's everything *else* that I seem to have trouble conveying."

"Please," said Ms. Argent, "just answer Mr. Gaines's questions."

Mr. Benedict proceeded to relate the facts. The Whisperer, he said, was powered by the tidal turbines his brother had invented and installed in Stonetown Bay. Due to their remarkable design, these turbines were capable of generating enormous energy (a mere fraction of which had once powered Mr. Curtain's Institute), but which currently remained unused save for the energy they transmitted to the Whisperer.

"Transmit?" interjected Mr. Gaines. "How? With cables? Wires? Speak plainly, Benedict!"

"Forgive me," said Mr. Benedict, and then, making liberal use of terms such as "electrical resistance" and "electromagnetic induction" and "receiver coils" — along with a great many terms that only Sticky, of all the eavesdroppers, even faintly recognized — he explained that the energy was transmitted invisibly, without cables or wires. "Is that plain enough, Mr. Gaines?"

"Er, yes . . . quite," Mr. Gaines replied after an uncertain silence. "Please continue."

"The Whisperer," continued Mr. Benedict, "was modeled after my brother's own brain, and was once responsive only to his mental direction. Given the similarities of our brains — I trust you're aware that Ledroptha and I are identical twins — I have managed to induce the Whisperer, with certain modifications, to respond to my own directions as well . . . but of course you will be familiar with all this from the case files."

Reynie felt a tickle at the end of his nose. A spider had descended by a strand of web and settled lightly upon him. In the ambient glow from Kate's flashlight, he could just make out the spider's doubled image (doubled because his eyes were crossed), and somehow resisting an urge to thrash about in panic, he moved his hand slowly and deliberately to brush it away.

"— of the original functions still in place," Mr. Benedict was saying when Reynie was able to concentrate again, "along with other modifications that have allowed me to aid its victims in recovering their memories. So as you can see, if the Whisperer were to fall into my brother's hands again, he would be an immediate threat. Not only could he suppress memories — as he has done before with devastating effect — he could *retrieve* them as well."

"You mean he could obtain key information," rumbled Mr. Gaines. "Sensitive information."

"Precisely. Passwords, codes, any bit of classified material a person might possess — he could have it all at his disposal. He would need only to be within range."

Ms. Argent asked, "And how far exactly would that range extend, Mr. Benedict?"

"It is not so much a question of distance as of focus. Ledroptha could use the Whisperer on anyone in his presence — any person toward whom he could direct his full attention."

Mr. Gaines said, "So if I were standing, say, in the courtyard outside this house, and he was looking down at me from a window . . ."

"You would be in range, yes."

"And he could, what do you call it, brainsweep me," Mr. Gaines said. "He could wipe away my memories. Or extract my memories for his own purposes — essentially read my mind."

"Yes."

"And if there were a whole crowd of people in that courtyard?"

"In theory they would all be at risk," said Mr. Benedict, "though in reality perhaps not. The Whisperer responds only to very specific, very powerful mental direction, and the concentration required to use it is exhausting. My brother has a fierce mind and could certainly do a great deal of damage, but he is human, after all. He would need to rest."

"You keep saying your brother," said Mr. Gaines slowly, "but what about you, Benedict? The Whisperer responds to *your* mental direction, too. So couldn't — in theory, I mean — couldn't you do all those things we've just mentioned?"

"In theory, yes."

"But he wouldn't!" Rhonda cried.

Mr. Gaines's demanding tone had become conciliatory now, almost ingratiating. "Oh no, I never meant to imply Mr. Benedict would use the Whisperer for the wrong reasons. But if it were for a higher purpose, I mean? For the good? Take for example these captured former Executives. Your questioning of them has produced no useful information —"

"On the contrary," said Mr. Benedict. "I have found it helpful indeed."

"No offense, but the committee has deemed that information useless," said Mr. Gaines. "Psychological motives and personal foibles aren't exactly facts, you know. Or perhaps you don't — well, let's not argue, Benedict. The point is with the Whisperer you could find out more *definite* things, could you not? Secret information that would lead us to your brother?"

"I doubt it," said Mr. Benedict. "Ledroptha has never trusted even his closest assistants to keep his most guarded secrets. He chooses instead to spread information around selectively, and to season it with red herrings . . . by 'red herrings' I mean false leads."

"I *know* what a red —"

"I may have misinterpreted your look of confusion," Mr. Benedict said quickly. "Perhaps you simply don't understand my position. So let me be clear: I will not use the Whisperer on anyone — anyone, Mr. Gaines — against that person's will. It is an intrusion, a violation. One's mind is one's most valuable, private possession. I would no sooner break into your memories, Mr. Gaines, than I would break into your home."

"We're not talking about *me*!" protested Mr. Gaines. "We're talking about criminals, Benedict! Listen, I can understand your hesitation with these Executives — I've read your arguments about how they were captured as children and raised up under Curtain's influence, how they should therefore be shown some lenience, even forgiveness, and so on — but leaving them aside, I don't see how you could refuse to probe the minds of these wicked fellows who worked for Curtain, these . . . what do you call them? These elegant thugs your man Milligan has brought in?"

"The agents call them Ten Men," said Ms. Argent. "Because they have ten different ways to hurt you."

"Right. These unsavory Ten Men. Nothing they've said has helped us get one step closer to your brother. In point of fact they've hardly said anything at all."

"Nor will they," said Mr. Benedict. "Not so long as they perceive any chance of Ledroptha gaining power."

"So you admit it! You admit your brother may yet be seeking a way to gain power! But you won't use the Whisperer on these vicious —?"

"Tell me, Mr. Gaines, have you ever spoken with Milligan about the years of crushing sadness he endured because of the Whisperer's effects? Or the mental anguish he experienced while trying to resist being brainswept in the first place?"

"I don't need to speak to Milligan about it. His is a different case entirely. In this case, couldn't you —"

"I have nothing further to say on this matter, Mr. Gaines."

There was a long pause, during which the eavesdroppers strove to keep still and quiet. Sticky was especially tormented — his natural fidgetiness was at its peak in moments like this — but the others were struggling, too. In Kate the reminder of those lonely years she and Milligan had lived apart had stoked an old, low-burning anger, and she felt like running, jumping, climbing, fighting — anything to work off the emotion. And Reynie, as he often did when his mind was racing, felt a powerful urge to pace.

Instead the three of them stood frozen, ears to their listening glasses, waiting.

At length Ms. Argent broke the silence. In a tentative voice, as if she herself didn't much like what she was about, she said, "What about your new side project, Mr. Benedict? Don't you wish to pursue that work?"

"What new project?" asked Mr. Gaines. "Why am I just hearing of this?"

"Mr. Benedict believes the Whisperer might be used to alleviate the symptoms of his narcolepsy. By way of a kind of hypnosis — is that right, Mr. Benedict? A sort of fooling of the brain's habitual responses to stimuli?"

"I'm impressed, Ms. Argent," said Mr. Benedict in an amiable tone. (Reynie imagined him tapping his nose, as he often did when someone gave a correct answer.) "You remember perfectly something I never mentioned to you."

"I'm sorry, I —"

"That's quite all right. I've made no real secret of my project, and it does interest me to see how information travels."

"We're offering you a deal," said Mr. Gaines, having instantly latched on to Ms. Argent's implied suggestion and making it his own. "You can get rid of your narcoplexy, or whatever you call it, and in the meantime you'll use the Whisperer as we see fit. That's a fair trade, Benedict. You know it is."

"I know nothing of the kind. It was not just my own situation I hoped to improve, Mr. Gaines, but that of countless people with similar conditions, since it stands to reason that what works on me might work on others. Regardless, I am not sure my ideas are even practicable; to determine that would require considerable research and experiment. But even if I *were* sure, Mr. Gaines, we would have no deal, for I simply will not do what you ask of me."

"I guess you like falling asleep willy-nilly?" said Mr. Gaines angrily.

"I certainly prefer it to laying aside my moral concerns."

"Very well," said Mr. Gaines, and there was a harsh scraping sound as he rose abruptly from his chair, "you leave us no choice. We're taking the Whisperer. There's no longer any justification for you to have it here. You've already restored all the memories that your brother —"

"Not all of them," Mr. Benedict corrected.

Mr. Gaines snorted. "Do spare me your pointless distinctions! The captured Executives had their chance and refused it. If they don't trust you, what do you expect me to —?"

"I wasn't referring to the captured Executives."

"Well, I'm afraid I can't begin to care!" Mr. Gaines snapped. "Your time is over, Benedict. The Whisperer is to be moved. And don't try to argue that you're the only one who can use it. All of our top scientific advisers are being assembled right here in Stonetown next week to deal with this very matter."

"That was not the argument I intended to raise," said Mr. Benedict calmly. "I'm sure you'll do everything you can to find a way to use the Whisperer — and I do worry about the choices you'll make if you succeed — but my more immediate concern is that you'll lose possession of it altogether. If you transport the Whisperer, you expose it. You make it vulnerable."

"A weak argument, Benedict. We have our top security people involved. No, I'm afraid the greater risk, as the committee sees it, would be to leave such a powerful tool in the hands of someone who refuses to heed our directions. There is growing concern that we cannot trust you anymore." Mr. Gaines made a disgusted sound. "Ms. Argent, if you please, stop looking so horrified. He wants us to be frightened — the better to protect his position. Now then, Benedict, should you choose to cooperate, you'll be allowed to supervise the removal of the Whisperer and its computers from the premises. We would welcome your technical input, and a good-faith effort on your part might help repair some of your damaged credibility."

"And if I choose *not* to cooperate?" Mr. Benedict asked.

"Then you'll be required to remain in your study throughout the removal process."

"I see," said Mr. Benedict. "And when is the removal to take place?"

"This very evening," said Mr. Gaines. "I have the paperwork right . . . well, where the devil is it?"

"You've mislaid the papers?" Mr. Benedict said. "But Mr. Gaines, you know you cannot take action in my home without proper authorization."

"I had it . . . right . . . What's happened, Ms. Argent? Did I not have it right here with these other —?"

"Forgive us," said Ms. Argent. "Obviously we'll need to find these papers, or else have them run through committee again. If that's the case it will be some time before we can proceed."

"Very well, Ms. Argent, I thank you," said Mr. Benedict. "Now if you'll excuse us, Rhonda and I must return to work. Milligan is waiting outside the door to show you down."

Mr. Gaines spluttered indignantly. "I'm not leaving until I've —"

"Actually, you'll be leaving right now," said Rhonda, whereupon the study door opened, and Milligan's voice — quite cheerful and polite, yet managing at the same time to suggest how unwise it would be to contradict him — said, "If you'll be so kind as to follow me, sir, this is your best opportunity to exit without conflict."

"Please, Mr. Gaines, let's go," said Ms. Argent.

With a snort and a few muttered protests, Mr. Gaines stalked from the room, followed by a silent Ms. Argent. The study door closed.

"Rhonda," said Mr. Benedict after a pause, "when they've gone, please ask Milligan to bring those papers up. We'll want to look them over. Number Two should come as well."

"Of course. But Mr. Benedict, can it really be that —?"

"Before we continue, Rhonda, I must ask another favor. Would you also fetch Reynie, Sticky, and Kate? Escort them all the way here, please. I want no one to speak with them before I've had a chance to do so myself."

"Certainly," Rhonda said. "I'll tell the others and then go find them."

"Oh, finding them won't be necessary," said Mr. Benedict, and Reynie heard a tapping sound inches from his ear. "They're right behind this wall."

～:～

The eavesdroppers were feeling grateful it was Rhonda who'd been sent to escort them — Rhonda's sternness being tempered somewhat by her amusement — when they discovered Number Two and Constance waiting for them outside the study. Both wore expressions of furious disapproval.

"Eavesdropping!" Number Two hissed, crossing her arms.

"Without *me*!" Constance said, doing the same.

Milligan came along the hallway behind them. Playfully tapping Kate on the head with a bundle of papers he said, "This is hardly appropriate behavior, young lady. Spies have *rules*, you know."

"Milligan, tell me you aren't making light of this!" said Number Two.

"Absolutely not," said Milligan ambiguously, with a wink at the children.

Mr. Benedict opened his door and smiled at the crowd gathered in the hallway. "Won't you all come in? Or must I stand at the wall with a glass?"

As everyone got settled — those without chairs sat amid piles of books on the floor, Milligan remained standing near the door, and Number Two hovered beside Mr. Benedict, who leaned against his book-cluttered desk — the older children fumbled to explain themselves. Mr. Benedict waved them silent.

"I haven't called you in here to apologize," he said, "though it *is* rather bad form to eavesdrop on your friends. In the future you must please bear that in mind." He held up the papers Milligan had given him. "This business is what I mean to discuss. What you three heard is far more important, at the moment, than how you came to hear it."

"And what was *that*?" Constance demanded. "Why am I always the last to know!"

"In this case," said Mr. Benedict, glancing through the papers as he spoke, "I believe it's because you were in the kitchen pretending to help clean up. Reynie, would you kindly summarize my conversation with Mr. Gaines and Ms. Argent? Milligan and Number Two need the details, as well. In the meantime, Rhonda, please memorize the names on these forms — Milligan and Number Two will already have done so — and then destroy them."

As Reynie sheepishly related the details of the conversation, Rhonda flipped through the papers with a keen eye. She had an excellent memory, almost as good as Sticky's, and in the few short minutes it took Reynie to give his account, she finished her task, shredded the papers, and took a seat on the floor next to Kate.

"An excellent summary, Reynie," said Mr. Benedict. "Thank you. Now, I believe Constance has some questions —"

But Constance had already butted in, crying, "How did you know they were eavesdropping, Mr. Benedict? Why didn't you send them away? It isn't fair! And is this true about using the Whisperer to get rid of your narcolepsy? How could it do that? And how dare they think they can take it away from you! Who do they think they are?"

The little girl, her pudgy cheeks gone quite crimson with the heat of her emotions, seemed unable to decide whether to be envious, outraged, hopeful, or worried, and in her agitation — she wasn't getting answers quickly enough to suit her, though she hadn't allowed time for Mr. Benedict to respond — she began to repeat her questions from the beginning.

Mr. Benedict held up his hands until she fell silent. "Let me answer your questions in order, my dear. First, I have used this study for so many years, any shift in acoustics — I mean the way sound carries — is bound to draw my attention. But by the time I realized that the hollow space in the wall behind me was no longer quite so hollow, it was too late to send away the wicked spies" — he smiled at the spies in question — "without calling Mr. Gaines's attention to their presence. That would not do, you see, for it would subject them to all sorts of disagreeable inquiries, and no doubt the Washingtons and Perumals would be dragged in as well.

"As for using the Whisperer to diminish the symptoms of my narcolepsy, what I told Mr. Gaines was the truth: It's possible. My hope was to adapt the machine to transmit powerful messages — instructions, essentially — that could redirect certain faulty mental impulses. Whenever my brain, for instance, sent a signal to fall asleep at inappropriate moments, these new, more powerful instructions would be to ignore the signal."

"Basically a form of hypnosis," said Sticky, and Mr. Benedict tapped his nose.

"And you thought it might work on others, as well," Reynie said, not a little wonderingly, for the real potential of Mr. Benedict's project was only just now sinking in. "That would mean thousands of people — no, even more than that — why, *millions* of people might be helped . . ."

Mr. Benedict nodded. "You see why I thought it worth pursuing, even though my chances of success were slim at best."

"And your nightmares?" Constance persisted. "The Old Hag and those other terrible hallucinations? Would it take care of those things, too?"

"Again, it's possible," Mr. Benedict said. "Indeed, a great many things were possible — possible if not probable. I even entertained some small hope of using this project to persuade my brother to surrender. Under the right circumstances, if Ledroptha found himself in a terrible spot, with no good options before him . . . well, I thought the promise of relief might just draw him in the right direction. A less desperate and thus more peaceful one. But as I say, my research had only just begun, and now —"

"Well, get to it!" Constance cried. "You have a little time, right? Or even more if Milligan snatches their papers again!"

"That trick isn't likely to work twice," said Mr. Benedict. "At any rate, we cannot afford to dwell on those possibilities now, however grand they might have been to contemplate.

The situation has changed, my dear. There is no more time. Our concern now must be what we *know* the Whisperer can do if it falls into the wrong hands."

"Gaines's hands are the wrong ones, I can verify that," said Milligan. "He doesn't seem to be a spy for Curtain, but he has a lot of power and no judgment."

"A bad combination," said Number Two.

"He might as well be a spy," said Rhonda. "If he succeeds in getting the Whisperer removed, he's doing exactly what Curtain would want."

"Because taking it out into the open makes it vulnerable?" said Kate, remembering what Mr. Benedict had said earlier.

"Yes," said Rhonda. "When we first moved the Whisperer here — right after your mission to the Institute — Curtain was on the run and could do nothing to intercept us. He's had time to prepare now, though. He has spies, and he most certainly has a plan."

"I've been pressed to move the Whisperer before," said Mr. Benedict. "Usually the Monk Building is suggested as a preferable location. As you know, I've maintained an office there — for reasons only those of us in this house are aware of — and the government has offered to secure additional space in the building for me. But it has been clear for some time that their real aim is to separate me from the Whisperer. They've tried to use quiet measures, small steps. Now that those have failed, they are prepared to take more extreme action."

"Who is 'they'?" said Constance.

"Certain well-placed officials," said Mr. Benedict. "Some

are likely spies for my brother seeking a way to return his Whisperer to him. Others are more interested in seeing what they can do with it themselves. And still others, such as poor Ms. Argent, are hapless individuals caught up in the process, trying to do their jobs, uncertain where their loyalties should lie, and not quite up to the task of deciding."

"So what do we do now?" asked Kate.

"Your lessons," said Number Two, checking her watch.

The older children cried out in protest, and Constance wrapped her arms tightly around her knees and hissed like an angry cat.

"Perhaps we can delay the lessons," Mr. Benedict said, laying his hand on Number Two's arm. "I know it's difficult to be kept in the dark. Naturally, I hate it myself. But you must understand that I cannot tell you everything, for in certain cases ignorance is your greatest protection."

"What *can* you tell us?" asked Reynie. "How about these 'psychological motives' and 'personal foibles' that Mr. Gaines mentioned, the things you've found useful but the committee hasn't?"

Mr. Benedict tapped his nose. "That is something I can tell you about. In my opinion my brother Ledroptha's motivations are worth a great deal of consideration. Not just what he does, but why he does it. The better we know these things, the better we can predict his next move, and I believe my conversations with his former Executives have been most instructive in this respect."

"I've wondered how instructive they could be," said Sticky. "We know Martina wanted revenge against Mr. Curtain for abandoning her — but she didn't really know much, did she? And Jackson and Jillson were Executives a long time, but I can't imagine they've been very cooperative."

"Oh no," said Mr. Benedict with a chuckle. "They have done their best to be obstructive. But in the process they have given away more than they realize. Most notably, they revealed that S.Q. Pedalian received far more sessions in the Whisperer than the other Executives did."

The children frowned in surprise. They all knew from their mission to the Institute what these "sessions" were about; Mr. Curtain had given them to his Executives as a reward, which helped ensure their loyalty. And Reynie and Sticky, in particular, remembered all too well how "happy" the machine made you feel when you thought what it wanted you to think — what Mr. *Curtain* wanted you to think — an effect it accomplished by suppressing your greatest fears. Even if you knew the truth about the Whisperer's darker purposes (as the boys had known), the feeling it gave you — that fleeting yet powerful illusion of well-being — left you yearning for more.

"Why would S.Q. get more sessions?" Kate asked. "He was already the most loyal Executive in the bunch!"

"Maybe he was loyal *because* of the extra sessions," Sticky suggested.

"But why would Mr. Curtain give them to him?" Constance said. "Why would he want to keep S.Q. around in the first place? That guy's about as smart as a lump of oatmeal."

"Poor fellow, it's not his fault," said Kate. "And he's really kind-hearted, you know."

"I *do* know," said Constance, "which makes me wonder even more why Mr. Curtain would want him."

"You are asking all the right questions," said Mr. Benedict, "and I am making it your assignment to reflect upon the best answer to them. You must continue with your other lessons in the meantime, of course."

"Can't you tell us what *you* think?" Sticky asked.

"Now where would be the fun in that?" said Mr. Benedict, and he took a folded slip of paper from his desk. "As a compromise gesture, however, I have composed a modest riddle that I believe to be pertinent. No doubt you'll soon have solved it."

"Oh, but please!" pressed Kate, rising along with the other children (all straining for a glimpse of the riddle). "If you think we can solve it so fast, then why must we wait . . ." She trailed off, noting Mr. Benedict's raised eyebrows, a sure sign that she had missed something. She turned to Reynie, who shrugged resignedly and said, "The assignment isn't to *find* the best answer, remember? It's to reflect upon it."

Mr. Benedict smiled. "Sometimes the answer is only the beginning, as you well know. Now, I promise we'll discuss this again, but in the meantime we must all turn to other tasks. Lessons, in your case, which reminds me . . ." Mr. Benedict laced his fingers together and gazed in an encouraging way at Constance. "Your friends have agreed to participate in a new exercise I've devised. I wonder if you would be willing yourself? I think you might enjoy this one . . ."

By the time Mr. Benedict had explained his idea, Constance was clapping her hands and bouncing in place, quite giddy with anticipation. The other children looked at one another and shifted uncomfortably.

"Wonderful!" Mr. Benedict said. "How about tomorrow, then? Moocho tells me he has the necessary ingredients, and Milligan has agreed to secure the ice cream, so if tomorrow suits you — say, just after lunch?"

"As soon as possible!" Constance cried.

"Tomorrow it is, then," said Mr. Benedict. "In the meantime, my friends, you'll have my riddle to consider —"

"And their afternoon lessons," prompted Number Two, snatching the slip of paper before the children could grab it.

"And your afternoon lessons," Mr. Benedict agreed. "So off you go!"

What May Be Perceived

As soon as they had finished doing their lessons (or in Constance's case, avoiding them), the children raced up-stairs. All afternoon the coveted slip of paper had peeked tantalizingly from the pocket of Number Two's yellow blazer, but at last they were in possession of it. They had a full hour before supper, time enough to take a crack at the riddle.

Flinging her jacket onto a peg, Kate threw open the win-dow (the girls' room was on the overheated third floor), then collected her friends' jackets and cardigans and hung them

tidily in the closet. This room was the tidiest in the house —
no small miracle considering who occupied it, but not even
Constance's willful slovenliness could withstand the atten-
tions of her tireless roommate. Kate would no sooner leave
shoes out to be tripped over than she would leave her bottle
of super-strength glue uncapped. The girls' room, therefore, with its uncluttered, spotless rug, was always the natural place for the Society's meetings.

"Hurry *up*, Kate," said Constance, who had just sat down.
"You're always making us wait!"

"I know, it's terrible," Kate replied carelessly, and she
somersaulted onto the rug next to Constance as Reynie and
Sticky settled down across from them.

Reynie unfolded the slip of paper. "Okay," he said, glancing up at the others, and after a short, tension-filled pause,
he began to read aloud:

> The answer to this riddle has a hole in the middle,
> And some have been known to fall in it.
> In tennis it's nothing, but it can be received,
> And sometimes a person may win it.
> Though not seen or heard it may yet be perceived,
> Like princes or bees it's in clover.
> The answer to this riddle has a hole in the middle,
> And without it one cannot start over.

"It's a trap!" Sticky cried with such vehemence that
Reynie wrenched around, half-expecting to see a Ten Man
leering from the doorway, and Kate snatched up her bucket
and flew to the window.

Sticky glanced wildly about, his heart pounding. "What is it? What's going on?"

Kate was peering intently into the courtyard, where Mr. Bane sat on the bench eating sunflower seeds and spitting out the shells. "All clear outside, as far as I can gather. Constance, is there someone in the hall?"

"N-no, I don't think so," said Constance in a shaky voice.

"What makes you think there's a trap?" said Kate, spinning around to look seriously at Sticky. "What kind of trap?"

Sticky blinked in confusion. He turned to Reynie, who had just covered his face with his hands. At first Sticky thought he was sobbing — his shoulders were shaking — but then with a great spluttering guffaw Reynie collapsed backward onto the floor, laughing and laughing.

"What's so funny?" Sticky said. Then his eyes grew wide. "Wait, did you think I meant . . . an *actual* . . . ?"

Kate's jaw dropped. "And *you* thought *we* . . . you mean you didn't realize . . . ?"

Soon everyone was rolling on the floor except Constance, who refused to see what was so hilarious about having the wits scared out of her. "For crying out loud, Sticky," she complained as the others chortled and groaned, "you can't go yelling stuff like that! We've seen too many *real* traps!" But they were all laughing too hard to pay any attention. (And they let themselves go on a while, too, for after such a fright the laughter came as a relief.)

Eventually, however — with tremulous sighs, dabs at their eyes, and weak little chuckling aftershocks — they sorted themselves out. Kate retied her ponytail, Sticky resettled his spectacles, and Reynie smoothed the crumpled slip of paper in his hand. Ignoring Constance's dark looks (she had one for each of them) they returned to the riddle.

Kate said, "I don't think 'trap' is the answer, Sticky. It fits some of the clues but not all of them."

"No, I see that now," Sticky admitted. "I just got excited when it occurred to me, because you *can* fall into one, you know, and the part about the clover reminded me of the drapeweed traps at the Institute."

"What do you think that's about, anyway?" said Kate. "What's a prince doing in the clover?"

"It's a figure of speech," Sticky said. "If you're 'in clover' it means you're wealthy — like a prince. Do you suppose the answer has something to do with money?"

Kate snapped her fingers. "Maybe S.Q. has a secret fortune! An inheritance, maybe, or some other kind of treasure Mr. Curtain wants to get his hands on. That would explain why he's kept S.Q. around, wouldn't it? And gave him those extra sessions in the Whisperer?"

"You can say a person 'falls into' money if it comes unexpectedly," Sticky mused, "in which case it's 'received' . . ."

"And you can win it!" Constance blurted out (forgetting, in her excitement, that she'd meant to be sulking).

"Hey, and Mr. Curtain needed money to start over!" Kate said. "After he became a fugitive he had to find new ways to get it, right? That's why he worked out that diamond scam with Mr. Pressius!"

For a moment their eagerness was dampened by the thought of Mr. Pressius, the wealthy businessman whose fraudulent activities had recently enriched Mr. Curtain — not to mention himself — yet who had managed to escape any charge of wrongdoing. They'd never actually met Mr. Pressius, but they'd suffered considerably because of him and held him in particularly low esteem.

Sticky reached for his spectacles, checked himself, and instead laced his fingers behind his head. "There's a problem with 'money,'" he said, pressing on with the riddle. "You can see it, right? And sometimes hear it — a pot of gold tends to jingle."

"True, but what if the answer isn't 'money' but 'wealth'?" Constance suggested. "You can *perceive* wealth if a person has expensive cars and mansions, without actually seeing or hearing it."

"Hey, I think that works!" said Kate. "Now we just have to explain the 'hole in the middle.'" She turned to Reynie, who usually would have offered a suggestion by now — or even a solution — but Reynie only looked thoughtful and said nothing.

"The hole isn't the only thing," said Sticky. "There's also the bit about tennis. And I suppose we should consider why there are bees in the clover and not just princes."

Kate snorted. "Sometimes you amaze me, Sticky! You know everything in the world but you don't know why bees like clover?"

"I think what Sticky means to say," Reynie put in, "is there must be a reason the bees are mentioned." With a curious hesitation, as if he expected argument from the others, he added, "My guess is it's to show there's more than one way to be in clover."

"What other way might there be?" Kate asked, but Reynie only shrugged, and when no one else volunteered an answer she said, "Well, at least the bees don't automatically rule out wealth. And I don't think the tennis part does, either."

"Can't we just ignore that?" asked Constance hopefully. "'In tennis it's nothing,' right? I'll bet that's just in there for the sake of the meter, and to set up the part about 'receiving' and 'winning.' I'm a poet, you know, I have experience with these things."

"But hold on," said Sticky, lighting up. "In tennis there's a net — and nets have *holes* in them!"

"You can fall into a net, too," Kate reflected. "I did it all the time in the circus . . . but it doesn't seem to fit the rest of the riddle. What about 'service,' though? In tennis you *receive* a serve — and you can *win* it, too! Maybe Mr. Curtain keeps S.Q. around because he likes having a *servant*. That's what S.Q. really is, you know — he's always at Mr. Curtain's beck and call."

The others mulled this over. It seemed to make perfect sense at first, but one problem with riddles is that wrong answers so often *do* seem to make sense at first, only to fall apart under closer examination. So it had been with Sticky's idea, and so it was with Kate's. "Service" seemed promising, but in the end they all realized it couldn't work. And they went on like this for some time, trying out one possible solution after another, none of which seemed right.

"I give up," Constance said finally. "I think it has to be 'wealth.' Maybe we can't figure out why the bees are in there, or what the hole in the middle is, but 'wealth' still seems like the best answer."

Kate sighed and unraveled her legs. "Well, we've been at this almost an hour. At the very least we could talk about something else and come back to the riddle later."

"We don't *have* to come back to it," Constance protested irritably. " 'Wealth' is the answer!"

Kate turned to Reynie. "Well, Reynie, what do you say? I don't think I've ever seen you so quiet when we were working on something."

"Hey, that's true," said Sticky, who'd been concentrating so hard on the riddle that he hadn't noticed Reynie's silence. "In fact, I'm surprised you haven't solved it by now."

Reynie seemed taken aback. "But I *have* solved it."

The others stared at him.

"Excuse me if I'm missing something," Kate said after a pause, "but, um, were you ever going to tell us?"

"Are you joking?" Reynie replied. "You asked me not to!"

"I did?"

Reynie cocked his head. "Well, Constance did, and you and Sticky didn't argue, so I figured you must agree."

"When did all this happen?" Sticky asked, exchanging a nervous look with Kate.

"When I was unfolding the paper!" Reynie cried. "Constance said, 'I know you're probably going to solve this, Reynie, but for once we'd like to have a chance to figure it out ourselves.' So I said 'Okay,' and then I read the riddle out loud, remember?"

"You did say 'Okay,' " Sticky recalled. "I guess we just didn't hear what Constance said."

"That's because I didn't say it," Constance said.

Kate rolled her eyes. "Well, either *you're* lying or Reynie is, and if I had to —"

"I thought it," Constance said, somewhat abashedly.

"You . . . you what?"

"I didn't *say* what Reynie said I did . . . I only *thought* it."

There was a silence, during which Reynie sagged backward onto the floor and stared at the ceiling.

Then Kate muttered, "Oh boy."

"So now Reynie can read minds, too?" Sticky asked.

"I didn't read any mind but my own," Reynie said. "Constance just put her thoughts into it."

"Sorry," Constance mumbled. "I didn't mean to, you know." And it was clear she was telling the truth, but at the same time there was a hint of impishness in her expression, as if she had just realized for the first time what her gifts might allow her to do.

There followed another long pause, and then, rather hesitantly, Kate said, "Okay, I realize this mind-reading thing, or whatever you call what Constance did —"

"Mental telepathy," said Sticky in an awed tone.

"Right, mental telepathy," Kate said. "I realize it's kind of a big deal. But, um, would anyone mind if I took a second to ask Reynie, just really quickly . . . I mean, I'm sorry, but it's driving me nuts not to know . . ."

" 'Love,' " Reynie said, swiveling his eyes toward her. "The answer to the riddle is 'love.' "

Kate sighed with relief. " 'Love'?" she repeated, grinning. "Well, how about that! I wonder if . . ." She trailed off, recollecting herself. "We can talk about it later, of course. Er, anyway, thank you, Reynie."

"No problem," Reynie said, and went back to staring at the ceiling.

◦:◦

"It's hot in here, isn't it?" asked Constance the next day. She was sitting at the dining room table with the other children, two of whom were eating pie and ice cream with expressions of immense satisfaction.

"Is it? I hadn't noticed," Sticky said irritably. He turned his back toward Reynie and Kate, who smiled at each other and kept eating. "Let's concentrate and get through this, all right? The sooner you finish, the sooner you get your treat."

"And the sooner Sticky gets his," murmured Kate, who like Reynie had drawn a long straw and thus avoided going last.

It was just after lunch, the adults had all dispersed, and the children were engaged in the first exercise Constance had ever been excited about — the exercise for which the older ones had only reluctantly volunteered. In a move designed to motivate Constance, Mr. Benedict had asked Milligan to bring home a gallon of ice cream and Moocho Brazos to bake one of his famous pies. Furthermore (and this was the part they were reluctant about), he had asked the older children to think of an embarrassing memory — one that Constance would be amused to discover — and give the younger girl the opportunity to fish it out.

Constance's eagerness to do the exercise had made the others shudder — no doubt their embarrassments would soon be put down in rhyming verse, possibly to be laughed at by future generations. But they recognized the importance of learning more about Constance's developing gifts (even more so now, given what had happened with Reynie the day before), and so with resigned hearts they all tried to think of experiences that had been just a *little* embarrassing, rather than outright humiliations.

"Honestly, you don't think it's hot?" Constance said, more loudly this time, with a sidelong glance at Reynie. "Maybe it's just me. I think I may faint if I don't cool down."

Reynie wagged his spoon. "Give it up, Constance. You aren't getting any of my ice cream."

Constance humphed — caught out — and Reynie chuckled to himself. It was small consolation for having Constance shine her unnerving spotlight into his mind, but he was determined to enjoy his treat nonetheless. The pie was Moocho's best ever, with a flaky crust and a tart, sweet, piping-hot cherry filling, and Reynie was taking time to savor each bite. Not so with poor Kate, who had already finished her own slice, then gulped her ice cream too quickly and now sat clutching her throbbing head.

"Fine, Sticky," Constance sighed, "let's have a peek inside that head of yours."

Her matter-of-fact tone, and indeed the whole exercise, reminded Sticky rather too much of going to the dentist with a mouth full of cavities. He tried to steel himself, but no sooner had Constance fixed her gaze on his face than he cried out, "Wait, wait! Let me . . . let me choose a better image."

Constance banged her fists on her knees. "Oh, for crying out loud! Now you're stalling! Will I *ever* get to eat ice cream?"

"Give me just a second," Sticky said, and sitting on his hands to keep them at bay, he hurriedly sorted through his embarrassing memories again (he had no shortage of them) trying to decide which he could stand to share and how best to represent it. Mr. Benedict had suggested that images would probably be more effective than words — images being unmuddied by grammar and easier to hold steady in the mind — and he had also asked the children to pay close attention to the "telepathic experience," if indeed any occurred, and to be prepared to report anything peculiar.

Reynie and Kate had experienced nothing more peculiar than an intense dread of having Constance poke around in their minds, followed by a natural feeling of annoyance when she succeeded — but for Sticky this prospect alone was enough to throw him out of sorts.

"I think it's best to just get it over with, Sticky," advised Reynie, who during his own turn had pictured Seymore the orphanage cat, over whom he had once tripped and fallen while others looked scornfully on. Constance had instantly guessed "some kind of slinky animal with whiskers, I'd say a weasel from the look of it." This was close enough, and per their agreement Reynie had been compelled to tell the whole story, much to Constance's amusement.

Kate, for her part, had pictured herself hanging upside down from a tightwire and flailing about. After brief consideration Constance had guessed "a hideous baby bat waking up," which may or may not have been an intentional insult, but regardless was good enough to earn her the story of Kate toppling from the wire with a shriek and just barely catching it with her legs. "The clowns got a kick out of that one," Kate had said, then added defensively, "I was only eight, you know."

Now Sticky was ready to try again. Taking a deep breath, he rapped on the table with his knuckles and tensed as if bracing for a blow.

"Is it ice cream?" Constance asked. "Ice cream and pie?"

"Of course not," Sticky said wearily, and he sank back into his chair. "Forget the sweets and try to focus on *me*, will you?"

"I *was* focusing on you! How do you know I wasn't?"

"You guessed ice cream and pie, Constance!"

They began to bicker, their tones growing more strident with every word, and Reynie was grateful for the distraction when Moocho Brazos swept into the dining room, all muscle and mustache, and swarthy as a sailor. Over his elegant tailored shirt and trousers Moocho wore the bright red apron the children had given him for his birthday. He wielded an ice cream scoop and a spatula (in his huge hands they looked like a child's playthings) but observing Sticky and Constance in the midst of their heated argument he lowered the utensils and shook his head.

"I see they aren't quite ready," Moocho intoned. He chuckled and took a seat (or rather, two seats) next to Kate. "I trust you enjoyed yours?"

"You know we did!" Kate laughed, reaching up to smooth a stray lock of Moocho's well-oiled black hair. She and the strong man had been friends for years, and she felt very motherly toward him.

"I'm so glad," said Moocho, and idly inspecting his spatula he said, "By the way, I believe I've finally solved that riddle you gave me last night. The answer is 'love,' isn't it? What a relief! If I'd known anything about tennis, perhaps I'd have managed sooner, but sadly I ignored that part for the longest time — 'in tennis it's nothing,' after all."

"That threw us, too," said Kate. "Or some of us, anyway. How did you finally figure it out?"

"I consulted an encyclopedia. Imagine my surprise when I learned that in tennis 'love' is a score of zero! Suddenly everything made sense! Or almost everything, I should say. Most of the lines came clear right away — a person can *fall in* love and so on — but a few aspects still puzzle me: the hole in the middle, the clover, and the part about starting over."

"Shall we tell you?" Reynie asked, speaking up to be heard over Constance, whose voice had gone quite shrill. "Or would you rather figure them out?"

"Oh no, if you please, I'm anxious to be rid of them. They've been hanging over me like a cloud."

"Well," said Reynie, "the hole in the middle is the letter O in 'love.' So the bit about 'falling in it' refers to falling in love — just as you guessed — and not to falling in the hole. You can read that first line either way."

"Clever," said Moocho, writing out "love" in the air with his spatula. "Although, in my defense, the O is not precisely in the middle but slightly to the left."

"Funny, that's what Constance said," Kate observed. (Moocho stiffened ever so slightly.) "Anyway, the last line of the poem does the opposite — it refers to the O, not to 'love.'"

"You can't start over without an O? Why not?"

"Try writing the word 'over' without the O," Reynie said. "It's hard to start, isn't it?"

Moocho slapped his forehead with the spatula.

"As for the clover," Kate went on, laughing, "take a close look at the word and you'll find 'love' in it. Bees, princes, and love — they're all in clover, just in different ways."

Moocho thanked them heartily for the explanations, and after a brief exchange about the weather (Constance had predicted rain by evening), the conversation turned to some meat scraps Kate had asked to be set aside for Madge. Reynie quickly tuned it out and dove into his own thoughts, for after so long with nothing new to consider, he suddenly had much more to think about than he had time to think. Last night he'd lain awake for hours thinking about that strange incident with Constance, and in his few spare moments today he'd been trying (true to their assignment) to reflect on the solution to the riddle.

Mr. Curtain had kept S.Q. around out of *love*? It seemed impossible — Mr. Curtain seemed incapable of love. But if you could make yourself believe otherwise, then Mr. Curtain's tolerance of S.Q., his least competent Executive and now his last remaining one, no longer seemed so mysterious. Still, just as Mr. Benedict had said, sometimes the answer is only the beginning, and Reynie found that the riddle's solution raised even more questions in his mind than it answered.

He would have given a lot to be able to put those questions

to Mr. Benedict, but since yesterday afternoon Mr. Benedict had spent every waking moment (and no doubt a few sleeping ones) down among the computers in the basement. At supper Number Two had taken a plate to him, and at breakfast this morning Rhonda had. Not even when they told Rhonda about Constance's latest feat had Mr. Benedict made an appearance; in fact Rhonda hadn't even summoned him.

"Don't get me wrong, what you're telling me is important, but he's asked not to be disturbed except in certain cases," Rhonda said, without specifying what those cases might be. "He has a great deal of work to do in a very short time and is permitting himself few breaks."

Rhonda wouldn't tell them what Mr. Benedict was doing or why it was so urgent, but in last night's meeting of the Society Constance had speculated he was seeking the remedy for his narcolepsy. She hoped so, anyway, since he would lose his chance forever once the Whisperer was taken away. She had spent the rest of the meeting railing bitterly against Mr. Gaines "and that twitty committee," for Constance loved Mr. Benedict (though she never exactly said so aloud) and felt every bit as protective of him as Number Two and Rhonda did. In fact she would have been his adopted daughter by now if only the authorities would recognize her existence, but due to the mysterious absence of certain official papers they had refused to do so. This was yet another reason for her bitterness. Few things infuriated Constance more than being ignored, and having her existence denied struck her as the worst insult imaginable.

"An empty box!" Constance cried now, breaking in on Reynie's thoughts. She and Sticky had finally resolved their argument and resumed the exercise. "An empty box, sort of tilted to the side!"

"Yes!" Sticky said with obvious relief, but then his face fell. "Oh, great, but now I have to tell you about the memory." Mustering his resolve he began, "One time in a quiz championship I was asked to draw a rhombus. I froze up from the pressure — you know how I used to do that sometimes . . ."

"Oh yes," said Constance with an arch look. "You *used* to do that."

Ignoring this comment, Sticky pressed on, "Well, instead of a *rhombus*, which is an equilateral parallelogram — that's the tilted box shape you saw — I got it into my head that I was supposed to draw an *omnibus*."

Constance frowned. "What's that?"

"A bus — 'omnibus' is essentially an old-fashioned word for 'bus.' I knew what a rhombus was, of course, I just got so flustered and . . ." Sticky grimaced and reached for his spectacles. "When I think of how carefully I drew the wheels," he muttered, "how I even put little faces of people in the windows, thinking I was being creative, while everyone there must have been shaking their heads, appalled that I thought this was a rhombus . . ."

Constance was staring at Sticky with a look of extreme disappointment. "That's it? Your empty box is just a dumb old rhombus? That's the most boring embarrassment I've ever heard of!"

Sticky's eyes flashed, and he was about to argue when he suddenly realized that he'd gotten lucky. "You think so? Well, sorry, Constance, that's the story." For a moment he contemplated his spectacles, which he'd removed without thinking. He put them back on again. "And guess what? We get our pie and ice cream now."

"You're right!" Constance exclaimed. "I guessed all three! Moocho, did you hear that? I guessed all three!"

"Congratulations," said Moocho with a grin, and to Sticky he said, "and also my sympathies. Allow me to give you both your just desserts." He wriggled his heavy dark eyebrows, obviously pleased with himself.

"Moocho!" Kate cried, laughing boisterously and clapping her hands. "What a joke! Oh, I wish I'd thought of that! *Just desserts!* Did you hear that, everyone?" She followed him into the kitchen and back, repeating his play on words over and over and laughing afresh each time.

A short time later, having already eaten all of her ice cream and most of her pie, Constance was staring at her remaining few bites with exaggerated dejection. "Moocho didn't give me as much ice cream as you," she complained to Sticky, "and now I don't have any to eat with the rest of my pie."

Leaning across the table, Reynie pretended to study her bowl. "I think you just misjudged your pie-to-ice-cream ratio, Constance. You took two bites of ice cream for every one bite of pie."

"Moocho gave you both the same," said Kate, who was in the corner of the dining room doing handstand push-ups. "I saw him scoop the ice cream."

"No, he didn't!" Constance snapped. "Sticky's scoops were bigger!"

Warily, Sticky slid his bowl closer to him and shielded it with his arm. "Well, you're not getting any of mine."

"Oh no? Maybe I should just fish out some more of

your embarrassing memories," Constance growled, leaning forward and poking her finger at him. "I'd love telling people about them!"

"Constance!" cried Reynie and Kate, horrified. "You wouldn't!"

The forceful reproach in their tone and the expression on Sticky's face — an unsettling blend of revulsion, fear, and fury — cowed Constance a bit. "All right, all right," she said, leaning back again. "I wouldn't do that, I guess." But she felt angry and resentful now, and she scowled at Sticky with a ferocity unusual even for her. She crossed her arms, her face turned bloodred, and with her nose wrinkling and her pudgy cheeks bunching up, she narrowed her bright blue eyes to slits.

Reynie was impressed, but Sticky didn't seem to notice. He was staring at his ice cream, blinking uncertainly, as if considering whether he could even enjoy it under the circumstances. And then, much to Reynie's surprise, he seemed to come to that very conclusion.

"Here," Sticky said, shoving his plate toward Constance, who set upon the ice cream with a look of triumphant glee. "I don't much like vanilla, anyway."

"You don't?" Kate said, amazed. She dropped onto her feet and walked over to see what was going on.

"I thought vanilla was your favorite," Reynie said.

Sticky's eyes widened, and he looked at Reynie in confusion. "It . . . it *is* my favorite. Why did I say it wasn't? For a second I actually believed it."

Slowly, disbelievingly, they all turned to Constance, who had already finished half the ice cream and was now clutching her head, much as Kate had done earlier. Her eyes were squeezed tightly shut.

"What's the matter, do you have a cold headache from eating *my ice cream?*" Sticky said, his voice rising. "It serves you right, if you just did what I think you did! *Did* you, Constance? Did you make me think I didn't like vanilla?"

Constance opened her eyes, the anguish in them so apparent that Sticky drew back in surprise. "I did!" she wailed, and to Sticky's even greater astonishment she burst into torrents of tears. "All right? I told you to think that! Now stop talking! Please! My head is splitting! Oh, it's horrible, really horrible!"

"Whoa," Kate murmured, with a worried look at Reynie. "She said please."

Disconcerted, Sticky was frantically patting Constance's arm, trying to soothe her. "Easy, Constance. You'll be okay. You can . . . you can eat the rest of my ice cream, okay? Don't you want it?"

But this only made Constance sob all the more. "I can't! I feel too sick! My head . . . my stomach . . . oh, I feel just *awful!*"

The little girl's wails had brought all the adults running, including Mr. Benedict (panting from the stairs), and straightaway she was carried up to her bed, where she lay moaning and crying for more than an hour, until finally, with Mr. Benedict holding her hand and her friends listening anxiously at the door, she mumbled, "I don't believe I'll do that again," and fell into a fitful sleep.

The Unwelcome Visitor

Hours later, Constance awoke looking as though she'd been ravaged by the flu. Pasty pale skin, red-rimmed eyes, hair a tangled mess. Nonetheless she felt much improved, and was surprisingly well-mannered, even meek, as she listened to Mr. Benedict's stern admonitions. She quite agreed that she'd behaved badly and must never do that sort of thing again, and at any rate nothing could induce her to risk another bout of such agony.

"But what caused it?" Constance asked, kicking free of her tangled sheets. "I mean, hearing people's thoughts and all that never hurt me — it's just sort of like having a conversation. But when I changed Sticky's mind . . ." She shuddered and hugged her knees.

"I suspect the main difference was the intensity of focus and mental effort involved," Mr. Benedict said, patting her arm reassuringly. "If telepathy is like a mental conversation, then changing someone's mind — essentially hypnotizing someone, as you did with Sticky — is like winning a long and exhausting argument, except that the entire argument is compressed into the space of a moment. In other words, I believe your sickness was simply the result of strain, my dear."

"So you think I can avoid it? Is that what you're saying?"

"If you are careful and prudent," said Mr. Benedict. He raised an eyebrow. "Do you think you can be prudent? You haven't had a great deal of practice."

"Oh, I can be!" Constance said. "I will be!"

Reasonably satisfied, Mr. Benedict went back to his work, though not without some reluctance and a final, concerned glance from the doorway. "We'll leave aside the mental exercises for now," he said mildly, "and return to them when I can be more fully involved. In the meantime, my dear, rest and play — rest and play." And with Number Two attending him he left Constance with the other children and hurried down to the basement.

"You don't have to say it," Constance muttered to Sticky as soon as they were alone. "I'm sorry, okay? I really am."

Sticky regarded her solemnly. Then he put a hand over his heart and said, "I shall always remember this moment," and Kate and Reynie laughed until Constance, blushing, covered her head with a pillow.

That evening a cold rain set in that did not let up for days. There was no going outside, and in the drafty rooms of the house even the brightest lamps seemed somehow to cast more shadow than light. It was gloomy, in other words, and adding to the gloom for Reynie was an unpleasant realization that had come to him slowly: Once the Whisperer had been removed from Mr. Benedict's care, the government would no longer think it necessary to guard the children and their families. All of them would be free to return to their lives.

Which meant saying goodbye to his friends again. This time, perhaps, forever.

The prospect put Reynie in a terrible mood. He ate little and spoke even less, and kept to himself more than usual. He saw no point in mentioning any of this to his friends — no point in depressing them, too — and he especially avoided Constance, who might divine his thoughts without even trying. Miss Perumal noticed, of course. She checked him for fever every day, and asked more than once if the incident with Constance had upset him more than he was letting on. But Reynie always insisted he was fine. He had many reasons for not wishing to discuss his concern with her, not least his dread of having his fears confirmed.

Reynie was already troubled, therefore, when he bumped into Kate one afternoon in the kitchen. But what she told him made his stomach flop.

"I just overheard Number Two telling Rhonda," Kate

whispered, glancing around to be sure they were alone. "The order's gone through committee again."

"When?"

"This morning, apparently."

"No, I mean when are they coming for the Whisperer?"

"The day after tomorrow. Wednesday afternoon. They don't intend to tell us until that morning. They don't want to worry us."

"We'd better call a meeting," said Reynie.

Sticky had to be rescued from Mrs. Washington, who was once again begging him to let his hair grow out, and Constance had to be roused from a long nap that she had strenuously argued she didn't need, but the Society eventually held its meeting. Sitting around the rug in the girls' room as they had done so many times before, they spoke aloud their questions in hopes of generating an answer, or at the very least a clue.

What would happen to the Whisperer when it left the house? Did Mr. Curtain's spies know it was to be relocated on Wednesday? Even if not, even if the move was uneventful, would Mr. Benedict finish what he was doing before then? What *was* he doing, anyway? It had been several days now, and still he was down in the basement, working feverishly among the computers.

"I suppose we'll find out on Wednesday," said Sticky, when after much discussion no answers emerged. "One way or another, we'll get some answers then."

"One way or another," Reynie repeated grimly.

There followed a long silence, during which the three older children stared glumly at the rug. Finally Constance heaved an exasperated sigh and said, "Can we just talk about this and get it over with? You're all thinking the same thing, you know. And don't get mad at me for knowing, either. I can't help it — your thoughts might as well be screaming at me."

Startled, they all looked at Constance, and then at one another, with expressions half-sheepish and half-relieved.

"Sorry," Kate said. "I know I've been avoiding everyone —"

"You have?" Sticky said. "I have, too! I didn't want . . ." He hesitated. "Well, it just didn't seem decent to be worried about what happens to *us*, not when there's this much more important question . . ."

Reynie shook his head wonderingly. "I thought I was the only one thinking about it."

Kate snorted. "Are you kidding? It's all I've been able to think about for days. And is it just me, or does anyone else think Mr. Benedict gave us that riddle as a distraction? Something to take our minds off what's going to happen?"

"I've wondered about that," Reynie said. "And the exercise with Constance, too. It seems like quite a coincidence that he gave us so much to think about all of a sudden."

"Well, it didn't work, I can tell you that," Constance said peevishly. "I've been constantly worrying about what will happen if that nasty man gets his hands on the Whisperer again, and I can't stand to think that Mr. Benedict might not have enough time to find a cure for his narcolepsy, and on top of it all there's this thing with, you know . . ." She pointed at her head.

"What, are you worried it will go off?" Sticky asked.

"Ha ha," Constance said, making a face at him. "You wouldn't think it was so funny if you'd been through what I went through. I've never felt so sick in my life."

Sticky refrained from saying that the experience had not been exactly pleasant for him, either. "Listen, though, Constance, do you still think that's what Mr. Benedict's working on — a cure for his narcolepsy? You aren't getting any thoughts or vibes or whatever that it's something else?"

Constance rolled her eyes. "For one thing, I haven't seen him any more than you have. And for another, I've been trying to keep my thoughts to myself, if you know what I mean. But I hope that's what he's working on, don't you?"

"I hope a whole lot of things," Sticky said.

"So do I," Kate said.

"So do I," Reynie said.

And they were all telling the truth, yet somehow, strangely enough, none of them felt very hopeful at all.

꒰꒱

On Tuesday afternoon, the day before the Whisperer was scheduled to be removed, Mr. Benedict was still at work. If it was a remedy for narcolepsy he sought, he obviously had not found it yet, for when an unexpected visitor arrived and Number Two hurried down to tell him who it was, he fell straight to sleep in his chair. He had seemed quite startled, Number Two told Rhonda upstairs (forgetting, in her fretfulness, to keep her voice down) — startled and even upset, and now she was having trouble waking him.

"I'll go back down with you," said Rhonda gravely. She turned (they were just outside the dining room) and saw Constance in the doorway, listening. "Constance, would you go tell Milligan —?"

Milligan appeared behind her. "I already heard. Constance, scoot along upstairs, won't you?"

By the time Number Two and Rhonda had managed to wake Mr. Benedict, everyone in the house knew what had happened and who was at the door. The children were crowded at the girls' bedroom window, which was open for the sake of the cool air, and were peering down into the courtyard for a glimpse of the infamous Mr. Pressius.

"That's him?" Constance muttered as Kate held her up. The rain had only just subsided, and on the shining wet stones of the front walk a well-dressed man stood talking to Ms. Plugg. He was evidently quite tall — he towered over the guard — and under his arm he carried a bouquet of pink carnations in the way some businessmen carry newspapers. "That's the rich creep who made the deal with Curtain?"

"Must be," said Sticky. "If he couldn't prove who he was, Ms. Plugg wouldn't have let him in through the gate."

After a while the front door opened and Milligan stepped out, dressed in his usual weather-beaten attire, and said something to Mr. Pressius in a low tone. The children strained their ears, but from this height it was impossible to make out his words. They saw Mr. Pressius jab a finger rudely — perhaps he thought Milligan was the gardener — and make some short reply.

Ms. Plugg spoke up then, gesturing at Milligan as if explaining who he was, and Mr. Pressius took a hasty step backward.

But Milligan only laughed (that much was easy to hear) and motioned for Mr. Pressius to follow him inside. Then he looked up at their window — clearly he'd known they were watching — and subtly shaking his head, he mouthed the words, "Don't come down."

Mr. Pressius followed Milligan's gaze. To their surprise, he smiled and waved as if perfectly delighted to see them.

"Great," Kate said, lowering Constance to the floor. "I suppose it's no use pretending we couldn't tell what Milligan said."

"Why is that awful man here?" Constance demanded.

"Hard to say," Reynie replied, still gazing out the window. "They've had their dealings, you know, and Mr. Pressius has government connections. Maybe he's making some kind of proposition. His timing makes me think it has to do with the Whisperer."

"It would have to be a slimy proposition," Kate suggested, "in which case their meeting will be short. Mr. Benedict won't even consider it."

"Probably not," Reynie said in a hesitant, troubled voice. "And yet . . ."

The others looked at him.

"Everyone was clearly surprised he's here," Reynie said. "Even Mr. Benedict was surprised — Number Two said so. And Mr. Benedict isn't usually surprised by this sort of thing."

"Gosh, that's true," said Kate. "That can't be good, can it?"

Their mood shifted then from indignant curiosity to anxious anticipation. Everyone hoped that Kate's prediction would prove true — that Mr. Pressius would quickly be shown the door — and that afterward a barrage of questions might yield some answers. The older children agreed that they would politely but resolutely insist upon their right to know what was going on. Constance, for her part, practiced making herself cry.

Exactly twenty-three minutes passed — they were keeping close track by the wall clock — and then Rhonda came up to say, with an odd catch in her voice, that Mr. Benedict wanted to see them in his study. Even before she'd finished speaking Kate had tossed everyone their jackets and sweaters, and they dashed to the door.

It occurred to Reynie as they bustled downstairs that they hadn't seen Mr. Pressius leave, despite keeping watch at the window. Were they about to meet him? The prospect made him uneasy. But then Milligan arrived at the study just as they did, reporting to Mr. Benedict that he'd ushered their visitor to the gate "without further incident," and Reynie had the sudden conviction that Mr. Benedict had timed his summons so that they wouldn't see Mr. Pressius leave. But why would he do that?

"Please make yourselves comfortable," said Mr. Benedict, who looked anything but comfortable himself. A red mark was plainly visible on his forehead — the apparent result of a sleep-induced tumble — and a stack of books that had fallen from his desk lay in disarray about the floor where he now sat. He greeted the children with his usual warmth, smiling at each in turn, but rarely had he appeared quite so haggard and worn.

As they found places to sit on the floor, Reynie also

noticed that the pink carnations were lying on Mr. Benedict's desk, not far from his humble potted violet, but that two or three petals lay on the floor near the wastebasket — as if someone had thrown the flowers away only to think better of it afterward.

Milligan went out, closing the door behind him, and Rhonda and Number Two sat in the empty chairs. When everyone was settled Mr. Benedict stroked his ill-shaven cheek, apparently seeking the proper words.

"I know you're all wondering why Mr. Pressius was here," Mr. Benedict said at last, "and I'm afraid I must tell you. First, however, allow me to offer a bit of background. Some days ago the government, which as you know is desperate for funds, sold my brother's tidal turbines to Mr. Pressius. The terms of the deal are obscured by a certain amount of legal embroidery, but suffice it to say that the Whisperer shall retain its power source and the government shall be able to pay off a few debts."

"How could they sell the turbines?" said Constance. "I didn't realize the government even owned them."

The other children groaned.

"We've talked about this," said Sticky, "about a hundred times. The government seized them after Mr. Curtain escaped." And before Constance could make a retort he said, "But there's been nothing in the newspapers about selling them, so the deal must be a secret. Is that right, Mr. Benedict?"

Mr. Benedict tapped his nose. "*Unofficial* is the preferred term, I believe. The arrangement calls for Mr. Pressius to sell back to the government — at a very modest rate — most of the electricity produced by the turbines, which his private technicians shall have operating at maximum capacity soon. The government will save a great deal of money on energy costs, and over time Mr. Pressius will earn a reasonable profit. These are the stated reasons for the arrangement."

"The stated reasons," Reynie repeated, significantly. "So what about the real ones?"

"*Those* surely have to do with my brother. After all, if Ledroptha plans to regain control of his Whisperer, he must also think of securing its power source. I'm certain Mr. Pressius is acting on his behalf — no doubt he stands to gain far more than a 'reasonable profit' for doing so."

The children, aghast, muttered and shook their heads.

"The government will continue to provide heavy security," Mr. Benedict went on, "but Mr. Pressius will cover the costs. Thus the authorities enjoy the illusion — I should say delusion — of retaining control of the turbines, and meanwhile they may pat themselves on the back for making such a clever arrangement."

"They need more than patting," Constance grumbled.

"What were they thinking?" Sticky said.

"I suspect my brother's spies did much of the thinking for them," Mr. Benedict said. "Indeed, confident assurances and promises of fortune, when whispered into the right ears, often serve as substitutes for thinking at all."

"Well, this is hideous news, all right," said Kate. "But why did Mr. Pressius want to tell you about it?"

"He didn't," Mr. Benedict said. "It's doubtful he even knows I'm aware of it. The transaction was meant to be kept secret from me. I've told *you* about it so that you can better understand the reason Mr. Pressius came here today. The real reason, I mean. I believe his visit was timed to distract me, you see, for tomorrow —"

"They're coming for the Whisperer," said Constance impatiently. "We know already."

Mr. Benedict raised an eyebrow, and the corners of his mouth twitched. "Forgive me, I should have guessed you would. Well, then, there you have it. The gears of my brother's machinery are turning once again, and he is doing what he can to prevent my throwing a wrench into them. That is the reason Mr. Pressius came here today, I have no doubt."

"The real reason," Reynie clarified. "And what about the stated reason? Is that important?"

Mr. Benedict hesitated. "Please understand that I am not worried about what Mr. Pressius had to say. If I seem troubled it is only because I'm concerned about how you will respond to it yourselves. Be assured, however —"

Constance spluttered in exasperation. "For crying out loud, what *is* it? What did he tell you?"

Mr. Benedict took a deep breath, let it out, and looked Constance in the eyes. "He said, my dear, that you are his long-lost daughter."

THE LITTLE GIRL IN THE BIG CHAIR

"It's a lie, of course!" Mr. Benedict hastened to say, and he reached to take her hands. Constance didn't resist as she normally might, but sat quite motionless, blanching, reddening, and blanching again so quickly it was as if someone were adjusting her color by remote control. The other children gaped in disbelief.

"I assure you," Mr. Benedict said with unusual vehemence, "this is a ploy, nothing more — a wicked attempt to distract us at a crucial time. You must not believe it for a moment."

"But . . . if it's a lie," said Constance, her voice rising and rising, "then why is everyone so upset? You, Rhonda, Number Two — you're all . . . all of you . . ." Before she could find the words to describe what she sensed intuitively, Rhonda and Number Two were at her side.

"We're just worried about you," said Rhonda with tears in her eyes, and Number Two added in a choked, furious voice, "And angry with *him*. It's such a vicious deceit!"

"We feel protective, you see," said Mr. Benedict with an uneven smile. (He was clearly striving to remain calm — and thus awake.) "We consider you a part of our family, even if our ties have yet to be made official. For Mr. Pressius to argue otherwise was terribly offensive to all of us."

"And perhaps a little upsetting," said Rhonda with a weak smile of her own.

"It's an outrage!" snarled Number Two. "And for him to have done so much to prove . . ." She bit her tongue, evidently having said more than she intended. But seeing there was no hiding the details from Constance now, she said, "Mr. Pressius has had some false documents produced. Expert forgeries — they must have cost a fortune — but forgeries nonetheless. We're intimately familiar with this sort of thing, you know."

Constance seemed encouraged. Still she looked to Mr. Benedict for assurance. "You're sure they aren't real?"

"Quite sure," he said, squeezing her hands. And when he saw she believed him, Mr. Benedict smiled more naturally this time, obviously relieved. He took a carrot from his pocket and handed it to Number Two, remarking that she had not eaten since lunch, and that was almost an hour ago.

"Furthermore," Mr. Benedict continued, "if these papers had come from the proper offices, we would have located them ourselves long ago. We've sought them most strenuously, you know. But no such papers have been found, no records at all, and though we could have produced false ones — even better forgeries, I daresay, than the ones Mr. Pressius has — we wanted nothing that smacked of falseness to be associated with your adoption. We all felt that this would be important to you."

"You're right," said Constance, after considering a moment. "It would have bugged me. So what happened, Mr. Pressius just walked in with flowers and expected me to call him Daddy?"

"Perhaps he did," said Mr. Benedict with a shrug. "His understanding of children seems to be as poor as he is rich. But more likely he hoped to upset you, and thereby to upset *me*. I admit he succeeded at first — I even threw away his flowers."

"And knocked your head in the bargain," said Number Two, somewhat less peevish now that she'd eaten the carrot to a nub. "And spilled your books everywhere."

"Very true," said Mr. Benedict, giving her an apologetic look. "After I woke up and composed myself, however, I realized the flowers must certainly be yours, Constance, to do with as you please. At any rate —"

Mr. Benedict broke off, for just then Constance jumped to her feet, snatched the bouquet from his desk, and hurled it into the wastebasket with all the force she could muster — so hard that flower petals flew up out of the wastebasket like tiny pink butterflies. Then placing her hands against the wall to steady herself, she stomped one foot repeatedly into the wastebasket as if trying to put out a fire.

"I see we are of the same opinion," said Mr. Benedict as Constance returned to her seat, and the others congratulated her on her judgment. Then Mr. Benedict cleared his throat and said, "I'm afraid a few unpleasant details remain. Mr. Pressius means to have you removed from my custody. I will never allow this, of course, nor even admit him into the house. But the encounter will be disagreeable, and when it comes I ask you to keep away from the windows. There is no telling what Mr. Pressius will say or how distressing you might find his words, and I shall be far more efficient in dealing with him if I am not also worried about *you*."

"Efficiency is important," Rhonda said when she saw Constance's suspicious look. "There's little time, and Mr. Benedict still has work to do."

Constance crossed her arms. "Then you had better do as I say."

Puzzled, Rhonda said, "What do you mean?"

"*You* know what I mean," said Constance, looking at Mr. Benedict. "You have to do it right away! If you say no, I'll throw a fit, I'll make trouble . . . I'll — I'll make sure you can't get any work done!"

The others glanced uncertainly at one another. Only Mr. Benedict seemed unsurprised, though he sounded rather disappointed as he said, "Threats are unbecoming in you, my dear, and you know perfectly well they won't work on me." He ran a hand through his tousled white hair. "I understand your feelings, however. In your position I would feel much the same."

"Then you have to do it!" Constance cried, turning crimson with passion. "Oh, you have to use the Whisperer, Mr. Benedict! You *have* to!"

⌣⋮⌢

In times past Mr. Benedict had steadfastly declined to use the Whisperer to uncover Constance's hidden memories. If they existed at all, he said, they might be traumatic, for a person's mind will sometimes bury painful memories as a means of self-protection. Then again there might be nothing to uncover. Her prodigious mental gifts aside, Constance had been just a toddler when she came to him, and most children that age had yet to form lasting memories. Mr. Benedict had felt the risks of using the Whisperer outweighed the possible benefits.

But circumstances had changed. Mr. Pressius's visit had stirred up emotions that Constance could scarcely understand, much less handle with aplomb. She longed for the real story of her past, longed to know beyond doubt that the vile Mr. Pressius was not her father. The forged documents didn't prove he *wasn't* her father, she argued (a point that Sticky rather unhelpfully conceded was logical), and the only way to be sure was to use the Whisperer. And her only chance for *that* — her only chance forever and ever — was right now.

"I can handle it," Constance said. "I know it might be upsetting, but I have to know. You said it yourself, Mr. Benedict — you'd feel the same way!"

Number Two pointed out that when Constance was older Mr. Benedict could attempt to recover her memories using hypnosis. "You'll be more stable then," she said, which was perhaps an unfortunate choice of words.

Constance leaped to her feet. "*I'm* stable as a table! *I'm* sturdy as an elephant! Not like you, dumb Number Two! *Your* skeleton's like gelatin!"

When at last Mr. Benedict had calmed Constance down and persuaded her to withdraw, as he put it, "your disparaging remarks about Number Two's skeletal fortitude," he adjusted his spectacles and said, "The fact is I expected this and have made my decision already. It's one reason I've been so busy in the basement — I knew we would need to take time for this. Yes, hypnosis might work, but its results can be unreliable. If they led us astray, and if no other clues emerged, we might always regret our missed opportunity to use the Whisperer."

Constance put her hands to her head. "You mean you'll do it?"

"Let us proceed upstairs," said Mr. Benedict, rising, and Number Two and Rhonda leaped up to accompany him. He looked at the older children. "Will you join us? The process can be unsettling, even distressing, and Constance will feel safer with you there."

"Do you really think they'll make me feel safer?" said Constance impishly as they headed upstairs. She was in high spirits now that she'd won her long-fought battle. "The scariest things I remember have all happened when I was with *them*."

"An excellent point," said Mr. Benedict. "Perhaps you'd prefer to do this alone."

To this Constance made no reply, only muttered something under her breath, and her friends smiled privately at one another. They followed her up the stairs, shucking out of their overclothes as they climbed.

By the time they had reached the balmy third floor and filed into the appropriate hallway, Constance's steps had grown noticeably slower and oddly deliberate, as if she were trudging through deep snow. It was a perfectly familiar hallway, with familiar bookshelves lining the walls and several familiar doorways — the holding rooms on the left, the chamber door on the right — and the chamber guards were familiar, too. Yet with every step Constance took, the stranger and creepier everything seemed; even the light had a harsh and sinister cast. Her spirits, so high before, had now plunged equally low, for the truth had begun to sink in: She had an appointment with the Whisperer.

"Steady," Reynie whispered, laying a hand on her shoulder. "We're right here."

Constance looked up at him gratefully. He managed to smile, but he looked somewhat less than steady himself. So did the other two, for that matter. Sticky kept reaching for his spectacles then jerking his hand away again, and Kate had unthinkingly flipped open her bucket lid. The children's last encounter with the Whisperer had been most unpleasant, and of course they were all thinking of it now.

Mr. Benedict spoke cheerfully to the guards as he rummaged through the pockets of his suit coat. He and his guests were the only ones ever allowed into the chamber, whose door was secured with two separate locks. Mr. Benedict produced the first key from his pocket. Number Two had the other. In a moment the door swung open and the little group shuffled inside.

The chamber was a small, softly lit room, painted in a soothing shade of green very much like that of Mr. Benedict's suit. In one corner was an overstuffed chair where Mr. Benedict's guests usually sat; in the other, behind a decorative screen, was the Whisperer. Otherwise the room was empty. No windows, no pictures, no books. The sessions with the Whisperer required great concentration, and Mr. Benedict had eliminated all sources of distraction.

"Before we begin," said Mr. Benedict, gesturing for them to join him on the floor, "let us take a moment to review and prepare. Now, do you recall the effect the Whisperer had on those whose memories my brother edited? I refer not to an entire brainsweep, as he termed it, but to the hiding away of specific memories."

"Well," said Kate, "the kids he did that to at the Institute were kind of mixed-up and confused for a while."

"Dazed," said Constance.

"Addlepated," said Sticky.

Mr. Benedict tapped his nose. "The sudden disappearance of a few select memories may not be as disturbing as losing all of them — Milligan can attest to that — but it is disorienting nonetheless, and the sudden *return* of those memories often has a similar effect. We must not be surprised, therefore, if Constance does not seem quite herself after the session. And Constance, *you* must not worry if you find you cannot think as clearly as you like. Rarely do the effects last more than a day or two, and in some cases they are scarcely even noticeable."

"Will it be . . ." Constance's voice faltered, and clearing her throat she sat up straighter and tried again. "Will it be, you know, like . . . last time?"

"Not exactly," said Mr. Benedict in a reassuring tone. "It's true you will hear the voice of the Whisperer in your mind, and the voice will not seem like *my* voice. The Whisperer sounds different to different people; it's a matter of mental interpretation. Regardless, it will ask you the questions I tell it to ask. As you know, the machine identifies memories that the operator — *I* am the operator now, my dear — believes to exist. Under my brother's control the Whisperer would bury those memories, but under mine it only retrieves what has been hidden. A simple process, really, not unlike turning on a lamp in a dark room."

"Wonderful," said Constance, a bit snappishly. She was anxious to begin, anxious to get this over with. "Let's go turn on that lamp."

Mr. Benedict agreed, and everyone stood. The older children, feeling an urge to wish Constance good luck — as if she were going on a long journey — took turns shaking her hand. Number Two gave her a stiff hug (which Constance stiffly tolerated), and Rhonda, with an arm across the little girl's shoulders, led her over to the guest chair. Then Rhonda joined the others, now sitting quietly out of the way.

Mr. Benedict took a long look at Constance perched in the overstuffed chair with her legs dangling and her arms crossed. Such a long look, in fact, that Constance frowned and demanded to know what he was doing.

"Fixing your image in my mind," said Mr. Benedict without averting his gaze. "It is a means of concentrating my focus." After a pause he said, "I realize that, my dear, but I'm afraid it's a necessary step."

The other children sneaked looks at one another. It was not lost on them that Constance's complaint — whatever it was — had not been spoken aloud.

Presently Mr. Benedict nodded, smiled at Constance reassuringly, and turned away.

Constance took a last nervous glance at her friends. "Here's hoping I don't come out of this as dopey as old S.Q.!"

Mr. Benedict paused and looked back. "Why do you say that?"

Constance shrugged. "I was just thinking about how addlepated I might be. So naturally I thought of S.Q."

"Naturally," said Mr. Benedict with a curious glimmer in his eye — but that glimmer, which Reynie did not fail to notice, might as well have been a spotlight, for he suddenly saw with perfect clarity why S.Q. Pedalian was the way he was. Mr. Benedict knew the reason and no doubt had been thinking about it, and Constance had unwittingly picked up on his thoughts.

The revelation sent Reynie's mind racing after answers to new questions — questions he wanted to ask Mr. Benedict, but of course the timing could not have been worse. Already Mr. Benedict was ducking behind the decorative screen, and Constance was bracing herself for a long-awaited and now half-dreaded moment. Reynie's questions would have to wait.

In the heavy silence they heard Mr. Benedict climb into the Whisperer's seat, fit the helmet over his head, and take a slow, deep breath. Then he spoke his name quietly aloud. Instantly a faint humming sound began, barely detectable even in the still room, and all eyes turned toward the little girl in the big chair.

At the moment, that little girl was feeling extremely uncomfortable. Though her friends were here with her, they were huddled off to the side, and when Mr. Benedict had disappeared behind the screen Constance felt suddenly very lonely and exposed. It was rather like having your teeth X-rayed in a dentist's chair, when for a few moments you are left alone in the empty room, but those few moments seem much longer. And then, with a start, Constance heard the Whisperer speak inside her mind, and she abruptly lost awareness of anything else.

What is your name? the strange, toneless voice asked.

Constance took a breath and tried to relax, tried to remember it was Mr. Benedict behind the voice. She reminded herself that she wanted to be here, that she wanted answers. And so, slowly at first but then all in a rush, Constance opened her mind to the Whisperer's questions.

They began simply enough: *What is your name? Where are you now? What color are your eyes?* Constance's mind produced the answers effortlessly, without conscious thought.

Where had you been before you went to live in the Brookville library?

Constance stiffened, concentrated, repeated the question to herself. She imagined herself in that library, where she had secretly lived for months. Reading the newspapers every day. Searching for something. But what? And what had she been doing before? No answer came.

How do you know your age?

Again Constance was stumped. How did she know? She thought for some time but came up with nothing.

More questions followed: *What did you have in your hand when you went to the library? Did you walk to the library? Did you take a bus to the library? What was in your pockets?* Constance pondered all these questions and more; she concentrated as hard as she ever had; but every time her mind came up blank. Frustrated, she spluttered aloud.

There was a long pause, so long that Constance began to wonder if Mr. Benedict had given up. But finally the next question came: *What frightening thing happened the day you went to the library?*

And then, somewhere deep in the recesses of her mind, an image flickered.

Constance sucked in her breath. She clutched the arms of the chair. It had been only a flicker, but the Whisperer was racing toward it with alarming intensity and force. That was the sensation she had — the flickering image like a target in the darkness, the Whisperer hurtling toward it like an arrow, and Constance herself borne along in the great hurtling rush. Closer and closer she flew until she was shooting straight into the image — it was a folder, nothing more — and then flying through it as if through a bright window and out at last into daylight, where she saw everything clearly, saw where she was coming from, saw where she was going, and saw who it was she was trying to escape.

Leap Years and Napmares

"**H**ello, ducky," said the man in the suit.

His smile was bright and even, and when he leaned over the safety gate that confined Constance to the playroom, a strong, pleasant fragrance wafted over her. And yet her skin prickled in warning. She took a step back, tightening her pudgy hands into fists.

"What are you doing?" said a woman's voice. Myrtle. Her name was Myrtle.

"I was about to pat the dear on the head."

"Oh! I wouldn't do that! She's prone to bite strangers who reach for her."

The man straightened and turned to the woman. "A reasonable practice."

"And she won't do anything you ask," said Myrtle. "I mean she *can* do it, but she won't if you ask her to."

"Of course," said the man, taking Myrtle by the elbow and leading her several paces down the hall.

They spoke in low tones, but Constance could hear them if she strained her ears. The man was asking politely about the other children that lived here, their ages and what sort of outing they were on, and saying nice things about Myrtle's house, which Constance could tell he did not mean. And there was another person with them in the hall, although he had not spoken a word.

Padding softly over to the playroom bookshelf (she wore her thickest, warmest socks today), Constance began choosing books. She drew out the largest ones she could lift, holding them to her chest like prized possessions, knowing from experience not to trust her clumsy fingers. Fairy tale collections, picture dictionaries, half-destroyed pop-up books, volumes of a children's encyclopedia. One by one she carried them away from the shelf, staggering slightly under their weight, and began to stack them.

"Pardon me for confirming certain details," the man was saying now. His tone, though still friendly, had grown more businesslike. "Can she truly read, or does she simply give that impression? Is it possible, for instance, that she's citing familiar passages from memory?"

"Not only can she read," said Myrtle, "she can *write*. Of course it's hard to make out her handwriting, but —"

A pen clicked. "May I ask what sort of things she writes?"

"Complaints, mostly, though she also likes to make lists of rhyming words. And some things she tears up before anyone can read them. She's a private child and likes to be left alone. She seldom speaks."

"Was she very much traumatized by her parents' death?"

"Goodness, no! She was only a few weeks old. Train crash, you know. She had no other family, and the orphanage nursery was full, so we were contracted to take her on . . . but that's all in the files, of course." There was a ruffling of papers, and Myrtle said quickly, "I hope we don't seem uncharitable! It's just that the money's less than we might have thought, especially considering how much more difficult than the other children . . ."

"I'm sure," the man said mildly. "Your troubles are at an end, however. Our employer is interested in gifted children of all ages. If you have the papers . . ."

"They're all in the folder. Birth records, health records — everything you said. But is it true you — forgive me, I don't mean to offend, but were the other records really . . . destroyed?"

Constance paused in her stacking to be sure she heard the reply. Her heart hammered so loudly in her ears, she feared she would miss it.

"I gather you spoke with my associate, Mr. Crawlings. He often misspeaks, madam." A laugh. "No, I assure you, her records were not destroyed, only transferred to a more appropriate agency."

"Well, that's certainly . . . Still, can't you say more about what's to be done with her there? It's very irregular, after all, and though she's a troublesome child we do want the best for her."

"Madam, surely you are aware of our employer's vaunted reputation."

"Of course! And the Institute is famous! I just . . . it *is* peculiar, you know, with the arrangement being kept off the books . . ."

The man chuckled. "That's merely a matter of simplifying an over-complicated bureaucratic process. You know how it is, with the Emergency at such a pitch . . ."

"Oh yes, it's terrible!"

There was an uncomfortably long pause. Constance, alone in the playroom, could sense the tension without seeing the adults' faces. Indeed, she felt it in her own face, now quite rosy with heat. Shaking her head as if freeing herself from a spell, she returned to the shelf for the last volume of the encyclopedia.

"Madam, I hate to press you, but did you not already make your decision? As you were told before, our employer will take excellent care of the girl, will nourish her gifts and help her reach her fullest potential — and, as you know, will pay you handsomely for the opportunity. However, we dare not even mention the child to him if we cannot deliver her. Mr. Curtain is much too busy a man to be bothered with needless distractions, to say nothing of disappointments."

"Oh, I am sure, I am sure! Please, if you will just . . . allow me one minute to speak with . . . I'll be right back!"

Constance heard Myrtle hastening away to the den. And then for the first time she heard the other man's voice, speaking in a hush. "Tell me again why we don't just take her?"

The first man grunted. "McCracken says this is the preferred approach — much simpler, much easier, and far less risky. We *will* take her, of course, if these ninnies suddenly recover their scruples. But they need the money, and I'm confident — ah, here she comes. Yes, madam, have you decided?"

"My associate wonders if you might just show him what you showed me."

"You've pointed at the wrong briefcase, madam, but I assume you mean the money. That would be in *this* brief-case. And certainly we'll show it to him. Be so good as to lead the way."

The men followed Myrtle away down the hall just as Constance stacked the last book. Panting from her exertions, she moved back to inspect her work. Her fingers could not manipulate the safety gate's complicated spring latch (she had tried many times before), nor was she strong enough to haul herself over it — and so she had constructed stairs. The bottom step was two books; the second one was four; and so it went with the rest of the steps, which led right to the top of the gate.

Scattered about the playroom were dozens of stuffed animals, and Constance gathered these as quickly as she could, lifting them in bunches over the gate and dropping them onto the carpet beyond. When she had built a considerable pile, she walked up the book steps — taking great care not to lose her balance — and jumped over the gate. She fell into the pile of stuffed animals with scarcely a thump.

From the hall closet she took out boots, a sweater, and a red raincoat, all of which quite swallowed her — everything she'd been given to wear was too large — and carrying these in an awkward bundle she crept down the hallway toward the front door. She took a deep breath before shuffling past the den, where a falsely cheerful conversation was taking place beyond the half-open door. No one observed her.

In the entryway stood a low desk, and on the desk was a folder. Constance hesitated, looking back toward the den. Should she risk the delay? Then she remembered Myrtle's change purse in the bureau drawer. That settled it. She put down her bundle, eased the drawer open, and took out enough coins for bus fare, leaving the rest. Then she opened the front door (she needed both hands to turn the knob), tucked the folder into her shirt, gathered up her bundle again, and went out into the cold.

She had never dressed so quickly. Standing at the bottom of the steps she struggled into her sweater, fairly leaped into her boots, threw on the raincoat. Thus attired she marched awkwardly to the corner bus stop, squinting against snowflakes that had just begun to fall. She would have preferred a bus stop farther away from the house, but she had no idea where one might be. On previous outings they always had caught the bus here.

A tiny old woman stood at the bus stop, leaning on a cane. Small though she was, she towered over Constance. She wore red-framed spectacles as big as saucers. Constance asked her when the bus was expected. The woman peered down through her huge glasses, blinking. Constance repeated her question more loudly.

The woman pointed up the street with her wobbling cane. "Here it is now, dear." Sure enough, a bus had rounded the corner and was rumbling down the block toward them. "Are you riding by yourself? How old are you?"

Constance was unsure how to answer this. She did not know how old she was. She knew she was much too young to be out alone, though, and so at last she said simply that she was very small for her age.

The woman cackled. "So am I! We don't let that slow us down, do we?"

Holding her breath, expecting Myrtle and the men to appear any moment, Constance followed the woman slowly — so very, very slowly — up the bus steps. She sat next to the woman, and no one questioned her. The doors closed. The bus hissed, jerked, and then, grumbling and groaning, pulled away from the corner.

She had escaped.

For some time Constance thought of nothing else. Then, because it was itching her, she remembered the folder. She took it from under her shirt; it was creased and crumpled now. The first document was her birth certificate. She studied the information carefully. Her parents' names and occupations were meaningless to her, for she had no memory of them. After a while she turned to the old woman, who was squinting at a newspaper clipping with her owlish eyes, and asked her for the date.

"Why, it's leap year day, didn't you know?" The woman showed Constance the clipping, an advertisement for a one-day-only sale. At the top was the phrase "Leap Into Savings" followed by numerous exclamation points, and at the bottom was the date. "I've always loved this day," the woman said with a smile, "the way it comes out of nowhere then disappears again. Like magic, isn't it? And here it's snowing, too. Oh yes, magical day, magical day."

Constance nodded. It did feel like magic, she thought. She felt rather like leap year day herself. Again she looked at the birth certificate. She had been born on January first, which made her just barely two years old. Constance was impressed. She had thought she was at least three.

Thinking back, she remembered Myrtle giving her a cupcake that day. There had been no mention of birthdays, however. Constance had assumed the treat was part of the holiday festivities. Evidently Myrtle hadn't meant to be unkind, but neither had she wanted Constance to grow attached. Already she'd been planning to hand Constance over.

For a minute or so Constance wondered how it would feel to be wanted, and her eyes welled with tears. But then she got angry, and that was better. Gritting her teeth, she wiped away the tears with the sleeve of her raincoat.

The old woman was speaking to her again. She wanted to know where Constance was getting off the bus.

Constance frowned. She had not planned this far ahead. She had escaped, but where does a person escape *to*?

The woman repeated her question, and feeling pressed to answer Constance said the first thing that occurred to her. She was going to the library, she said — and having said it she realized it was exactly the right thing. Books had been her means of escape; now they would be her refuge.

"Which do you mean, honey, the main library or one of the branches?"

Constance almost said the main library, which was the only one she'd ever been to, but then realized she might be looked for there. So instead she said a branch library — the one that was farthest away.

"What, you don't mean the Brookville branch?" asked the woman, surprised, and Constance said yes, that was the one. She was to meet her family there.

The woman clucked her tongue and explained that Constance had caught the wrong bus. "Now you'll have to make — let's see — two transfers, dear. No, *three*. Do you have enough money?" said the woman, already opening her change purse.

By late afternoon Constance stood on the steps of the Brookville library, snowflakes ticking softly on her raincoat, eating a hot dog she had purchased with money the kind old woman had given her. Exhausted and anxious, she stood for some time staring at the front doors. Then she went inside and began searching for a good place to hide.

Eventually Constance found an unlocked storage room, in the back of which was a stack of boxes labeled "To be processed when funding is approved." The boxes were coated with dust; they appeared not to have been touched in years. Constance squeezed behind them into a narrow space just big enough for her to lie down. She folded up her raincoat to serve as a pillow. Hours later, long after the library had closed, she awoke.

Thus began Constance's life in the library. She made few appearances by day, and then only when the library was busy, so that people might reasonably assume she was with someone (the young woman over in nonfiction might be her mother, for instance, or perhaps the stooped old fellow browsing magazines was her grandfather). She was careful never to be seen emerging from the storage room, and only occasionally was she obliged to explain to concerned librarians or patrons that she was very small for her age. She made sure always to appear confident and happy so as not to seem lost or in need of help. And generally she kept out of sight.

Her meals were not especially healthful, but Constance found them satisfactory. By the end of her first night she had learned where the librarians kept their snacks (and whose were best), and when after some weeks of nightly raiding she discovered that mousetraps had been set out, she triggered them with pencils and ate the cheese. She also found the key to the vending machine in the staff breakroom. But she was careful not to overuse it, and to spread out her thefts as best she could, so that no one would suspect the truth. And at any rate, it only seemed fair.

Constance spent her waking hours reading newspapers and rhyming picture books. She did not much enjoy the newspapers, which were dreary and dull and filled with nonsense about something called the Emergency. She only read them to see if there was anything about a missing little girl. There never was. A few articles appeared about a young quiz champion who had run away, but these she gave the merest glance — they weren't about her, and that was all that mattered.

After the first week, Constance began to believe no one was looking for her. The few men in suits who visited the library were not the ones she'd run from, and nothing about them gave her goose bumps. Myrtle never appeared. Constance was free.

In reality, though, Constance was tormented, for every time she slept she dreamed of those men at Myrtle's house — and the dreams terrified her. Often she woke with a cry, her heart pounding in her ears. When this happened at night, and she found herself alone in the dark library, she would lie there a long time petrified with fear, trying to muster the courage to stand up and turn on the light. And when the dreams came during the day ("napmares," she called them), her relief upon waking was instantly replaced by the fear that she'd been heard crying out, and she would hold her breath and squeeze her eyes shut, dreading discovery.

This went on for weeks and weeks.

And then finally one night, waking in a fit of despair, Constance angrily commanded herself to feel better. Her face turned beet-red, her fists bunched into tight balls, and with all the fierceness she could muster (it happened to be no small amount) she said, "*Forget* it, Constance! Forget those men! Forget everything that's happened! Forget it, forget it, *forget* it!"

And so she had, until this very moment.

"I'm an orphan!" Constance declared joyfully, and an observer might have been shocked to see the enthusiasm with which her announcement was received. Everyone in the chamber leaped up, greeting Constance's news with warm, happy smiles and heartfelt expressions of congratulation.

Constance was very excited and not a little out of sorts. She rattled away about her narrow escape, walking up and down as she did so, but from time to time she stopped, confused, to look around. In these moments she seemed unsure where she was. Then Mr. Benedict would gently speak her name, and Constance would look at him in surprise, then laugh and return to her narrative, often starting at the beginning.

"And then I just made myself forget!" she said, when at last she came to that part of the story. "I went back to sleep and never thought about that stuff again. How in the world did *that* happen?"

"A form of self-hypnosis," said Mr. Benedict. "It is not unheard of, especially when motivation is sufficient. And of course your mind is most unusual —"

"I remember everything that happened after that, though," Constance was saying, not having heard a word he said, "like reading the newspapers — I just kept reading them every day with the feeling that I was looking for something, but I didn't know what I was looking for anymore! Bizarre! And then one day I read your advertisement, Mr. Benedict, and I thought, 'Oh! That's what I'm looking for! Special opportunities!'"

At this, Constance turned and walked straight toward the chamber door.

"Where are you going?" Kate asked as Rhonda made a subtle move to stand in the way.

Constance stopped and stared at Kate. "What? Oh!" She blushed and turned to Mr. Benedict with an expression of mild distress. "I thought I was leaving the library!"

Mr. Benedict smiled. "Some confusion between one's recovered memory and one's present reality is common. It will soon pass. In fact already you show signs of an unusually rapid —"

But Constance had moved on. "My parents were just ordinary people!" she cried. "I'd like to find out more about them —"

"We'll help you," said Number Two and Mr. Benedict at the same time.

"— but for now I'm just happy to know where I came from. Other than the public library, I mean. That nasty Mr. Pressius — I can't wait to rub his nose in it! Wait till we show him the *real* papers! Oh please, Mr. Benedict, you have to let me be there when he sees them!"

Reynie noticed a troubled look flicker across Mr. Benedict's face, but Constance noticed nothing of the sort, and she went on about the papers at some length — how they would make everything right again, and Mr. Benedict could finally adopt her, and it would be perfectly legal and real and official — until Sticky interrupted her.

"You left that part out before," Sticky said. "Are you saying you know where those records are? The ones in the folder?"

"Of course, silly!" Constance laughed. "I hid the folder in a book!"

"Well, that's terrific!" Sticky replied. "So where is the book? I mean, did you bring it with you or —?"

"Sticky," said Mr. Benedict quickly.

But already Constance was saying, "It's at the library, where else?" and Sticky's expression changed from excitement to horror.

"But that library *burned*! It was in the newspapers! I thought you knew! I thought you must have . . . must have . . ." Sticky fell silent, realizing what he'd done. He squeezed his eyes shut and tried to wish back his words.

"But . . . but without those papers . . ." Constance said, her voice trembling.

"Constance," said Mr. Benedict, "I promise you —"

But Constance did not stay to hear Mr. Benedict's promise. With a despairing wail she turned and ran to the door. Rhonda would have stopped her if Mr. Benedict had not tried to do so himself. Unfortunately, at the sight of Constance's anguished face Mr. Benedict had fallen asleep in mid-stride, and it was all Rhonda could do to catch him. In fact she and Number Two — who leaped in from the other direction — suffered cruel blows as their heads collided, and Kate found herself struggling to support the dazed young women as they in turn supported Mr. Benedict.

Sticky, his eyes still tightly closed, saw none of this. But hearing a sound rather like two coconuts knocking together, followed by moans from Rhonda and Number Two, he opened his eyes to find everyone toppling slowly to the floor. Everyone but Constance, who had unlocked the door and fled the room, and Reynie, who had gone after her.

"I'm so sorry!" Sticky cried. "It was an accident!"

Kate groaned. She had managed to prevent the adults from falling quite so hard as they might have, but even so they were all tangled and jumbled, and lying with her back arched across her bucket she was in considerable discomfort.

"You're not to blame," said Rhonda through gritted teeth. A bump was rising on her forehead. "We should have warned you to keep quiet about that."

"Rhonda's right," said Number Two. "But who could have guessed Constance had those records with her at the library?" She struggled to her knees and began patting Mr. Benedict's arm, trying to wake him. "We knew the Ten Men had burned it down, of course, but —"

"What?" said Sticky and Kate together.

"Oh yes," said Rhonda. "You didn't think it was a coincidence, did you?"

Sticky frowned. "The newspapers said the cause was unknown."

"To most people it *was* unknown," said Number Two. "Not to us." She was still absently patting Mr. Benedict's arm although he had opened his eyes now and was blinking up at her. "Somehow those Ten Men — at that time they were called Recruiters, of course — discovered that Constance had been at the library. Most likely one of their informants saw her come out, because it was on that very day that the brutes showed up and threatened the librarians. Who told them nothing, incidentally."

"The same thing happened in Holland," Kate reflected. "You'd think these guys would learn their lesson — librarians know how to keep quiet."

"It helps to ask politely," said Mr. Benedict (startling Number Two in mid-pat). He sat up, his expression melancholy but his voice determinedly even. "And in this case the librarians had little to tell. They had seen Constance on occasion but had no idea she was living in the building."

"The Recruiters ransacked the library," said Rhonda, "then set it on fire to cover their tracks. And I'm sure you know what happened to the librarians."

"The Recruiters kidnapped them," said Sticky grimly.

"And Mr. Curtain brainswept them," said Kate, equally grim.

"A common fate," said Mr. Benedict, "of anyone my brother found inconvenient. I'm pleased to say they're better now, though; their memories were restored in this very room. At the time, of course, the librarians were not even thought to be missing — that being one of the Whisperer's pernicious effects — but we always followed such matters closely. By nightfall Milligan was on Constance's trail."

"Which led him straight back here to Stonetown, right?" said Kate. "Because she came to take your tests."

Mr. Benedict tapped his nose. "And we all met her the day after that. Presumably she stopped reading newspapers once she left the library and so never heard about the fire. I saw no reason to mention it." He held up his hand, anticipating Sticky's response. "Put your mind at rest, Sticky. I would have told her soon regardless. There's more to the story, you see, and had Constance not been in such a volatile state of mind, perhaps she would have stayed to hear the details."

Sticky perked up. "What details?"

"Not all the books were lost," said Rhonda. "A few were salvaged by a librarian who had managed to hide from the Recruiters in a storage room."

"Constance's storage room!" Kate exclaimed.

"Most likely," said Rhonda. "When this librarian smelled smoke she began loading boxes of books onto a cart, and as soon as she knew the Recruiters were gone she fled the building — taking the cart with her. It was from her that we learned all these details."

"We made sure none of this was reported to the newspapers," Number Two said. "Otherwise the Recruiters would have returned to finish their job. We helped the librarian go into hiding, and we took the books for safekeeping."

"You mean the books are *here*?" cried Kate.

"In your *house*?" cried Sticky.

"In the attic," said Number Two. "Four boxes of them."

"They must be awfully overdue," Kate said.

Mr. Benedict, his eyes still melancholy, laughed nonetheless. "We intended to return them when the library was rebuilt, but construction has been delayed due to lack of funds. At any rate, if Constance's papers are not among these books, we can assume they were destroyed in the fire. In either case I shall know the best way to proceed. Constance has nothing to worry about. In fact she should be encouraged."

"Wouldn't you like to go tell her that, Mr. Benedict?" asked Rhonda. "You're clearly worried about her."

"I had better not," said Mr. Benedict, with a wave to acknowledge Rhonda's concern. "I suspect she has locked herself into her room, in which case she won't let me in for some time, and at the moment I haven't any to spare. It's also possible that Reynie is with her — I assume that's where he's run off to — which would be for the best. She's unlikely to listen to me right now, but she may respond to him."

"Speaking of which," Kate said, for just then Reynie stepped back into the chamber.

"She wouldn't open the door," Reynie said, after confirming that Constance had indeed locked herself into her room. "I'm not even sure she could hear me knocking. She was sobbing pretty loudly and throwing things around."

Mr. Benedict received this news with a somber nod. But then he drew himself up and said briskly, "Well, we must remind ourselves that she is going to be fine. The disorienting effects of her session will soon fade, and there is nothing but good news for her ahead. I will let your friends tell you what I mean by this, Reynie, for now" — he was checking his pocket watch — "yes, even now Mr. Pressius is on his way back here, and I must be calm and focused when I deal with him."

⚬∴∾

"Calm and focused" was what Reynie, Sticky, and Kate agreed they must be, too. After a quick discussion about the best way to handle things, the three of them hurried back to the girls' room only to discover that Constance was no longer there.

"She knew we'd come," Reynie surmised, looking around. "I guess she really wants to be alone."

Constance had thrown an impressive tantrum — the floor was such a mess there was hardly room to step — and Kate, clicking her tongue, right away set about straightening up. "Maybe we should give her a little time and then go look for her," she said as she returned pillows to beds and clothes to hangers. "What do you boys think?"

The boys readily agreed. Though no one wished to admit it aloud, the truth was they were all relieved, for in her current state Constance would have been close to unbearable. Half-guilty and half-glad, the three of them settled onto the rug, which Kate had tidied with typical frenzied speed.

"I think I've figured something out," said Reynie. "Something about S.Q. and Mr. Curtain."

Sticky and Kate listened intently as Reynie reminded them what Constance had said in the chamber. Neither of them had noticed the look in Mr. Benedict's eye or given any thought to his interest in Constance's comment about S.Q. Pedalian. Kate (who disliked waiting) had been wondering how long the session would last, and Sticky had been secretly wishing he were somewhere else, for just being in the same room with the Whisperer made his head sweat.

"Suddenly it all made sense to me," Reynie said now, his voice an excited whisper. "Jackson and Jillson said S.Q. got extra sessions in the Whisperer, right? They thought he was getting rewarded for his loyalty, but *I* think Mr. Curtain was burying some of his memories!"

"So *that's* what made him seem so dimwitted?" Kate said.

"Well, my guess is he wasn't the sharpest file in the drawer to begin with," Reynie said, "but I'll bet a lot of his confusion came from losing memories all the time. If *we* kept losing memories, I imagine we'd be mixed-up, too."

"But why would Mr. Curtain go to so much trouble?" Sticky wondered. "What was it he wanted S.Q. to forget? To *keep* forgetting?"

"Think about the riddle Mr. Benedict gave us," said Reynie.

Sticky looked puzzled. "Mr. Curtain wanted S.Q. to forget 'love'?"

"Um . . . no," Reynie said. "But love is the reason Mr. Curtain went to so much trouble."

"Okay, you just lost me," said Kate. "First of all, I still have a hard time believing Mr. Curtain loves anything but control. But if he does love S.Q., why would he do something so awful to him?"

"To keep his loyalty," Reynie replied. "Can you think of anyone else as dedicated to him? The Ten Men follow Mr. Curtain for money, the Executives did it mostly for power, but S.Q. seems genuinely to admire him. He does whatever Mr. Curtain wants, sticks with him despite miserable treatment — he's as loyal as anyone could possibly be. And why? We've seen it ourselves. He thinks Mr. Curtain is trying to do *good*."

"I never could understand how he managed to believe that," Sticky said, "despite all evidence to the contrary. But I suppose if Mr. Curtain kept removing his memories of that evidence . . ."

"Exactly," said Reynie, "and I think there's even more to it than that. The Whisperer can also suppress your greatest fears, right?"

"Right," said Sticky. "So?"

"So S.Q. was an orphan when he got to the Institute," Reynie said, "and Mr. Curtain was the closest thing to a father that he had." He shrugged. "S.Q. *wanted* to believe good things about him."

"You mean S.Q.'s greatest fear —?"

"Is the truth," said Reynie. "The truth about Mr. Curtain."

～:～

For a while the three of them, in growing excitement, discussed the implications of this new idea. Without the

Whisperer at his disposal, Mr. Curtain had been unable to continue S.Q.'s sessions. Wasn't it likely, then, that S.Q. would find it harder and harder to avoid the truth? Hadn't they already seen some evidence of that during their last encounter with him? True, Mr. Benedict had been compelled to trick S.Q. in order to save the children, and this was surely a setback — but wouldn't S.Q. eventually see that he was wasting his admiration on the wrong twin? That it was Mr. Benedict who was good and Mr. Curtain who cared about no one but himself? And when that moment arrived, might not S.Q. Pedalian prove to be the chink in Mr. Curtain's armor?

"No wonder Mr. Benedict took such an interest in what Jackson and Jillson said," Sticky reflected, "even though Mr. Gaines and his crowd didn't think much of it."

"I wonder if Mr. Curtain knows," Kate mused. She was staring off at nothing in particular, absently retying her ponytail as her right foot jiggled with pent-up energy. Or perhaps it was her left foot — her legs were so twisted up it was difficult to tell.

"Knows what?" Reynie asked.

"Hmm?" Kate saw the boys looking at her expectantly. "Oh, I was just wondering if Mr. Curtain realizes he cares so much about S.Q.'s opinion. Or if he gives himself some excuse for going to all that trouble, when it would have been so much easier to just brainsweep S.Q. and get rid of him. Mr. Curtain wouldn't like to think himself weak, you know."

"Good question," Reynie said.

"Well, I wouldn't like to say I sympathize with him," Kate said, "but for a long time I refused to believe I needed anyone myself — and *I'm* not an egomaniac madman like Mr. Curtain. I'm sure he's capable of —"

As if to affirm just exactly what Mr. Curtain was capable of, at that moment the angry, shouting voice of Mr. Pressius came in through the window. They jumped up and ran to look out.

Mr. Pressius stood at the closed gate, gesticulating wildly, his face inches away from Mr. Benedict's own. On the sidewalk around him, and even spilling into the street, were at least a dozen police officers, as well as a handful of government agents in suits and sunglasses. Mr. Benedict stood calmly in the courtyard, his hands resting atop the iron gate. Behind him stood Milligan and Ms. Plugg, observing the exchange with close attention.

"What do you mean I need more signatures?" Mr. Pressius roared. "Whose signatures could I possibly need? I have a *court order*! Right here!" He shook a piece of paper in Mr. Benedict's face.

A government agent stepped forward and spoke in Mr. Pressius's ear.

"But that's preposterous!" Mr. Pressius cried, turning on the agent. "My daughter is being held captive by this very man before you! And you mean to say I need an entire committee's *permission* to go in and get her? Or else I need *his*? This *criminal*? That's outrageous! You told me —" The agent quickly spoke into his ear again, and Mr. Pressius, furiously rattling the gate, shouted, "But why didn't you say anything about this when I *asked* you? What kind of bureaucratic nonsense is this, with you fools and your top-secret —"

Suddenly Milligan's voice rang out. He spoke quite clearly and calmly even though he had to shout to be heard over Mr. Pressius's ranting. "Mr. Shields," he bellowed to the agent standing beside Mr. Pressius, "you know your orders. Any person who disregards protocol and jeopardizes the project by publicly revealing —"

Even before Milligan had finishing speaking, Mr. Shields had clapped one hand over Mr. Pressius's mouth and another firmly on his shoulder. The astonished Mr. Pressius's eyes grew huge, and he was too flummoxed to resist as the agent wheeled him about and marched him toward a car at the curb. A few uncertain police officers made as if to intervene, but another agent, flashing her badge, indicated that they were free to let the disagreeable man be taken away. The officers relaxed and smiled, obviously relieved. They had a brief, hushed conversation with the agents there on the sidewalk, then a quick word with Ms. Plugg at the gate (Mr. Benedict and Milligan had already gone inside), and then everyone shook hands all around. A minute later the sidewalk was empty.

Reynie, Sticky, and Kate, who had witnessed the entire scene, were fairly breathless from cheering and laughing and talking at once.

"Mr. Benedict *knew* he couldn't take her! He knew it all along!"

"But Mr. Pressius had no idea! Did you see his face?"

"He sure isn't used to being contradicted, is he? That would have taken a lot longer if he hadn't blown his top."

"I'll bet that's what Mr. Benedict was counting on!"

And then all together when the last police officer had ambled away: "Let's go tell Constance!"

They felt sure Constance would be cheered by the story of Mr. Pressius's defeat — perhaps she'd even seen it herself — but first they'd have to find her. After a quick search of the third floor they hurried down to the dining room, where Mrs. Washington and Miss Perumal were at the window discussing the incident.

"— a relief," Mrs. Washington was saying to Miss Perumal. "He'd brought so many with him, after all, and at first I thought they would bash in the front door and storm the house!"

"I had the same thought," Miss Perumal admitted. "I felt sure it would come out all right, but perhaps not without a nasty hullaballoo." She turned as the children came into the room. "Hello, you three! Everyone fine? I assume you watched the proceedings just now."

"Yes, and we're looking for Constance," Reynie said. "Have you seen her, Amma?"

"Not since she went outside," said Miss Perumal — she checked her wristwatch — "almost an hour ago. Has she not come back in?"

"We haven't seen her," said Reynie. His heart, for no reason he could make out, had begun to speed up. "You gave her permission?"

"Certainly," said Miss Perumal. "Rhonda had told me she was excused from lessons, and it's finally nice out. She wanted to kick a ball in the backyard, and I —"

"Which guard is posted back there today?" Reynie asked, his heart beating even faster now.

"Mr. Bane. Why, what's the matter, Reynie? You look upset. In fact, you all do."

Reynie didn't take time to respond. He turned and dashed to the stairs, his friends close on his heels. Kate, in fact, was about to leap past him — but then they saw Mr. Bane himself appear at the bottom of the stairs. They froze, staring, wondering what to do. Their thoughts were a wild jumble, and no one was thinking exactly the same thing, yet all of them — not two seconds before — had felt sure that Mr. Bane had done something wicked. Now here he stood.

"Um," Kate said hesitantly as the man started up toward them, "Mr. Bane? Have you seen Constance?"

"Move aside," said Mr. Bane, brushing past them none too gently. The children looked at one another in confusion, then turned and followed him. He strode briskly down the hall and knocked on the door of Mr. Benedict's study. "We have a problem," he said when the door swung open. "Constance Contraire has left the premises."

DARKNESS FALLS

Mr. Benedict was only asleep for a minute. Milligan never even let him touch the floor, but held him sagging in his arms while Rhonda dashed off to alert Number Two. Then like a suddenly animated marionette Mr. Benedict stiffened and sprang forward to stand on his own. He had scarcely opened his eyes before he began interrogating Mr. Bane, whose answers were simple enough:

After kicking the ball around the yard awhile — presumably to throw off suspicion — Constance had "accidentally" sent it rolling under the hedge, and complaining bitterly about the mud and wet grass she had wriggled under the hedge to retrieve it. When she didn't emerge, Mr. Bane had called for her to come out. He had called several times, had thought she was being stubborn. She was known for being stubborn, wasn't she? It had never occurred to him that her size allowed her to do what most people could not — squeeze between the palings of the iron fence beyond the hedge — or that she would ever choose to do such a thing. Why would she wish to leave the safety of the yard?

"When was this?" Mr. Benedict said curtly. He was in the hall now, headed for the dining room with Mr. Bane hurrying along beside him and the three children following behind. (Milligan, after a rapid, whispered exchange with Mr. Benedict, had already left.)

"I came up here the moment I realized she was gone," said Mr. Bane.

"No, when did she first go under the hedge?" Mr. Benedict stopped outside the dining room and fixed the man with a piercing gaze. "Be sure of what you say, Mr. Bane. I see from your muddy knees that you did indeed kneel to look beneath the hedge, and yet I can tell you are choosing your words carefully. Now you had better leave off any excuses and tell me the exact truth whether you like it or not. How long did you wait before you went to check? Five minutes? Ten?"

Mr. Bane swallowed. He looked defiantly at Mr. Benedict, but only for a moment. Then he looked away. "About ten minutes, yes."

Mr. Benedict stared at him, assessing his words. "Unfortunately, I believe you. You'll notice, Mr. Bane, that I do not ask how loudly you called for Constance to come out. At the moment I have no time to watch you squirm and protest. You were negligent, and I —" Here Mr. Benedict hesitated. He took a breath, glanced probingly at the children, and in a slightly less cold tone said, "I should like to think that you're sorry for it."

Mr. Bane looked up, his jaw twitching. He coughed into his fist. "I am, of course. Very sorry indeed." He did not look at all sorry, Reynie thought, but he did look as though he were trying to.

"You've done good work until now," said Mr. Benedict stiffly. "I shall bear that in mind when I speak with your superiors."

"Thank you," said Mr. Bane in a flat tone.

Mr. Benedict nodded. "And now, if you will please inform Ms. Plugg what has occurred, I shall take a moment to speak with my friends."

Mr. Bane stalked off, and Mr. Benedict — after listening for the man's footsteps on the stairs — led the children into the dining room. According to some privately understood arrangement, Number Two and Rhonda had assembled everyone in the house (not including the guards), and they all stood close together, talking agitatedly. On every face was an expression of deepest concern. Miss Perumal and her mother drew Reynie close as soon as they saw him; the Washingtons did likewise to Sticky. Moocho Brazos beckoned Kate over and stood with one huge hand resting protectively on her shoulder. Mr. Benedict raised his hands for attention, and everyone immediately fell silent.

"You know what has happened," Mr. Benedict said, his words quiet and quick. "Constance has run away and is now in danger. Milligan is contacting his sentries and will notify those authorities we can trust, but I intend to begin a search right away. There is not a moment to lose." He gestured toward the dining room table, where Number Two and Rhonda were already spreading a large map. "We shall designate different sectors to any of you willing to help search. I must remind you that anyone who leaves the house runs a risk." He paused to let his words sink in. "Now please forgive my directness, but there's no time for delicacy. Who will help?"

Every hand in the room went up, including the children's.

"Thank you all," said Mr. Benedict. "You children, of course, must remain here in the guarded house." (The other adults nodded firmly at this, and the children lowered their hands, knowing this was no time for argument.) "The rest of us will be divided into search parties as follows: Miss Perumal, Moocho Brazos, and Mr. Washington will go with Number Two — you'll be afoot. Mrs. Perumal, Mrs. Washington, and I will accompany Rhonda in the station wagon."

The adults gathered around the table, where Mr. Benedict, a pencil in each hand, swiftly marked perimeters on the map as Number Two and Rhonda explained their search strategy. Reynie, Sticky, and Kate watched helplessly from across the room.

"Why do you think he put my parents on different teams?" Sticky murmured.

"For the same reason he separated Amma and Pati," Reynie said grimly. "If something bad happens to one of them, we'll still have one guardian left."

Sticky's eyes widened. He cast a worried look toward his parents.

"They'll be fine," Kate said reassuringly. "I'll bet Mr. Benedict knew they would worry about that, so he just took care of the problem up front. That doesn't mean he's really worried himself."

Sticky nodded, half-convinced, but his fingers twitched maddeningly nonetheless, and this time he couldn't resist giving his spectacles a polish.

A final flurry of instructions at the table; the group broke up. The children were hugged and kissed and their shoulders were squeezed, and two minutes later they were alone.

Never had the house felt so empty. The three of them stood at the dining room window, looking down into the courtyard and the street beyond. Any minute, they said to themselves, they would see Constance come back through the gate and demand petulantly that Ms. Plugg let her into the house. Or the station wagon would pull up with Constance in back, arms huffily crossed. But after twenty minutes of staring they had seen only the occasional pedestrian or car, and Ms. Plugg in the courtyard pacing to and fro and speaking into her radio. Meanwhile the shadows were lengthening. It would soon be dusk.

Finally Sticky suggested they go up to his and Reynie's room and look out the back. "At least it would be a change," he said, and with gloomy nods they headed to the third floor. Their footsteps sounded unusually loud on the stairs, for the house was unnaturally quiet.

As Reynie and Sticky stood at their window looking down

into the backyard (where Mr. Bane, like Ms. Plugg, was pacing and speaking into his radio), Kate busied herself by straightening their room. The boys' room was not exactly a shambles, but compared to hers it was a disaster, with sloppily made bunk beds, socks on the floor, and every inch of the desk's surface covered with newspapers, books, writing tablets, and whatever came out of their pockets at the end of each day. Kate felt grateful for the mess; she had desperately wanted something to do. The boys, for their part, were glad that her bustling about covered up their strained silence. Everyone was extremely upset and trying not to show it.

"I wonder which direction she went," Sticky said at last. He pointed to the lane beyond the hedge-lined fence. "Either way, the hedge would have hidden her from Mr. Bane."

"I'm not sure that mattered," said Reynie. "Didn't you get the feeling Mr. Bane knew what she was up to? And let her do it?"

"I sure suspected him of something," said Kate, using her Swiss Army knife tweezers to pick up dirty socks and toss them into a hamper. "I didn't know what, though."

"I did, too," said Sticky, "but then Mr. Benedict mentioned his muddy knees. So obviously Mr. Bane went to the trouble to look for her, right? I don't like him, but if Mr. Benedict, of all people, is willing to drop his suspicions . . ."

"The muddy knees were a cover-up!" Reynie said, barely keeping the frustration out of his voice. He felt ready to lash out at the least thing. "Don't you see? Mr. Bane handled it all so slyly. He knew Mr. Benedict would notice his knees, so he didn't bother pointing them out himself — that would have seemed too obvious." He shook his head. "And I don't believe Mr. Benedict dropped his suspicions. He only pretended to. Did you see the way he glanced at us? Something's not right."

Reynie found he was clenching the edge of the window-sill so hard his fingers hurt. He loosened his grip and kept gazing into the backyard, avoiding Sticky's eyes. He felt sure that eye contact with his friend would cause him to shout angrily or burst into tears — he wasn't sure which. He suddenly realized he was terribly hot, and tearing his jacket off he fairly ruined the zipper.

"You're right," said Sticky after a pause. There was a tremor in his voice, and he was steadfastly avoiding Reynie's gaze as well.

"Of course he is," said Kate from the top bunk, where she'd been smoothing wrinkles from the covers. She vaulted the rail, twisted in the air, and dropped catlike to the floor. She was moving lightly and nimbly as ever, as if she hadn't a care in the world, but this was simply how Kate always moved. Her voice was grave as could be. "Do you think Mr. Bane lied about her running off, then? You don't think someone *took* her, do you? Mr. Benedict didn't seem to think so. He organized the search parties, after all."

"No, I think Mr. Bane was telling the truth — at least about those basic details — and I could tell Mr. Benedict believed him, too." Reynie glanced down at the pacing figure of Mr. Bane, now chafing his hands against the evening chill, and then turned from the window with a feeling of revulsion. "I'm pretty sure she ran away. She was really upset and mixed-up. In fact, come to think of it, this business with Mr. Pressius must have felt an awful lot like her recovered memory."

"Hey, that's true," said Sticky. "Some odious man working for Mr. Curtain intends to take her away? It's very similar. But this time she had friends. She had *us*. So wouldn't you think —"

"Maybe she left a note!" Reynie cried, and he ran to the desk, which Kate had just begun to organize. Already the pens and pencils had been gathered into a cup, the newspapers folded and stacked. "You're right," he said as he rifled through papers, "she does have friends this time, and maybe, just maybe . . ."

"I didn't see one," said Kate, wishing she had. "But you should double-check to be sure."

Reynie did, and then Sticky did, too. There was no note. Still, the possibility lingered, and they decided to search the house — starting with the girls' room, even though Kate hadn't seen a note when she was tidying the room. This time they rummaged through Constance's chest of drawers. But though they found lots of candy wrappers, four or five moldy muffin bottoms, and several reams of poetry (Sticky read through all of it in two minutes), there was no note.

Kate searched the closet. Hardly had she begun before she slapped her forehead and groaned. "Why didn't I notice this before? Her old red raincoat's gone! And her boots! She didn't just throw a tantrum, she was getting ready to run away! If I'd realized that, we might have stopped her in time . . ." She fell silent, looking bitterly at an empty clothes hanger in her hand.

"Don't blame yourself," Reynie said. "We weren't look-ing for clues, remember? We had no idea she was planning to leave."

"*You'd* have noticed it. Even if we weren't looking for clues."

"Maybe, maybe not," said Reynie. "But we do different things, right? Isn't that why we're a team?"

"I suppose," said Kate, then forced a thin smile and said, "I mean yes. Anyway, let's drop it. I'm just upset by this whole business, and standing here isn't going to make it bet-ter. Let's look for the note."

There was no note to be found, however. They searched all the likely places, and some unlikely ones too, casting about for telltale scraps of paper. They searched for two hours and more. But there was nothing.

Nor was there any sign of the search parties, and it was long past dinnertime. Taking apples from the pantry, they bypassed the dining room (its empty table seemed strangely mocking to them now) and went back upstairs to eat them, hoping the boys' bedroom would feel cozy enough to ward off the atmosphere of emptiness.

A vain hope, as it turned out: Reynie could not help but think of all the empty space in the house beneath him. For some reason he imagined himself high in the crow's nest of a ship, far above a treacherous sea. It was a lonely, scary, unnerving feeling, so much so that he had difficulty swal-lowing even the smallest bites of apple. And he had only managed two or three of these when the scary feeling got much worse — for suddenly, without warning, the lights went out.

Reynie heard the metallic twang of Kate releasing the hidden catch on her bucket's flip-top. An instant later her flashlight beam swept across the room, falling first on Sticky's face (rigid with fear) and then his own. He squinted and shielded his eyes.

"You boys okay?" Kate said, already moving toward the window.

"The . . . the last time . . . ," Sticky began. His voice faltered.

"I know," said Reynie. How could any of them have forgotten the last time the lights went out? Two of Mr. Curtain's men had broken into the house, looking for children to kidnap. The only thing that had stopped them was Milligan. And this time Milligan wasn't here.

"It isn't just our house," Kate announced. "The whole street has lost power."

"That seems good," said Sticky hopefully. "Right? There's just a line down, or else a problem with the neighborhood grid."

The boys joined Kate at the window. Sure enough, the windows in all the nearby houses were dark. In some of them figures could be seen passing back and forth with lamps and flashlights.

"It seems darker than you'd expect," Sticky said.

Reynie was gazing at the sky, where the night's first stars twinkled more brightly than any other time he could recall — at least in the city — and with a sinking feeling in his belly he realized why. He pressed his face to the glass and peered toward downtown. "It isn't just our neighborhood. It's Stonetown."

"The whole *city*?" cried Sticky. "The whole . . . the whole . . ." In his mind's eye he saw darkness spreading out in all directions, impenetrable black ink spilling from an infinite inkwell.

"Look downtown," Reynie said. "Normally you can see the tops of some buildings from here."

Sticky couldn't bring himself to look, but Kate saw that Reynie was right. Where there should have been lights shining from the top stories of Stonetown's taller buildings, now there was only blackness.

In the distance a siren wailed; some of the neighborhood dogs began to howl along. Then they heard Mr. Bane and Ms. Plugg shouting back and forth to each other from opposite sides of the house. Mr. Bane, standing on the back steps, was saying something about his radio, which appeared to have stopped working. Ms. Plugg shouted back that hers was out, too.

"Their *radios* are out?" Sticky said. "Oh no, this isn't normal. This isn't right."

They looked gravely at one another.

"I can't hear you!" Mr. Bane shouted, and they watched him trot around to the front of the house.

No sooner had he rounded the corner than Reynie noticed something in the lane. A large, shadowy mass, darker than the darkness through which it moved. The shadow moved smoothly down the lane the way a car might, but it was much larger than a car. And unlike a car, it made absolutely no sound.

"Kate!" Reynie hissed. "Do you —?"

"I see it!" Kate pointed her flashlight out through the darkness. By the time it reached into the lane the beam was wide and diffuse, but there was no mistaking the familiar shape it fell upon.

Sticky's breath escaped him with an audible whoosh. He reached for Reynie's arm only to find Reynie grabbing for his.

"Not good," said Kate.

The Salamander was crowded with Ten Men.

As they fled the room Reynie kept seeing the terrifying image in his mind's eye: the elegant men with their briefcases, standing in the armored vehicle like business executives on a commuter train.

"Head for the front door!" Kate said, slapping her flashlight into Sticky's hand. "I'll warn the chamber guards!"

The boys didn't even think to argue. Stumbling and tripping in their panic, the flashlight beam skidding wildly across walls, ceilings, the floor again, they raced down the stairs, flight after flight. From above they heard Kate shouting her warning to the chamber guards (they were taken aback and she had to repeat herself twice), and then as they descended the final flight of stairs they felt a body rushing past them in the darkness — Kate sliding down the banister. She had her penlight clenched between her teeth; by the time the boys reached the bottom she was directing it at the alarm keypad by the front door.

The warning light was off. Kate's fingers flew across the keys anyway, but there were no familiar chirping sounds. "Alarm's out," she said, speaking around the penlight.

No alarm, no radios, no power. No help.

The door flew open and Ms. Plugg filled the doorway. "What's going on? I heard shouts!"

"Bad men in the lane!" Sticky gasped. "Very bad men!"

Ms. Plugg's face hardened. "Get back inside and lock the door. We'll —"

But Kate and the boys surprised her by hurrying down the front steps, at the bottom of which stood Mr. Bane, looking completely out of sorts. He was anxiously running the zipper up and down on his jacket and staring all around. Ms. Plugg spun on them and barked, "I said get *inside*! It's not safe! Mr. Bane, for heaven's sake, grab them!"

Mr. Bane stopped his zippering, but he only blinked at Ms. Plugg as if he didn't understand.

"It isn't safe inside!" Reynie cried. "The whole thing's a setup, Ms. Plugg! You should run, too! There's no stopping them now!"

Ms. Plugg's eyes widened as his words sank in. But she shook her head resolutely. "No . . . no, I can't run. You three go. Find a place to hide. I'll —"

"Quiet!" Kate hissed, and in the sudden silence they heard heavy footsteps coming from the side of the house, moving toward the front. A large man, running purposefully.

Before the others could even register what they were hearing, Kate had snatched her flashlight from Sticky's hand and — narrowing her eyes, calculating carefully — flung it toward the corner of the house. The flashlight hurtled twenty yards through the air, spinning end over end, and arrived at the corner at exactly the same moment as the Ten Man. There was a loud *crack*, and with a sharp cry the man dropped his briefcase and staggered backward out of sight, clutching at his head.

"Now, Mr. Bane!" roared Ms. Plugg, leaping down the steps. "Follow me!"

The children bolted for the gate. As Kate threw it open Reynie glanced back to see Ms. Plugg disappearing around the side of the house. Mr. Bane stared after her, his hand still frozen to his zipper. Reynie looked away, trying not to think of what was about to happen. Against a Ten Man, even a stunned one, Ms. Plugg stood no chance.

"Where do we go now?" Kate said, turning in the dark street.

"The cellar," Reynie panted, pointing to the little house across the street.

Kate was off like a shot, streaking across the yard to the cellar doors, sliding the metal bolt, and lifting open one of the doors just as the boys caught up. Sticky ducked down the cellar steps into blackness while Reynie paused long enough to make sure they weren't being watched. The courtyard was empty now, but there were shouts and crashes in the house —

Then Kate shoved him roughly through the door and jumped in after him, pulling the door closed. Reynie stumbled down the steps, bumping into Sticky at the bottom, and the two boys went sprawling onto the cellar floor.

"Stop groaning," Kate whispered as they picked themselves up. "I saw Crawlings and Garrotte coming out the front door."

The boys stopped groaning. They had encountered these Ten Men before and could picture them easily — Garrotte a bearded man with a face like a bat, Crawlings strangely spidery, leering, a bald man missing an eyebrow. The thought of them here sent shivers through both boys.

Kate shone her penlight toward the steel door that led to the secret passage. "I don't suppose there's any chance that Milligan was careless . . ."

Fumbling his way through the blackness, Sticky tried the door. "No," he said bleakly, "it's locked."

"Then we'd better hope they aren't looking for us."

Just then Garrotte's voice rang out from a distance: "Which way did the chickies run? Did you see?"

"Oh, that's *really* a shame," whispered Kate, reaching into her bucket.

"Somewhere off in that direction," replied Crawlings, followed by quick footsteps on pavement. The Ten Men were crossing the street. "It's a pretty night for this, isn't it? The stars are beautiful, and it's so cool out. Feels like early spring."

"It *is* early spring," laughed Garrotte. "You can stop hibernating now, old fellow."

The Ten Men's voices, so unnervingly casual and relaxed, grew louder and more distinct as they walked into the yard.

Kate had the penlight in her mouth again; the boys could just see her face in the glow. She was squinting at the fastenings that held the sliding bolt to the wood, gauging the distances between them. Then she lifted something into the light — her magnet — and Reynie's heart leaped as he realized what she was about to try.

With utmost concentration Kate placed the magnet against the cellar door. Then, like a thief cracking a safe, she pressed her ear to the flimsy wood as she slid the magnet up, then down . . . and then her eyebrows lifted. She'd heard what she wanted to hear. Steadily, carefully, ever so slowly, Kate slid the magnet along the wood.

They heard Crawlings again. "Look, Garrotte! A perfect hidey hole for scared little bunnies!"

Heavy footsteps, a disappointed grunt. "*Almost* perfect, my dear. You'll notice the bolt is fastened from the outside."

"Ah!"

"I suppose we should hurry back and help the others," said Garrotte with a sigh. "A pity, though — he'd have been so pleased to have the urchins."

"Think positively, Garrotte! His other plan may work. And perhaps we'll find the fussy one before Benedict does! She's the greatest catch, at any rate . . ."

The Ten Men's voices faded as they withdrew.

"So they don't have her yet," Sticky whispered. "That's something, at least."

"But they're looking for her," Kate said. "And didn't it sound like Mr. Curtain has some other plan for catching us?"

"It did," said Reynie. "But you know the Whisperer's being loaded into the Salamander at this very minute — the Whisperer and all its computers. So why would Mr. Curtain need *us* anymore? What would he need to bargain for?"

These and other unpleasant questions they considered for several minutes, sometimes whispering, sometimes sitting quietly in the dark. They dared not peek out of the cellar doors until they were sure the Ten Men had gone. After the initial sounds of conflict, no sound had come from the direction of Mr. Benedict's house, but for all they knew the eerily silent Salamander was parked in the street.

"I never expected to see anything creepier than Mr. Curtain's wheelchair rolling toward us without making any noise," whispered Kate. "But the Salamander topped that and then some. It reminded me of an alligator gliding along through a swamp."

"Obviously he's improved his noise cancellation technology," Sticky reflected. "And, of course, signal disruption in general."

"Signal disruption?" said Kate.

"Oh yes," said Sticky. "Knocking out Stonetown's power is one thing — naturally he'd need spies in the right places, and probably a malicious computer program or two, but for Mr. Curtain it can't have been all that hard. The communications, though? The fact that the guards' radios failed? For that you need some awfully sophisticated technology, really high-power stuff."

"That's Mr. Curtain's cup of tea," said Reynie. "Energy, invisible signals, wave forms —"

"And creepiness," Kate said. "And madman-iness . . ."

She went on like this, but Reynie heard none of it, for he was suddenly experiencing the most curious thing. All at once he had begun to feel strangely frightened — more frightened, that is, than he already was — as if there were some new threat in the darkness of which he'd previously been unaware. He felt his heartbeat quickening.

"Kate," he breathed, interrupting her, "shine your penlight around the cellar, would you?"

His tone was unnerving and serious, and Kate quickly shone the light around in every direction. The cellar was empty.

"What's the matter?" Kate asked, shutting the light off to spare the batteries.

"Nothing," Reynie said, his heart still pounding. "Nothing, just a — a strange feeling."

Even as he spoke, however, the sensation grew stranger still, and then out of nowhere a sequence of numbers and letters flashed into his mind: **133 N292**. What in the world? Was this a memory? If so, of what? Some kind of code? Reynie shook his head, trying to clear it, but the sequence still hung there in his mind, unchanging, shining brightly as if lit by neon. Not since his sessions with the Whisperer had he experienced anything like it.

Oh no, Reynie thought, breaking into a cold sweat. *Oh no, oh not the Whisperer.*

He tried to calm himself, tried to think clearly. Surely it couldn't be the Whisperer causing this. Mr. Curtain hadn't appeared to be in the Salamander, so there was no one who could be operating it — not yet, anyway. No . . . no, it must be a memory, something important he noticed somewhere. But where? And why was it so important? Reynie began to calm down a bit as his mind set to work on the problem. The sequence seemed vaguely familiar now, but perhaps only because he was getting used to it.

"Reynie?" Sticky said. "Do you still have that feeling? You have me kind of spooked."

Reynie didn't have a chance to answer, for though none of them had heard approaching footsteps, a man's voice suddenly spoke from so close by he might have been inside the cellar with them.

"Now don't attack me when I open the doors, Kate," the voice said, and Reynie thought he might faint with relief.

It was Milligan.

SETUPS, CLUES, and LIKELY STORIES

$\mathbf{T}$he children emerged from the cellar into a night strobed
by blue lights. A very young police officer stood beside his
patrol car at the curb, trying in vain to use his radio. When
the power went out, Milligan said, he'd shown his creden-
tials to this officer and commandeered the car. He knew he
needed to get back to the house at once, but he was on the
far side of Stonetown, in the Quarryside neighborhood, and
thanks to the non-functioning traffic lights the streets were
completely snarled. Even using the patrol car's blue lights

and siren (not to mention sidewalks and front yards) it had taken him twenty minutes.

"Of course I shut off the siren when we got close," Milligan said, "but stealth was beside the point — they'd already gone. I was just relieved to see they hadn't taken you with them. Officer Williams, these are the children I told you about."

The young officer lowered his radio with a trembling hand. He smiled weakly at the children, who could not help but notice his unnaturally pale face. "Pleased to . . . glad you're . . . um . . ."

Milligan clapped him on the shoulder. "You should sit down, friend. You're about to faint."

The officer obliged by collapsing into his patrol car, and Milligan ushered the children through the front gate, saying, "I'm afraid my driving didn't quite agree with him. Or perhaps it was my description of the Ten Men. I thought it only right that he know about them, since they might be here when we arrived."

As Milligan led them around the side of the house, he related what he'd learned in the last few minutes. "There are the broken pieces of your flashlight, Kate," he said, shining his own into the grass, "and that depression in the earth is where the man's briefcase fell, and over here" — he passed the beam over a mutilated patch of ground — "is where Ms. Plugg grappled with the fellow for a full minute, at least. She was a wrestler in school, you know, an All-American. Obviously she sensed he was trying to get at his briefcase — you can see how he kept working his way toward it, but Ms. Plugg kept dragging him back."

The children, who saw nothing of the sort, could only nod. Milligan led them on toward the back of the house. "In the end he got his handkerchief to her nose, and that put her right out. She'll be fine, though — she's tough as they come. Woke up when I got here and insisted on helping me, despite her grogginess and no doubt a raging headache. I sent her inside to check on the chamber guards. With luck they'll have been dispatched quickly, with shock-watches and handkerchiefs. If the briefcases came into play I'll need to administer first aid."

"You haven't been inside yet?" Kate asked.

Milligan arched an eyebrow. "I've only just arrived, Kate. It may surprise you to learn that you were my top priority."

They entered the backyard, where the deep tracks of the Salamander's treads ran right up to the back steps. Across the yard the demolished iron fence lay flat upon the crushed hedge, whose branches poked up through the fence palings, twitching and springing. The children had the disconcerting impression of a hapless creature pinned by a great weight, and as they told Milligan what they'd seen, the rustling sounds and jerky movements of the branches in the darkness kept causing them to jump and stare.

"Noise cancellation for the Salamander?" Milligan frowned, bemused. "I hate to say it, but that was a brilliant stroke. In the darkness, with no lights and no sound — it was perfect for a sneak attack, perfect for getting away on the river."

"The river?" Kate said.

"The Salamander is amphibious, after all, and Stonetown River is just blocks away. Dark alleys and lots were all that lay between them and escape. And a security fence or two, but the Salamander is no respecter of fences, as you can see."

A window opened above them, and Ms. Plugg called down that the chamber guards were all right — just frazzled from the shock-watches — but she hadn't seen Mr. Bane.

"What a surprise," Sticky muttered.

"There's something else," Ms. Plugg added, in a deeply troubled tone. "Oh, I can hardly bear to . . ." The poor woman's face, framed by the window, was the very picture of shame. "That *chair* is destroyed! The special chair in the chamber! I'm so sorry, Milligan. What an utter failure we were . . ." She withdrew from the window, unwilling to hear any words of forgiveness or comfort Milligan might offer.

Baffled, Milligan looked back at the children. "Destroyed? They *destroyed* the Whisperer?"

The children were just as baffled as he was. They'd assumed that the Whisperer had been stolen — that even now the Salamander, laden with the Whisperer and its computers, was headed downriver to Stonetown Harbor, or else upriver to some unknown landing, to be delivered once again into the waiting hands of Mr. Curtain.

"I'd love to believe it," Reynie said, shaking his head. "I really would — but I don't."

"Come with me," Milligan said, and they followed him into the house and down the hidden stairway into the basement, where his flashlight beam illuminated a jumbled mess of blackened, mangled, half-melted computers.

Kate whistled in amazement. "They burned them? That makes no sense! Why wouldn't he just *take* them?"

"He did," Reynie said.

"But the computers —"

"These aren't the Whisperer's computers. If they were, we'd be coughing like crazy."

"Of course!" Kate cried, sniffing the air. "No smoke!"

"So it's some kind of setup," Sticky said. "But why would Mr. Curtain do it this way?"

Milligan grunted. "To convince the authorities that the Whisperer no longer exists — that it no longer poses a threat."

"No, I realize that," Sticky said. "What I mean is, why did Mr. Curtain do such a bad job of it? If *we* can tell those computers weren't destroyed here tonight, everyone else can, too."

Reynie groaned and put his hands to his head. "Who was the only person with regular access to the Whisperer? Who was the one about to lose control of it?"

"Mr. Benedict," Sticky whispered, as if he didn't want anyone to hear.

Reynie started to pace, found no room for it, and dropped onto the bottom stair. "So it was all arranged from the beginning," he muttered angrily. "The only person who could say for sure that these aren't the Whisperer's computers is Mr. Benedict, but *he'll* be suspected of sabotaging them — out of spite, I suppose, unless they come up with some other ludicrous reason. They won't trust anything he says. The truth will disappear right along with the Whisperer."

"But the Ten Men!" Kate said.

Milligan shook his head. "Thugs with a personal vendetta against Mr. Benedict and me. Not necessarily thieves. That's how it will be portrayed. They'll say Mr. Benedict seized upon this attack as an excuse, as a cover for something he did himself. They may even suggest he arranged it." He knelt down and gathered the children close to him. "Listen, this is all about to get a great deal more complicated, and I'll need you to do exactly as I say. Can you do that?" With a smile he added, "For once?"

They nodded. Milligan pursed his lips and looked at them askance.

"We *will*," Kate insisted.

"Thank you," Milligan said. "All right. Mr. Benedict and the others will be getting back any minute now, and my sentries will arrive as a team, and no doubt Gaines and all his crew will come, too. This whole place will be bedlam, with listening ears all around you, and you must say nothing about any of this — not a word — unless you're absolutely certain you're alone with one of us."

"Won't we be questioned?" Reynie asked.

"You can say I ordered you not to speak to anyone. That will put them off for the time being," said Milligan. As he spoke, they heard car doors slamming and familiar voices talking excitedly in the courtyard, and two sirens that had been keening in the distance began to grow louder. "You'll need to be moved. There's no help for it. My sentries and I have to track the Salamander if we can, so I can't stay with you. Meanwhile Ten Men are still on the prowl for Constance, who may well lead them right back here — and I can't leave enough sentries behind to protect you properly."

"Won't moving us be risky, too?" asked Kate, who would rather be near the action than shut away somewhere with no idea what was happening.

"Everything is risky now, I'm afraid, but the safest thing is to relocate you, and as soon as possible."

"My parents —" Sticky began.

"They'll agree with me. Anyway, I'll be moving them, too. But we'll all want you out of harm's way first. Meanwhile, Kate, here is the key to the security door in the cellar — if we get caught off guard again, this time you'll have a safer place to go."

Milligan finished in a shout, for the sirens sounded from just outside now. And their stupendous blaring persisted for some time, which made the courtyard reunion between the children and the adults a frustrating ordeal of yelling and gesturing. Only Mrs. Perumal, who was hard of hearing, seemed unaffected by the clamor; she stood placidly by Reynie, patting him and nodding as everyone else plugged their ears and pulled their hair. Officers and agents gesticulated on all sides; neighborhood residents spilled into the street to gawk; and high overhead a much-agitated Madge wheeled and darted, her dreams of pigeon-hunting rudely disrupted.

Then, abruptly, the sirens were cut off, and the roaring voice of Mr. Gaines broke over the scene: "And where were *you*, Benedict? Tell me that!"

The shout came all the way from the backyard, where Mr. Benedict had gathered with several others to inspect the scene. His response was too quiet to hear, and the courtyard hubbub resumed, this time at a lower pitch. The Washingtons, the Perumals, and Moocho Brazos — who had not found Constance — were bombarding the children with expressions of concern and questions about what had happened. But the children, cleaving to Milligan's instructions, fended the questions off until later, for the courtyard remained crowded with agents, officers, and dazed-looking house guards.

Rhonda appeared in the front doorway with a lantern. "Quickly now, everyone," she said, beckoning the families inside. "We have new arrangements to make."

The arrangements were discussed by lanternlight in the foyer, away from prying ears. In one hour, Rhonda said, an armored car would take Mr. Benedict and the children to the police station. The drivers could be trusted; they were top sentries, handpicked by Milligan. Once the children were safely deposited, the sentries would return for the adults.

"Why the police station?" Miss Perumal asked.

"Mr. Benedict has to go there anyway," Rhonda said. "That much has been made clear to us. Resisting will only waste time, and we haven't a second to spare. Nor can we spare more than two sentries to drive, or trust anyone but Milligan's sentries to do it. The police station is reasonably secure and not very far. Even with the traffic jams we should have everyone there in a few hours."

"What about Constance?" Reynie asked.

Rhonda rubbed her temples. "She wasn't where he hoped to find her. Number Two and I will stay here in case she wanders back, and Milligan will organize a new search once he determines whether the Salamander can be tracked. He fears it can't be done — not past the river — but he has to make an attempt while the trail is fresh. If there's any chance at all . . ."

Here Rhonda checked herself, but it was clear enough to Reynie that she thought the situation desperate. She mustered a resolute smile, however, as she distributed flashlights and sent everyone off to pack overnight bags. "Bring only essentials," she said, already hurrying out, "and meet back here in one hour."

The children insisted they would be fine going upstairs alone, not least because they wanted to talk in private. As they mounted the dark staircase into the even deeper darkness above, they whispered about the dread they had heard in Rhonda's voice. This wasn't the best way to bolster one's courage, it turned out, and before they were halfway up the stairs Reynie and Sticky were both longing to go back down. Even Kate felt a strange prickling at the back of her neck, as if she were being watched. She kept spinning to shine her flashlight into some black, empty corner, then frowning and pressing on as the boys clutched their hearts and gasped for breath.

"I have an uneasy feeling," said Kate at the top of the stairs. "I think we should stick together while we pack."

"If you insist," Reynie said, wiping a sweaty palm against his shirt, and Sticky made a faint squeaking sound that was almost certainly a murmur of assent.

"But first let's have a look at the chamber," Kate said, and she darted off before the boys could reply. Gathering themselves as best they could, they hurried after her bobbing flashlight.

The hallway was in order, with no signs of a struggle (there hadn't been much of one), but the unguarded, open chamber door was a strange sight — especially since they had expected to find it smashed in. A quick inspection revealed that the Ten Men had focused laser pointers on the door's two locks. A turn of the knob and a hard shove had accomplished the rest. And in the chamber, beyond the overturned decorative screen, lay a pile of blackened components that certainly looked like they had belonged to the Whisperer.

"If we didn't know better," Kate muttered, casting her flashlight beam over the pile, "I'd say that was really it."

Sticky sighed. "Don't you wish it was? Then this whole nightmare would be over instead of just beginning."

The word "nightmare" reminded Reynie of Constance, somewhere in the city, no doubt staring fearfully into darkness even now, just as she had used to do upon waking from her terrible dreams.

"Do you think she's still confused?" asked Kate, evidently thinking about the same thing.

"Maybe," Reynie said. "Or maybe she's snapped out of it and wishes she hadn't."

"I wonder if she has any idea that Ten Men really are searching for her," Sticky said.

"I can hardly stand to think about it," Reynie said, shaking his head. "Let's get out of here."

In a solemn silence they made their way to the hallway where their bedrooms lay. They reached the boys' room first, and Kate grabbed the doorknob only to leap back when a voice inside cried, "What? Who's there?"

"It's Mr. Bane," said Reynie in a choked voice, and realizing he was right Kate flung open the door and shone her flashlight in.

Mr. Bane sat in the middle of the floor, squinting in the powerful flashlight beam, his face a mixture of confusion and alarm. He tried to shield his eyes with one hand. "Was that Reynie's voice I heard? Is that you, Reynie?"

"What are you doing in here?" Kate demanded, not lowering the light.

"And Kate, too," said Mr. Bane, still squinting, his head turned away from the light. He took his jacket from beside him and held it up to block the beam. "Would you lower that flashlight? My head's killing me."

Kate shone the beam a few seconds longer — just to make a point — then lowered it and again demanded to know what Mr. Bane was doing in there.

"I . . . I'm not sure. They must have dragged me in here," said Mr. Bane, looking around the room as if seeing it for the first time. "I . . . well, you saw me in the courtyard. I was completely taken aback, I'm sorry to say. I got mixed up and thought Ms. Plugg had run into the house. When I came inside, though, she wasn't there. Then I heard the chamber guards shouting and ran up here to help. I followed noises down this hall. It was dark, and in my hurry I bumped right into a man with one eyebrow."

The children exchanged glances.

"He was coming out of your room," Mr. Bane said to Kate. "He pressed a handkerchief to my nose. It must have been dosed with something — I blacked out and only just woke up. When I heard you at the door I thought you might be one of them. But they've all gone, obviously, or you wouldn't be poking around in the dark." Mr. Bane climbed to his feet. "Now what's happened? How are the others? How long have I been out?"

"You'd better report downstairs," Reynie said. "People have been looking for you."

"Well, you're just full of answers, aren't you?" Mr. Bane said coldly, and with a sniff he pressed past them and fumbled away down the hall without benefit of a flashlight. They shone theirs after him until they were sure he was gone, then went into the boys' room.

"He's lying," said Reynie, going straight to the window.

"Of course he's lying," said Sticky. "He's trying to cover for being a coward. I'll bet he just ran up here and hid where he thought it was safe."

"I don't know," said Kate. "Why bother lying to *us*? He's never taken two seconds to speak to us before, so why start now? Maybe Crawlings really did knock him out, and he's too groggy to think straight."

"Or he's hoping the more people he tells, the better his chances of being believed," said Sticky.

Reynie watched Mr. Bane skulk out of the house into the backyard, where Mr. Benedict, Mr. Gaines, and several others remained in hushed but heated conversation. Flashlights moved about the yard and the dark lane beyond like fireflies on a summer night. Mr. Bane began his animated explanations, his voice rising to the window in a plaintive, unintelligible murmur. He was anxiously fiddling with his zipper again, having put the jacket back on.

"Tell me," Reynie muttered, "when do you suppose is the

best time to take off your jacket — right before you run inside to fight intruders, or right after you wake up in the dark, thinking they might be just outside the door?"

"His jacket *was* off, wasn't it?" Sticky said.

"It's hot up here," Reynie said. "He was probably sweltering. And I think we surprised him. We were quiet coming down the hallway. Otherwise I'll bet he'd have put it back on before we saw him."

"Well, what else is new?" said Kate. "We knew we couldn't trust that guy."

Reynie felt he was missing something, but when he tried to concentrate he kept seeing that strange sequence of numbers and letters in his head. He decided to wait a bit and try again — sometimes answers came to him when he was thinking of other things — and in the meantime he and Sticky hurriedly packed their bags. Then they all went down to Kate's room.

The door was open as she'd left it — no surprises this time — and with a quick sweep of her flashlight Kate verified the room was empty. "He might have told the truth about Crawlings," she said, crossing to the window, "even if he lied about everything else. I did see Crawlings come out of the house, after all, and we all heard him tell Garrotte which direction we ran. He could have seen us from this window." She went to her bed and dragged an overnight bag from beneath it.

"They were looking for us," Sticky said. "We know that much already."

"Yes, but doesn't it seem they knew which rooms to search first?" Kate said, smoothing the bedskirt, which she had only very slightly disturbed. "It was only a few seconds before they came out after us." Out of habit she glanced around for other things to tidy. Even in the dark she managed to locate a wrinkle in the rug, an errant scrap of paper, and a floor lamp Sticky had accidentally knocked crooked with his bag.

"Sorry," Sticky said as she straightened the lamp (and put his bag in the hall). "So you think they ran directly up here? You think Mr. Bane told them?"

"I don't know who else —" Kate cut herself off. Reynie was staring at her. "What, am I missing something?"

Reynie shone his flashlight at the scrap of paper in her hand. "What's that, Kate?"

Kate looked down in surprise. "This? Oh, just a scrap I saw on the rug. I was going to throw it away . . ." She looked up again suddenly, her eyes wide. "But, hey, didn't I —"

"Leave the rug spotless? Yes, you did. We stood right here and watched you."

"So someone —"

"Crawlings!" Sticky said. "Remember how McCracken was always saying how careless he was?"

Kate turned her flashlight onto the paper. "Only a number here. *2100*. And looks like an *h* after that . . ."

Reynie went to the wastepaper basket. There were more scraps of paper inside. "He tore something up and threw it away!"

"And in the darkness he didn't notice that he'd dropped a scrap," Kate said.

Reynie pieced the scraps together on the rug. Some came from an envelope that had been unsealed with a letter opener

.("Remember those letter openers?" Sticky muttered with a shiver) and bore on the front the single letter *C*, which they thought probably stood for Crawlings. The rest formed a note: *Rendezvous and search Abbot Edifice 2100 hrs.*

"I think I see what's happened," Reynie said. "The Ten Men were carrying sealed instructions — to be opened in certain circumstances, maybe, or else just when they got here."

"It makes sense," said Sticky. "Mr. Curtain knew they couldn't use radios or phones, and he doesn't trust anyone to know all his plans ahead of time."

"He was careful enough to be pretty vague," said Kate. "I know '2100 hours' is nine o'clock, and 'rendezvous' means to meet somewhere — but where? And who or what is this 'Abbot Edifice'? Is it a person or a place?"

Sticky furrowed his brow. "It's kind of both. An edifice is a building, and an abbot is the superior of an abbey or —"

"Slow down," said Kate. "An abbey's a kind of church, right?"

"It can be," Sticky said, speaking slowly. "'Abbey' usually refers to a convent or monastery under the supervision of an abbess or abbot. But sometimes the church in one of those places is called the abbey, as well."

"Okay!" said Kate. "So they're going to meet up again at nine o'clock at a certain convent or monastery —"

"Definitely a monastery. The note says 'Abbot,' not 'Abbess.'"

"A monastery, then, and they're going to search one of the buildings," Kate said. "But which monastery and which building?"

"Wait!" Reynie said, jumping to his feet. "A monastery is where monks live, right? So isn't the abbot a monk, too? Mr. Curtain isn't just being vague — he's using code words!"

"Of course!" Sticky said. "So Abbot Edifice is code for —"

"The Monk Building!" Kate cried.

"But why search there?" Reynie said, his eyes darting back and forth. "Unless . . . Okay, Mr. Curtain must know that Mr. Benedict has a connection to the Monk Building. So maybe — if the Ten Men didn't find everything they expected to find *here* —"

"Then Mr. Curtain's instructions would send them to look *there*," Kate said, and glancing at the wall clock (which fortunately was battery powered), she added, "in fifteen minutes! We need to tell Milligan!" And she dashed from the room.

Reynie and Sticky followed as quickly as they could, but Reynie stumbled over Sticky's bag in the hall, and Sticky stumbled over Reynie, and by the time they got downstairs Kate was waiting for them, bouncing up and down impatiently. "We're too late! He's off with his sentries already!"

"What about Mr. Benedict?" Reynie said. "Or Rhonda or Number Two?"

"They're all surrounded by officials, and Mr. Bane's right there with them — and, oh, we don't have *time* for this! It'll take ages just to get Mr. Benedict by himself, but if the Ten Men are looking for something important, then we need to get there first!"

With a jolt of alarm Reynie realized that Kate meant to go to the Monk Building herself. But before he could argue how crazy this was, she held up the key Milligan had given her.

"I can take the secret passage! They'll never see me. I'll check the peepholes first, so if they're already in the office I won't blunder in on them — and if they *are* there I can spy on them!"

"Whoa, slow down, Kate," said Sticky. "We need to —"

But there was no slowing her down. She was off to the front door before Sticky could finish.

Reynie said, "If we can't stop her —"

"I know," Sticky said, hurrying after her. "We'll have to go, too."

When they reached the front door Kate was halfway across the courtyard and heading for the gate. Striding along with her (though none too steadily) was the bedraggled Ms. Plugg. The police officers had moved off to usher neighbors back inside their homes, and the dazed chamber guards still sat on the steps. No one appeared to question what Ms. Plugg and her young charge were doing.

"...said you were to stand guard in the yard," Kate was saying as the boys caught up to them. "And absolutely no one else is to know."

"What is it you hope to find down there?" asked Ms. Plugg, who seemed grateful to have been given a duty.

"I can't say, but it's important! And you're not to say anything or let anyone come down there. And we have to keep quiet ourselves —"

"We?" Ms. Plugg turned and saw Reynie and Sticky behind her. "Oh, hello, boys —"

"So don't bother calling down to ask if we're all right," Kate continued, and when the guard's brow wrinkled she added quickly, "Sorry, Ms. Plugg, I'd explain more, but we have to hurry! The car gets here in half an hour."

"Half an hour," Ms. Plugg repeated, and checked her watch. They were across the street now and hastening toward the cellar doors.

Sticky was pleading with his eyes for Reynie to stop them, and Reynie *wanted* to, yet he couldn't bring himself to do it any more than Sticky could. All it would take was one word to Ms. Plugg about what Kate really intended. But then what? Confusion, argument, delay; the Ten Men would get there first; and then what might be their only chance to stop Mr. Curtain would be lost. Reynie couldn't fathom living with that knowledge. So despite the warning bells in his head and the revolt in his belly, he held his tongue, and down into the cellar the three of them went.

"Glad you're coming," Kate whispered, "but you know I can't wait for you. I need to run fast." Holding her flashlight under her arm, she directed it at the metal door and inserted the key into the lock. "If I'm in trouble when you get there, you can hurry back here for help." She turned to reassure them as the door swung open. "Don't worry, though, I won't be in trouble."

"Wait!" Sticky said, jumping forward to catch her by the arm. He missed — she was already several paces down the secret passage — but she stopped and turned expectantly. "Your flashlight! Remember to turn it off before you go into the anteroom — if it's dark in the office your light will show through the peepholes!"

"Gosh, glad you thought of that," said Kate. "Thanks!" And then she was gone.

It was more than a year since they had been in the secret passage, and the boys entered the dank, narrow, gloomy tunnel with no little trepidation. Their crisscrossing flashlights swept not just the floor but the walls and ceiling, too, annoying several spiders and centipedes into skittering retreat.

Reynie swallowed hard. "Ready?"

"Not really," said Sticky, "but I suppose it doesn't matter."

Together they counted to three, took a deep breath, and ran into the gloom after Kate.

Tricky Lines and Heavy Traffic

Reynie and Sticky stopped at the end of the passage to catch their breath, then again when they neared the top of the dark, winding, seemingly interminable stairs. It wouldn't do to be panting and wheezing when they crept into the secret anteroom, located on the Monk Building's seventh floor. Mastering his breath as best he could — knowing perfectly well that under the circumstances it would never fully settle, nor his heartbeat stop racing — Reynie kept up the count he'd begun in the back of his mind almost fifteen minutes ago. Almost fifteen minutes, but not quite. The Ten Men shouldn't have arrived yet, which meant Kate should have had her chance to search the office. So why hadn't the boys met her coming back in the passage? He feared he knew the answer, and a minute later Kate confirmed it.

"I stuck around to spy," she whispered when the boys appeared at the top of the stairs. She was kneeling by the far wall of the anteroom, her eye to a peephole. She had set her flashlight on the floor lens-down, so that only a dim glow emerged from around its rim. Kate tapped the flashlight. "Don't worry, I only turned that on for you two. I'll turn it off when they show up."

"When they show up?" Sticky breathed. "Are you out of your mind? Did you search the office or not?"

"There was nothing there. Nothing at all. Empty file cabinets, empty desk drawers. It's all just for show. Or else the Ten Men got here early and took everything, but it doesn't look that way. The place doesn't look ransacked — just empty. I want to hear what they say when they discover the same thing."

"But . . . but . . . ," Sticky stuttered, trying to think of a way to change Kate's mind. The Ten Men were probably already in the building! They were probably coming up the main stairs! But he didn't want to leave Kate behind. "That wall isn't very thick," he finally managed. "You realize that, don't you? If they heard us in here, they could smash right through it."

"Oh, no doubt," Kate agreed. "So you'd better get settled. They'll be here any second."

Reynie hurriedly glanced around to get his bearings before Kate switched off her flashlight. As long as he avoided the stairs there was nothing to trip over or bump into; the floor was barren. So was the entire anteroom, save for the various garments, wigs, and hats hanging on the side wall (these were the disguises the adults donned on errand days) and a lever near Kate's head that opened the secret entrance into the office.

Don't bump that, Reynie told himself as he knelt at one of the peepholes. *Whatever you do, don't bump that!*

Sticky must have been thinking the same thing; he veered so widely around the lever it might have been a cobra. Then he took his position at the final peephole, Kate switched off the flashlight, and everything was suddenly, impenetrably black.

As if conjured by darkness, there came the sound of footsteps.

The footsteps were followed by a thoughtful grunt, then a man's muted voice. "This one isn't marked. It would appear to be 7-B, though."

"Open it," said another, deeper voice.

Peering through the tiny hole Reynie saw a red glow in the darkness, like a hot burner on an electric stove. The lock, he realized. A Ten Man had just aimed his laser pointer at it. The glow faded as quickly as it had brightened, Reynie heard the doorknob turn, and with a thump and a heavy shudder the office door opened. Flashlight beams swept across the office. Reynie instinctively drew back. When he pressed his eye to the hole again he saw two men. One of them, a huge, powerful figure with shining, well-coiffed brown hair, was undoubtedly McCracken — the leader of all the Ten Men, and by far the most formidable.

McCracken made an adjustment to his flashlight and stood it upright on the empty desk, where it shone like a lantern. With his intelligent eyes narrowed, he turned his head slowly from left to right, surveying the office. Beside him the other Ten Man — a familiar bespectacled man named Sharpe — was doing the same, with exactly the same expression and movement of the head, so that the two men looked eerily like robotic figures you might see in an amusement park ride.

Again at the same moment, the men set down their briefcases.

"Not terribly promising," Sharpe observed.

"I never trust promises anyway," said McCracken in his too-familiar, cool bass tones.

"It's clearly out of use. Why does Benedict keep it?"

"Perhaps he hasn't found anyone to take it off his hands. Times are hard for the gainlessly employed, my dear Sharpe. In fact Benedict used to maintain several offices here, but now he's down to just this one. At any rate, it only makes less for us to search — and search we must, if only as a matter of form."

By "we" McCracken clearly meant Sharpe, who cheerfully set to yanking out file cabinet drawers. As he did so Reynie studied the office himself, wondering if Kate had overlooked anything. He recognized the room, of course. 7-B had been the site of one of Mr. Benedict's tests. How well he remembered peering through these very holes with Sticky — they had only just met — as Kate negotiated a challenge the boys had passed moments before. The floor then had been painted in a checkerboard pattern, and the secret entrance had been a regular door. Now 7-B resembled exactly the sort of dull office found behind every other door in the Monk Building, with a desk, file cabinets, bookshelves, a wastepaper basket, and a potted ficus tree that had seen better days. Reynie saw nothing important in it at all.

Nor did Sharpe, who appeared to enjoy the search none-theless. With a satisfied smile he upended the desk, tossed file drawers here and there, ripped pastel paintings from the wall and punched his fist through them. For good measure he roughed up the ficus, whose last remaining leaves fell to the floor like sad confetti. Then he took a cloth from his brief-case and polished a scuff from one of his gleaming black shoes. "When will the others come?" he asked, breathing hard.

McCracken checked his large silver wristwatch. Then he checked his other one. "Crawlings and Garrotte arrive in two minutes. The others hold their positions, of course."

"I do hate to wait," said Sharpe. "Mightn't we get on with the instructions? It will save time."

McCracken laughed. "Sharpe, what a fellow you are! All of us have to be present or the number won't come out cor-rectly. Would you like to follow the wrong instructions? Do you think Mr. Curtain would be pleased?"

Sharpe rapped his knuckles on his head as if sounding for contents. "Excellent point, McCracken. Well taken. No, since you put it that way, I believe we should wait."

Two and a half minutes later Crawlings and Garrotte strode into the office.

"You're late," said McCracken.

"Sorry," said Crawlings. "We thought we might have seen one, but no such luck."

"And no sign from the roofs?"

"No."

"Very well," said McCracken. "Let's cite our numbers, beginning with Crawlings."

Each Ten Man spoke a number aloud. McCracken nodded. "The sum is odd. That indicates you, Garrotte."

Garrotte reached inside his suit coat and took out a sealed envelope. He handed it to McCracken, who had already unsheathed a wicked-looking letter opener. McCracken slit the envelope, removed the letter, and let the envelope fall. As an afterthought he sliced the envelope in two as it drifted to the floor — he didn't even look at it — before unfolding the letter and looking it over.

Read it aloud, Reynie pleaded in his mind. *Read it aloud!*

But McCracken only said "Ah," and passed the letter around for the other Ten Men to read.

"Excellent!" said Crawlings, the last to have a look. He crumpled the letter and tossed it toward the wastepaper basket. "That gives us plenty of time for coffee and scones. I don't know about you fellows, but I'm famished."

"You forget," said McCracken. "We have to make another sweep for the girl. But take heart, my dear — if we don't track her down this time we'll set up a watch in the neighborhood, and you can have something then."

Sharpe looked hopeful. "Do you think she'll turn up before we have to go? I would so love a bonus! But of course we can't miss the rendezvous."

"With luck she'll go crying back to Benedict's house well before then," said McCracken.

"With real luck we'll track her down right away!" said

Crawlings, and with a comical smile he pantomimed drinking from a coffee cup and rubbing his belly. The other Ten Men chuckled.

"As for that," said McCracken, "I have a few more ideas. Let's signal the others and get moving."

The Ten Men filed out of the office, leaving it in darkness, and the young spies listened to their footsteps fading away. Not daring to whisper, Reynie mentally willed his friends to be silent until they were sure the Ten Men had gone for good. For a long time he listened with straining ears, and was just about to switch on his flashlight when Kate switched on hers.

"Did you see that?" Reynie whispered excitedly. "Crawlings left the instructions!"

"I saw it, all right," Sticky said. "Let's go . . ." He trailed off, distracted by the sight of Kate heading for the stairs — and by the crumpled letter in her hand. "Wait, you already *got* it?"

Reynie was staring, too. "I didn't even hear you!"

"I've been practicing," Kate whispered, already starting down the stairs. "Now come on! We're going to be late!"

It was agreed Kate would run ahead in hopes of showing the letter to Milligan or Mr. Benedict as soon as possible. And for the first time in ages, Reynie actually *had* hopes. From the Ten Men's discussion it sounded as though they wouldn't make their next rendezvous for some time, and Reynie felt sure Mr. Benedict could decipher his brother's instructions — whatever they were — quickly enough to act. It was a most promising turn of events, and Reynie couldn't help feeling proud of his part in it. Nor was he alone: Kate's feet had flown even faster than usual, and Sticky, puffing along beside him in the secret passage, kept spontaneously breaking into a grin.

The boys' high spirits were diminished considerably, however, when they staggered up out of the cellar to find a miserable-looking Kate being chastised by Ms. Plugg, who had her by the elbow. A short black limousine with its lights on idled in the street — this must be the armored car — and from Mr. Benedict's house, in tones of rising alarm, the adults could be heard calling their names.

"They're here!" roared Ms. Plugg, and relieved faces appeared in several windows.

The guard plunged back into her tirade without missing a beat: "— looking for you, and no one seems to have had any idea of these orders Milligan supposedly gave me! And what was I to do? Even though I began to doubt your word, what if I was mistaken? No! I had to keep my mouth shut! I had to shrug and play it off as confusion! Meanwhile the Washingtons are panicking! Miss Perumal is worried sick! Her mother had to take a pill! Do you know how it felt for me to stand here not saying anything to console them? Do you realize —?"

"I said I'm sorry!" Kate cried. "And I really am, Ms. Plugg! I can't explain how important it was, or why we had to do it that way, but —"

Ms. Plugg was hardly mollified. "Did Milligan give those orders or not? Did you or did you not have to search for something important down in that cellar?"

As the *exact* truth would surely have released fresh torrents of recrimination, Kate simply held up the crumpled letter. "I have to show this to Milligan or Mr. Benedict — it's urgent, Ms. Plugg!"

Ms. Plugg snorted like a bull, glancing at the letter in Kate's hand. "What is it? No, let me guess, you can't tell me."

By now Reynie had regained his breath enough to come to Kate's aid. "We're sorry, Ms. Plugg, but it's true — we can't discuss it with you. But it *is* extremely important."

Ms. Plugg's steely gray eyes roamed from face to face. All three children tried to look both humble and beseeching. At last she nodded curtly. "Milligan isn't back yet. You can speak with Mr. Benedict in the car. Milligan's sentries just went in to fetch him. Here they all come now."

Sure enough, out of the house spilled not just Mr. Benedict and the sentries (two men in plainclothes whose alert eyes darted ceaselessly all around) but also the Washingtons, the Perumals, Rhonda, Number Two, and finally Moocho Brazos carrying four small brown bags. The children eventually discovered that the bags contained snacks for the police station, but first they had to endure such tongue-lashings as they had never experienced — a frantic, furious scolding from all quarters, amplified by a need for haste.

"Across the street—!"

"— without permission—!"

"— without *telling* any of us! And in that cellar, of all places! Why on earth —?"

"— searched high and low! Have you any idea, young man —?"

It went on like this, at great speed and considerable volume, for about twenty seconds. Then all at once it ended, and in a rush the three of them were swept up and clutched and patted and even wept over, and their hair fussed with (in Reynie's and Kate's case) and clothes brushed off (they all had cobwebs and beetles on them), and in her confusion of emotion the crying Mrs. Washington declared that Sticky was getting so *big* — and then with earnest pleas to be careful and tearful promises to see them at the station, the children were bustled into the backseat of the armored car with Mr. Benedict.

Throughout all this commotion they had said nothing to defend themselves. In part this was because they'd been given little chance, but it was also because Mr. Bane had sidled up and was observing the group with keen attention. Reynie, his eyes downcast as he mumbled apologies, had steadied himself with the knowledge that soon they could speak privately to Mr. Benedict.

But it was Mr. Benedict who seemed to have the most pressing things to say. As soon as the car doors closed he said, "I realize you have something to tell me. I see it on your faces, and obviously you had reasons for leaving the house. I have things to tell you as well, and the sooner the better. How urgent is your news? Must we discuss it here, or can it wait a few minutes?"

The children glanced at one another. They were bursting to show Mr. Benedict the letter — and to see it themselves, for that matter — but they all had the sense it could wait a few minutes.

"Very well," said Mr. Benedict. "We can begin after we've made a brief stop in the next block. There's no sense interrupting ourselves at the outset." And at a signal from him the driver eased the car away from the curb. (It occurred to Reynie that they had left behind their bags and jackets, but that hardly mattered now.) "This is Mr. Hardy, by the way, and in the passenger seat is Mr. Gristle."

The sentries glanced over their extremely wide shoulders and gave jaunty salutes to the children. Their faces, however, were deeply serious. Hardy was a tall, wiry man, with tall, wiry hair that brushed the ceiling; Gristle was a blockish, balding fellow with wisps of gray hair like scattered clouds. Their shoulders were so broad that they met between the front seats, and between them the children had no view at all of the road ahead.

But as the car headed out of the neighborhood and turned toward downtown, they saw through the side windows that traffic had begun detouring out of the congested main streets. With headlights as its sole source of illumination, the city seemed to exist only at street level. And yet what it appeared to lose in height it was gaining in breadth, as the normally dark back alleys were lit now by a growing stream of traffic.

It was in just such an alley that the limousine pulled over behind a dilapidated taxi parked against a wall. Car horns blared as the sentries jumped out and stopped traffic. Mr. Benedict explained that they were changing cars. Bemused yet anxious to keep moving, the children quickly got out — squinting in the myriad headlights — and packed themselves into the back of the taxi. Then Mr. Benedict and the sentries leaped in, the tall-haired driver gunned the engine, and the taxi shot away up the alley, its rattling muffler echoing off the walls.

"There," said Mr. Benedict, and as if they had just sat down to tea he folded his hands in his lap and said, "Now that that's settled, we can have a proper conversation. I'll begin with why we've changed cars, and why we aren't going to the police station."

"We aren't going to the police station?" cried Sticky, already disturbed to have traded an armored car for a mere taxi.

"The police station was the cover story," said Mr. Benedict. "We're going to a different secure location, and Milligan will meet us there when he can. The subterfuge was necessary because of Mr. Bane, who — as I believe you already suspect — is a spy for my brother."

"We knew it!" Kate exclaimed, drumming triumphantly on her bucket (she was holding it in her lap). "We knew something fishy was going on ages ago, didn't we? But you said . . . what did he say, Sticky? That it would be . . ."

"Imprudent to speak of it further," Sticky said.

"I'm afraid it would have been," said Mr. Benedict. "If you had known Mr. Bane was a spy, you would have found it difficult to behave normally around him. It is a strain always to be acting, and I preferred to spare you that. Furthermore, I could not chance Mr. Bane's discovering that I suspected him, and were he to overhear an incautious comment — from Constance, for example, in a fit of temper — we would lose a key component of our defense."

"But how is letting a spy guard your house a *defense*?" Kate asked.

"We discovered that Ledroptha had worse plans," said Mr. Benedict. "He intended to make a desperate, terrible attack that would have resulted in far greater casualties than we've yet seen. But this was risky to my brother as well, whereas with a spy in place he could wait for information that might lead to a better opportunity. And so I allowed Mr. Bane to be kept on, having already determined him to be the least dangerous of my brother's spies. He is not thoroughly wicked, you see, though he has a weak character. As you saw tonight, he was terrified by the Ten Men. I believe he got in over his head, as they say."

"So you weren't worried about him trying to kidnap us or anything?" Kate asked.

"Actually," Mr. Benedict said, "that was one of the few things I *didn't* worry about. I had set an abundance of precautions in place, you see — far more than you're aware of, since by necessity many were kept secret. And at any rate I considered the four of you more than a match for Mr. Bane."

(Kate beamed at this last remark, so obviously sincere and stated so matter-of-factly, and with which she entirely agreed. And the boys, somewhat less confident, felt a stirring of pride nonetheless.)

"Not that I expected you to be tested," Mr. Benedict continued. "Milligan's sentries were on high alert, and if not for this complete power and communication outage — which I am sorry to say I failed to predict — the Ten Men could never have reached the house. As for Mr. Bane, I was confident he would never personally harm any of you — not directly, I mean."

"It's true he never did anything worse to us than snap and snarl," Sticky reflected.

"Until today," said Mr. Benedict with a pained expression. "As we have just seen, under certain circumstances even indirect action can do terrible harm. Indeed, my task all along has been to manage the circumstances so that everyone was safe — and I do mean everyone — from any potential wicked actions, indirect or otherwise." Mr. Benedict started to say something else, no doubt an apology or an expression of regret, but then seemed to think better of it, perhaps to avoid the children's inevitable protests.

"That was an awfully tricky line for you to walk," Reynie said after a pause.

"A treacherous one," Mr. Benedict said in a somber tone. "But necessary, and it had the potential of creating a lead to my brother. This was why I didn't have Mr. Bane arrested on the spot after he let Constance run away, and why I tried to mask my suspicion. He may not have offered much of a lead, but he was all I had. He still is, I'm afraid. Arresting him might spoil our chances of retrieving the Whisperer — and Constance — before it's too late."

The children were eager to reveal that they possessed a *new* lead to Mr. Curtain, but before any of them could speak Mr. Benedict's head lolled forward, his spectacles slipping from his nose.

As Kate tried to shake him awake, it dawned on Reynie that Mr. Benedict's voice had faltered at the mention of

Constance's name. Of course. He was incredibly worried, upset, probably guilt-ridden — he'd let Mr. Bane guard his house, after all, and Mr. Bane had let Constance go! Yet his manner had been as calm as ever, and Reynie, his mind in a whirl, hadn't realized that Mr. Benedict's composure was the product of great effort. In fact it was a house of cards, and just the thought of Constance in danger had sent it tumbling down.

"Try tickling his nose," Sticky said. "That worked once."

But before Kate could try it Mr. Benedict started and sat up straight. He turned apologetically to the children, resettled his glasses, and without wasting a moment said, "I'm afraid that may happen again, so let me speak quickly, for if the situation worsens there are things you must know. The timing of my brother's attack is no accident. He arranged everything so that it would come to pass today. If Mr. Pressius had succeeded in removing Constance from the house, Ledroptha knew I would go after her, and that Milligan would accompany me as a bodyguard. My absence and Milligan's was key, of course, for my brother knew that if he attacked while I was home, I would sabotage the Whisperer before he could possess it — and that Milligan would ensure I had enough time to do so."

Mr. Benedict grimaced. "I would never have allowed that to happen, and yet I made a different, foolish mistake by not anticipating what Constance, in her agitated state, might —"

He fell asleep again.

"Good grief!" Kate cried.

"What's the matter?" Hardy said, glancing in the rearview mirror to see Kate holding Mr. Benedict's spectacles with one hand and shaking him with the other. "Is he all right?"

"No!" said Kate, exasperated. She caught herself. "Sorry, I mean yes, he's fine. He's asleep again, but he's fine."

"Well, the traffic isn't," Hardy returned darkly. "Even the sidewalks are packed, and I'd hoped to use them."

It was true. All over Stonetown, stranded subway trains and hopelessly stalled buses and taxis were emptying out, their passengers abandoning them to walk instead. This was a novelty for many people, whose confusion, combined with the apprehension the blackout caused, led to a disorderly crowd that spilled around the cars and flowed along the sidewalks like water streaming around boulders and gushing down gullies.

Mr. Benedict opened his eyes, rubbed his face, and instantly pressed on: "It goes without saying that Constance caught us off guard by running away. It was a lucky break for Ledroptha that Mr. Bane was posted at the back door today, though no doubt this was part of his original plan. If we had left the house to deal with Mr. Pressius — as my brother hoped — then Mr. Bane could make some excuse and abandon his post just as the Salamander arrived, thereby eliminating any chance of a warning."

"That's exactly what happened!" Sticky said. "We saw him go around the front to talk to Ms. Plugg, and the very next second we saw the Ten Men!"

"Yes, it was well orchestrated, and I'm afraid it was only the beginning. Do you recall Mr. Gaines saying that the government's top advisers were being convened to deal with the Whisperer? If Ledroptha has his way, the Whisperer will deal with *them*. I am certain he plans to obtain highly classified codes and passwords from those advisers, then use those secrets to his advantage. It will be the very sort of thing he's accomplished tonight in Stonetown, but on a much grander scale.

"I'm telling you this now, children, because the next twenty-four hours will be most chaotic, and we are likely to be separated. If the situation worsens, you and your families must leave Stonetown and go into hiding. Mr. Hardy and Mr. Gristle here will be assigned to help you and protect you."

The children exclaimed in alarm. They were to go into *hiding*? Without Mr. Benedict? But what did he think was going to happen? What —?

Mr. Benedict, sadly affected by their dismay, fell asleep again.

"Look, what he was trying to get across to you," said Hardy sympathetically, when a long bout of pleading and shaking failed to wake Mr. Benedict, "is that things could change fast. Mr. Curtain will want to get rid of anyone who knows the truth — anyone who knows the Whisperer still exists and what it's used for. That means you and your families, kids, sorry to say. Us, too, of course. Anybody associated with Mr. Benedict, and of course Mr. Benedict himself."

"Especially him," said Gristle. "But not before Curtain gets what he wants out of him."

"What would that be?" asked Reynie, feeling shaken. His voice was barely strong enough to be heard over the blatting muffler.

Hardy shrugged. "Answers about this sleeping problem they both have. Curtain knows Benedict was working on something that could stop it, right? Everything else, Curtain can figure out for himself. But he wants to put the kibosh on this narcology —"

"Narcolepsy," Sticky corrected.

"— this narcolepsy, right, and he'll do whatever it takes. And he holds the cards now — he's got the Whisperer — so Benedict's got to find a way to catch him off guard. But that's not going to be easy, is it? We don't even know where he is. And even with Milligan on his side, and Gristle and me and the other agents he can trust . . . well, the odds aren't exactly good."

By now Kate was shaking Mr. Benedict so vigorously she looked to be attacking him. Like the others, she wanted to believe Mr. Benedict could solve this problem if only he could stay awake for it. But he was not to be wakened. His haggard, drawn face betrayed just how far he had pushed himself. Now his exhaustion was pushing back.

In the front seat Hardy and Gristle were muttering to themselves about the traffic ("Like a herd of turtles," Gristle kept saying) and how best to proceed. At present they could hardly be said to be proceeding at all. Ten minutes passed, then twenty, and Kate had no more luck waking Mr. Benedict than the sentries did reaching the next intersection. At last the men made a decision.

"Look, we didn't want to draw attention to ourselves," said Hardy to the children, "but we're never getting anywhere if we don't do something. You three sit tight." He and

Gristle got out of the taxi and began speaking to the drivers of the cars ahead of them, flashing badges and gesticulating. Apparently they had some plan for clearing a lane.

A plan would be good, Reynie thought. So much was happening at once it was hard to keep even the simplest thoughts in mind before others flew in to replace them. Constance, the Ten Men, Amma and Pati, Mr. Curtain, Constance again . . . And behind them, flashing with still more urgency now, was that mysterious sequence — that code or whatever it was. **133 N292**. What *was* that, anyway? For the first time since it made its appearance, Reynie had a moment to concentrate on it. He closed his eyes and tried to organize his thoughts.

"I give up," said Kate. "I've tried tickling, patting, hair-pulling — you name it. Nothing's working."

"Maybe we should go ahead and look at those instructions," Sticky suggested. "We could try to work them out ourselves."

"You're right," Kate said, opening her bucket. "Reynie, are you ready?"

But Reynie was thinking, *Organize my thoughts!* Organize — *that's it!* "Sticky," he said, his eyes popping open, "what do you think this sequence is?" He described the code exactly as he saw it in his mind, including the space in the middle.

"Sounds like a call number," Sticky said instantly. "You know, for a library book — a Dewey decimal number."

"That's what I thought!" said Reynie. "Listen, I think I know where Constance is!"

"What? How?" Kate asked.

"No time to explain! Sticky, does that call number belong to any book you know? A book in the Stonetown library system? You memorized the entire catalog, right?"

Sticky thought a moment. "Well . . . yes. It's the call number for *The Myth of ESP* by Perry Normal. I've read that book. It isn't very good. Sketchy research, and —"

"But where is it shelved?" Reynie interrupted. "Is it at one of the branch libraries, or . . . ?"

"Oh. No, there's only one copy in the system. It's at the main library."

"Constance is at the main library!" Reynie cried.

Kate closed her bucket, ready to move. "That's not far from here. I can be there in five minutes."

"I should come, too," Reynie said. "If she's still mixed up, she might give you trouble. Sticky, if Mr. Benedict wakes up you can tell him where we went."

Sticky frowned. "The Ten Men are prowling around looking for her, right? What if you get cornered somewhere, or Constance runs off again and you have to go after her, or . . . ?" He shook his head. "We have to stick together. You might need me."

"He's right, Reynie," said Kate. "It should be all three of us."

"And the sentries, too, yes?" asked Sticky, trying to blink sweat from his eyes. (His forehead had suddenly begun to perspire.)

"I wish, but then who would protect Mr. Benedict?" Reynie said. "He'd be a sitting duck sleeping here all alone. Hardy and Gristle wouldn't leave him even if we wanted them to. Anyway, they probably wouldn't believe me — I can't exactly prove what I know."

"So we go alone," said Kate, "and we go now. The Ten Men could be closing in on her this very minute."

Reynie reached for the door handle, then stopped and slapped his forehead. "I'm not thinking straight! We should leave a note in case he wakes up before we get back, or . . ."

"I'm on it," said Kate, taking out a pen. She wrote MAIN LIBRARY on the palm of Mr. Benedict's hand, where it couldn't be lost or overlooked. Mr. Benedict twitched, snuffled, sighed heavily . . . and continued sleeping.

Reynie was watching the sentries. They were several cars ahead now, talking to a bus driver. After a moment they nodded, glanced back at the taxi to be sure all was in order, then moved ahead to speak to another driver.

"Now!" Reynie hissed, throwing open the door. He leaped into the crowded street and was almost swept away by the throngs of people pushing their way through the stopped traffic. He clung to the door until his friends got out, too, and then — hanging on to one another and frowning in the headlights and exhaust fumes — the three of them made off into the night, hoping they weren't too late.

COWDOZERS and RENDEZVOUS

STONETOWN
MAIN LIBRARY

The children soon discovered that the fastest way to reach the library was to cut through the downtown buildings. The streets were too congested to move freely, and though the buildings were dark — indeed, *because* they were dark — they were relatively empty. The boys had unthinkingly left their flashlights behind, but Kate still had hers, and she led the way through whatever hotels, late-night restaurants, and corner malls they could find whose doors had been left unlocked. In some cases, doors had even been propped open to allow people to pass through, for the electrical mechanisms that opened them were not functioning.

It won't be long till that changes, Reynie thought. If the power stayed off much longer, people would forget about convenience and start worrying about security. Everything that could be locked would be locked. But for the time being people seemed to think the blackout would end any moment — or hoped it would, anyway, and were acting as though they believed it.

In some places they found it necessary to backtrack, in others to cut across a parking lot, which was what they were doing when Kate suddenly stopped in her tracks and looked up. Even in all the hubbub, she thought she had heard a familiar piercing cry. Sure enough, circling in the darkness above, along with a dizzying number of nighthawks and bats, was the much larger, instantly recognizable shape of her beloved peregrine falcon.

"Oh, Madge! You *followed* me!" Kate shook her head wonderingly. She was very impressed — Madge must have seen her get into the limousine and followed it, then followed the taxi, then kept track of her despite all her shortcuts through buildings. She wanted to call the falcon down and reward her with a treat, but there simply was no time. "Oh, do be careful, Madge!" she cried, already pressing on. "I know it's confusing out here tonight!"

The boys took little notice of this exchange. Sticky was too busy keeping an eye out for well-dressed businessmen with briefcases, and Reynie was busy berating himself for not thinking clearly. Why, for instance, had he not thought to leave the Ten Men's instructions with Mr. Benedict? Sticky could have memorized them with a glance and folded the paper into Mr. Benedict's hand. Too late now. And shouldn't he have realized sooner what the mysterious code in his head was? After all, he knew what Constance was capable of now — or at least he thought he did — and there had been other clues, too. Hadn't she been confused when she ran off? Hadn't it seemed she was reliving that fateful day when she'd sought refuge in the library? It should have been obvious to him that the code was a call number, Reynie thought. He needed to get his head straight and keep it that way.

The Stonetown Main Library was a massive structure with columns in front and a peaceful courtyard in back. Like many of the buildings in the city, it was equipped with emergency lighting, but this consisted mostly of dim, battery-powered bulbs posted above doorways and in stairwells. The security guard, used to having more lights on, had found the vast empty building too creepy to suit him and was now sitting on the front steps watching the traffic and the crowds. Rather than risk his refusal, which would only slow them down, the children circled the building seeking a way in.

Kate found one in the form of an unlocked window on the second floor. (She discovered it by climbing up a drainpipe and checking window latches while Reynie and Sticky covered their eyes, terrified she was going to fall.) A minute later the emergency door at the top of the fire escape opened and Kate appeared, smiling in triumph. Propping open the door with her bucket, she came down and lowered the fire escape ladder for the boys.

They all knew the library fairly well, but it was Sticky who remembered exactly where every section was. They were on the right floor, he said; they just needed to bear left. Soon Kate was shining her light along a row of books as they read call numbers. This was the spot. They could even see a gap where the book in question had been. And on the floor beneath it was a cellophane wrapper smeared with peanut butter and flecked with crumbs.

"She must be close by," Kate whispered.

No sooner had she spoken than from a shelf near her knees a head popped out and a voice cried, "It's you! You came! You got my message!"

Reynie and Sticky yelled and tottered backward, bumping into each other and knocking books from the shelves, and Kate suddenly found herself looking down from the topmost shelf, having instinctively scrambled up like a startled monkey.

The head, of course, belonged to Constance Contraire. They had found her.

❧⋮❧

Constance was wearing her old red raincoat and boots, both of which were too small for her to be comfortable. But her excitement at being found caused her to miss a perfectly good opportunity to complain; in fact it made her positively chatty. Riding piggyback on Kate as they hurriedly made their way back to the taxi, Constance chattered all the while.

"It was so strange! Like one of those dreams where people from all different places and times in your life are together in one spot. It really felt that way to me — like everything that had happened to me before was happening to me right then, even though somehow I was in this new place with different people around me. But it was the past — my memory, I mean — that felt the most real. Oh, it's hard to explain how strange it all was!

"I caught a bus," she continued, "and asked the driver to take me to the library branch that was farthest away — just like before, right? — but he checked his watch and told me I ought to go to the main library instead. He said because of the funding shortage the branches had reduced their hours, and the one I'd mentioned would be closed by the time we got there."

"Well, that was nice of him," said Kate, "though I wish he'd have told you to go back home instead. It would've saved us a lot of trouble."

Kate's tone was somewhat breezier than she actually felt. She and the boys were having a hard time suppressing their irritation. It was clear from what Constance had told them that she hadn't been in her right mind when she ran away, and they knew it was unreasonable to blame a frightened four-year-old for causing them such intense worry and trouble. Still, after all they'd been through on her behalf, the others would have appreciated a little more apology and a lot more gratitude.

"So you meant to go to a branch library," said Sticky in as neutral a tone as he could manage. "That explains why Milligan was in the Quarryside neighborhood. The branch library there is the farthest one away from Mr. Benedict's house — it's all the way across town."

"Mr. Benedict must have guessed what you'd do," Reynie reflected. "But he didn't know exactly when you left, or what bus you might have caught — if you even managed to catch one — or whether you'd come to your senses and change your mind, or anything . . ." He cocked his head and looked at Constance curiously. "Hey, did you not try to send *him* the call number, too?"

"No, I was scared when the lights went out, but I felt pretty mad at him — I know, I know! I was mixed-up, remember? — so I focused on you instead."

"Well, he's really worried about you. You should know that."

"Is he?" asked Constance, clearly pleased. "I guess he'll be glad to see me, then."

"You don't have to be so happy about it," Sticky snapped. "We've *all* been worried, you know — and we've been through a lot."

"Have you?" said Constance, as if this had never occurred to her. "Probably not as much as I've been through, though. Can you imagine what it was like for me when I realized what I'd done? Exactly the most dangerous thing possible, right? Here I was, in the middle of the city with no protection, and then the lights went out, and people were frightened and hurrying for the exits — oh, they tried to act calm, but their fear might as well have been shouting at me, it was all I could feel — and I wanted so much to come back to the house, but I was terrified, you know. I got this feeling that there were people out looking for me. Ten Men, actually. Maybe my mind was playing tricks on me, I don't know, but I was really scared."

The others made an effort not to look at one another or even to think too much about the truth. They happened to know that the Ten Men *were* looking for Constance — but it wouldn't do any good for Constance to know that herself. And then, as if to make a final play on their sympathies, she did what they'd all felt she should have done at the very beginning; she asked about *them*.

"So you really have been through a lot?" Constance asked. "Like what? You have to tell me about it!" She was looking about her with curious, wondering eyes. They were passing through a dark hotel lobby, where a few weary travelers sat reading newspapers by flashlight. It was all very strange, and she felt rather as if she had awakened from one dream only to enter another, but in this one, at least, she felt less frightened and alone.

"Later," said Kate, coming to a stop in the open doorway. "Right now we have a problem." She pointed down the street. The taxi was where they had left it — but it was unmistakably abandoned. Vehicles were creeping around it on both sides, blaring their horns and knocking bumpers in the confusion. The sentries and Mr. Benedict were nowhere to be seen.

"Where did they go?" Sticky cried.

"You mean they left without you?" said Constance, stunned. "Why would they do that?"

"Well, if Mr. Benedict woke up," said Kate, "then he probably saw the note we left on his hand — in which case they'll be looking for us back at the library."

"And if he didn't wake up?" Constance asked.

This was Reynie's question exactly, and once again he wanted to kick himself for not having thought everything through. "We should have left a note where the sentries could see it, but we left it on Mr. Benedict's *hand*, where they wouldn't think to check. So they would have had no idea where to look for us, or whether we intended to come back. They may well have carried him away, thinking it was their duty to get him to that secure location."

"I hope it was a hard decision," Sticky muttered.

"Well, where *is* this secure location?" asked Constance, looking round at them. Her face fell. "Oh . . . you don't know."

"The way I see it, we only have one decent choice," said Kate. "If they aren't looking for us, they could be anywhere, right? It'll be almost impossible to find them. So I think we should go back to the library in case they went there. But this time we stay out on the streets, because if they did go to the library that's how we missed seeing them — by cutting through the buildings. What do you think?"

"Makes sense to me," said Sticky.

Reynie didn't answer for several seconds. He was determined to consider more carefully this time. "You're right," he said at last, "we should go back. Even if we don't find them there, Mr. Benedict has to wake up eventually, and this way he'll know where we are."

"We should've just stayed there," grumbled Constance.

"Oh, great point, Constance!" said Kate, rolling her eyes.

They went back to the library. It took them much longer this time, and more than once they were jolted by the sight of a briefcase-toting businessman among the crowds. But these always proved to be *actual* businessmen, not Ten Men, and the children arrived at the library without incident.

Mr. Benedict and the sentries weren't there.

Kate opened the emergency exit again to let the others

in. After they had used the restrooms and Constance had produced an armload of snack crackers ("The librarians would understand," she insisted, and the others were too hungry to argue), they settled down to wait in a stairwell, where the emergency lighting would spare Kate's flashlight batteries. They didn't intend to wait idly: Kate still had Crawlings's instructions and they were keen to decipher them.

As the Ten Men had done earlier, so the Mysterious Benedict Society did now: The paper was passed from hand to hand, each member reading it in turn. But whereas the Ten Men had merely glanced at the instructions and grunted in understanding, the children shook their heads — partly in bafflement, partly in excitement — and quickly passed the paper on, mumbling to themselves. Constance was the last to see it. On the front was a note:

Gentlemen,

I have arranged for you to meet my most highly placed contact in government. He may be accompanied by certain associates, but you must bring him to me alone. Above all, you must be discreet — if our enemies learn his identity, all is lost. Do not fail me. Your rendezvous instructions are opposite.

Sincerely,
Your Employer

"What does *rendezvous* mean?" Constance asked. She pronounced the word as if it rhymed with "Ben says mouse."

"It's French," said Sticky. "It's pronounced RON-day-voo. It means a meeting at a certain time and place. 'Your rendezvous instructions are opposite' means the instructions for determining that time and place are on the opposite side."

"Oh!" said Constance, flipping the paper over. "I mean, I knew that."

"If we can figure those instructions out," said Kate, "we'll know where the Ten Men are supposed to meet this 'highly placed contact' — someone whose identity Mr. Curtain needs to keep secret at all costs. In other words, Constance, this is big."

Constance, frowning, had flipped the paper back over to study Mr. Curtain's note. "But what about the Z?"

It took the others a moment to realize what she was talking about.

"It's silent," Sticky assured her.

Constance's frown deepened. "Well, that's stupid. Why not just leave it out?"

"How about we save grammar discussions for another time?" Reynie suggested.

Kate took the note from her and reread the instructions, which were as follows:

In the root
By the mover
To the north
At noon

"He's using code words again," Kate said, "or maybe just vague language he knows they'll understand. We ought to be able to figure it out though, right? We figured out the last one. So let's put our heads together!"

But though "to the north" and "at noon" were easy enough to understand, "in the root" and "by the mover" were not, and after several minutes of consideration the children had yet to come up with anything like an answer.

"I can't believe those guys figured it out so quickly," said Kate. "It hardly took them a second."

"They must have some trick," said Sticky, "some strategy they apply to decipher the instructions."

Reynie sat up straight. "You know what? Mr. Curtain *gave* them the trick! He said the instructions were *opposite!*"

"So?" said Kate. Then she brightened. "*Oh!*"

Constance scowled. "But Sticky said 'opposite' meant —"

"It isn't Sticky's fault," Reynie said. "That's exactly why Mr. Curtain wrote it that way, to throw off anyone who wasn't supposed to read this note. He's being careful, see? But the Ten Men must have known about the trick ahead of time. They're probably familiar with all these code words, too — the instructions just make things easier for them."

"They *must* be familiar with the code words," said Kate, "because it isn't exactly the easiest thing in the world to guess the opposite of 'root,' is it? Or maybe I'm speaking too soon — maybe you boys know the answer already."

Reynie shrugged. "'Stem'? 'Flower'? It's hard to know what he means by 'opposite.'" He scratched his head. "Or what he means by 'root,' for that matter. It has lots of different meanings, now that I think of it. You can root for your favorite team —"

"The opposite of that would be 'boo' or 'jeer,' maybe," said Kate.

"You can root around for something in a bag —"

"So the opposite would be to hide something?" Constance said. "That doesn't make sense."

"Well, there's the square root of a number," Sticky suggested, "the opposite of which would be the square . . ." He faltered when he saw Reynie giving him a strange look. "Right. I know. Obviously the Ten Men aren't going to meet in a math problem somewhere. I was just —"

"But they *can* meet in the *square*!" interrupted Reynie. "A city square! I think you've got it, Sticky!"

"I . . . I guess you're right!" said Sticky, surprised. "Now we just have to figure out *which* square!"

"There's more than one?" Constance said, making a face. "Oh, brother. For a second there I was getting my hopes up."

"He says 'by the mover,'" said Kate. "Do you think he means an earth mover? You know — a bulldozer? Are they doing construction in any of the squares, Sticky?"

"You're forgetting it's supposed to be the opposite," Constance said. "There's no opposite of a bulldozer, is there? Is there any such thing as a bull*waker*? Or a cowdozer? Come on, Kate, use your head!"

"You know, I'm starting to regret finding you," Kate muttered.

"Let's think about this," said Reynie before Constance could respond. "A mover is someone or something that moves. So what is the opposite of that?"

"Someone or something that doesn't move," said Sticky.

"A statue!" cried Kate and Reynie at the same time.

Sticky sucked in his breath. "Guess what? Only one square in Stonetown has a statue, and that's Ferund Square! The others all have fountains or parks!"

"Okay," Reynie said, rubbing his chin, "so they're to meet in the square, by the statue, on the south side — I think we can agree that south is the opposite of north — and, well, I guess the opposite of noon must be midnight, right?"

"We've done it!" said Kate. "We've figured out their rendezvous! Oh, and this is *perfect* — the observation deck of the Pittfall Building is on that square, and it gives a direct view of that statue! It's even on the south side! If I go up there —"

"You?" Reynie said.

"Oh, well, Milligan then. Whoever. The point is you would be in a perfect spot to spy on their rendezvous without being seen yourself. It's all glassed in with reflective windows and everything. We couldn't have asked for a better setup! This is going to work out brilliantly!"

It did seem perfect. The only catch was that no one knew about the rendezvous but them. Mr. Benedict still had not shown up, and midnight was less than an hour away. What if he was still asleep, wherever he was? What if he was awake but something had happened? What if he was trying to come to the library but was delayed? What if he wasn't coming at all?

After mulling these possibilities over, Kate jumped up. "Sorry, but I just can't risk it! I can't sit here and give up what may be our last chance to stop Mr. Curtain. I have to go! You three can tell Mr. Benedict everything when he comes.

I'll be careful, I promise!" She was already strapping her bucket to her belt.

"You aren't serious, are you?" Sticky said. "Oh, wait, it's you — of course you're serious."

"It's only eight blocks," Kate said. "I can be there in no time."

"Kate, I don't feel right about this," Reynie said.

"I know, I know — you think you should come with me. Well, I won't force you to stay if that's how you feel. But we need to make tracks. Right now the Ten Men are probably still watching Mr. Benedict's house, so this is absolutely the safest time to go. We'll be less likely to bump into them on the streets, and we can be on the observation deck before they even show up."

"No . . . no, that's true," Reynie said. "I don't think you should go alone, but . . . I don't know, I can't explain it, something just feels wrong. I don't think *any* of us should go."

Kate hesitated. She trusted Reynie's judgment, yet she was not one to be shaken from her course without good reason. "Look, if you can tell me why, I'll stay. But if it's just a feeling . . ." She shrugged. "Well, we're all nervous, right? I'm nervous myself. But nothing could be safer than that observation deck. It will be dark up there, easy to hide, and if I leave right now no one will see me."

They were all looking at Reynie, waiting for him to explain his reluctance. But he couldn't. There seemed to be a hundred things to think about at once, and he couldn't pin down any of them. His only clear thought was that Kate was right, that this really might be their last chance. And what a chance! *If our enemies learn his identity,* Mr. Curtain had written, *all is lost.*

"Okay, but please be careful," he said at last. "I mean extra careful. Like if you were me and not you."

"You got it!" Kate said with a laugh, and she flew down the stairs without waiting for another word.

"She didn't even say goodbye," humphed Constance.

Reynie was staring after her in dismay. He had realized, an instant too late, that they hadn't discussed what Kate would do afterward. Would she come back to the library? Would she wait there? And — the thought suddenly occurred to him — what if she didn't get a good look at this secret contact? Would she try to *follow* the Ten Men? Surely she wouldn't!

But even as he thought it, Reynie knew better. Kate surely would. And she had purposely hightailed it out of the library before Reynie had a chance to talk her out of any such thing.

"Should we go after her?" Sticky said, when Reynie had shared his concerns. "Maybe we could talk some sense into her, or cling to her legs or something."

"Even if she did follow them, I don't see how dangerous it could be," said Constance. "For all this talk about how careful he is, Mr. Curtain has been awfully careless. I think he's gotten overconfident, don't you? I mean, it's ridiculous — couldn't he have had his Ten Men learn some harder codes? Sure, we had to work a little, but it took us, what, a few minutes? He's not working all that hard to cover his tracks."

"So are you saying we shouldn't worry?" Sticky said. "I find that kind of hard, you know, since —"

"Oh no," said Reynie, in a tone of deepest dread. "Oh no, oh no! That's it! What Constance just said — that's it, that's what's been bothering me! Mr. Curtain isn't being careful enough! Not at all! Finally everything makes sense, and oh — it's the worst kind of sense! We *have* to go after Kate! She's walking right into a trap!"

Breakable Codes
and Findable Clues

This time, despite the rising feeling of panic in his gut, Reynie remembered to leave a better note. Scribbling as fast as he could, he explained everything to Mr. Benedict, folded the paper together with Mr. Curtain's note, stapled them both closed, and ran out the front door of the library, where he did his best to explain himself to the startled security guard. He was forced to trust the man — he had little choice — but he kept his request simple: If someone came looking for the children, would the guard please pass along this note and say it was urgent? Then, just as Kate had done to Reynie minutes before, Reynie sprinted away before the confused man could argue.

Sticky and Constance were waiting behind the library. He had told them he would explain everything, and so he did, speaking between gasps, for the three of them were running full tilt. The boys took turns giving Constance piggyback rides, and sometimes she ran on her own legs, but they all knew that even with their best effort they could never catch Kate. They only hoped to reach her before the Ten Men did.

For Reynie saw now, in his mind's eye, all the pieces of a puzzle that earlier he hadn't even known existed. The first piece had been Mr. Bane's odd behavior upstairs: Reynie realized now that Mr. Bane had been waiting to tell them privately — and them specifically — about Crawlings leaving the girls' room. He'd needed to make sure they went in and discovered the torn-up note. No doubt the Ten Men had collared him and told him what to do.

The second puzzle piece was the note itself: Yes, Crawlings was careless — and Mr. Curtain probably knew that the children knew this — but would he really have left those instructions in the wastepaper basket? Not without expecting them to be found.

And then there was McCracken: He hadn't seemed to expect to find anything in the Monk Building. He'd even said the office must be searched "if only as a matter of form." In other words, the search had to appear to explain why they'd been there. *That was their stated reason*, Reynie thought grimly. But their *real* reason had been something quite different. It was the same reason that McCracken — normally so cautious — had not objected when Crawlings threw the wadded instructions away in the office. He'd even dropped the envelope to the floor himself.

Breakable codes and findable clues. Everything had been done on purpose.

Mr. Curtain knew what the children were like; he knew they would take risks to stop him if given a chance. And so — quite cleverly, careful not to overdo it — he had given them that chance, had left them a trail they couldn't resist following. Hadn't they overheard Crawlings and Garrotte saying that Mr. Curtain had another plan for catching them? Well, this was it. And most distressing of all was that it was still working. Kate was running right into a trap, and her friends were running right after her.

"He had nothing to lose," Reynie panted as they moved down a crowded sidewalk, keeping close together near the wall, "and everything to gain. He knows we're Mr. Benedict's greatest weakness — that's how *he* sees it — and if he catches us he can use us to get what he wants. There was no reason not to try. He hasn't even put himself at risk."

"So they were hoping to lure us to the Monk Building, but they didn't know about the anteroom?" Sticky asked, still trying to make sense of what Reynie was telling them.

Reynie stopped to let Sticky take over carrying Constance, who suddenly seemed to weigh more than a piano. "If they had known," he said, starting off again, "they'd have grabbed us right then, wouldn't they? McCracken mentioned something about roofs — I think he had Ten Men hidden all around the building keeping an eye out for us. He was hoping we'd come running up the street.

When we didn't show, they knew to leave another clue just in case."

"But what if we had told Mr. Benedict?" Sticky asked.

"Mr. Bane made it hard for us to do that, didn't he? But I'm sure Mr. Curtain was prepared for that possibility. Maybe he even hoped for it. Maybe he hoped Mr. Benedict would fall for the trick, too, and walk right into his ambush. Those instructions didn't leave much time to consider everything — just enough to make a snap decision and rush to the scene."

"Like Kate did," Sticky said, his voice thin with strain. He hitched Constance higher on his back. "And we did."

"The first time we just got lucky," Reynie said. "We could use the secret passage. This time we just have to hope we have enough of a head start."

However badly they needed that head start, it was hard work running on crowded sidewalks and trying to keep together, and they were soon forced to stop to catch their breath. Hands on his knees, Reynie looked up at the street signs. They were only four blocks from the square.

Beside him, Sticky was just about to set Constance down when she cried, "I see Crawlings and Garrotte!"

Reynie straightened abruptly, and the blood rushed to his head. Desperately trying to blink away stars, he followed Constance's gaze. In a moment he spotted the Ten Men on the opposite corner, just about to step off the curb into the crush of pedestrians. They were laughing and talking, swinging their briefcases as if headed out to do something fun after a productive day at work. He glanced quickly around.

"This way!" he said, making for a subway station entrance a dozen paces away, and Sticky, fairly stumbling, followed close behind.

"Did they see us?" Reynie said as he hurried down the steps.

"I don't think so," said Constance, who had been looking over her shoulder.

It was very dark, and Reynie stopped at the first landing, unsure of his footing. His eyes were still adjusting to the gloom. Sticky dropped Constance beside him and fell gasping to his knees. Below them, far away from the shifting glare of a thousand headlights, the steps descended into even deeper darkness. Together they stared fearfully up at the open entrance. Seven or eight people filed past, jostling and bumping one another — and then Crawlings and Garrotte appeared.

Reynie knew they would be almost impossible to see down here, yet he suddenly felt so sure of being spotted he could almost hear the Ten Men's voices echoing down to the landing, "Oh, chickies! Here chickies!" But the men didn't even glance in their direction, and an instant later had passed out of view.

Reynie fell back against the wall. Sticky lowered his head to the floor. For a few moments the only sound they made was heavy breathing, and their only feeling was one of intense relief.

Then Constance said, "Well, what do we do now? They're ahead of us!"

"Oh no," Sticky groaned, hauling himself to his feet again. "I hadn't got that far yet. What *do* we do?"

"The next subway stop is the square," Reynie said. He peered down the steps into the blackness. "And there's no crowd down there. We might even move faster than we could on the streets."

"You mean run through a pitch-black subway tunnel?" Constance said. "Are you out of your mind?"

"I'm starting to feel that way," said Reynie. He had perceived a faint blue glow at the bottom of the steps, and without waiting for more objections he hurried down toward it. The tunnel was their only hope, but only if they moved now — and as fast as they could.

"Come on," Sticky said, grabbing Constance's hand.

The blue light turned out to be a subway system employee carrying an emergency glow stick. He was a pale, skinny man in a white uniform, and in the weird light he looked ghastly and strange, an apparition drifting up from the abyss.

"Subway's closed, kids," he said as they approached. "I'm the last one out. What do you want down here anyway? Don't you realize there's a blackout? Subways don't run in blackouts, you know."

"Can we have your glow stick?" asked Reynie quickly. "We're scared and we don't have flashlights."

The man seemed torn. He turned and looked back into the blackness out of which he had just emerged. "There's a whole box of them on the platform. I was giving them out to the passengers. But to tell you the truth, it gives me the willies down there in the dark, and if you don't mind —"

"Thanks!" Reynie said, and to the man's astonishment he snatched the glow stick and hurried down into the darkness with Sticky and Constance at his heels.

"What? Oh, okay, uh, I'll — I'll wait for you here!" the man called after them. "Or actually — just, I'll just be up there at the top of the steps. Where it isn't so dark . . ."

They paid him no attention. In moments they had ducked under the turnstiles and reached the station platform, where they found the box of glow sticks and helped themselves. Sticky lowered himself onto the tracks, and Reynie lowered Constance down to him, his arms trembling so much he almost dropped her.

"I *really* don't want to be doing this," said Constance, staring into the blackness.

"Just keep talking," said Sticky. "Maybe that'll scare the rats away."

Their passage through the black tunnel was frightening indeed, with their glow sticks casting faint, strange shadows, and noises of unknown origin sounding in the dark. And when, not far along the tracks, they came suddenly upon the abandoned train — like some monstrous creature lurking in the dark — they all cried out at once. They collected themselves and dashed past it, past car after empty car, expecting at any moment for someone or something to peer out at them through a window — or worse, to leap out at them. But they got beyond it, and indeed all the way to Ferund Square station, without incident.

"We made good time," Reynie puffed as they mounted the station steps. "We might just have a chance."

They had wheezed out their plan as they ran, and when they reached the street entrance they lost no time. Reynie knelt down, and Sticky helped Constance onto his shoulders. He stood up shakily, with Sticky supporting him, until

Constance had a fairly decent view of the square. "See anything?" he gasped. "Or, you know, sense anything?"

Constance was looking all around. "I don't. But it's so crowded . . ."

"We'll have to chance it," said Reynie, already letting her down again.

Into the square they plunged, weaving through people on the sidewalks, constantly looking over their shoulders, laboriously making their way through the crush to the Pittfall Building. The observation deck, three stories up, could be seen but dimly, a wide, windowed outcropping whose outline was barely evident against the starry sky. It had been designed to offer the best view of the historic square — high enough to position the observer above street-level obstacles, low enough to eliminate the need for coin-operated telescopes. But it might as well have been specifically designed as a trap. Because it was enclosed, there could be no shouted warnings to Kate. Nor would any cries for help be heard from inside it.

At last, their hearts pounding, their lungs and legs burning, Reynie, Constance, and Sticky reached the front door of the Pittfall Building. It was the sort of door that could be locked only electronically, and since it had not been locked when the power went out (the building usually remained open until late) it was conveniently unlocked now.

Conveniently, Reynie thought, if you were setting a trap for a certain headstrong girl. Upon passing through this door, in the weak glow of emergency lighting, Kate would have seen what they saw now: a hand-printed sign at the security desk that said "Observation Deck Closed Until Further Notice" and another that said "Gone For Batteries — Back In 15 Minutes." Kate would have been thrilled, Reynie realized — no need to sneak past the security guard or concoct some false explanation for needing access to the deck. She could just bolt up the stairs and get situated with her spyglass.

Reynie headed for the stairs, propelled by urgency yet trembling with fatigue and a terrible mounting dread. They were exhausted, there was no time to rest, and the instant they reached Kate they must turn right around and run out again. Could they possibly make it? Would it be better to try to hide somewhere in the building? No, that would be faster, but then the Ten Men could simply block the exits and make a thorough floor-by-floor search. They had to get out.

"I . . . can't . . . keep . . . up," Constance huffed from several steps below. She was struggling valiantly, using both her hands and feet to climb, but was hardly moving at all.

"I'll stay with her," Sticky said, waving Reynie on. "We'll wait for you here. Hurry!"

Reynie didn't waste breath answering — he had none to spare — but pressed on as quickly as he could. He had reached the second-floor landing now, only twenty more steps to go. It felt like a hundred, but at last he stood on the third-floor landing, staring at the door to the observation deck, its sign illuminated by a buzzing emergency bulb. He gathered himself — pushing away the frightening thought that he might be too late — and flung the door open. Instantly a flashlight shone into his eyes.

"Reynie!" whispered Kate's voice. "What are you doing here?"

"A trap," Reynie gasped. "We have to —"

He was interrupted by the sound of shouting in the stairwell. A scream, a scuffling sound, a man's voice crying, "She bit me! The naughty little duck bit me!" And another man laughing and saying, "Proper caution, Crawlings! Will you never learn? Come, Sharpe, give me a hand with Mr. Spectacles. Garrotte, you take this . . ."

Kate had lowered her flashlight. Reynie could see her round eyes. There was no further explanation necessary. He shook his head helplessly, his heart in his throat. They had been so close.

"Hide this!" Kate hissed, reaching into her bucket. She handed him her rope, still neatly coiled, and as he hurriedly tucked it under his shirt she slipped something else into his front pocket. Her Swiss Army knife. Then she leaped back, shouting, "What's going on, Reynie? Who's out there?"

An enormous figure appeared in the doorway. The floor groaned beneath his weight.

"Oh dear," said McCracken. "Oh dear, oh dear. Were you not expecting us?"

⌒∙∼

"Tell me," said McCracken, setting down his briefcase, "did you leave a note telling your mommies and daddies where you were going? I assume you didn't have permission to come here alone."

"What do *you* think?" said Kate, irritated that she couldn't think of a more cutting reply.

McCracken tapped two fingers together. "What do I think? I think we had better leave soon. But first let us get reacquainted."

The other Ten Men sauntered in with their captives. Constance was still struggling, her teeth clicking audibly as she tried to bite Sharpe and Garrotte, each of whom had a hand under one of her arms. Her feet, several inches off the floor, kicked futilely this way and that as if she were dancing. Sticky, for his part, walked sullenly along under his own power. Behind him came Crawlings with a furious expression and sucking his thumb (which Constance had bitten), so that he looked like a giant toddler on the verge of a tantrum. The smell of expensive cologne hung heavy in the air.

"Constance, my dear," said McCracken, "if you don't stop trying to bite my associates I'm afraid we'll have to start your nap time." Constance glowered at him and stopped struggling. McCracken broke into a toothy grin. "Ah, much better!"

"I see you've had some dental work done," said Kate pointedly, for she remembered (with no small satisfaction) that McCracken had lost teeth in his last encounter with Milligan.

"Ever the cheeky one," said McCracken, still grinning. He flicked one of his front teeth with his tongue; it popped out and fell neatly into his hand. Squeezing it between two fingers, McCracken stepped close to show Kate the tiny sharp serrations now protruding from its edges. He held it close to her face, but Kate did not shy away. She lifted an eyebrow, doing her best to appear unimpressed.

McCracken nodded and stopped squeezing the tooth. "Black-market dentistry," he intoned as the sharp points retracted. "You'd be surprised. Now, my dear, I need you to set down your bucket, turn out your pockets, and hand over your shoes. You mustn't think I've forgotten what a clever girl you are."

To resist would be pointless — not to mention painful — and Kate did as she was told. McCracken inspected her shoes and tossed them back to her. "Better give us that belt, too," he said, warily eyeing the buckle. Finally satisfied, he handed Kate's bucket and belt to Crawlings and said, "Very well, darlings, let's move along."

"Where are we going?" Reynie demanded. He was trying to formulate a plan. If he could goad McCracken into giving him some information . . .

McCracken looked at him intently. "Goodness, you seem frightened, Reynie! Are you worried about what terrible things we'll do?" He bent forward and spoke in a hushed, singsong tone, as if offering instructions to a much younger child. "What you need to worry about, Reynie, is not *what* terrible things we'll do, but *when* we'll *do* them. And the answer, if you're very good, is 'perhaps never.' But if you're the least bit naughty, then the answer is 'right now.' Do you understand?"

Reynie swallowed and nodded. The other Ten Men laughed.

"Mr. Curtain prefers that you be awake, alert, and of reasonably sound mind when we deliver you," McCracken said. "But we have permission to wipe your little noses with our handkerchiefs should circumstances require it."

Reynie was at a loss for what to do then, and the Ten Men were so brisk and efficient (not to mention intimidating) that the children had been hustled downstairs, out a backdoor, and into a waiting van before anyone could think of a productive way to resist. Then the doors were slammed shut, and it was too late.

"My name is Garrotte and I'll be your driver today," said Garrotte, grinning impishly from behind the wheel as McCracken squeezed into the passenger's seat. The other Ten Men chuckled and took seats in the back with the children. "Don't forget to buckle up! We want a safe and pleasant ride."

"You may as well get comfortable, sweets," murmured Sharpe, folding up his spectacles and closing his eyes. "We'll be riding around awhile."

It turned out that by "awhile" Sharpe meant several hours. Miserable, interminable hours, during which the children were not allowed to move or speak as the van crept along the jammed city streets. And all the while the Ten Men seemed completely relaxed. They sat calmly, comfortably, sometimes dozing (though never all at once), sometimes engaging in amiable chatter. From time to time one would rise to peer out the windows in the back doors of the van, then return to his seat, smiling to himself.

Reynie spent the first part of this long ride trying to calm down and come up with a plan. He was having trouble with both. His nerves were shot; his mind was fatigued; his body was exhausted. But after more than an hour of searching for bright spots, Reynie suddenly had an encouraging thought — their situation was undeniably awful, but wasn't it also an opportunity? After all, they were being taken to Mr. Curtain, and Mr. Benedict needed to *find* Mr. Curtain.

Reynie began to get excited. If he just paid close attention to where they were taken, then found a way to let

Mr. Benedict know — there had to be *some* way — the tables would be turned! Not only could they be rescued, but Mr. Curtain could be captured once and for all!

Heartened by his idea, Reynie glanced around, meaning to give his friends covert looks of encouragement. To his surprise he found them all dozing, their heads lolling heavily on their necks. He almost laughed. Even considering all they had been through, it was hard to imagine sleeping at a time like this. And then, in less than a minute, Reynie had joined them. And like them he spent the following hours repeatedly jolting awake, finding himself miserable, cramped, and scared, then succumbing yet again to the powerful need for sleep.

This happened over and over again, and time passed strangely between the weird dreams Reynie experienced while sleeping and the very real, equally weird nightmare he faced each time he awoke. But eventually, finally, the cycle ended; the van stopped. It idled in one place for much longer than it had done before, and Reynie, noticing this, slowly grew alert. Despite the hours of driving they were still downtown; through the high windows in the back doors he could see a distant traffic light. But something had changed, and after a moment he realized what it was. The traffic light was red. The power was back on. And the night's unusual darkness was giving way to familiar gray dawn.

"Good morning, sunshines," Sharpe yawned, resettling his spectacles and scratching his head. He sprayed a misty breath freshener into his mouth and smiled sleepily at the bleary children.

In the front of the van McCracken's radio crackled, and a man's voice — Reynie recognized it with a shiver — said, "What is your status?"

"We have secured the goods and await orders," McCracken replied.

Mr. Curtain's gleeful tone was unmistakable even through the radio. "You secured the goods? Confirm that — you secured the goods?"

"Confirmed," McCracken said, laughing. "We have indeed secured the goods."

"Then proceed to base at once!" Mr. Curtain barked, followed by a screechy sound that someone else might have thought was radio interference but that Reynie recognized as Mr. Curtain's laugh.

McCracken tucked his radio into his suit coat and nodded at Garrotte, who instantly swerved across the sidewalk and into a parking garage, zooming up to the first empty level. Garrotte and Crawlings leaped out of the van with boxes under their arms. At once there came a banging overhead, and a prolonged scratching noise rather like the sound of a person unstripping package tape. Meanwhile McCracken and Sharpe were taking out blindfolds and securing them over the children's eyes — and Reynie's hopes were plummeting. So much for paying close attention to where they were going.

"Mr. Curtain's orders," said McCracken in a falsely apologetic tone. "One can never be too careful."

Garrotte and Crawlings got back in. "We'll make good time now," Garrotte called back to them cheerfully. "Just listen to *this*." He threw a switch, and overhead a siren began to wail. The Ten Men had disguised the van as an ambulance.

With the siren blaring the van was able to move steadily through the city, occasionally slowing but never stopping, until at last, having pulled free of the heavier traffic, the siren was turned off. The van moved swiftly now; its tires hummed on open highway. But *which* highway? Reynie wondered. Headed to where?

"Little bunny," McCracken said to someone, "you had best stop wriggling your eyebrows. If that blindfold slips loose, you will most sincerely regret it."

That had to be Kate, Reynie thought. He hoped for her sake that she would do as she was told. They were already in deep enough trouble, and Reynie could see no way out of it.

THE SHARK AND HIS PREY

They rode for a time in silence. Despite their dread of what lay ahead, the children were all hoping the trip would end soon. They were horribly uncomfortable from sitting for so long, the early-morning sun shone painfully into their eyes even through the blindfolds, and everyone was thirsty. Constance made a point of uttering dry, rasping noises and smacking her lips until Crawlings growled and told her to stop.

"Garrotte," said Sharpe, "be a good fellow and switch on the radio, will you? I'm curious what people are saying about last night."

Garrotte switched on the radio. The children perked up their ears. A news reporter was speaking excitedly:

". . . entire city! Again, it's a wondrous display of efficient technology, Martha, and real leadership on the part of Jim Pressius. The turbines, apparently, were not even connected to the grid yet, but Pressius's technicians pulled off an overnight miracle."

"It's really something, John! And for the benefit of those just tuning in, will you quickly repeat what you've learned about Stonetown's new power source?"

"Right, well, just after the shocking crash of the computer systems that manage the city's power grid, Mr. Jim Pressius, the wealthy entrepreneur, stepped forward to offer an emergency alternative. It seems Mr. Pressius owns a tidal turbine system invented by Mr. Ledroptha Curtain, the noted scientist and educator. The turbines are located in Stonetown Bay — the National Guard was immediately deployed to protect them, incidentally — and thanks to the urgent efforts of Mr. Pressius and his experts they began supplying power to Stonetown just before dawn. All this is according to the government's official statement, Martha, which was released after communications were restored about twenty minutes ago."

"And still no explanation for the communications outage?"

"Unfortunately, no. Obviously it was connected to the blackout, but authorities are at a loss to explain it. In fact according to Mr. Pressius, there's only one scientist in the world with a sufficient understanding of energy anomalies and invisible waveforms to explain what happened, much less prevent its happening again — and that's his friend Ledroptha Curtain."

The children sucked in their breath. Could this really be going where they thought it was going?

"I'll remind our listeners that Mr. Curtain is the man who invented the tidal turbines," said the anchorwoman. "So has Mr. Curtain been involved in any of this, John?"

"Apparently not, Martha. He's a famously private individual, extremely reclusive, and in fact his current whereabouts are unknown. Our listeners may recall that his well-regarded Institute closed over a year ago under mysterious circumstances —"

"It wasn't mysterious to *us*!" Kate snarled, unable to contain herself.

"Hush, kitty," McCracken murmured.

"— his alleged involvement in possible criminal activity —"

"Alleged!" Kate muttered indignantly. "Possible!"

"I won't warn you again," said McCracken. "Some of us are trying to enjoy the program."

"— as you said, John, and follow up on any developments as the government seeks to contact Mr. Curtain. Meanwhile, we're receiving a lot of reports of *actual* criminal activity due to the outages, isn't that right?"

"Yes, indeed, Martha. Apparently looters and burglars had a field day — or field *night*, rather — in Stonetown during these long, dark, and quiet hours . . ."

At McCracken's behest, Garrotte checked to see what was being said on the other radio stations. It was all the same: a terrifying night; mounting fears that it would happen again; Mr. Pressius a civic hero; and an urgent need to locate and consult the preeminent scientist Ledroptha Curtain.

The radio voices went on and on, and Reynie was developing a fierce headache. The relentless bright sunlight wasn't helping — its glare intensified as it passed through the windows, and even with the blindfold and his eyes closed he could feel its heat on his face. He dared not cover his eyes with his hands for fear the Ten Men would think he was trying to remove his blindfold, and when he tried to shift positions Sharpe ordered him to sit still. But physical discomfort was the least of Reynie's concerns at the moment, for he saw quite plainly what Mr. Curtain was hoping to achieve — and that everything was going exactly as planned.

Mr. Curtain's "possible criminal activity" had always been classified. The public knew nothing of it, and most of the people in government who did were simply accepting what their superiors told them. If just a few high officials' minds changed, so too would the official position on Mr. Curtain's guilt. After all, the most important piece of physical evidence in his case — the Whisperer itself — was believed to have been destroyed. No matter that some people, including the children, knew what *really* happened to the Whisperer. These were already being dealt with.

After about an hour on the highway the van turned off, wound along a twisting side road for perhaps five minutes more, then finally came to a stop. "We're here," McCracken announced into his radio.

"I see you," a man's voice replied. "We'll open up."

There came a rattling, clanking sound, as if a large gate or drawbridge were being opened, and the van started forward again. After some maneuvering, some muttered cursing, and some jibes from the other Ten Men about Garrotte's parking, the van doors were flung open and the children unloaded. They were marched into a building and up several flights of stairs, where (thanks to Constance's incessant whining) they were given water to drink and one minute apiece in a cold bathroom. But not until they had been corralled in a bright, stark room were their blindfolds removed. The Ten Men whipped them off with a flourish and withdrew to the doorway.

The first thing the children saw was Mr. Curtain. His appearance startled them, for though the Ten Men had kept up their cheerful banter, no one had heard Mr. Curtain's voice or any other indication of his presence. But here he was in all his creepy glory, the spitting image of Mr. Benedict save for his haughty expression, his more carefully combed white hair, and the slightly different plaid pattern of his green suit. He was squatting, not sitting, in the seat of his wheelchair, his forearms resting atop his knees — and he was silently circling them like a shark around its prey. His cold green eyes darted from face to face. He licked his lips, then pressed them tightly together, suppressing a smile. His wheelchair made absolutely no sound at all.

He circled them once, twice, three times, expertly maneuvering his wheelchair with subtle manipulations of a handheld remote control. He circled so close that he could easily have reached out and scratched them — and perhaps he would, Reynie thought; he did have the air of someone planning something nasty — and to make matters even more unsettling, the children found themselves quite inside the wheelchair's eerie bubble of silence. (Kate was frowning in irritation, having let fly a snappy comment only to have it pass unnoticed, while Sticky, for his part, was grateful no one had heard him whimper.) And still Mr. Curtain circled and circled.

Though helpless to act, none of them wished to give Mr. Curtain the satisfaction of seeing them so frightened, and after his fifth or sixth circuit they stopped twisting to keep their eyes on him when he passed behind them. Fixing their gazes ahead, they endured this bizarre and menacing behavior with what little composure they could manage.

Reynie took the opportunity to study the depressing, unvarying features of the room: Large empty metal bookcases stood against each of the three walls he could see, their shelves coated in dust; a desk (equally empty and dusty) stood right up against one of them; and everything looked slightly askew — the furniture seemed to have been shoved against the walls to clear space in the room. Behind them, he knew, was the door through which they had just entered; otherwise the room appeared to have no exits. (Not even for Kate, unfortunately — the ceiling was plaster, the heating register too small to squeeze through.) Judging from the decor and the dust, the room was a dull office that had been some time out of use.

Mr. Curtain glided before them a seventh time, then an eighth, fully smiling now (no longer trying to suppress it). Reynie glanced nervously at him, then quickly glanced away. Who knew what this madman was up to? Was he trying to disorient them? Confuse them?

The wheelchair came round again. With a start, Reynie saw that it was empty.

"Boo!" roared Mr. Curtain from right behind them, and the children fairly leaped out of their skins. They spun to see him leering down at them from his full height. Delighted by their startled faces, he let loose with his grating, screechy laugh and waggled his fingers at them.

"You see?" Mr. Curtain said as his wheelchair circled round to him again. "If you grow too used to something, too complacent, you are easily caught off guard. I am afraid you children grew far too used to having luck fall your way — and far too bold because of it. So very much like Benedict. Not that I am complaining, of course. Your predictability has served me well."

"Is this your new office?" Kate said, glancing about in an appraising way. "Cold, dusty, empty — it suits you, I think."

Mr. Curtain's smile faded. From the doorway came the sound of a hastily swallowed chuckle. Mr. Curtain glanced at the Ten Men (Crawlings was staring at his feet), then reached inside his suit coat and took out a pair of shiny silver gloves. At the sight of these the children flinched and recoiled, recalling with painful clarity how it felt to be touched by them. "Ms. Wetherall," said Mr. Curtain as he tugged the gloves on, "did you not hear what I just said about being too bold?"

"Mr. Curtain! Mr. Curtain, sir!" cried a familiar voice, and barging into the room (squeezing with some difficulty through the group of Ten Men) came none other than S.Q. Pedalian. "The van's here!"

Mr. Curtain scowled and turned on him, waving his arms. "Of *course* the van is here, S.Q.! Look around you — what do you see? Hmm? Through whom did you just pass to enter this room? Are they not the very men we expected to *arrive* in the van? And who are these children before me? Are they not the very ones I expected to be *brought* to me in the van?"

S.Q. blinked and looked over at the snickering Ten Men. "I'm . . . I'm sorry, sir. I just got excited when I saw it, and . . ." He started to nod in greeting at the children, caught himself, and turned away from them. "It won't happen again, I promise."

Mr. Curtain rolled his eyes in exasperation. "Of course it won't, you idiot! How could it?" He held up one hand to stop S.Q. from speaking. "Do not try to answer that." Shaking his head, he contemplated his gloves a moment, then sighed and slowly began taking them off. "And now, thanks to your interruption, I find my enthusiasm for using these has passed. Perhaps later."

Kate looked gratefully at S.Q., but he would not meet her eye. She vividly remembered the last time they had seen each other. S.Q. had been deceived by Mr. Benedict and the children — the deception, unfortunately, was vital to their escape — and was utterly distraught. No matter that his distress resulted more from his fear of Mr. Curtain's anger than from anything else, it was the deception he had fixated on, and Kate wondered how he felt about it now. If she hadn't known better, she might have thought his blundering entrance was a ruse meant to spare her those silver gloves.

But *did* she know better? As Mr. Curtain tucked away the gloves and climbed into his wheelchair again, Kate studied S.Q.'s bland, impassive face. What was he really thinking? He looked the same as ever, though perhaps he had grown into his gangly frame a bit — yes, he had almost certainly filled out — and the boots on his oversized feet had developed gaps along the seams; he desperately needed new ones. But Kate and the others knew Mr. Curtain's dark secret now; they knew how he had managed to manipulate S.Q.'s kind nature. Time had passed — was passing still — so might not S.Q. be starting to grow beyond the man's influence?

If so, his subservient manner wasn't revealing it. If anything, he seemed more eager than ever to please Mr. Curtain, or at least to avoid incurring his wrath. Even the eternally optimistic Kate had to admit the possibility that S.Q. still felt loyal to Mr. Curtain — and still felt betrayed by Mr. Benedict and the children. They certainly couldn't count on his help.

"I shall not abide further interruptions," Mr. Curtain said. "Therefore I advise you children not to speak unless you are specifically told to do so. Do I make myself clear?"

Kate and the boys nodded. Constance opened her mouth to respond, but Kate quickly clapped her hand over it.

Mr. Curtain smirked. "Much better. You may have noticed that I often prefer silence." His wheelchair backed away from them, and crossing his legs in a relaxed manner he continued in scarcely more than a whisper, forcing them to lean forward and strain their ears.

"Here is what I expect of you. You will remain quietly in this room, causing no disturbance whatsoever. Failure to comply shall result in immediate punishment. You will eventually be given some food, so do refrain from asking for it. The same is true for bathroom visits. In fact, your best course of action — the one least likely to result in punishment — would be to lie still on the floor with your eyes and mouths closed."

Mr. Curtain stared at them a long moment to be sure he'd been understood. Then he whirled about in his wheelchair and rocketed out the doorway, moving with such speed and force that if the Ten Men had not expected it and stepped neatly aside they would have been scattered like bowling pins. With winks and smiles they followed their employer out, and S.Q. brought up the rear, hurriedly closing and locking the door behind him with nary a glance at the children.

⌣∶∾

As soon as the door had closed Kate turned to the others and whispered, "I'm so sorry! I should have waited for Reynie to think things through. We'd never have gotten into this mess if I had. I would have said so sooner, but we were never alone. Oh, this is all my fault!"

"Forget it," Reynie said. "You just wanted to stop Mr. Curtain. We all did."

"I still do, actually," said Sticky. "Before he does . . . well, whatever it is he's going to do to us."

Constance, who had slept almost the entire time in the van, was still groggy and exceedingly cross, and now — in response to Kate's apology — she said, "You're sorry?

We get packed in a van like sardines in a can,
I have to sit by a stinky Ten Man,
Thirsty and terrified hour after hour,
Certain that Curtain has us in his power . . .

And you say you're sorry? You think sorry covers it?"

"Constance!" Reynie scolded, and Sticky shot her a disapproving look.

Kate bit her tongue. In recent months she had finally come up with a rhyming response for the next time Constance attacked her in verse (at long last she had hit upon "remonstrance" as a suitable rhyme for "Constance"), and she'd been most eager to use it. But the timing was all wrong, and so she said lightly, "Sorry will have to do for now, Connie girl."

Constance, ashamed of her outburst but in no mood to admit it, sat on the floor and covered her eyes with her hands. The events of the past several minutes had all seemed far too loud and upsetting, and at the moment she simply wished she could hide inside her own shell like a turtle.

Kate turned to the boys. "So what do you think he intends to do with us? Why did he tell the Ten Men he wanted us awake and alert?"

"He wants to trade us for something, right?" Reynie said. "I think he means to show Mr. Benedict we haven't been brainswept. That way he can threaten to use the Whisperer on us if Mr. Benedict doesn't give him what he wants."

"So he wants us to be able to prove we still have our memories?" Kate said. "My, how practical of him. Well, guess what? If it comes to that, I'm going to pretend to be brainswept — just to get his goat!"

"Let's not let it come to that," Reynie said, walking over to the light switch. "We need to get out of here."

"So you're . . . turning off the light?" asked Sticky, perplexed.

"I'm looking for the window," Reynie said, throwing the switch. The room went dark, but not completely so — a faint glow of sunlight filtered out from behind one of the big metal bookcases. "We need to move that bookcase," he said, turning the light back on.

Kate hurried to inspect the bookcase. "Awfully heavy," she murmured. "It'll be noisy to slide it. Anyway, we'll want to be able to put it back fast. Here, give me a hand with that desk."

With the boys on one end and Kate on the other (and Constance uncovering her eyes to supervise), they carried the desk to where Kate wanted it. Then, moving slowly and with the utmost caution, they tilted the bookcase forward until its top rested against the desk. The metal shelves groaned and twanged, but only a little, and after a tense few moments of listening they decided no one was coming to check on them. Crowding into the narrow space behind the tilted bookcase, they peered out the large, dirt-streaked window they had exposed.

The view was not very encouraging. Three stories below them lay a kind of bleak, square courtyard sparsely covered with dead brown grass and surrounded by four brick buildings — or rather four wings of the same building — four stories high. The wings were identical, with identical flat roofs and identical long rows of dirty windows. The arrangement reminded Reynie of a hospital he had visited once, and Sticky of a dreary office complex where his mother used to work. But there was no obvious clue as to what this place was — or used to be, rather. The only thing that seemed certain was that it had been abandoned and neglected for a while.

"What do you think?" Reynie murmured to Kate. "I still have your rope."

Kate was craning her neck this way and that. "I'm glad, but it's not going to be much use. We're too high up." She studied the roofs across the courtyard for clues about the roof directly above them, then shook her head. "There's no good way to climb up, either — not even a gargoyle to lasso, just standard old gutters. Although . . ." She frowned. "No, never mind, that wouldn't work."

"What were you about to say?" Sticky asked. "Maybe if the rest of us hear it —"

"No, really. It won't work."

It wasn't quite like Kate to say something couldn't work, much less to refuse even to discuss it. Everyone looked at her quizzically. She might be an accomplished trickster around her enemies, but to her friends she was remarkably transparent.

"What are you trying to hide, Kate?" Reynie asked. "What's going on?"

Kate had walked away from the window as if to dismiss it out of hand. "Nothing. I'll tell you later. Right now we should put the bookcase back up."

"She thinks she could get away!" exclaimed Constance, who had been staring keenly at Kate's troubled face.

Kate looked stunned, then quickly tried to recover. But try as she might, she couldn't hide her guilty expression. She could hardly have looked more shamefaced if she'd been caught stealing.

"Is that right, Kate?" Sticky asked, his eyes growing round with hope. "But that's great! Why wouldn't you tell us?"

Kate shook her head, fretfully knitting her brow. "I'm sorry — I couldn't help it! It's not like I can keep from having ideas, right? I didn't *mean* to . . ."

Reynie was going to ask Kate what in the world she was talking about — she seemed to have misunderstood Sticky's question — when suddenly he understood. Kate believed *she* could get away, but not the rest of them. And she wasn't about to leave her friends behind. She was ashamed even to have thought of it.

"Kate," Reynie said urgently, "listen, you have to do it! If you think you can, you have to — it's our best chance! You could figure out where we are, then find your way back to Mr. Benedict and the others. They'll know what to do to rescue us, don't you see?"

Kate was bouncing on the balls of her feet, her face tense with distress. (In fact she looked like someone who desperately needed to find a bathroom.) "Oh, of *course* I see, Reynie! But how can I possibly —? No, I just can't do it!"

Sticky grabbed her arm. "Yes, you can, Kate. You can and you will! Don't worry about us, we'll be all right — but only if you go and get help!"

Rarely had Sticky spoken with such force, and Kate was somewhat taken aback. She stood blinking at him a moment, then gave a small, tight nod. "You're right. I . . . I know you can manage without me, of course, and . . . all right. I'll go."

Her decision made, Kate was once again her usual self — and her usual self was all action. Retrieving her rope and Swiss Army knife from Reynie, she wrapped the rope around her waist, tucked her shirt in over it so that it was hidden, then opened a short blade on the knife. She had already noticed that the window was painted shut, and with precise, deft strokes she began to work her way along the frame, cutting through the paint.

As Sticky and Constance watched her work, Reynie was watching Sticky. Now that his forceful speech to Kate was finished, he seemed more anxious than ever; in fact he was gazing mournfully at Kate as if he would never see her again, and Reynie was struck by a sudden realization. Sticky had done his best to convince Kate to go, not because he thought she could save them — a doubtful prospect at best — but simply because he hoped she could save herself.

And he said exactly the right thing, too, Reynie thought. *He knew she needed to see that we'd be all right.*

Reynie turned away, fairly overcome by a surge of emotions — pride in his friend, concern for Kate's safety, and fear that Sticky was right, that they might not ever see Kate again. He started pacing the room, averting his eyes. Kate needed to go at once; she didn't need distractions. And so Reynie paced, and as he did his thoughts circled around Kate's escape attempt. What if someone was watching out one of those other windows? What if she had to break a window or pick a lock to get out of that courtyard? Could she do that quietly? And how did she mean to get down into that courtyard, anyway? Reynie went over these questions again and again, until he was so distracted himself that Constance had to speak his name twice to get his attention.

"Clean out your ears, Reynie," she said. "Kate's ready!"

Reynie turned to see the others looking at him. Kate had gotten the window open and, apparently, had already said her goodbyes to Sticky and Constance. She was beaming at him — her old confident self — and despite his strange turmoil of emotion, Reynie couldn't help but smile back. He hurried over and hugged her.

"Be careful," he said.

Kate winked. "You know me."

And with that, she leaped out the window.

SECRET COMMUNICATIONS

Noneof them was prepared for Kate's dramatic exit.
They gasped in unison and jumped forward to grab her. But
she was already out of reach, and bumping together at the
open window they saw what Kate had done. At the last instant she had spun and kicked off against the window ledge —
kicked off sideways, so that she hurtled several feet through
the air, parallel to the wall, in a trajectory that brought her
to a metal drainpipe, which she had latched on to with her
astonishingly strong hands. Already she was scrambling down

it toward the ground far below, as comfortable as a monkey in a tree. But once again Reynie and Sticky couldn't help covering their eyes. They might trust Kate's agility, but they had little reason to trust the drainpipe's sturdiness.

"She's down!" Constance whispered, to their relief. "She's running around checking doors!"

Now the boys felt even more anxious, but they forced themselves to look. There she was, darting first to one door and then the next, trying each one gingerly, quietly, cautious lest someone be standing on the other side. After several tries one of the doors in the opposite wing opened, and Kate disappeared.

They watched the vacant courtyard for a while, but Kate didn't reappear, and with a strange mixture of sadness and hope they closed the window. The boys applied themselves to righting the tilted bookcase. It was much harder to do without Kate, even more so to do it quietly, but with a good deal of straining they got the bookcase up again. At least now if someone glanced into the room it wouldn't be instantly apparent that something was amiss. Anything more than a glance, of course, would reveal that an entire *person* was amiss — but Kate could use as many valuable extra seconds as her friends could give her.

In the tense minutes that followed, they stood perfectly still in the middle of the room, listening for sounds of an outcry or alarm. Then, just as their tentative hopes were blossoming into real optimism, they heard exactly what they had been listening for — exactly what they had wanted so badly not to hear. Distant shouts and crashes. Radios squawking. And worst of all, someone laughing. They looked at one another and then away again, not wanting to believe it, and too upset for words.

Eventually Constance hung her head and mumbled, "Here they come."

Footsteps echoed in the hall, the door was unlocked and flung open, and Kate came sprawling into the room. She was panting and wobbly from her struggles, her hair had come loose from its ponytail, and her cheeks were bright red, but she seemed unhurt. Indeed, no sooner had she hit the floor than she was back on her feet and charging (staggering, really) at McCracken, who had so unceremoniously tossed her into the room. He was ready for her, and with a careless sweep of his arms he spun her about and sent her crashing to the floor again. This time her friends caught hold of her and held her back.

"Tsk, tsk," said McCracken. "I thought we agreed to part on peaceful terms."

"I never agreed to anything of the sort!" shouted Kate, still very worked up.

"Hmm," said McCracken as Mr. Curtain, scowling, rolled into the room behind him. "It certainly *sounded* like you agreed. But then I was holding you upside down at the time, so perhaps I misunderstood you."

"You didn't waste any time, did you, Miss Wetherall?" Mr. Curtain snapped. "Any of *your* time, I should say — my own valuable time is a different matter. I have work to be doing!" Springing from his wheelchair, he strode angrily over to the huddled children. "Did I not say that any disturbances would be punished?" he said, already pulling on his shiny silver gloves.

"Fine!" Kate cried, raising her chin defiantly. "Get it over with and go back to your precious, nasty work!"

"As you wish," Mr. Curtain said, and elbowing Kate aside he seized Reynie by the arm.

Reynie felt as if he'd been struck by lightning. Everything flashed white and red and flew apart, as if the room itself had exploded, and searing pain seemed to erupt from every part of his body at once — his face, his hands, even his toes — and then he was lying on the floor. When the fiery pain subsided and his eyes regained their focus, the familiar faces of his friends swam blearily above him — and Kate was weeping.

"It isn't fair!" she was shouting furiously through her tears. "It wasn't Reynie who tried to escape! You never said —"

"I decide what is fair and what isn't," Mr. Curtain said coolly. "You will all do well to remember that. Especially you, Miss Wetherall. The next time my work is interrupted, I shall extend the punishment to everyone." He leaped into his wheelchair again and spun it about. "McCracken, have S.Q. come see me in my work space. Apparently I must remind him how to lock a door."

"Funny," said McCracken, his brow wrinkling, "it was locked when we came in just now." He looked at Kate askance. "Were you really so clever as to lock it behind you to throw off suspicion?"

"A monkey would have thought of that, McCracken," said Mr. Curtain irritably. "Perhaps in the future I shall *hire* monkeys — they certainly couldn't do a worse job. In the meantime you will post a guard in the corridor as an added precaution." With that Mr. Curtain shot from the room, and McCracken, wagging his finger at the children in amused disapproval, followed after him and locked the door.

It took some time for Kate to calm down. She kept apologizing to Reynie, then railing against Mr. Curtain as her friends tried to shush her. Finally, when Reynie managed a weak smile and laid a finger to his lips, she got control of herself. "Right," she said, wiping away her tears. "Sorry. I'll be quiet. I've already done enough."

"Not you," said Sticky through clenched teeth. "Them."

"He's right," Reynie said. "It isn't your fault. We all wanted you to go, didn't we? So stop beating yourself up. Anyway, I'm already feeling better. You know it doesn't last that long."

Kate remembered all too well how long it lasted — Mr. Curtain had used those gloves on her before, too — and if memory served her, Reynie probably still felt queasy and shaken but was putting on a brave face. She nodded and said nothing more, busying herself instead with retying her ponytail. It was no help dwelling on what was already done. But she still felt terrible, all the same.

"What happened out there?" Constance asked her.

"We're in some sort of complex," Kate muttered. "There are high walls all around it, and they've put razor wire on top of the walls. Sharpe spotted me before I could find a way out."

Kate didn't much feel like talking, but naturally the others kept asking questions, and soon she had told them everything. She had sneaked through several corridors of the building without encountering a soul, then gone out an exterior door and found herself in what looked to be an abandoned construction site. There were great mounds of rubble and debris everywhere, and scattered heavy equipment, all surrounded by those high walls. She'd been spotted right away, unfortunately, and was too busy running for her life to investigate properly, but it was clear the complex was in the process of being demolished or renovated. Or had been, at any rate — there were no workers anywhere, and everything was as still as a graveyard.

"It's like a fortress or a military base or something," Kate said. "I don't know. I was pretty focused on finding a gap in that wall. One part at the back of the complex looked ready to topple — I think there was an accident; there's a huge crane nearby — but there wasn't a single hole big enough for even a rabbit to squeeze through. And there's a gate at the front, as high as the walls and topped with the same kind of wire, and it was guarded by Ten Men, but I got an idea that I could maybe smash through it with the Salamander, except that I worried about that wire coming down on top of me —"

"Wait a minute," Reynie said. "Back up. You were driving the Salamander?"

"I was *going* to. On my first time running around I saw it parked in a sort of big temporary shed, so I doubled back to it after I got the idea about the gate. I wasn't sure I would go through with that, but I figured I would have time to decide that after I stole the Salamander, provided I could get to it. That part turned out to be easy. The Ten Men weren't really running, they were just kind of closing in on me, strolling along all casual and relaxed — you know how they do — about seven or eight of them by the end. But they'd left open a clear path to that shed, and I made a beeline for it . . ." Kate made a disgusted face. "I'll bet you can guess who was sitting inside it, waiting for me."

"McCracken," the others said.

Kate nodded. "He was kneeling down so I couldn't see him over the sides. I basically jumped into his arms. The only bright side is they didn't think to search me again. I still have my rope and knife."

"There's more bright side to it than that," Reynie said. "At least now we can figure out where we are."

"We can?"

"Well, Sticky probably can, right?" Reynie said.

"Sure, we can at least narrow it down," Sticky said, though he seemed uncertain why it should matter. "Only a few places in the Stonetown area fit Kate's description — complexes of one kind or another that were being renovated when the funding ran out. It's a big deal when work gets suspended on projects like that. It's always in the papers."

"Of course!" Kate said, her aspect brightening considerably.

"And from the sound of it," Sticky continued, "I'd say we're in a prison. Did you happen to see any guard towers?"

"Yes! Sharpe was up in one when he spotted me and called out to the others! Oh, how is it I didn't realize it was a prison? An actual prison!" Kate rolled her eyes and snorted good-naturedly. Now that they were figuring something out, her miserable, guilty feeling was rapidly draining away. (Some people might have felt guilty for cheering up so quickly, but as it was in Kate's nature to be cheerful, and to look excitedly forward instead of glumly backward, the thought didn't even occur to her.)

"My guess is you were distracted by the Ten Men trying to capture you," Reynie said with a smile. "Anyway, there can't be many abandoned prisons within an hour's drive of Stonetown, right? Sticky, is it Solipse Prison? I'm sure I remember reading about that one."

Sticky shook his head. "I wish it were that easy. Solipse Prison and Third Island Prison were both slated for major renovation. Their prisoners were temporarily transferred elsewhere — at least it was supposed to be temporary — while the work was being done. The cell blocks and out-buildings were all to be demolished and rebuilt."

"So quit beating around the bush," Constance said. "Which one are we in? Haven't you seen pictures of them somewhere? Surely both of them didn't have a weird square building like this, with four sides going around a pathetic little courtyard."

"Actually, that's exactly the problem," Sticky said. "Both prisons were built according to the same plan, and they were being renovated according to the same *new* plan. The administration buildings were to be left intact while everything else was torn down and rebuilt. I think it's safe to say we're in the administration building of one of those prisons — but I have no idea which one."

"Good grief," Kate said. "And we were so close!"

"We aren't finished yet," said Reynie. "Solipse Prison is due north of Stonetown, isn't it, Sticky? And Third Island is due west?"

"That's right," Sticky said.

"Then I know where we are," Reynie said. "And what's more — I have a plan!"

Constance had her doubts about Reynie's plan, but then Constance had doubts about everything. Everyone else was optimistic. Hadn't Constance shown that she could transmit thoughts when she was sufficiently motivated? And when could she possibly be more motivated than now, when she was trapped in a prison and just waiting for Mr. Curtain to do his worst?

"Yes, but it's an awful lot of information to communicate," she said in a low, worried tone, "and I've had hardly any practice."

"Come on, Constance!" Kate said, grinning. "It's going to be great! Just like Reynie said, it'll be perfect! We can let Mr. Benedict know where we are, but Mr. Curtain will have no clue that we did! Mr. Benedict will have the advantage again — he'll have the element of surprise!"

Reynie chose not to point out that with the four of them being held hostage Mr. Benedict would still have a very tricky situation to deal with. The best thing now was to boost Constance's confidence. In fact, that was why he had called for an "official meeting" of the Society. Outwardly it might seem that sitting in a circle on the floor was hardly different from what they had been doing before. But Reynie hoped it would remind Constance of the success they'd had in the past, and that the familiar arrangement and tone would have a calming effect on her.

"Well, okay, but I can't really picture it," Constance said doubtfully. "When I was in the library I just stared at the call number on the spine of that book. Mr. Benedict said images probably get through more easily, so that's what I tried. But there's not much to look at here . . ."

"We'll help you decide what to think," Reynie said, and the others agreed.

And so the Society began to brainstorm about the best way for Constance to communicate their situation to Mr. Benedict. It wouldn't do for him to plan a rescue attempt at the wrong prison, after all. He needed to know that they were being held in Third Island Prison, something they wouldn't have known themselves had Reynie not remembered the too-bright morning sun glaring through the van's rear windows. The sun, of course, rose in the east; therefore they had been heading west.

They were in Third Island, no doubt about it. And between Sticky and Kate, they had a fairly good idea about the place. For Constance's benefit Kate laid out in greater detail what she had seen outside, and Sticky explained that the prison was situated on an island (the third one upstream from the bay, hence its name) along the widest stretch of Stonetown River.

"What is it with this guy and islands?" said Constance, rolling her eyes.

"It makes good strategic sense," Reynie said. "The prison's a defensible position, and if things go awry he can shut down the power again and use the Salamander to escape on the river."

"Do you really think he could shut it down again?" Kate said.

"I don't see why not. He still has his spies in place, and

soon he'll have the Whisperer up and running again. I assume that's what he's working so busily on."

"I'm sure it is," Sticky said. "He'd want to run through all the computer programs first to see the things Mr. Benedict changed, and make sure —"

"Stop, stop!" Constance growled. "You're cluttering my head up. I just need to concentrate on where we are and what we know for sure, right?"

"Yes," Reynie said. "I think it's best to keep this simple. You should try to tell him what we know — focusing on the most important details — and to be safe you should probably conjure up as many images as you can. Like a neon sign flashing the words 'Third Island,' maybe —"

"And maybe the three of us looking out from behind prison bars," Kate suggested.

"But that might be confusing," Sticky said. "I'm sure he knows that the prison cells here were demolished."

"Yes, but it's symbolic," Kate argued.

"I *know* it's symbolic," Sticky said. "My point is for the sake of clarity we should —"

Constance frowned and shushed them, looking at the door. "Here's S.Q.!"

Sure enough, the lock turned, the door swung open, and S.Q. Pedalian entered the room with a large plastic bowl of popcorn. He closed the door behind him. "Before you say anything, you should know that speaking to me will get you punished. Mr. Curtain made that very clear to me — *very* clear — and it will be my duty to report you if you do. So please don't. No funny business, either.

Garrotte is posted in the hallway and will come running if I call out."

S.Q. set the large bowl on the floor and stared at it apologetically. "I'm afraid it's a bit stale, and there's no butter. But Mr. Curtain says that nutrition is not our main concern at the moment. He just wants to prevent your whining about your empty stomachs." For the first time, S.Q. looked up and made eye contact with the children. "Just so you know, I don't hold a grudge against you for what happened back on that island. I've given it a lot of thought since then, and I realize you were just scared. If I were you I might have tricked myself, too. Not that I could trick myself, of course — I mean, not without . . . never mind. All I mean to say is I have no hard feelings. Okay? Don't answer that!"

From S.Q.'s anxious expression they could all tell that he'd meant what he said, that he would report them if they said even one word to him. Still, he seemed reluctant to leave, and lingered there by the popcorn bowl, nudging it with his tattered boot as if to encourage them to eat. Finally, with a heavy sigh, he turned to go out.

"Kate," Reynie said quickly, "I hope S.Q. realizes that we don't have any hard feelings toward him, either. I mean, I hope he knows that we understand he's just trying to do what's right."

"Surely he does, Reynie," said Kate, instantly catching on. "We've always gotten along with him, haven't we?" And Sticky and Constance (in rather awkward, self-conscious voices) hastened to agree.

S.Q., listening intently, turned back to them with a grateful smile. "Thanks," he said. "That's pretty clever of you, incidentally."

"Sticky," Reynie said (though he was looking imploringly at S.Q.), "I wonder if S.Q. would be willing to tell us what's going on. I'll bet he can imagine how frustrating it is to be held captive and not even know why. Like he said himself, we're just scared."

S.Q. looked troubled. "I don't know . . . I mean, my orders don't specifically state . . ."

"You're right, Reynie," Sticky said, "it would be very kind of him."

S.Q. pressed a knuckle against his lips and glanced at the door. "I suppose it wouldn't hurt just to — well, it's all very simple, really. As you'd know if you hadn't been deceived by malicious false reports, Mr. Curtain only wants to stabilize the country. He wants to protect it! But there are powerful people in the government who don't listen to reason — they only want to hold on to their power, no matter how bad it is for everyone else."

"You think Mr. Curtain is just trying to *help*?" Constance said incredulously. Then seeing her friends' horrified looks, she quickly added, "I'm asking Reynie!" and somewhat desperately she went on, "Well, Reynie? Is that what you think, Reynie? *Is* it, Reynie?"

"I don't know, Constance," said Reynie. "Maybe he is."

Plainly relieved, S.Q. said, "I assure you he is. And he has several friends in government who understand this. That's why they've arranged to bring the very best government advisers to have a secret meeting with Mr. Curtain later this afternoon. Together they're going to work out a way to ensure all the major cities have a safe and steady power supply. Thanks to Mr. Curtain's expertise, new tidal turbines can be built, power grids updated and vastly improved, new systems put in place — trust me, it's all going to be much, much better for everyone. And once the higher-ups see what Mr. Curtain really means to do — what he's been trying to do all along — well, they'll change their minds and support him. He'll no longer be considered a criminal." S.Q. paused, then added with feeling, "And neither will I."

The children looked gravely at one another. They had no doubt that these "friends" S.Q. spoke of were actually spies — and that this very afternoon Mr. Curtain would be using his Whisperer to extract valuable secrets from the advisers that his spies were bringing to him. And afterward he could simply sweep away their memories of that unpleasant experience, and no one would be the wiser.

"Reynie," said Kate, "I still don't understand why Mr. Curtain needs *us*."

"Oh! That part is more complicated," S.Q. said. "Even I have trouble understanding it. But it comes down to other people — foolish, wicked people — trying to ruin Mr. Curtain's chances. He's been forced to use some unusual methods to clear up this situation. He only has one weakness, really, and Mr. Benedict has information that would help him get rid of it — but Mr. Benedict has been corrupted and is unwilling to help — so Mr. Curtain has had to involve you. I'm not sure why, but the important thing is that it will all work out fine if you just do as he says."

"Constance," said Reynie. "I wonder if S.Q. really, truly believes that."

S.Q.'s face clouded at this. For a moment he stood frozen, his eyes darting quickly this way and that as if seeking answers — or comfort — in the corners of the room. "I have to go," he said abruptly, and hurried to the door. "Garrotte will wonder what's taking me so long."

Reynie, forgetting himself, almost called out after him. And then S.Q. was out the door, and they all heard the turning of the lock.

Time was growing short. By this afternoon, Mr. Curtain might be too powerful for anyone to have any chance of stopping him. Everything now seemed to depend on Constance's ability to send her thoughts, clearly and accurately, across an unknown number of miles, into the mind of Mr. Benedict. It was no surprise that she was feeling the pressure. She had once thwarted the Whisperer itself, but that fight had called for her straightforward, stubborn resistance; her courage and obstinance had saved the day. This time was different, the task far more complex.

Never had Constance worked so hard or for so long. Minutes passed, and then an hour, and still she worked. And all it seemed she was doing was lying on the floor with her eyes squeezed tightly closed. In reality, her friends knew, she was sending out her thoughts again and again, then "listening" carefully for any kind of response. Reynie, Kate, and Sticky maintained perfect silence, breathing as softly as they could and trying hard (in Sticky's case, extremely hard) not even to scratch their itches or stretch their legs. They knew that Constance's ability to concentrate was of the utmost importance, that their fate, and indeed the fate of everyone they held dear, depended on Constance's success.

Thus it was not a little disconcerting when Constance began to snore.

"Constance!" they cried, alarmed. "Constance! Wake up!"

Constance sat up with a start, then scowled and rubbed her eyes. "What? What is it, what's wrong?" Lowering her fists, she noticed their stricken looks and said, "Oh. I guess I fell asleep . . ."

"Constance, how could you?" said Kate, shaking her head.

"I don't know. I didn't realize I did. I'd sent out the message for about the hundredth time, and each time I thought maybe I could hear Mr. Benedict saying something to me. But it was muddled and quiet, I couldn't make out a word of it, and as far as I know it was my own imagination doing it. Right? I mean, if what you want more than anything is to hear someone's voice in your head . . ." She yawned and stretched. "I can't believe I fell asleep, though. I was a nervous wreck until — oh!"

"Oh what?" Reynie said.

"I remember what happened," Constance said, closing her eyes and putting her fingertips to her temples. "I got this picture in my head, and it was so comforting it made me relax . . ." She opened her eyes. "I think I was so exhausted that relaxing for even a second just put me right out."

"The same thing happened to me in the van," Reynie said. "What was the picture?"

"It was Mr. Benedict and everybody. They all looked funny, dressed up in silly costumes, and all of them grinning at me." Constance smiled. "Better yet, they were all holding pies — Moocho Brazos's pies. I could practically smell them."

"Sounds to me like you were already dreaming," Sticky said.

Constance considered this. "Maybe so. It *was* an awfully silly image to have pop into my head."

Reynie, however, was growing excited. "Constance," he said urgently, "don't you think it might have been a message from Mr. Benedict?"

"Oh! I don't know . . . I suppose it might have been!" She pursed her lips, thinking. "If so, I can't imagine what he meant by it. Maybe he just wanted to make me laugh and feel better . . . maybe it was his way of telling me everything will be all right. That was the feeling it gave me, anyway."

Unconvinced, Reynie pressed for details. Who had Constance meant by "everybody"? What were the silly costumes? And how did she know they were Moocho Brazos's pies? Constance replied matter-of-factly that "everybody" meant Milligan, Rhonda, and Number Two; that the costumes were just silly disguises — big fake mustaches, trench coats, and hats; and that of course the pies had been made by Moocho, because who else would have made them?

"It's true they were shaped oddly, though," said Constance upon reflection. "They were baked in the shape of *S*'s."

"Like the letter *S*?" Sticky said. "What for?"

"How on earth would I know? Maybe it stands for something — safety or security, maybe. Like I said, the picture made me feel better. Maybe it was supposed to give me a feeling of being safe at home."

"Assuming it wasn't just a dream, after all," said Kate, looking at Reynie to see what he made of it.

Reynie was rubbing his chin. "Are you sure that was the only image you saw, Constance? And there weren't any words to go along with it?"

"Oh sure, there were *lots* of words, but I couldn't possibly tell you if they came from Mr. Benedict or from me. They were all in a jumble, and anyway they were all words I'd been thinking myself — all that stuff about Mr. Curtain's plan, and the prison, and the spies bringing those advisers here, basically everything I'd been trying to send to Mr. Benedict, only it was in fragments and snippets. Sometimes it seemed like they were in my own voice and sometimes in Mr. Benedict's. I don't know — if he was trying to tell me something he wasn't doing a very good job of it."

Constance found herself suddenly famished, and as Reynie and the others discussed what the image might mean, she made short work of the stale popcorn, cramming it into her mouth by the handful.

The more they talked, the less certain Sticky and Kate were that the image actually came from Mr. Benedict. Reynie, on the other hand, strongly suspected that it did; he felt the image seemed meaningful somehow, but for the life of him he couldn't say why. And even if it did come from Mr. Benedict, whether he had sent it on purpose or Constance's probing mind had cobbled it together out of his thoughts seemed impossible to gauge. Furthermore, if he *had* sent it on purpose, it may well have lost some of its supporting detail in the transmission. So the image, tantalizing though it was, seemed unlikely to do them any good.

"Maybe we should take a little break," Constance said, when they had exhausted themselves talking about it (and she had stuffed herself with popcorn). Her eyelids had begun to droop. "Just a tiny short one to sort of" — she yawned — "sort of rest a minute while we think about this some more. I can tell you're all tired . . ." And without further ado she curled up on her side and fell asleep with her mouth open.

Sticky looked at her enviously. "I wish I could do that."

Reynie shook his head. "I think the strain took a lot out of her. She isn't used to working very hard, you know."

"That would be an understatement," said Kate, checking the popcorn bowl. It was empty, of course.

... .STATE D...REA SONS.....

AND...... ....S UDDEN.. ....

....IN SIGHTS.

As Constance slept, Sticky and Kate began discussing other ways to get out of their predicament, for neither of them had any confidence that Mr. Benedict had received Constance's message. Reynie still felt otherwise, however, and he continued to ponder what the strange image in her head could possibly have meant. He kept thinking he could make sense of it if he tried hard enough, or thought about it in the right way, but it was no easy matter to find significance in silly disguises and S-shaped pies. For a long time he paced along the far side of the room, tuning out the whispers of

Sticky and Kate, who knew to leave him alone at times like these. Finally, though, taking a break to clear his thoughts before trying again, he realized they were arguing.

"You *have* to do it," Sticky said.

"No way," Kate said emphatically. "Just drop it, okay?"

"What are you talking about?" Reynie asked, coming over to them.

Sticky looked up at him beseechingly. "You realize she could try again, don't you? Mr. Curtain thinks S.Q. left the door unlocked — no one realizes she got out through the window."

"That's true!" said Reynie, surprised. "Why didn't I think of that?"

"But I'm not going to do it, and that's that," Kate said.

"But you know more this time!" Sticky insisted. "You could have a plan, and we could make a distraction or something."

"For what?" said Kate, waving him off. "A chance to save my own skin and leave the rest of you to be punished? Maybe even brainswept? And then live the rest of my life knowing I escaped when you couldn't? Forget it!"

Reynie quickly took Sticky's side in the argument, pointing out that she could try to contact Mr. Benedict and tell him where they were. But it did no good. Kate was adamant.

"We know now that we're a long way from anywhere, right? So it's a long shot at best. I might manage it in time, but then again I might not. Look," Kate said, her expression softening, "don't think I'm not aware of what you're suggesting. You're both willing to risk some awful punishment just so I can get away. But *I'm* not willing to risk it, especially since our chances are better if we stick together."

"But you don't know that!" Reynie protested. "I keep messing up! I forget things . . . I don't think clearly . . ." He cut himself off, biting his lip in frustration.

Kate clucked her tongue. "That's another thing, Reynie. You're being too hard on yourself. You can't think of everything all the time — no one can. I can't do any of this alone, neither can Sticky, and neither can you. You know that. Maybe you just forget it because you feel responsible. But you aren't responsible for all of us, you know. I mean, we're *all* responsible, right?"

Reynie looked away, feeling strangely embarrassed. "I know that, of course I know that. It isn't like I think I have to solve every problem . . ." But even as he said it, he realized that he did. "Anyway," he went on quickly, "the point is you can't count on me to figure a way out of this. You should make a break for it while you can."

"I didn't say I count on *you* to figure a way out," Kate said. Then she frowned. "I guess it's true I usually do expect you to, which is my own way of being too hard on you, isn't it? Sorry for that. But I'm not counting on you this time, I promise. I'm counting on *us*. Just because we don't have an answer right now doesn't mean we won't have one soon. So you can quit trying to get me to go, both of you. I'm through talking about this. Got it?"

Reynie and Sticky had no good answer for this. At any rate, they both felt encouraged by Kate's speech. For wasn't she right? Didn't they always manage together?

"Got it," said Sticky.

"Got it," said Reynie.

"Good," said Kate, and all of them smiled.

Reynie's mind had wandered from the problem of the image Constance had seen to the very real prospect of being brainswept by the Whisperer — something he had been trying hard not to think about — and he had just arrived at the despairing thought that soon he might not recognize the faces of his friends, that these trying moments might well be the last ones the Society ever spent together. It was hard to imagine, and even harder to bear, so it was almost a relief when Constance's eyes sprang open and she sat up.

Almost, but not quite.

"Crawlings is here," Constance said.

Reynie shivered, unnerved by the feeling that some ghostly Ten Man was among them without their knowing it. Kate and Sticky, feeling much the same, stopped whispering and looked toward the door.

For a long minute no one spoke or moved. There were no footsteps, no noises in the hall. Even Constance began to suspect she'd been wrong. But then the lock turned, the door inched open, and, like a turtle easing out of its shell, Crawlings's pale bald head slowly poked in through the door. He wriggled his eyebrow and leered at the children. "Oh, come now, kittens. Don't stop whispering on my behalf."

"But that would be rude," Kate replied. "We were whispering about you, after all, and I'm afraid we weren't saying very nice things."

"Crawlings doesn't care about rudeness," Constance said. "Or doesn't he know that it's rude to listen in on people?"

Crawlings snickered. "Oh yes," he said, sauntering on into the room, "that would be very rude indeed, but I don't quite count children as people, you see. It's true they rather *resemble* people — but then so do puppets." His brow wrinkled and he began fiddling with the clasp on his briefcase as if considering whether to open it. "Now what did I come in here to do? I'm trying to remember."

"Let us go?" Sticky ventured weakly, his eyes fixed on the briefcase.

Crawlings pretended to consider this. "No . . . no, I don't believe it was that," he said. He tapped his chin with his long, spidery fingers. "Something to do with my briefcase, maybe?"

The children watched him in silence. Crawlings was clearly toying with them, but still their nerves stood on end as they waited. He went so far as opening his briefcase and peeking at them to observe their response. They only stared blankly at him, however, and looking faintly disappointed that they hadn't whimpered or begged for mercy, he closed it again and snapped his fingers.

"I have it! I'm to bring you to Mr. Curtain's work space for a quick word. Emphasis on quick — he's very busy. So chop chop, little puppets, let's hurry along!" And like a loving father Crawlings grabbed Kate by the hand and swung it playfully back and forth between them. "I believe I'll keep you close, my dear. The rest of you may walk in front of us."

They had hardly taken two steps before Crawlings stopped, released Kate's hand, and flexed his fingers with a troubled expression. "I'm impressed with your grip, Katie-kins, but you had better stop squeezing so hard or mean old Crawlings may have to squeeze back."

Kate looked up at him innocently. "But I *wasn't* squeezing hard," she said, batting her eyelashes.

Crawlings narrowed his eyes and took her hand again, telling the others which direction to go. They proceeded down a long corridor and into an elevator. "Mr. Curtain put you as far away from him as possible," Crawlings explained as the elevator descended. "He has so much work to do, and children can be so noisy, you know. Though I suppose you don't notice this yourselves."

"We're more bothered by smells," Constance said, holding her nose, for in the close confines of the elevator Crawlings's cologne was almost overpowering.

Crawlings grunted and muttered something about inferior sensibilities. When the elevator door slid open he leaned out and whispered to someone in the corridor. "Is he ready for them?"

"He was," came the whispered reply, "but you were late, so now he's speaking to McCracken." (Reynie perked up his ears at this; sure enough, he could just make out Mr. Curtain's voice in the background.) "You're to go in the instant they're finished talking."

"Am I really late?" Crawlings asked, checking one of his watches. He frowned and checked the other one, looking concerned. Perhaps now he regretted the time he'd wasted intimidating the children.

"Did you at least fetch his juice from the basement?" whispered the other Ten Man. "He called for it again."

Crawlings's eyebrow rose in dismay. "I'll go right now and bring them back —" His eyes shot over to Reynie, who had abruptly begun pressing the elevator buttons for all the higher floors, including one for the roof. With an angry cry he slapped Reynie's hand away from the panel. "You little fool! What are you doing?"

Rubbing his stinging hand, Reynie stepped away and averted his eyes.

Crawlings gritted his teeth. "We'll settle this later," he hissed. "Get out, all of you!" As the children filed out he whispered down the corridor to the other Ten Man: "I'm taking the stairs. Keep an eye on the urchins, will you? Send them in if he finishes with McCracken."

"Crawlings, old sport, you know it isn't *my* job to —"

But Crawlings was already scuttling off and pretended not to hear.

The other Ten Man sighed and regarded the children from his post outside an open doorway. He was unfamiliar to them, a slight, swarthy man in a dapper seersucker suit, with a bandage on his forehead that Kate suspected was the result of the flashlight she had thrown outside Mr. Benedict's house (in the darkness she hadn't gotten a good look at the man she'd hit). If they hadn't known he was a Ten Man they might have thought he was kind, so gentle was his expression and so friendly the smile he leveled at them. He was holding a newspaper, working the crossword puzzle with an expensive-looking gold pen. Laying the pen to his lips, he indicated that they should wait quietly where they were.

They nodded and stood perfectly still — all the better to listen. For this was exactly why Reynie had pressed those buttons, and the others knew it: From here they could hear Mr. Curtain and McCracken. If they had accompanied Crawlings to the basement, they would have missed their chance to eavesdrop.

Mr. Curtain's voice emanated from a doorway just beyond the one the Ten Man appeared to be guarding. But even from this distance his tone of satisfaction was unmistakable. ". . . here within the hour! Can you imagine that, McCracken? Has it ever occurred to *you* to fulfill my orders exactly on time? Oh, how rare! I'm very pleased. I cherish expedience, you know."

"As do I," said McCracken. "And in this case it is a benefit, no doubt, of your associates not having to engage with government agents. Such challenging tasks as *that* you leave to my men and me."

Mr. Curtain screeched — or rather, laughed — and said, "Try not to be defensive, McCracken! Or are you simply angling for greater compensation? I believe I pay you handsomely enough. Now here is what I expect. You will post all of your men in the two foremost guard towers. From there they shall be in perfect position to rain down destruction should anything not go as expected. Do you agree?"

"Certainly. You expect treachery, then?"

"Of course not! I said 'should anything *not* go as expected,' didn't I? I am careful, McCracken — you should know that by now."

"Indeed I do," said McCracken. "So careful, in fact, that you've never revealed to me the identities of these friends you are expecting. Don't mistake my meaning — I admire your caution — but do tell me how I'm to know whether to admit them. I assume there is a password?"

"I was getting to that, McCracken," Mr. Curtain said irritably. "Yes, there will be a password — but you'll see that I am cautious even with that. When the van arrives, you must radio me from the gate and describe the driver. I shall then give you a question to ask, and you must relay the response you're given. If it is correct, you'll open the gate. If not . . ."

"If not, we'll set about earning our pay," said McCracken. "Now, may I make one suggestion? I have more than enough men to handle any complications at the gate. Allow me to leave one in the building with you, just as an added precaution."

There was a pause. "I sense there is something more to your suggestion than you are letting on, McCracken. Tell me what it is."

"To be frank, sir, I do not entirely trust your assistant. I know he is loyal to you — and you must think so yourself, having kept him for so long — but he seems to have a soft spot for our young prisoners, and I worry he may try to help them somehow."

"I see," Mr. Curtain said in an icy tone. "You disapprove of my choice in assistants. Very well, McCracken, I shall deploy S.Q. to the gate with you and your men, and you may leave behind whomever you wish — your own choice in associates being so impeccable." When McCracken shrewdly chose not to reply to this, Mr. Curtain snapped, "Take Crawlings, for instance. Give him two simple tasks and he accomplishes neither on time." And raising his voice he called out, "I don't suppose Crawlings is here yet, is he, Hertz?"

"He's gone for the juice," answered the Ten Man in the corridor, with a wink at the children. "But the cherubs are here when you're ready for them."

"I am beyond ready. Send them in."

Hertz lifted his newspaper and waved the children down the corridor. As they passed the room he was guarding, they caught a glimpse of the Whisperer in the corner, surrounded by various tools and parts. On a shelf above it sat a familiar red bucket. Kate hesitated only a moment to gaze at it, but in that moment Hertz took his pen and flicked her on the head so cruelly that her ears rang. She moved on, glowering at him over her shoulder. She could feel a knot rising but refused to put her hand to it. Hertz smiled cheerfully at her, tapping the gold pen against his bright white teeth.

"You okay?" Sticky whispered. "It sounded like he hit you with a lead pipe."

"Felt like it, too," Kate whispered back, and though her head was throbbing she added, "I'm fine. A little pain never hurt anybody, did it?"

Sticky looked at her askance. "Um, actually —" he began, but Kate quieted him with a wink.

They found Mr. Curtain in a large oval-shaped room, sitting in his wheelchair with his back to them. The walls of the room were lined with computers, and on four separate monitors arrayed against the far wall dense blocks of complex computer code streamed endlessly past. "Keep an eye on our guests, McCracken," said Mr. Curtain, whose own eyes were fixed intently on the screens. "Bludgeon anyone who touches anything but the floor."

McCracken, standing off to the side, chuckled. "Happy to oblige."

"I am making final preparations, children," Mr. Curtain said, still watching the monitors, "making certain that all is in order. This includes you. Later today you will be allowed to speak with your beloved Mr. Benedict by radio. He will no doubt ask you questions, and you are to be prompt and truthful in your replies. If you do this, you shall see him shortly thereafter. If not, you will be punished severely.

"I tell you this now so that you may prepare yourselves. I will not allow any childish nervousness or desperation to create wrinkles in an otherwise smooth operation. I would dislike it extremely, for instance, if in a panic you lied to Benedict, or attempted to tell him something that might disrupt my plans. I assure you such action would be fruitless, and it would be a shame, would it not, to suffer the painful consequences of disobedience for no reason?" He paused. "You may answer."

"For all we know," Reynie said, "obedience will bring painful consequences, too. What assurances can you give us that it won't?"

Mr. Curtain cackled. "None! You shall have to take my word for it, but what else do you have? Tell me that!" He cackled again, his shoulders shaking. He was evidently in a wonderful mood. "I do give you my word, however: If you do as I say, you will soon be reunited with your dear Benedict. I am telling the truth, am I not, Miss Contraire? I recall you have a gift for divining such things."

It wasn't lost on Reynie that Mr. Curtain had made no mention of actually letting them go free. And Constance, at any rate, refused to follow Mr. Curtain's lead. "I'm even better at divining *dumbness*," she retorted. "You really think Mr. Benedict will give you what you want?"

At this, Mr. Curtain's shoulders stiffened. But after a short pause they relaxed again, and he said evenly, "For you and your friends, Miss Contraire, I believe he'll do whatever is necessary. He clearly prizes his little club of admirers above all else. Without you, no doubt, he feels he is nothing, for that is the sort of weak person he is. Let me ask you, then: How could I possibly care about such a person if everything else — *everything* else — is in my control? Benedict and his followers are mosquito bites, scarcely worth the scratching. When I have what I desire, I shall gladly be rid of you. You may go off and do whatever silly little things you wish. It will be of no consequence to me."

"Because you think you'll be ruling the world?" Kate asked contemptuously. "Just like last time?"

Mr. Curtain's wheelchair bucked and spun about, and he glared at her with such fury that even Kate could not help but shrink away. Then his eyes closed, and his chin dropped to his chest.

"Don't move," ordered McCracken in a wary tone, as if they had blundered into a den of hibernating grizzlies. "For that matter, don't speak. And if you value your little legs, don't smile or smirk or any such thing. I would prefer not to have to drag you out afterward. I've had to drag out more than my share of men who smiled at moments like this. It's inconvenient, to say the least, and I have a great deal to do."

The children held still and waited. One minute passed, then two, and then Mr. Curtain jerked, snorted, and raised his head. For a moment his expression was one of unmistakable embarrassment, and his eyes darted from face to face, assessing the mood of everyone present. The embarrassment was swiftly overcome by anger — his eyes flashed dangerously; his hands trembled — but with an effort he suppressed it by lifting his gaze to the ceiling, lacing his fingers together, and taking several deep breaths. Finally Mr. Curtain checked his watch and glanced over his shoulder at the still-scrolling computer code on the monitors.

"Stop scrolling!" he snapped, and the code stopped scrolling. "Go back one hundred and twenty-seven lines." The code began scrolling in the opposite direction, and Mr. Curtain turned back to the children and looked at them coldly. "Your impertinence often surprises me, Miss Wetherall. But I am resolved not to let it happen again. As for your question about ruling the world . . ." He waved his hand dismissively. "For the moment I shall be content to run this country. The world will follow soon enough."

Kate nodded in mock approval. "Baby steps," she said. "That's always best."

Mr. Curtain's eye twitched and his lips pressed together in a line.

"So what will you do?" Constance demanded. "Knock out the power in every city until everyone comes begging for your help? Why not just take everything over? Why do you have to be *thanked* for it, too?"

At this point Reynie broke into a terrible fit of coughing, forcing himself to hack so violently his eyes watered. He was sure Constance had touched a dangerous nerve (Mr. Curtain's stricken expression confirmed it), and anxious to draw attention away from her he croaked, "I think what we're wondering, Mr. Curtain, is why you want things to seem some way they aren't. You're a genius — everyone knows that — so why not devote yourself toward *actually* making things better?"

Mr. Curtain had regained his composure now (Reynie had done his best to give him the opportunity), and in a condescending tone he said, "Your question betrays your naïveté, Reynard. Making things seem a way they aren't *is* making them better."

"But it's just an illusion!" Sticky blurted out, then clapped his hands over his mouth.

Luckily Mr. Curtain seemed more amused than perturbed. "You must understand something, George. The world's leaders create catastrophes and resolve them — all at their own whimsy — every single day. It is how the world runs. Lacking anything else to believe in, common people need to believe in their leaders' abilities to save them. It's true! Their emotional well-being — and yes, their fate — depends on the intelligence and skill of those who manipulate the days' disasters. And it should go without saying that the one who succeeds in taking the reins of leadership — by whatever means — is the most intelligent and skillful, and therefore most qualified to lead."

Noting the children's dubious looks, Mr. Curtain shrugged in a resigned manner. "In your simplicity you often mistake my motives, I'm afraid: I do not dislike people, I only mean to control them, for I cannot stand seeing the complex business of the world being so badly mishandled. I am a perfectionist; I cannot help it. In the end everyone shall benefit from my inclinations, with the rare exception of individuals such as yourselves, who are perennially dissatisfied."

"And you're perennially boring!" said Constance (who wasn't sure what "perennially" meant but felt sure it applied). "I think you just want people to call you a hero, and this is the only way you could figure how to do it!"

Again Mr. Curtain pressed his lips together. "What you think hardly matters, Miss Contraire. In truth I have no idea why I waste my time trying to enlighten such foolish creatures. I must have a soft spot for those doomed to fail. McCracken, take them away and send in Crawlings — I spy him lurking in the corridor there."

"As you wish," said McCracken, herding the children toward the door. "And when shall I dispatch my men to the positions we discussed?"

Mr. Curtain checked his watch. "The van should exit the highway in thirty minutes, and the approach along the access road takes precisely five. Just be sure your men are in position when the van arrives at the gate. In the meantime, tell Hertz I need his assistance moving the Whisperer."

"He's afraid to touch it, you know," said McCracken with a grin.

"Precisely why I'm choosing him. He won't paw it unnecessarily."

McCracken acknowledged this with a nod, and in the corridor he drew Crawlings briefly aside. They spoke in hushed tones, but the children heard enough to deduce that Crawlings was the Ten Man McCracken intended to leave behind. Perhaps this choice was meant as a barb flung at Mr. Curtain; perhaps it simply reflected some private, strategic consideration. Regardless, Reynie knew it was a terrible choice for him and his friends. Crawlings would surely take the first opportunity to punish them for what Reynie had done in the elevator.

"I have a bad feeling about Crawlings," Sticky whispered.

"Me, too," Kate whispered back, "but I think that will change."

"Really?"

"Oh yes," Kate whispered. "I'm pretty sure it will get worse."

⌣∴∾

Alone in their third-floor room, the Society quickly gathered in a circle to discuss their next step. Kate suggested they figure out a way to pass information to Mr. Benedict when they spoke on the radio. "In case he didn't get Constance's message," she said. "We can come up with a code of some kind, something only he will understand."

"That's awfully risky," Sticky said. "Mr. Curtain will be looking out for just that sort of thing."

"I know, but we don't want to *help* him, do we?"

"Mr. Benedict is smart," Sticky said. "Maybe he can find a way to rescue us even if we just go along with Mr. Curtain."

"His biggest concern is going to be our safety," Reynie said. "He'll sacrifice himself if he has to — you know he will."

"Of course he will," Constance said angrily, and tears started to her eyes. "But it won't do any good! Mr. Curtain doesn't intend to let us go — he never did and he never will! Oh, I don't *want* to be brainswept! I *like* remembering who I am, and who my friends are, and . . . and . . ." She clenched her fists, clamped her mouth shut, and uttered a strange sort of internal scream that sounded like whale song.

"Easy, Connie girl," Kate soothed. "I'm afraid you'll pop."

"I'm not really excited about getting brainswept, either," Sticky said in a low tone. "I just hope our families get away . . ."

A gloomy silence fell over them. It seemed impossible to Reynie that this was really happening. But the facts insisted upon themselves. Mr. Curtain had the Whisperer and the children, and no one was ever going to know. And things were only going to get worse from here, for weren't Mr. Curtain's spies bringing him what he wanted at that very moment?

As if Reynie had spoken this aloud, Constance scowled and muttered, "McCracken called them his 'friends in government.' Ha! Why don't they call them what they are? Nasty, weaselly old spies!"

"Who else would be his friends?" said Kate. "Thugs, thieves, and spies — that's his crowd, isn't it?"

"Spies . . . ," Reynie murmured, his brow wrinkling.

Constance glanced at him — then stared at him. And then her eyebrows shot up (at exactly the same time Reynie's did) and she cried, "Oh! *Spies!*"

"Fake mustaches and trench coats!" Reynie exclaimed. "Those S-shaped pies —!"

Kate and Sticky gasped.

"S-pies!" Constance said, and she was suddenly so delighted she clapped her hands. "So he did get my message! And he *answered* me — he told me their plan!"

Reynie jumped up and started to pace. "I think he was trying to give you the details, Constance, but the words didn't come through as well. But he also sent you that coded image —"

"And that was the only thing that came through clearly," Constance said, nodding excitedly. "It's right, it *feels* right! And that comforting feeling — he was trying to tell me everything was going to be fine, that he had a plan, that they were coming to rescue us!"

"He used the information you gave him to hatch his plan," Reynie said. "They must have waylaid the real spies somehow, and they're coming in their place."

"Milligan's going to be busy," Kate said with a hint of nervousness. "There's a bunch of Ten Men. But at least he'll be taking them by surprise — he always says that's the most important thing with them — and once he's inside . . . *oh no!*" She sprang to her feet. "The password! The question Mr. Curtain's going to ask them! They won't know the answer!"

"They'll be attacked before they ever get through the gate," Sticky said, and he covered his face as if he couldn't bear to look, as if he were already witnessing what was about to happen. "They won't have a chance . . ."

Reynie started to speak, then seeing Constance's eyes squeezed shut and her hands over her ears, he froze and kept quiet. Sticky and Kate noticed, too, and silently the three of them watched her, trying to be hopeful. But when

Constance opened her eyes again, she still looked very much alarmed.

"I tried to warn him, and I . . . I'm pretty sure he heard me — but they're still coming! They're still going to try!"

"Are you sure?" Sticky asked.

"Well, I didn't get words, just a sort of feeling, but . . . no, I'm sure of it. They're going to risk it for our sake! Oh no, oh no . . ." Her lips began to tremble and she closed her eyes again, this time to stop herself from crying.

"It's a pretty desperate gamble," Sticky said grimly.

"They must think it's their only chance to save us," Reynie said.

"But there's just no way!" Kate cried. "They'll be in the worst possible position! Forget about us — who'll save *them*?"

There was a long, heavy pause. And then, in the back of Reynie's mind, a gear began to turn. And then another. And then he looked round at his friends and said, "It'll have to be us."

Sticky blinked. "You . . . you realize that we're still prisoners, right? That we were counting on them to save *us*?"

"That's step two," Reynie said. "Step one is getting them inside."

Kate was starting to smile. "Wait, are you saying we have to save *them* so they can save *us*?"

"That's exactly what he means," said Constance, peering at Reynie's face.

Kate laughed and clapped her hands together. "I love it! So where do we start?"

"Where do you think?" Reynie said, his eyes flashing. "We escape."

The Window of Opportunity

Their escape attempt would be dangerous, to say the least, and the timing would have to be perfect. As Reynie pointed out, they had had some practice already; they just needed to make a few important adjustments. But even so, as they frantically set about making preparations, Sticky was so anxious he almost threw up, and perspiration streamed down his head and dripped from his ears. Reynie, for his part, kept stopping to review the plan, worried that he'd overlooked something, and Kate was utterly serious for once. Constance just covered her eyes and waited with a growing sense of dread. They knew that Crawlings would come to the room as soon as the other Ten Men were dispatched to the guard towers — and everything, *everything* depended on their being ready when he did.

✧

The elevator door opened, and Crawlings stepped out and walked briskly down the corridor. He had his radio out and was listening to the other Ten Men bantering as they took their positions. They were in high spirits, and why shouldn't they be? Unlike Crawlings, none of *them* had just been threatened by Mr. Curtain. And *they* might have a chance to wreak terrible damage soon, whereas Crawlings was relegated to guarding the building. But he was determined to have his fun, regardless. When he drew near the room where the children were being held, he turned down the radio and began to tiptoe.

Setting down his briefcase ever so quietly, Crawlings unlocked the door and flung it open in one quick movement, hoping to startle the children. Much to his delight, his entrance prompted a cry of alarm — in fact the children appeared not just startled but completely dismayed. And the reason was immediately apparent. They were up to something.

Across the room, a bookcase had been moved aside to expose a large window, which had been raised, and a big desk that previously had been shoved to one side of the room was now sticking halfway out the window. It had been flipped over so that its writing surface was balanced on the window ledge and its legs stood up in the air like those of a petrified animal. The two boys stood frozen by the desk, each holding a leg, and they gaped at Crawlings with horrified, guilty expressions — very much like petrified animals themselves. Beside them the pudgy little girl was scowling ferociously.

"Well, well, chickies!" Crawlings cried. "What are we up to?" As he spoke, he noticed a rope tied around one of the desk legs. They were trying to escape! This was even better than he'd hoped! Now he had a good excuse to punish them.

But just as he was about to stride across the room and snatch the boys violently away from the window, he noticed that the rope stretched across the room and disappeared behind the open door. Crawlings hesitated, his eyebrow twitching with suspicion, and for a split second he considered investigating. But then, seized by the conviction that nothing important was behind the door, and that even now the older girl was outside the window climbing down, Crawlings plunged confidently forward.

A swift, furtive movement from behind the door caught his eye, and he whirled just in time to see Kate's lasso dropping over his head and shoulders. "Now!" she shouted. Crawlings felt the lasso tighten, pinning his arms to his sides. Worse, he felt himself being drawn irresistibly backward, and with rising horror (and a humiliating yelp) Crawlings realized that the boys had shoved the desk out the window — and that he was now tied to the desk.

Completely off balance, Crawlings couldn't keep from staggering backward. But when he came to the wall he managed to fling his legs out, bracing his heels against it, and dropping the radio he caught awkwardly at the window ledge with his hands. He snarled at the boys, who were anxiously dragging Constance out of harm's way. For some reason she looked quite ill, but all Crawlings could think about was getting loose — getting loose and getting even — without being yanked out the window. He couldn't get at the rope without letting go of the ledge.

Kate, meanwhile, had snatched up his radio. "We'll be taking this," she told him as she hurried to the door, "and your briefcase. You won't be needing them, you know, since you're *all tied up* at the moment!" And cutting Crawlings off in mid-curse, she closed the door and locked it.

"That was pretty lame, Kate," said Sticky, already picking up the briefcase.

"I had to say *something*, didn't I? Hey, what's wrong with Constance?"

"Carry her, will you?" Reynie said with a worried look. "I'll take the radio. We can talk while we run."

At the end of the corridor they hid the briefcase in a closet (it was too heavy to keep carrying), then sent the elevator up to the fourth floor and slipped into the stairwell. Their hope — indeed their plan — was that when Crawlings finally got free he would try to recapture them himself, since reporting their escape would be humiliating. Even if he wasn't fooled by the elevator trick, he would probably search for the children in all the wrong places, because the children were going to the last place he would expect — straight to Mr. Curtain.

As they hurried down the stairs, Reynie whispered, "I think you saved us, Constance. I don't think he was going to fall for it."

Constance, clinging weakly to Kate's back, managed the faintest flicker of a smile. "I didn't even mean to," she muttered. "I just saw that he looked suspicious, and we so badly needed him to . . ." She groaned and put a hand to her head. "Oh, but I feel so sick! I feel horrible!"

The others exchanged worried looks, and Sticky whispered, "Do you think she can manage it now? Should we try something else?"

"But what else can we try?" said Kate.

Just then McCracken's voice came over the radio announcing that the van had arrived at the access road and would be at the gate in five minutes.

"I can do it," Constance moaned, resting her head against Kate's shoulder. "I *have* to do it."

"We don't have much choice," Reynie said after a moment's deliberation. "It's now or never. Hang in there, Constance!"

⌣∴⌣

Mr. Curtain was expecting word from McCracken any minute when he heard a suspicious noise in the next room. It was a surreptitious, scraping sound — the sound of someone taking something quietly from a shelf. "Crawlings!" he roared, rocketing out into the corridor. "You have no business —" He screeched to a halt in the neighboring doorway, staring in disbelief.

Four guilty faces stared back at him. Kate had frozen in the process of belting her bucket to her hip. The other three were crouched in the corner, where the Whisperer had been before he and Hertz moved it to his hidden staging room.

All of them looked as if they'd been caught stealing from a cookie jar.

"Snakes and dogs!" Mr. Curtain bellowed. "You? Here? Now? Where is Crawlings? No, never mind — I haven't time for this!" He leaped from the wheelchair and reached into his suit coat.

"We're sorry!" Reynie cried. "Please don't punish us! We'll do whatever you say — you don't have to get the gloves out!"

"Oh, you *will* be punished!" Mr. Curtain snarled, but then he hesitated. He cocked his head, listening — he had left the radio in the other room — and after considering for the briefest of moments he snapped, "It will have to wait until later, however. Come with me at once!"

The children obeyed and soon were in the other room, sitting compliantly in a corner where Mr. Curtain could see them. Grumbling and glaring, he wheeled back and forth between different computers, making minute adjustments and checking readouts. Computer code no longer streamed across the four monitors; he seemed to have finished whatever he'd been doing before.

"Your timing couldn't be worse," Mr. Curtain said, shooting the children an icy look. "But no doubt you planned it that way. Somehow you knew the building was empty. What better time to steal your ridiculous bucket back?"

"It isn't stealing," Kate began, "not if —"

"Do not speak to me!" shouted Mr. Curtain, suddenly looming over Kate like a thundercloud. "Speak to me again and face the consequences! One day you will learn to hold your tongue, Miss Wetherall! Now give me that bucket —

there must be something important inside for you to have taken such a chance retrieving it."

Kate had no choice, and Mr. Curtain was rummaging through the bucket, muttering irritably to himself, when McCracken's voice sounded over the radio: "Mr. Curtain, the van has arrived at the gate. The driver appears to be a red-haired man with glasses. He has called out that his name is Mr. Rubicund."

Mr. Curtain shot over and snatched up the radio, smacking his lips. "Excellent! Very good, McCracken, very good indeed! Ask Mr. Rubicund to answer correctly the question he once missed as a student at my Institute, the question he was sent to the Waiting Room for missing. He'll know what I mean."

"One moment," McCracken said. "I'll ask him now."

The older children were watching Constance out of the corners of their eyes. She appeared to be gazing intently at Mr. Curtain, but she was so pale and shaky she might have been slipping into a daze. After a moment her eyes widened and she whispered, "Something about energy waves produced by the acceleration or the oscill . . . oscill . . ."

"Oscillation?" Sticky whispered frantically. "Energy waves produced by the acceleration or the oscillation of an electric charge?"

Constance nodded. "What you said. But that's just the *question*. I can't . . ." She shook her head in despair. "I can't see the answer . . ."

"Electromagnetic radiation!" breathed Sticky. "That's the answer, Constance — electromagnetic radiation!"

Constance squeezed her eyes closed. Perspiration trickled down her pale cheeks.

McCracken's voice came over the radio again. "He says
the answer to the question was electromagnetic radiation, Mr.
Curtain. He says he still can't believe he missed that one."

"Ha!" Mr. Curtain shouted, and he raised his fists in triumph. "That's it! It really is Rubicund! You may open the
gate, McCracken! Deliver everyone to the conference room
immediately. I have one final adjustment to make, and then
I shall be with them."

Mr. Curtain laughed again. Then, half-closing his eyes,
he began snapping his fingers and jerking his wheelchair
side to side as if dancing. After a moment Reynie realized he
was dancing. He was humming a tune barely audible over
the sound of the wheelchair's rubber tires, which made sharp
chirping noises against the floor, rather like the squeak of
sneakers on a basketball court.

With a final flourish — a somewhat awkward attempt to
make ocean-wave motions with his arms — Mr. Curtain
stopped and leered smugly at the children. "I am exulting,"
he said, "for it is not every day that one's plans, so painstakingly developed and so often delayed by resistance, finally, at
long last, fall so perfectly into —"

He was interrupted by a distant boom. He froze, listening. The boom was followed by a series of crashes and bangs.
"What's happening?" he whispered to himself.

Kate couldn't resist answering his question. "Gosh, Mr.
Curtain," she said, "maybe it's just me, but I think it sounds
kind of like your Ten Men are getting bushwhacked."

It took a moment for this comment to settle in Mr. Curtain's brain. Then his eyes grew very wide, and he slowly turned to fix them on Constance, who was lying on the floor whimpering, too miserable even to gloat. "Contraire!" he gasped. "She . . . she . . ."

"Read your mind?" Kate finished. "Yes, she did."

"And she . . . but she can't possibly have . . ."

"Given the answer to Mr. Benedict? If you say so."

Just then Mr. Curtain's radio crackled, and into the room came the most wonderfully welcome sound in the world — the sound of Milligan's voice. "Constance," he shouted (for in the background was an incredible clamor of crashes and shouts), "you and the others stay where you are! I'm coming for you! I'll be —" His voice cut off, giving way to static.

Mr. Curtain, staring at the radio, began to pant rapidly like a puppy. Anyone else might have thought he was panicking, but Reynie understood he was trying to calm his surging emotions. He could not afford to fall asleep at this most inopportune of times. Slipping the radio inside his suit coat, he shot over to a computer and tapped a rapid sequence onto its keyboard. Then he spun his wheelchair about and barked, "Come with me!"

"Sorry, but no," Reynie said. "We're going to do what Milligan said and stay where we are. You're welcome to wait here with us if you'd like."

"I'm welcome to —?" Mr. Curtain bit his lip, quivering with anger and considering what to do. His eyes were wild, but his voice seemed to regain its assurance as he said, "No, thank you, Reynard. I haven't time for pleasantries. But I encourage you to enjoy the next few minutes — they are all you have." His wheelchair zipped to the doorway, where he paused for a final word without bothering to look back at them. "Oh, you should be aware that I have engaged a defense mechanism. If anyone attempts to disable or destroy my computers, they will explode. Miss Contraire can verify that I am telling the truth."

With that Mr. Curtain shot silently away.

The children exhaled with relief, but they were still much too frightened to congratulate one another, for they had no idea who was winning the battle that raged outside. Kate retrieved her bucket, which Mr. Curtain had left behind, and Reynie patted Constance, who still lay curled up on the floor. Otherwise all they could do was wait and hope.

A long minute passed, during which they continued to hear strange cries and noises from beyond the walls, before Constance opened her eyes and said, "Milligan's coming down the corridor!"

They were still cheering when Milligan burst into the room. His jacket was torn and his face was streaked with dirt and sweat — but he seemed in good shape and even better spirits. "Kate!" he cried, laughing and sweeping her up. "Oh, how glad I am to see you're all right — that *all* of you are! Except, is Constance —?" He went to kneel beside the miserable girl.

"I'll be okay," Constance muttered with her eyes closed, "if you'll just stop talking."

Milligan smiled. "You did very well," he whispered. "Mr. Benedict understood everything perfectly. And now I am going to get you out of here." He glanced quickly around the room. "We had better wreck these computers first."

The children hastily intervened, explaining what Mr. Curtain had done.

"That figures," Milligan said. "He still hopes to use the Whisperer against us. We need to move now."

"Crawlings is down the hall!" Constance suddenly announced. "He's getting off the elevator!"

"How far is that, Kate?" Milligan muttered. He reached into his back pocket and took out a pair of rubber gloves.

"Sixty feet," Kate hissed, watching him with concern. "Um, shouldn't you be getting out your tranquilizer gun?"

"It's jammed," Milligan said, putting on the gloves. "I took an awkward hit. My radio's busted, too. Now go stand against the wall, please. Everything's going to be fine."

The children ran to the wall just as Crawlings's head appeared in the doorway. It only flickered there for an instant — a shiny pate, a single eyebrow — and then the doorway stood empty again. But in that instant Crawlings had perceived that Milligan was unarmed — indeed, Milligan had his hands up to demonstrate this — and when he reappeared his arms were extended and his silver shock-watches gleamed under the fluorescent lights.

Everything happened in a flash: a whiff of cologne, an electric hum, two wires streaking from Crawlings's watches. In the same instant Milligan made blindingly quick snatching motions in the air before him, and then he stood grasping the wires, one in each gloved hand, like a chariot driver holding the reins. Even before Crawlings could look shocked, Milligan had yanked him across the room. Then Crawlings did look shocked (indeed the bristly hairs of his eyebrow all stood on end), and Milligan lowered the unconscious Ten Man to the floor.

The children were beside themselves with amazement.

"Nice trick!" Kate cried, dancing up and down.

"You liked that?" Milligan said. "All right, everyone, time to go."

"You grabbed the wires!" Sticky said, as if Milligan himself didn't know what he'd done, and Reynie nodded excitedly in agreement. "You — you *grabbed* them, Milligan!"

"So I noticed," Milligan said. "And as I may have to do it again, Kate had better carry Constance. Let's get moving now. Oh, and brace yourselves — I'm afraid things are about to get dangerous."

The Courtyard Conflicts

Milligan intended to take them out through the prison gate, but not until it was safer. At the moment, he said, a battle was raging there between his sentries Hardy and Gristle and at least two Ten Men, possibly more. "It depends on how many McCracken dispatched to come after me," he said with a wry smile. "I guess we'll soon find out his opinion of my skills."

Leaning out the doorway, Milligan looked both ways, sniffed the air, then motioned for them to follow him. The children hurried out into the long corridor, where Milligan, having made some private decision, began walking in the direction opposite the elevator.

"Where are we going?" Kate whispered as they followed after him.

"Away from that room," Milligan replied. "The Ten Men will have heard me on the radio telling you to stay put, and by now Mr. Curtain has informed them where you were, so that's where they'll start their search. We don't want to make it easy on them, do we?"

"What about Mr. Benedict and the others?" Reynie asked, glancing apprehensively over his shoulder. "Where are they?"

"Still in the van. Mr. Benedict fell asleep when the battle started. Don't worry, he and the others are disguised as sentries, so the Ten Men probably won't risk a direct assault on the van. And I have twenty more sentries on the way. With luck Hardy and Gristle can hold their own for a while, especially if most of the other Ten Men are out looking for me."

"You mean us," Sticky gasped. He was suddenly having difficulty breathing. There was so much empty corridor behind them, and so many doors on either side, he hardly knew where to look. "We're *with* you."

"That's true," Milligan admitted, leading them around a corner onto the next long corridor. "But we'll stay on the move, and since they'll have to spread out to search for us, I should be able to deal with them one at a . . ." He stopped, cocking his head to the side as if he'd noticed something amiss.

Reynie, following his gaze, saw a door ahead that was

very slightly ajar. Milligan glanced at Constance, who had just lifted her head from Kate's shoulder with a look of confused suspicion. Her eyes were glassy and heavy-lidded, and her chin was shiny with drool, but her nose was wrinkled with distaste.

"Hold on a second," Milligan said. "My shoe's untied."

Sticky instinctively looked down at Milligan's boots, which appeared to be tightly laced. It was hard to get a good look, however, for Milligan was moving swiftly toward the door, and in the next instant had kicked it open and disappeared into the room. There was a shout, a thump, and — oddly — a thin twanging sound like a broken ukulele, and then Milligan reappeared carrying a briefcase.

"That was Garrotte," Milligan said, closing the door softly behind him. "He sends his regards."

Reynie needed a minute before he could hear Milligan over the sound of the blood roaring in his ears. When it had subsided a bit, he interrupted Milligan and asked him to repeat himself.

Milligan started over. Their plan, he said, would be to make a circuit through the building's four wings, each of which would have four corridors that formed a rectangle. "We'll work our way along the sides of each rectangle, do you see? Then we'll move on to the next wing and do the same thing. It's best not to backtrack — if Ten Men get on your trail they inevitably double up."

"Can't we hide in there?" Reynie suggested, gesturing toward the door Milligan had just closed. "If Garrotte's already down, wouldn't it be safer . . ."

Milligan shook his head. "The Ten Men make regular reports by radio. When Garrotte doesn't call in, they'll come running to this spot in full force."

"But how would they know to come *here*?" asked Sticky, who like Reynie much preferred the idea of holing up and waiting for reinforcements.

"Their radios are equipped with tracking devices," Milligan said. "Which, incidentally, is why I'm not using Garrotte's." He put his hands on the boys' shoulders. "Listen, I know it would probably feel better to hide, but in this case the safest thing is to keep moving. Just concentrate on the plan, and we'll be out of here before you know it. Are you ready, Kate?"

"Sure, but will you just move Constance's head to my other shoulder?" Kate said, wincing. "Her chin is starting to dig into my . . . Okay, that's better. Ready!"

With Milligan in the lead and Kate hard on his heels, the group continued down the corridor. The boys trailed some paces behind, looking constantly about and trying hard to focus on the plan. ("Rectangles," Sticky whispered to himself, "rectangles, rectangles, rectangles.") It was of course a very basic plan, hardly worth explaining, and Reynie felt sure Milligan had done so just to give them something less scary to think about. It probably did keep them both a little calmer. But Reynie still couldn't help anxiously wondering how many more doorways might conceal Ten Men, and Sticky kept reaching up and briefly, lightly touching his spectacles, as if to reassure himself they were still there.

Halfway down the corridor, they passed a set of double doors that opened onto the building's interior courtyard.

Through windows in the doors they caught a glimpse of the desk they had tied Crawlings to, now a broken pile of wood and metal, with a frayed length of Kate's rope still attached to one leg. Kate and the boys exchanged glances. Under the circumstances, it was hard to feel more than a flicker of pride at having set such a good trap — but they did, at least, feel a flicker, and it bolstered their courage as they stalked on.

At the next corner Milligan bade them stop. He sniffed the air and frowned. "McCracken," he muttered. "Him I'd rather avoid. We'd better turn around."

"I thought we shouldn't backtrack!" Kate whispered.

"We'll cut across that courtyard to a different wing," Milligan said. "When the time comes to face McCracken, I don't want you anywhere near."

"I agree with Milligan!" Sticky whispered.

Milligan winked at him and quickly ushered the children back to the double doors. Nostrils flaring, he stared out through the windows in the doors for several seconds before nodding and leading them into the courtyard.

Out in the open air, they could hear more distinctly the faraway sounds of conflict — screeches, bangs, and mysterious squawking noises reverberating off distant walls. The sounds were unnerving, and Reynie cringed at every one. But at least they proved the Ten Men hadn't won yet, he told himself as he hurried past the smashed jumble of desk; silence might have disturbed him even more.

Reynie was about to ask Milligan how long it would take the other sentries to arrive when a door in the opposite wing burst open — the very door they'd been heading for — and a madly grinning Sharpe leaped into the courtyard, both hands bristling with clusters of pencils.

His every nerve jangling with alarm, Reynie was still drawing breath to cry out when he found himself tossed to the ground on the far side of the broken desk. A half-second later Sticky crashed on top of him, and as they desperately disentangled themselves they discovered Kate already crouched beside them and Constance huddled at her feet. With hearts in their throats they peeked over the top of the desk.

The air positively swarmed with pencils. They were everywhere, a deadly horizontal rain. Indeed, as Milligan deflected them with Garrotte's briefcase, they made a rattling sound not very different from that of rain on a tin roof. And then the storm was over, and Milligan was still on his feet, although he had been forced to retreat several paces under the onslaught.

Sharpe regarded him cagily, no doubt expecting a return salvo of tranquilizer darts. Like Milligan he was crouching and holding his briefcase before him like a shield. When no darts appeared, however, Sharpe straightened, smiled, and casually adjusted his spectacles, as if he had all the time in the world. He reached into his briefcase again.

Milligan whipped something from inside his jacket and flung it hard across the courtyard. Sharpe saw the sudden movement and looked up, ready to shield himself, but whatever Milligan had thrown sailed off far to the right — a brown blur that missed him by at least twenty feet.

Sharpe hooted with delight as he reached into his briefcase again. "You're losing your touch, Milligan! What was that, anyway? Some kind of stick?"

"You could call it that," Milligan said, just as the boomerang — having arced around the rear of the courtyard — collided with the back of Sharpe's head.

Sharpe fell on his face.

The children jumped to their feet, cheering. But it wasn't over yet. Sharpe had popped right back up again, so fast it was as if he had rebounded into a standing position. His spectacles had been knocked off, his nose was bleeding from his fall, and he was wobbling unsteadily, utterly disoriented by the blow — but in his hand was a laser pointer, and he was aiming it at Milligan.

Everyone froze.

Sharpe's eyes wandered away from Milligan in a dazed, addled way, then wandered back again. With his empty hand he touched his bloody nose, winced, then frowned at the blood on his fingertips. He seemed to have no idea what had happened or where he was. Reynie saw Milligan's knees bend ever so slightly and knew that he was gathering himself for a spring. He had an awful lot of ground to cover, though, and Reynie's heart was hammering in fearful anticipation when — much to his amazement — Sticky cleared his throat and said, "Um, excuse me."

All eyes swiveled to focus on Sticky, including Sharpe's. Trembling with fright, Sticky nonetheless smiled in a friendly, helpful way, and then — moving slowly — he drew his polishing cloth from his shirt pocket and held it to his nose. Then he gestured toward the handkerchief poking out of Sharpe's breast pocket and nodded encouragingly, saying in a small voice, "You . . . you have one . . . right there . . . you can use to . . . um, to stop the bleeding . . ."

The confused Ten Man frowned again and looked down at his breast pocket. Seeing the handkerchief, he brightened with comprehension — a very muddled comprehension — and tugged it out and held it to his bloody nose.

This time he fell on his back.

"That . . . was . . . AMAZING!" Reynie said, throwing his arms around Sticky, and Kate, not to be left out, threw her arms around both of them.

"You'd better let go before I collapse," Sticky wheezed, but he was grinning ear to ear.

"Nice work," Milligan said, tucking his boomerang back inside his jacket. "Now let's move. I'm afraid your cheers may have drawn attention. Not that I didn't appreciate them."

Kate and Reynie let go of Sticky, upon which his knees wobbled a bit and his grin began to fade. (The reality of what he'd just done was beginning to sink in, and the effect was like blood rushing violently to his head.) He staggered to the side, and Kate shot out a hand to steady him.

"Um, Milligan?" Sticky said in a tremulous voice. "Are you absolutely sure we can't just hide somewhere until the other sentries arrive? Surely there's *some* place, right? Sorry, I just don't know how much more of this . . ." He trailed off, looking embarrassed.

Milligan regarded him seriously. "No," he said after a moment, "I'm the one who should be sorry. You've been so brave — all of you have — I forget what a toll this must be taking on you. But I'm still afraid we'd be tracked down and surrounded if we attempted to hide. I really am sorry, Sticky. You know I'd bustle you out the gate this instant if I could, but I simply can't risk getting you so close to that fight — not without knowing how it's going first."

"Milligan, what if we went to the roof?" Reynie suggested. "From up there we could see everything without getting in harm's way."

"Hey, that's true!" Kate said. "We know where the elevator is, Milligan."

"Sixty feet from the room where I found you," Milligan said. "I remember." He shaded his eyes and looked up toward the roof. "Well, I suppose we could cut through an adjoining wing, come at the elevator from the other direction . . ." He glanced sidelong at Sticky, whose face had lit up with an expression of intense hopefulness. "All right, that's not a bad idea. We'll go to the roof, I can see how Hardy and Gristle are faring, and if there's a clear path we'll make a break for the gate. How's that?"

"Great!" Sticky said, and Kate and Reynie nodded.

"If it looks too dangerous, though," Milligan warned, "we'll just have to come back down and keep moving." He stooped to lift Constance, who was still lying limp on the ground, and set her gently onto Kate's back again. "We can't dawdle up there or we might get trapped. Agreed?"

The children, who did rather prefer not to get trapped, agreed.

And so the group of fugitives made their way to the elevator, taking the route that Milligan had settled on. More than once they caught a whiff of expensive cologne, and each time Milligan would stiffen and narrow his eyes — and the children's hairs would stand on end — but they encountered no more Ten Men. And as the children crowded into the elevator with Milligan and felt themselves begin to rise, they felt their hopes begin to rise, too.

Then the elevator doors opened onto the roof, and the first thing they saw was McCracken.

"Stay in the elevator!" Milligan said, needlessly throwing out his arm to keep them back. Beyond him they could see McCracken engaged in a ferocious struggle with two other powerful figures who were striving to keep his arms pinned.

"Moocho!" Kate cried.

"Ms. Plugg!" cried the boys.

Milligan hesitated in the elevator doorway, gritting his teeth. He could not leave the children unprotected, but neither could he just walk away. Moocho Brazos and Ms. Plugg, strong and determined though they might be, were no match for the immensely powerful and treacherous McCracken. Their faces were strained and glistening with perspiration — indeed Ms. Plugg's was apple-red — whereas McCracken, however temporarily inconvenienced, had not even mussed his feathered brown hair. Already he was breaking free of their grip and grinning with expectation. He looked over at the children and laughed.

"Apparently we've all had the same idea!" McCracken called. "The roof's getting much too crowded, don't you think?"

Milligan was trying to think what to do when he felt himself shoved hard from behind. Stumbling forward, he caught his balance and spun to see the elevator doors sliding closed. "I made it easy for you!" Kate called, her tone bright and eager though her face was clouded with worry. "We'll be fine! Now go get him, Milligan!"

Then the doors were closed, and Kate let out a cry of anguish and covered her face.

"You were right to do it," Reynie said after a silence. "He was in an impossible situation. We couldn't just leave them. There was no telling what McCracken would do to them."

"Yes, but what about Milligan?" Kate cried. "His tranquilizer gun is jammed, and . . . and . . . oh, what have I done?"

"Milligan can take care of himself," Sticky said, trying to sound convincing. "The question is what do we do now? Should we . . . should we hide, or keep moving . . . ?"

But Kate could think of nothing except Milligan now. When the doors opened she leaped from the elevator, Constance bobbling wildly on her back. Heedless of the route, entirely forgetting the possibility of running into another Ten Man, Kate dashed down the corridor to the nearest double doors and burst out into the courtyard again. There she ran back and forth, craning her neck as she tried to see what was happening on the roof. Twice she almost stumbled over Sharpe's motionless body, but she paid him no mind whatsoever.

"Kate, you shouldn't be out here — it's too exposed!" said Reynie when he and Sticky had caught up to her.

Kate only shook her head and continued to run back and forth, staring toward the rooftop and grimacing with worry.

"What if Sharpe wakes up?" Sticky said. "We don't want to be here if that happens, Kate."

Kate glanced at the Ten Man, nodded, and putting Constance down she rapidly bound Sharpe's ankles and wrists with the fishing twine from her bucket. For good measure she rubbed his nose with his handkerchief again, then stood and backed away, squinting up toward the roof. It was all she could do not to hurry back up there and try to help. But her presence would only distract Milligan, and she knew it.

"Oh, but I can't bear to stand here doing nothing!" Kate cried aloud. She jumped up and down, staring and staring.

Constance laid her head on the ground and moaned. The boys began whispering urgently, trying to decide what to do. It seemed just as dangerous to go anywhere without Milligan as it was to stand here and wait — hope — for his return. They still could hear the distant skirmishes from somewhere out beyond the building, and who knew where Mr. Curtain was now? And where was the Whisperer? What if he'd moved it to a window or guard tower from which he could peer down and focus on anyone he chose? At the moment, any one place seemed as potentially dangerous as any other — except for the roof, where they *knew* things were bad.

"I see Madge," Kate said, almost absently. The boys looked up to see the falcon's familiar shape circling high above the roof. "She must have seen me getting into the van and followed it here. Oh, Madge, I wish I could see what you can see right now!" She was reaching into her bucket for her whistle when a whirling brown blur streaked out from the edge of the roof, arced, then streaked back out of view.

"Milligan's boomerang!" Sticky said, his voice tinged with hope.

But almost immediately the boomerang sailed out again, its arc much lower this time, and on its return trip it smacked against the edge of the roof and dropped down into the courtyard. It spun erratically and listlessly as it fell, clacking against the wall like a weird wooden bird. The children stared at it lying in the dead grass, the huge crack in it visible even from several paces away.

Kate turned and looked pleadingly at the boys.

"It's up to you," Reynie said after a heavy pause. "I really don't know what's best."

"Remember Constance, though," said Sticky in a low voice. "Reynie and I are too slow if we're carrying her. We need you to do that. We . . ." He trailed off, feeling guilty and helpless. There was Constance to think about, of course, but there was also their friends — and Kate's father — on the roof. "Listen, just do what you think's right, and we'll support it."

Kate's lips were pressed together, and her anguished eyes were fixed on the roof again, but she acknowledged his words with a tight nod. "Two minutes then," she said. "Give me two minutes, and no matter what, I'll come back to carry Constance."

"Go," said the boys.

And Kate went.

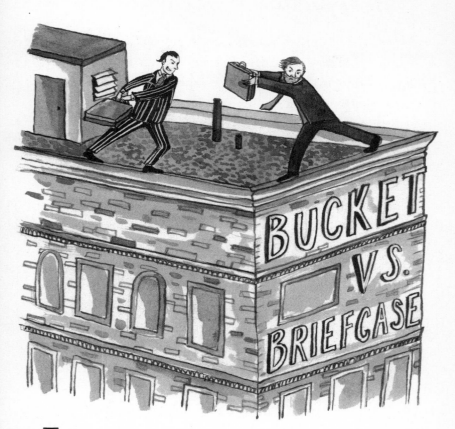

It had been a terribly difficult fight for Milligan. No sooner had the elevator doors closed than McCracken had slipped from the grasp of Ms. Plugg and Moocho Brazos — who had suddenly found themselves clinging to each other instead of the Ten Man — and then in one swift motion had ripped his handkerchief in two and put the separate halves to their noses. Moocho and Ms. Plugg had sagged to the rooftop. Just like that, it was down to McCracken and Milligan.

Only it had not been that simple, for Milligan had also needed to protect his fallen friends — no small task on that exposed rooftop, with a ruthless opponent willing to do whatever necessary to win. In just the first minute of the fight, Milligan had narrowly escaped being struck by a razor-sharp pencil; a spinning clipboard that shrieked like a whistle as it sailed past his ear; and a tiny white projectile — flicked toward his eyes — that appeared to be a tooth.

But Milligan was not without defenses. He still had Garrotte's briefcase, which he used to deflect some of McCracken's projectiles. And he had taken out his tranquilizer gun, which McCracken didn't know was jammed. At the sight of it the Ten Man had sprinted to take cover behind an air-conditioning unit, one of several scattered over the rooftop, and Milligan had kept him pinned behind it as he painstakingly dragged his friends to the elevator.

He had yet to fire a single dart, however, a fact not lost on McCracken, who called out, "You're being unusually stingy, Milligan! Don't tell me you're down to your last dart already!"

"Don't tell you?" Milligan grunted, keeping his broken weapon leveled at the air-conditioning unit. "But I thought we weren't keeping secrets from each other anymore."

"It's true we've grown quite close," said McCracken, peeking out in time to see Milligan leaping free of the elevator, into which he had successfully dragged Moocho and Ms. Plugg. The doors were sliding closed, and Milligan was tucking a utility tool into his pocket.

"Aren't you going with them?" McCracken called, ducking as Milligan raised the tranquilizer gun again. "You'll be joining them soon, anyway, you know."

"I hate elevators," Milligan said. "People are always getting stuck in them." As he spoke there came a clanging, screeching sound from behind the elevator doors.

"Ah, you've jammed it! To protect them, I assume? Surely you realize I can get the doors open."

"You won't waste time on that," Milligan said, reaching into his jacket. "You have other orders."

"Indeed I do," McCracken laughed, rising with his briefcase at the ready. "And now you've forced me to take the stairs! How wicked of you, Milligan! Such punishment! What will you do next — insist I eat broccoli?"

"Try this instead!" Milligan said, flinging the boomerang.

McCracken was far cleverer than Sharpe was. He knew a boomerang when he saw it, even one thrown at such a high speed, and gracefully ducked Milligan's as he moved to get into a better position. Worse, he had sniffed out the truth about the tranquilizer gun and was moving now with much greater freedom and speed.

Milligan caught the boomerang and prepared to throw it again. He knew he would never hit McCracken with it. He had known it the first time, in fact. But he also knew that McCracken would never let him reach the stairs, that the Ten Man was gathering himself for a furious attack, and that the only advantage left to him was surprise.

Milligan threw the boomerang again, this time much lower, and the throw seemed so obviously errant that McCracken glanced around to see if Milligan had been aiming at something else — something explosive, perhaps.

Seeing nothing, he looked back to find Milligan bearing down on him with startling speed.

McCracken had no time to reach into his briefcase. Indeed, it was all he could do to retain possession of it, for Milligan came after him with such astonishing swiftness and agility — sometimes swinging Garrotte's briefcase, sometimes flying out with his hands and feet — that McCracken was hard-pressed to defend himself. He was not a Ten Man for nothing, however, and backing away from Milligan he parried and countered with his own briefcase. And in this way, in close and furious combat, the two men moved rapidly across the rooftop, away from the courtyard, with Milligan constantly on the attack and McCracken struggling to keep his balance.

And then abruptly they arrived at the edge of the roof and found themselves battling there, balancing upon the very precipice, four stories above the rear of the prison complex.

Both men were perspiring. Both were smiling. But only one of them was winning — and both of them knew it. The Ten Man was stronger by far, and Milligan had been at a disadvantage from the beginning.

"It's almost over, Milligan," McCracken said, swinging his briefcase around with the force of a wrecking ball. "You see that, don't you?"

Milligan ducked — the wind from the briefcase ruffled his hair — then rose in a burst, swinging Garrotte's briefcase up toward McCracken's chin. "I can't," he panted. "Your big head's in the way."

McCracken leaned back just in time. He wobbled at the

edge, recovered, and brought his briefcase down like a cudgel, narrowly missing Milligan's twisting shoulder. But the dodge had put Milligan off balance, and in the next instant McCracken kicked the briefcase out of his hand. It went sailing out and away off the roof — and Milligan, in a desperate attempt to catch it, slipped from the edge.

Even as his keen eyes scoured the wall for a handhold, Milligan heard Kate's cry of horror from somewhere across the rooftop. But his eyes were focused on a tiny section of crumbled brickwork below him, with a gap in the mortar in which some long-ago bird had built its nest. Milligan managed to thrust his hand into this gap as he fell, and his strong fingers found their grip. Twigs and lint from the destroyed nest sifted down over his face as he hung there, twisting this way and that several feet below the rooftop.

"Kate!" Milligan shouted. "Kate, I'm all right! Run! *Run*, Kate!"

But Milligan was not all right, and Kate knew it. She had peeked out from the rooftop stairwell just in time to see him fall, and she understood the situation perfectly well. Maybe for the moment Milligan had found something to hang on to, but he was a sitting duck for McCracken, who glanced toward her with a delighted expression and called out: "Yes, do, Kate! Run off now and let the grown-ups speak privately!" He made a shooing motion with his hand. "I'll be along in a moment!"

Kate didn't budge, however. Her heart was pounding; she was boiling with anger and fear; and yet she was trying hard to think clearly, for she would need all her wits to save Milligan.

Seeing her still standing there, McCracken cocked his head to the side and raised his eyebrows as if to say, "Yes? Are you really going to be so bold?" And he was smiling as if he hoped she would be.

Kate flipped open her bucket.

McCracken laughed and reached into his briefcase.

Then Kate charged, and McCracken stopped laughing.

The Ten Man knew the girl was talented, but he was quite unprepared for the ferocity of the attack she now unleashed upon him. Though a great expanse of rooftop lay between them, the items from her bucket that she flung at him now arrived much faster than he would have expected — and all were thrown with uncanny accuracy. First came a barrage of marbles, mere nuisances he deflected with his briefcase, but then a horseshoe magnet winged past his face, narrowly missing him. Next came a flashlight, which actually managed to knock a pencil from his hand, stinging his fingers. With a twitch of irritation McCracken took out another pencil — more quickly this time — and whipped it toward the girl, who had already cut the distance between them by half.

Clink! went the pencil as Kate deflected it with her bucket, and then she was on the offensive again. What came flying at McCracken next were a bottle of extra-strength glue, an almost empty roll of twine, and a slingshot. These last attacks were pathetic, however, and as McCracken batted the projectiles away he reflected that she was running out of steam, not to mention things to throw. What was more, McCracken noticed that she was puffing hard on what appeared to be a broken whistle (it produced only a sort of thin squeal) — no doubt trying, and sadly failing, to summon help.

Then the girl threw the precious bucket itself. It came soaring along at such an enticingly slow speed that McCracken had time to laugh with anticipation before smashing it sideways with his briefcase. It made a satisfying metallic crunching sound as it flew away off the roof.

And now she was only ten paces away, still coming toward him, still puffing absurdly on that broken whistle — and apparently with one last thing to throw. She lofted it now, and it flew toward his face at a pitifully slow speed, a small dark object of indeterminate substance. McCracken was tempted to snatch it out of the air just to see what it was. But it appeared somewhat oily and nasty, and so he merely tilted his head to let it fly past without soiling him.

And then suddenly, out of nowhere, something larger and far more frightening appeared, something with glistening cold eyes hurtling directly toward his face, its wickedly sharp beak and talons extended — and the colossal, elegant McCracken could not help but cry out and flap his arms and shield his face like a panicked child trying to ward off a bee. He was so completely taken aback that he almost didn't notice his briefcase being yanked from his hand.

Then the moment passed, and McCracken dropped his arms. The falcon was sailing away with its piece of meat, and the girl — the clever girl! — was running off with his briefcase. Halfway across the roof she skidded to a stop, stooped to pick something up, and then calmly walked back in his direction. She was aiming Milligan's tranquilizer gun at him.

McCracken's mood improved at once. He straightened up again, smoothing his tie, and said, "I'm impressed, plucky! What a trick! Why, you have more talent than most of my men! You should be proud — your ploy almost worked!"

Kate, who had indeed been feeling proud (and not a little surprised) to have gotten McCracken's briefcase away from him, and even to have gained the upper hand, felt her confidence diminish. Why had he said "almost"? She stopped and said, "You can keep your compliments. Now get away from the edge of the roof."

"But why should I do as you say?" McCracken asked, crossing his massive arms like a petulant child. He was eyeing his briefcase.

"I assume you'd prefer not to fall off when I knock you out," Kate said.

"Oh! So you intend to shoot me with a dart?"

"I might spare you a minute or two if you do what I say," Kate said cagily. "Now why don't you take your tie off and leave it there? After I pull Milligan up, we'll decide what to do with you."

"Very well," said McCracken, and with a mysterious smirk he reached for his tie.

It had taken Milligan a few moments to understand what was happening above him, but now he shouted, "Kate! Run! He knows the gun's jammed! *Run*, Kate!"

Kate blanched. "Oh. Well, it *has* been two minutes, I bet. Do excuse me." And with that, she turned and bolted for the stairs.

Disappointed, McCracken watched her go. She really was impressively fast, even carrying his heavy briefcase. He hurried over to the edge of the roof and smiled down at Milligan, still hanging precariously by one hand. "I have to run, Milligan — the little vixen took off with my briefcase — but please do hang on if you can. I'll be back in a jiffy with something heavy to drop."

Milligan started to say something — anything to give Kate a better head start — but McCracken had already turned and run away across the rooftop.

In the courtyard, Constance and the boys were crouching behind Sharpe, whom they had propped into a sitting position against the wrecked desk. Their hope had been that anyone glancing out a window would be too preoccupied to look closely and spot them. It was like hiding behind a tiger to avoid lions, but at least the tiger was asleep.

"That was more like three minutes," Constance mumbled when Kate appeared. She hadn't even opened her eyes. Kate didn't seem to hear her, though, and Constance whimpered pathetically, too miserable to repeat herself.

Kate was panting hard, but there was no time to catch her breath. "We need to . . . hide the . . . briefcase!"

"What happened, Kate?" Sticky asked. "What's going on?"

"Where's Milligan?" Reynie asked.

"He's coming," Kate said between gasps, then with an apologetic look she added, "but I think . . . McCracken's coming first. That's why . . . we need to . . ."

She was interrupted by an explosion of glass and wood. What appeared to be an enormous cannonball — it was large, black, and round — had just burst through a second-floor window. The three of them went reeling backward in surprise. The object hit the ground rolling, then abruptly unfurled and straightened up, revealing itself to be a man in a dark suit. It was McCracken. He had taken a shortcut.

"Hello, dumplings," McCracken said with a gap-toothed smile. Gripping the lapels of his suit coat, he flapped and shook vigorously, sending bits of glass and wood splinters flying in all directions. "Goodness! I haven't hurried so in years. But, you see, I was afraid you'd be naughty and hide my briefcase."

They wanted to flee, but they had Constance to consider, and Kate was so winded she was still trying to get Constance off the ground when McCracken snatched the briefcase from her. In an instant he had reached inside and taken out his laser pointer.

"If one of you would like some attention," McCracken said, wiggling the laser pointer, "please try to run away. I'll be happy to single you out."

No one moved.

McCracken laughed. "So shy!" Keeping the pointer at the ready, he glanced around the courtyard. "I need to run back up to the roof for a minute — I have some unfinished business with Milligan — but I'm afraid there's nothing proper to chain you to here, and I can't have you wandering off . . ." He sighed. "Very well, I'm afraid it's nap time, children. I suppose I'll be carrying you later, but there's no help for it. Do line up."

The children huddled together. The older ones put their

arms around Constance, and they all steeled themselves and looked up at McCracken defiantly.

And in looking up, Reynie saw a figure on the rooftop. At least he thought he did. He quickly lowered his gaze so as not to draw McCracken's attention, and when he glanced up again a moment later, the figure wasn't there. He had thought — hoped — it might be Milligan. Was he so desperate that he'd imagined it?

"Excellent," McCracken said. "If you hold on to one another like that, this will go much more quickly." He cocked his head, squinted, and held up two fingers as if framing them for a photograph. "Yes, now hold it just like that . . ."

"Can't we get you in the picture, too?" Reynie said, as friskily as he could. He was trying to stall, and McCracken always seemed to enjoy bantering with his victims.

"I'm touched," McCracken said, amused. Then he snapped his fingers. "I know! Perhaps we should have Pandora in the picture as well!" McCracken reached into his briefcase again and took out an elegantly decorated cigar box. He gave it a shake. From inside came a squealing, snapping noise.

"Um, just for the record, I'm fine with not having her in the picture," Sticky put in.

"Me, too," said Kate. "She sounds fussy."

McCracken grinned. "Who's the fussy one?" he said. "Very well, perhaps later, after you've had a chance to get to know her." He set the box at his feet. "Well, then. I have enjoyed our conversation, but there is work to be done for us grown-ups. Hold still, please." He began shaking his arms.

It was clear there would be no more stalling. Once again they braced themselves, their eyes drawn irresistibly to McCracken's large silver shock-watches, which glinted menacingly as they came clear of his shirt cuffs. And as McCracken raised his arms, holding his palms toward them, Reynie and Kate were both thinking helplessly, *Milligan, where are you? Where are you? Where are you?*

❧

As it happened, Milligan was on the roof. He had arrived there by scraping away old mortar with his utility tool to create finger holds. Painstakingly, laboriously, he had made his way up the side of that wall, inch by inch and brick by brick, only to discover that the ever-cautious McCracken had locked the metal door to the stairs. Ordinarily this wouldn't have mattered; Milligan would have picked the lock or pried open the doors to the elevator. But his fingers — indeed his entire arms — were trembling violently from the arduous climb (it's no easy matter clinging to the side of a wall) and at the moment Milligan could scarcely grip his utility tool, much less wield it effectively.

And yet he must do something! Kate had saved him so that he could save *her*, and Milligan would do anything in the world not to fail her.

Looking down into the courtyard, he saw McCracken lining the children up. There was no question what he meant to do. Milligan cast about for something heavy to throw. He found various sharp pencils and other small implements, but nothing he could throw with any accuracy from this height, certainly not with his useless trembling fingers.

Precious seconds had passed. Another glance into the courtyard. Now McCracken was shaking those enormous arms . . . he was holding up his palms . . . the children were cowering together . . .

Desperately Milligan looked about him one last time for something to throw.

There was nothing.

⌣∶∾

"You'd better enjoy this," Kate was saying, her teeth clenched. "Because Milligan's going to make you pay pretty heavily for it."

"Oh, you can be sure I'll enjoy it," McCracken said with a wink. "And why don't you just let me worry about Milligan? For now, sleep well, my little cheeries!"

An electric whine filled the air, and all the children closed their eyes except Kate. It was only Kate, then, who saw McCracken suddenly flattened to the ground — struck from above by something very large indeed. Everyone heard the incredible *whump!*, however, and their eyes flew open to see McCracken lying unconscious before them. To their astonishment they saw that on top of McCracken was another person, also unconscious.

Milligan, having found nothing else to throw, had thrown himself.

⌣∶∾

"Oh, Milligan, not again!" cried Kate, rushing to his side as the boys stood helplessly by.

Milligan's eyelids fluttered open, and his gaze settled

upon Kate's face. He opened his eyes wide and blinked several times, trying to focus.

Kate laid her hand against his cheek. "Why do you keep doing this? Why do you keep getting hurt?"

"Bad habit," Milligan mumbled. "How's McCracken?"

"You knocked him out," said Kate. "He seems to have broken his Pandora's box with his face."

It was true. Bits of wire and spring were scattered all about the Ten Man's huge square jaw, some of them still twitching and making weird twanging sounds. Perched in a nest of coiled wire were two AA batteries. Pandora had been a terrifying threat, but evidently an empty one.

"Can you move?" Kate asked.

Milligan thought a moment, then raised his right arm. "I can move this," he said, wincing. "But never mind about me — you need to get out of here. It's much too exposed, and I can't protect you now. Go on, Kate. I don't want to have fallen four stories for nothing."

"We can't leave you! I'll — I'll rig something up with that broken desk . . ."

"No," Milligan said firmly. "No sledges this time. This isn't a race, Kate, it's cat-and-mouse. Just give me McCracken's laser pointer. Don't worry, I don't have to last long. Help is on the way, and anyway, it's you Mr. Curtain wants — he'll try to use you to bargain his way out of this. The crucial thing is for you to avoid being caught."

"But —"

"You'll only draw fire on me if you stay here, Kate. The safest thing for all of us is if you go."

This might have been a ploy, but it did the trick. "Well . . . but where should we go?" Kate asked reluctantly.

"Anywhere but here. Just keep moving, don't get cornered, and don't go near the Whisperer. Do you think Constance can tell you when someone's coming?"

She turned to Constance, who was curled up in a ball, shivering and whimpering.

"Maybe?" Kate said.

"Doubtful," said Sticky.

"Then keep your eyes open," Milligan said. "And your noses, too. When the other sentries arrive the Ten Men will sound an alarm. When you hear that, make your way toward the gate — but you still have to avoid being seen, is that clear?"

Kate nodded. "Oh, Milligan, it's clear, but . . ."

"We'll talk about how hard this was when it's all over, okay? Right now what I need from you is action, Kate."

That did it. Kate kissed him and stood up quickly, and the boys wished him luck. Then they helped poor Constance onto Kate's back, and the four of them hurried out of the courtyard, stopping only to look back one last time at Milligan. He waved to them from where he lay, looking perfectly relaxed, as if he had just settled down for a bit of a rest, and as if it were the most natural thing in the world to be using a Ten Man for a pillow.

THE
SORTING
OUT

"Let's check the gate," Reynie said when they had gone inside. "If it's clear, why not get out now?"

"We could scout it out from the roof," Sticky suggested.

"No, the elevator's jammed," Kate said. "I think Moocho and Ms. Plugg are in there. I hope so, anyway, because I didn't see them on the roof."

"What about the stairs?" Sticky asked.

"Too risky, don't you think? We might get trapped up there, and there's no other way down except the way Milligan came."

"Okay, forget the stairs," Sticky said.

"Come on," Reynie said. "We'll sneak as close as we can to the gate and take a peek."

And so, with their eyes peeled and their noses in the air, the Society set off. Running furtively down corridor after corridor, peeking around corners before hurrying on, they found their way at last to the building's main entrance at the front of the prison complex. There was an empty lobby there, with an empty reception desk and empty, dusty chairs. But the place was full of sound — shocking, enormous, violent sound — and as they crept forward to peer out through the front doors (large double doors with windows in them, like the courtyard entrances), the children already knew that the path to the gate wouldn't be clear. The incredible screeching, squealing, and banging warned of complete mayhem outside. And sure enough, looking out, they beheld a most intense and curious battle taking place.

Hertz, the Ten Man in the seersucker suit, was in a fight with two vehicles. Spinning, running, lashing out with his necktie (which he held like a bull whip), Hertz snarled and laughed as a sleek black van and the Ten Men's fake ambulance maneuvered around him like angry elephants — roaring, charging, backing up, and blaring horns. One moment Hertz's tie would wrap around a door handle and he would start to yank the door open; the next he would have to give up the attack and leap aside as the other vehicle bore down on him. The van kept sounding its horn, and the ambulance its siren, apparently in an attempt to disorient him. His briefcase lay open on the ground, but the vehicles weren't giving the Ten Man any chance to reach into it; the best he could do was kick it out of the way whenever one started to roll over it.

Through the windows they gaped with wide eyes and wrinkled noses (the odor of burnt rubber reached them even inside the building), trying to determine whether it would be possible to make it to the gate unnoticed. But some seconds passed before they could make any sense of the spectacle — not least because smoke from the madly spinning tires drifted in clouds over the scene, now obscuring one vehicle, now the other. But then a gust of wind momentarily cleared the air, and with a jolt they recognized the drivers of the vehicles: Rhonda and Number Two.

"Whoa!" Kate said.

"They're unbelievable!" said Reynie.

Sticky nodded, but he was already turning away. "We can't possibly go out there, though. So what do we do?"

"Let's go out the back," Kate said, trotting past him to take the lead. "I'm getting an idea."

Again they sneaked through the empty corridors, pausing to listen at every odd sound, and at one point narrowly avoiding discovery as two Ten Men burst out of a room and walked quickly toward the front of the prison. ("Are you serious?" one was asking the other. "But wouldn't that diminish the market value?" The other shrugged and said he only knew what he'd been told.) Luckily the children had smelled cologne in the corridor and slipped through a different doorway just in time.

At last they reached the rear of the prison complex. Peeking out another set of double doors, they saw S.Q. Pedalian loping along in the distance, speaking into his radio as he hurried around a corner of the building. He was carrying Garrotte's briefcase, the one Milligan had dropped from the roof. Then he was gone, and save for the widespread demolition debris and the looming crane near the wall, the area seemed clear.

Kate pursed her lips, listening, then led the boys toward the building's opposite corner, away from the one S.Q. had rounded. On a mound of rubble along the way she discovered her half-crushed bucket, its flip-top dangling by a sliver of metal — she removed the flip-top with a jerk, as one removes a loose tooth — and despite its poor condition she belted it on again as a matter of principle.

At the side of the building they saw the large open-sided shed she'd told them about. The Salamander was still there, sitting in plain view and seemingly unattended.

"Constance," Reynie whispered as they stole toward the shed, "is anyone hiding in the Salamander?"

Constance snorted, shuddered, and looked up with wild eyes. Several strands of Kate's ponytail clung to her damp face. "What?"

Reynie cringed, laid a finger to his lips, and repeated the question.

"Who cares?" Constance muttered, and buried her face in Kate's ponytail again. It was unclear whether she'd actually been awake. But obviously she wasn't going to be of much use.

Kate laid her gently on the ground and tiptoed over to inspect the Salamander. With a look of relief, she motioned the boys over. "I know how to drive it," she said, "but it would be great if we could activate the noise-cancellation thingy, wouldn't it? We could break out without anyone even noticing." She pointed to a complicated panel of switches and buttons.

Reynie looked at Sticky. "Can you figure it out?"

Sticky bent close to the panel, studying it. "I think this will do it," he said, throwing two switches and turning a dial. "It ought to —" His mouth kept moving, but no more words came out, for all sound around them ceased. It was the strangest sensation, like having one's ears plugged by invisible fingers. They looked at one another and nodded.

The boys took seats on benches near the front, their movements utterly, eerily silent. Kate leaped down and retrieved Constance, then started the engine — they could *feel* the vibrations but heard nothing — and took the wheel. The Salamander backed silently out of the shed, jerked to a stop, and eased toward the rear of the complex.

As they moved along, Sticky continued to study the panel of switches. Something had caught his attention — a curious little antenna he couldn't account for — and he started to mention it to Reynie and Kate, but of course he couldn't. The Salamander rounded the corner, and Kate pointed toward a section of the prison wall that seemed ready to buckle. Weblike fissures ran outward from a damaged, crumbling portion about ten feet up. Reynie looked from the wall to the gigantic metal beam suspended from the crane nearby. He suspected Kate was right; something had gone wrong with the crane, and that beam had struck the wall. As they drew closer he noticed the yellow hazard tape wrapped around the operator's cab of the crane, warning people away.

Kate steered the Salamander in a wide path around the dangling beam (even Kate could be sensibly cautious sometimes), then stopped and motioned for the boys to get out. With a flurry of gestures she indicated she intended to ram the damaged wall. She had mentioned this plan earlier, when they were running through the corridors. But she hadn't provided much detail, and now Reynie and Sticky responded with gestures that meant, "What about you?" Kate indicated that she intended to jump out before the collision.

Moderately satisfied, Reynie and Sticky climbed down and reached up to take Constance. They carried her a safe distance away, hearing after a dozen paces or so the crunch of their own footsteps and, from a distance, the continuing sounds of conflict.

"It's like breaking out of a prison of silence," Reynie said.

"Don't jinx us," Sticky said. "We haven't broken out of anything yet."

As Kate backed up the Salamander to get a good start at the wall, they did their best to make Constance comfortable on the ground. She mumbled and moaned — she was absurdly miserable — but there was little they could do for her at the moment.

"By the way," Sticky muttered to Reynie, "Mr. Curtain also added —" But he stopped speaking when they saw the Salamander lurch forward. Kate had gunned the engine.

The Salamander accelerated rapidly and was soon moving so fast that the boys were horrified at the thought of Kate's leaping out of it. Then they were horrified she might not leap out at all, for she was still at the wheel and the wall was fast approaching. But at the last instant she turned, ran, and leaped out the back, tumbling backward from the momentum when she hit the ground. Then she sprang up with a grin, threw out her arms, and took a bow, as if this weren't an escape attempt but rather a spectacle put on for an appreciative audience.

In truth it *was* a spectacle. Even as Kate bowed, the Salamander smashed into the wall behind her, sending up a great cloud of dust. The razor wire atop the wall snapped like twine and went furling away in both directions, and cinder blocks and vast chunks of cement fell down all around the Salamander. The debris hammered the armored vehicle with such force that it shuddered visibly with each impact, yet so soundlessly they might have been giant wads of cotton.

And then the show was over. The Salamander had come to a rest with its nose jutting out on the far side of the wall. Rubble lay all around and inside it, but beyond the Salamander the boys could plainly see Stonetown River rushing past. They were seconds away from freedom.

And yet the breakout was not as quiet as they had hoped. The crash itself may have been silent, but it was instantly followed by a curious whining sound that seemed to come from two separate directions, traveling along the tops of the prison walls. Reynie and Sticky grimaced at each other, realizing what it was. All around the prison the razor wires, vibrating from the Salamander's impact, were sending out a telltale, spooky song.

"Quick!" Reynie said, and Sticky stooped to help him get Constance onto her feet.

Kate was trotting away from the Salamander, smiling with satisfaction. As soon as she could hear her footsteps, she congratulated herself. "Not bad, Kate. Now you just have to —" Her voice was cut off in mid-sentence. Startled, she glanced behind her — and a cry of fright passed soundlessly from her lips.

The Salamander had reversed out of the wall and was rapidly bearing down on her. Already it was so close that it filled her vision completely. She had no time to leap out of the way, and with half a second's delay she would have been struck — but Kate didn't delay. She flung herself down and let the huge machine pass silently over her, its bulk blotting out the sun, its enormous treads churning the earth on either side. Then it was past, and leaping up Kate saw the boys dragging Constance out of the Salamander's path.

"— a remote control!" she heard Sticky saying to Reynie.

And looking past them she saw Mr. Curtain.

He sat in his wheelchair near the building's back door, his face livid with fury, manipulating a small device in his hand. "This is mine!" he snarled as the Salamander rolled to a stop beside him. (Evidently he'd switched off the noise cancellation.) "You are not to touch it!"

"Too late," said Kate simply. "And it's too late for *you*, too," she added, and was looking for a snappy way to elaborate when her brain registered the familiar red helmet he was wearing. Speech failed her. Her heart, already hammering, tripled its pace. The helmet was affixed to the back of his wheelchair.

Mr. Curtain had made the Whisperer portable.

So this was the final adjustment Mr. Curtain had been working on, this wicked improvement on his wicked invention. And yet so much had not gone according to plan, and his expression betrayed a complicated mixture of fury, disappointment, outrage, and triumph.

"You have spoiled my day, children," Mr. Curtain said sharply. "But as you can see, there is always the night. Now tell me, where has your protection gone? Can it possibly be that you have been left to fend for yourselves? Oh dear, how unfortunate for you!"

"The same could be said for you," Kate retorted.

"On the contrary, Miss Wetherall, I am once again in control. Come with me now and I will spare you the gloves. I may even let you keep your memories. You shall be my defense as I track down and eliminate my enemies."

"We won't do it, Mr. Curtain," Reynie said, and though he knew he should be terrified, he felt strangely unafraid. Was he just too used to being frightened? "We won't do what you say. You should know that by now."

Mr. Curtain narrowed his eyes. "You prefer to be brainswept, I see."

"You might want to save your energy," Reynie said. "There are twenty more agents on their way here right now, and Milligan's already taken care of McCracken and most of your other thugs. How tired are you right now, Mr. Curtain? Do you feel strong enough to brainsweep twenty agents?"

Mr. Curtain stared hard at him. "I do not trust you in the least, Reynard . . ." A shadow passed over his face, an expression first of doubt and then of angry wonder. "And yet . . . I sense you're telling the truth. There really are more agents on the way. And McCracken hasn't responded to my radio calls . . ."

"Because he's down for the count!" said Sticky, stepping boldly forward. "Just like Sharpe. Just like Crawlings and Garrotte. Try calling *them* on the radio! Reynie's telling the truth, all right."

Mr. Curtain hissed at him, and Sticky jumped back in fright.

"I thank you for your suggestion, Reynard," Mr. Curtain said coldly. "Perhaps I *had* better save my energy. Rather than waste my Whisperer on your little brains, I shall simply make use of my gloves. This is your last chance to obey. You will form a circle around me as we move —"

Reynie interrupted him. "If he comes after us, scatter," he said to his friends. "He can't chase us all down — he doesn't have time." Sticky nodded, and Kate slung Constance up onto her back. They prepared to run.

Mr. Curtain glared. "Your foolishness grows tiresome, Reynard. There is no need to catch all of you. One shall provide insurance enough. And the easiest to catch shall also be the most useful."

Everyone knew who he meant, including Constance, who opened her bloodshot eyes long enough to bug them out at him. Then she closed them and lowered her head again, too sick even to be impertinent.

Mr. Curtain snorted and looked at Kate. "Are you tired, Miss Wetherall? You look it, I'm afraid. You do indeed. And you have no chance of outrunning me. My wheelchair never tires, and you are carrying extra weight. Perhaps you should unburden yourself and make it easier on everyone."

"Fat chance," Kate growled. "Even if you catch me, I'll fight you. Believe me, you won't like it."

"Oh, I think I will," said Mr. Curtain dryly. He reached inside his suit coat and took out his gloves.

"We'll *all* fight you!" Sticky yelled, and he shook his fist at Mr. Curtain. (Then, feeling slightly ridiculous, he coughed and lowered his arm.)

"He's right," Reynie said. "You may be stronger and faster, and you may have those gloves, but there are three of us and only one of you. And you have to go soon or you'll risk being caught."

Mr. Curtain seemed extremely taken aback. "Risk? Caught? You dare suggest to *me* . . ." He began taking deep breaths to calm himself, and Reynie noticed that his knuckles were white from clenching the armrests of his wheelchair. Evidently he realized that they were prepared to do what they said. They were ready to engage in a fight they would certainly lose — indeed, painfully lose — in order to protect their whiny friend, and Mr. Curtain had no idea how to handle it.

Reynie pressed the advantage. "This isn't about winning anymore, Mr. Curtain. It's about getting *away*."

Mr. Curtain started to reply, then cut himself off, clamping his mouth shut and staring upward at the sky. He was breathing noisily through his lumpy nose.

"Your only chance," Reynie went on, "is to jump in the Salamander right now and drive out through that hole in the wall. Delaying will only get you captured. It's up to you."

Mr. Curtain slowly lowered his gaze to Reynie's face. "I see what you are up to," he said. "You think if I do what you suggest, I'll have to leave my Whisperer behind. You think it's too heavy for me to lift into my Salamander alone." He drummed his fingers on his armrests, his eyes darting back and forth.

"But you can see Reynie's right," Sticky said. "If you want to have any chance of escaping, you'd better do it now."

"Do not pretend to be interested in my welfare, George, and I will not feign interest in yours." Mr. Curtain was nodding to himself, as if he were arriving at a decision. "I assure you, if I must make my exit, it will not be without my Whisperer. It is everything I have, do you see? No, of course you do not see. No matter. It is my all, and I will protect it at all costs. Therefore at least one of you must come as my hostage."

"I think we've been through this already," Kate said tartly. "There's no way . . ."

But she didn't finish her thought, for Mr. Curtain had just taken out his radio.

"You think your Ten Men will come help you?" Reynie said, thinking fast. "They have problems of their own." As if to prove his point, a boom and scattered shouts rang out in the distance. (For all Reynie knew, this was a worse sign for them than for Mr. Curtain — but Mr. Curtain couldn't be sure, either.) "They're probably wishing they had a different employer right about now."

Mr. Curtain hesitated, offered Reynie a sardonic smile, then raised the radio and did exactly what Reynie had hoped he would do. "S.Q.! Come to the rear of the prison at once — at *once*, S.Q.! Do not make me —"

S.Q. could not have been far away, for almost immediately he appeared around the corner of the building, running at full tilt. There was nothing left to do now, Reynie thought, but hope he was right.

As S.Q. ran up, Reynie looked him straight in the eyes. "Don't do what he says, S.Q.! You know he wants to hurt us! You *know* he does, S.Q.!"

Stunned, S.Q. drew up short, looking back and forth between Mr. Curtain and the children. "But . . ."

"But?" Mr. Curtain snapped. "*But?* You may not say 'but' to me, S.Q. Pedalian!"

S.Q. cringed and turned apologetically to the children. "I'm sorry. You just don't understand . . ."

"But we do understand!" Kate said, shaking her head. "You want to do what's right, and you want to believe that Mr. Curtain is good — but he isn't, S.Q.! Think about it! What he tells you never *feels* right, does it?"

"I . . . well, I don't . . ." S.Q. shifted back and forth, clutching at his head.

"We know what it's like, S.Q.," Sticky joined in. "Not wanting to be alone, wanting to have a family. We've all been there. But you can have that and do what's right, too. Trust your instincts, S.Q.!"

Mr. Curtain was quaking with rage; his forehead pressed hard against the front of the Whisperer's helmet. "*S.Q.!*" he bellowed. "Stop chattering with them and do as I say! This is absolutely your last chance —"

"Or what?" Reynie challenged, turning on him. "You'll start removing his memories again?"

S.Q. gaped at Mr. Curtain, whose shock was plain enough. It was the shock of having been exposed, not of having been falsely accused, and S.Q. saw this as clearly as anyone. After a long moment he drew himself up and shook his head. "No," he said. "No, I won't do it, Mr. Curtain. I won't do what you say."

Mr. Curtain's jaw dropped. "You . . . but you . . ."

"Won't do it," S.Q. finished. "That's what I said." He glanced at the Salamander, then at the hole in the prison wall. "I'll help you get away, Mr. Curtain. I don't want anything to happen to you. I'll help you escape — but I'm not touching these children."

Mr. Curtain let loose a shriek of outrage. "Then *I'll* touch them!" he snarled, whipping his wheelchair around. "And I'll deal with *you* —"

The children were getting ready to bolt when the double doors banged open and someone shouted, "Ledroptha! Stop!"

Out through the doors came a frazzled Mr. Benedict, doubled over and breathing hard. His suit coat was torn, his shirt was half untucked, and in his hair were bits of red fuzz from the wig he'd worn as Mr. Rubicund. Staggering over to put himself between Mr. Curtain and the children, he panted, "Leave them . . . alone . . . Ledroptha. It's finished . . . anyway."

Mr. Curtain was so furious it was a wonder he was still awake. "How dare *you* tell *me* when anything is finished, Benedict? No! No! No! I shall tell *you* when it is over! And for you it is over right now!" And flipping a switch on his wheelchair, he glared at Mr. Benedict with such hideous intensity that it was alarming even to look at his face.

"Very well, Ledroptha, very well," Mr. Benedict intoned, and he turned to the children. He had recovered his breath somewhat, and with perfect calmness he said, "He's attempting to brainsweep me, I'm afraid. Now, how are you all? I see poor Constance is sick. Well, it's no surprise. She's had quite a day, hasn't she?"

The children were too astonished to answer. Not five paces away, Mr. Curtain was focusing on Mr. Benedict with all his might, yet Mr. Benedict was paying him no attention whatsoever, and seemed to be feeling no ill effects.

"S.Q.," Mr. Benedict said, smiling warmly, "it's good to see you again. I've never quite gotten over our last difficult parting. I hope I find you well?"

Like the children, S.Q. was too confounded to reply. Meanwhile, Mr. Curtain had begun to sputter. His face had grown pale and glistened with sweat, and his wheelchair twitched and bucked like a spooked horse.

Mr. Benedict glanced at him. "You may recall how much time I've spent in the basement lately," he said, turning back to the children. "Constance believed I was seeking a cure for my narcolepsy — and for secrecy's sake I chose not to dissuade her of this notion. But the fact is I was working on a program that would disable the Whisperer. It was a delicate business, for I had to disguise my work. Naturally, if Ledroptha regained possession of the Whisperer — and I knew he intended to try — I didn't want him to detect the program."

Behind him, Mr. Curtain gasped.

"You mean you sabotaged it?" Reynie cried.

"Indeed," said Mr. Benedict. "But my program didn't go into effect until, oh, about twenty minutes ago. You can imagine my dismay when Ledroptha stole the Whisperer *yesterday*, having cleverly deceived me into thinking he would make the attempt *today*, but it has all worked out well in the end, hasn't it?"

"It . . . has?" Sticky asked hopefully.

"Certainly! Why, thanks to you children, we were able to prevent Ledroptha from obtaining the secrets he desired. And now the Whisperer is no longer a threat to anyone. His computer programs — including the self-destruct mechanism — are all wiped clean away. I'm afraid he's wearing that silly helmet for nothing."

Reynie suspected that Mr. Benedict was attempting to infuriate his brother; after all, it would be easier to capture him if he fell asleep. If that was the strategy, it almost worked. Mr. Curtain's shock of disbelief was quickly overcome by fury, for the evidence was clear: The Whisperer was not responding to his mental directions. Everything — his invention, his great plans, *everything* — was ruined, and his face had gone quite purple as this realization took hold.

Still, even through the horror and anger Mr. Curtain saw that his fate depended upon staying awake. Panting and trembling, he began turning his wheelchair in a slow circle, trying to think what to do.

"Ledroptha," Mr. Benedict said quietly. "You have no one to call. Your government connections have been severed. Further orders to disrupt the city's power and communications will not be followed. Fleeing or fighting will be pointless now, and yet a peaceful surrender may earn you some degree of mercy before the court. Are you hearing me, Ledroptha? Your best course of action is to surrender."

Mr. Curtain scarcely even looked at him, but S.Q. was listening with utmost attention, and when Mr. Benedict had finished speaking he said, "He's right, Mr. Curtain. You should turn yourself in. But don't worry, you don't have to do it alone. I'll do it with you — we can do it together."

Mr. Curtain stared at S.Q. a moment, then pointed a finger at him and said, "You wish to help me, S.Q.?"

S.Q. nodded emphatically. "I do!"

"Then move!" Mr. Curtain barked, and his wheelchair suddenly shot forward.

With a nimbleness no one had seen in him before, S.Q. leaped aside just in time as Mr. Curtain barreled toward the prison wall. And then he had to leap again — indeed they all did — for the Salamander had launched into motion as well, following after Mr. Curtain like some vast creature under a spell.

S.Q. stumbled, recovered his balance, then jumped up and climbed into the Salamander as it passed by. "If you're going, Mr. Curtain, then I'm going with you!"

"Should we try to stop them?" Kate asked.

Mr. Benedict shook his head sadly. "We already have stopped them, Kate. This is just the sorting out."

And so Mr. Benedict and the children watched the sorting out.

Near the prison wall Mr. Curtain had slowed to let the Salamander catch up with him. Like a stunt rider standing in the saddle, he rose and balanced on the seat of his wheelchair, and from there he leaped over the Salamander's side — smacking straight into S.Q., who had staggered forward to help him.

"They're going to crash!" Reynie said, for the Salamander had narrowly missed the construction crane and was headed to the right of the gap in the wall.

Mr. Curtain, however, had taken the wheel and applied the brakes, and just in time he brought the Salamander to a grinding, skidding stop. With a curse they could hear even from a distance, he ordered S.Q. to give him room, then reversed the Salamander to take a better angle.

Mr. Curtain's abandoned wheelchair, meanwhile, was now rolling crazily along on its own, but Mr. Curtain paid it no mind, as if the wheelchair, like everything else, was something he meant to escape from forever. Round and round it looped, at greater and greater speed, until its course brought it crashing headlong into the construction crane with a violent crunch. The red helmet dropped to the ground like fruit from a tree, and a lone wheel wobbled off and twirled to rest like a spun coin.

The wheelchair would never be used again, but it had not done its final damage. High above, the crane's cable slipped visibly, and the enormous metal beam began swaying back and forth. An ominous groaning echoed off the building and the prison wall. Mr. Curtain looked up in alarm as the beam's shadow passed over the Salamander.

"S.Q.!" he ordered. "Get into the crane and grab that lever!"

In a flash S.Q. had climbed into the cab of the crane — breaking through the yellow hazard tape, which now hung from him like streamers — and grabbed a large lever. "I can feel it trembling! I think it's slipping!"

"Of course it's slipping, you fool!" Mr. Curtain shouted. "You need only hold it until I'm through the gap!"

Overhead the beam swung back and forth, back and forth, now over the gap in the wall, now over the crane itself. The groaning grew louder.

"I don't think I can!" S.Q. shouted.

Kate gasped and started to run forward, but Mr. Benedict, predicting this, had already grabbed her. "You mustn't risk it," he said, his face rigid. "No matter what you do, that beam is going to fall."

Mr. Curtain had maneuvered the Salamander into the gap now. He was almost to the river. "Come, S.Q.! Come on, you idiot!"

"But if I let go . . ." S.Q.'s face was a mask of fear. High above him the beam swung and swung.

"Snakes and dogs!" Mr. Curtain bellowed. He gazed up at the swinging beam, then at S.Q., and then turned to stare at the dark river flowing past. Under the circumstances his hesitation seemed very strange indeed. He seemed to stare a terribly long time. And as he stared, his shoulders seemed to sag, as if a great weight had settled upon them.

Perhaps, thought Reynie — standing with the others, still watching anxiously from a distance — perhaps the full force of despair had finally hit him. Hadn't he said that the Whisperer was his all? Hadn't he lost it forever? So what did that river have to offer him? If one had nothing to escape to, what did escape really mean?

And then Mr. Curtain turned his back on the river, leaped from the Salamander, and climbed into the cab of the crane. As he did so, a loud, wailing alarm sounded from the direction of the prison gate ("The sentries have arrived," Mr. Benedict said to the children), but Mr. Curtain seemed not even to notice. Elbowing S.Q. aside, he snatched hold of the trembling lever. "Get into the Salamander and pull it forward, S.Q. — I will follow after."

"But you won't be able to —"

"I'm stronger than you, S.Q.! Now do as I say!"

S.Q. leaped down from the cab and ran to the Salamander. But instead of pulling it forward, he backed it out of the hole in the wall, turning it so that its back end was almost to the crane. Mr. Curtain was shouting furiously at him, but S.Q. shouted even louder. "Jump down and get under the Salamander! Then I'll drive it out! You'll be protected if the beam falls!"

Mr. Curtain gaped at him as if astonished. "But of *course* it's going to fall, S.Q.! Couldn't you tell that? And now . . ." He shook his head. His arms were visibly shaking with the effort of holding the lever firm. "I will not go to prison, S.Q., and yet . . . I am so weary of trying to control what ought to be controlled, so weary . . ."

"It's all right!" S.Q. called desperately. "You can still be all right, Mr. Curtain! I'll help you! Just . . . just let go of the lever and jump down . . ."

Mr. Curtain looked very tired — very tired, and almost relieved. Gazing at S.Q., who was gazing back with a helpless, concerned expression that Mr. Curtain had never seen from anyone, at least not directed toward *him*, he seemed to settle something in his mind. "Yes, I suppose it's time I relinquish control — at least I can control the relinquishing.

Very well, S.Q., I'll let go of the lever! Let go and let chance take over at last . . ."

Mr. Curtain released the lever and threw up his hands in defeat.

The lever slipped. The beam dropped.

But before the lever slipped and the beam dropped, S.Q. — who had started moving the instant he saw what Mr. Curtain meant to do — leaped into the cab of the crane, seized him, and leaped out again, falling hard to the ground. The beam came down just as S.Q. was dragging Mr. Curtain beneath the Salamander. It struck the cab and the Salamander both, crushing the cab like an aluminum can and nearly flattening the Salamander's sides.

But when Mr. Benedict and the children came running to pull the men from the wreckage, they found them unhurt. S.Q. was holding Mr. Curtain tightly, so that they had to drag the two men out together, and Mr. Curtain was cursing him, berating him, snapping at him. "You fool! You fool! You miserable, unthinking . . ."

But Reynie noticed — and so did they all — that Mr. Curtain was clinging as tightly to S.Q. as S.Q. was to him, and in the brief moments before his emotions sent him to sleep, Mr. Curtain's eyes expressed something quite different from the words he was uttering with such ferocity. His words were venomous, and his face was twisted with despair, yet there was something in his eyes that might have seemed familiar in anyone except Mr. Curtain. It was relief, perhaps, or perhaps something even stronger.

It might even have been hope.

PROJECTS and POETRY

Mr. Benedict awoke with a start and ran his fingers through his rumpled hair. Glancing about, he found himself in his study chair, flanked by Rhonda and Number Two. Across the desk sat a frowning Mr. Gaines and a worried-looking Ms. Argent.

"Ah," Mr. Benedict said. "You were saying, Mr. Gaines?"

"Have you already forgotten?" growled Mr. Gaines. "Apparently you found it quite humorous."

"Oh yes!" Mr. Benedict said with a smile. "You were warning me of the consequences of failing to cooperate. I apologize — I thought we had established that the Whisperer no longer functions, so your threat to deny me access seemed like a joke."

Mr. Gaines stared at him coolly. "We thought with proper incentive you might be persuaded to *restart* the Whisperer."

"To do so I would essentially have to reinvent it, Mr. Gaines, a project that would take many years — and in which I have no interest."

Mr. Gaines grunted doubtfully. "We'll return to this subject later, then. Right now we have some straightforward questions, and you would be well advised, Mr. Benedict, to answer them honestly."

"I shall do my best," Mr. Benedict declared, patting the hand of Number Two, who had bristled at Mr. Gaines's words. (Rhonda reached across and handed her a banana.) "Why don't you ask them all together? It will be more efficient that way. Oh, and if you don't mind, please start at the end of the list and work your way backward. Changing the order of things often helps clarify my thinking."

Mr. Gaines rolled his eyes and turned to Ms. Argent, who nervously flipped to a different page on her clipboard, cleared her throat, and began reading questions from a long list, starting at the bottom. As promised, the questions were fairly straightforward, but to anyone unfamiliar with the case they would have seemed like jokes and riddles:

What were the strong man and the security guard doing in the prison elevator? Who hit the man in seersucker with the fake ambulance? How did the secret agent come to be in the courtyard with so many broken bones — and why did he seem so cheerful about it? What exactly happened to the Salamander, the Whisperer, the wheelchair, and the crane?

These and several other questions Ms. Argent read with a straight face and an even, deliberate tone. Mr. Benedict listened attentively, looking thoroughly entertained. When she came to the end he said, "All excellent questions, Ms. Argent. In response, allow me to offer a short narrative of the pertinent events. If you prefer, I shall start at the beginning rather than the end."

"Oh, please do!" said Ms. Argent, and Mr. Gaines nodded brusquely.

"Very well. The beginning is this: My brother's spies deceived your top advisers — the group of experts you conveniently summoned to Stonetown, Mr. Gaines — and were taking them to meet my brother at the prison, where he intended to use his Whisperer to extract top-secret information from them. When we learned of this, my associates and I intercepted their vehicle, and Milligan and two of his sentries apprehended the spies, all of which I believe you know already. And when I informed your advisers of my brother's plot, they agreed it would be preferable for them to exit the vehicle and seek shelter beneath a highway overpass.

"Extreme haste was necessary in order to save the children, for if the van did not arrive on time, I believed my brother would grow suspicious and move to another secret location. Therefore, although Milligan sent instructions for several more agents to follow after us, we could not wait for them to organize their team. Our plan was for Milligan and his sentries to infiltrate the prison and bring the children back to the van. The rest of us were to wait at the van in our disguises (I've neglected to mention our disguises, but I assure you we looked quite dashing) pretending to be sentries ourselves — and thus, we hoped, staving off any reckless attacks on the part of the Ten Men.

"Unfortunately things went awry, and when Milligan did not communicate with us (his radio had been broken), Moocho and Ms. Plugg decided to go in after him. They managed to get to the roof with the intention of scouting the area, but McCracken arrived at the same time, and a struggle ensued. Eventually Milligan intervened and secured them inside the elevator for their own protection, but his conflict with McCracken culminated in a fall from the roof into the courtyard. I believe this explains the broken bones."

Ms. Argent nodded without looking up from her clipboard. She was frantically taking notes. Mr. Gaines was studying Mr. Benedict with narrowed eyes, as if he suspected trickery and was intent upon discovering it.

"Now then," Mr. Benedict continued, "during this time Milligan's sentries were engaged with another Ten Man, but they, too, were defeated — shocked unconscious — at which point Rhonda and Number Two thought it necessary to enter the fray. I was still asleep at this time, but I believe it was Number Two who hit the Ten Man with the fake ambulance, am I right, Number Two?"

"It would be more precise to say that he hit *me*," said Number Two in a satisfied tone. "He was pursuing me at full tilt when I applied the brakes. Rhonda took advantage of his discomposure by securing him with a chain from his briefcase."

"He was terribly annoyed," Rhonda put in.

"What of the other Ten Men?" Mr. Gaines pressed. "Your report stated that Milligan's agents rounded up a 'baker's half-dozen,' which we took to mean seven, since that number corresponds to our own information. I must admonish you, Benedict — it's highly irregular and inappropriate language for an official report."

"So you did receive my report!" Mr. Benedict said, then scratching his head with a puzzled expression he asked, "Why, then, have you asked all these questions? I'm certain I've already addressed them."

"You've addressed almost nothing!" said Mr. Gaines indignantly. "For one thing, you hardly mention the children in the report, and in your so-called 'narrative' just now, you've omitted their role entirely."

Mr. Benedict raised an eyebrow. "The children were kidnapped and held hostage, Mr. Gaines. That was their role in this affair. There is little to discuss. Indeed, now that I know you've received my report, I see no point in continuing this conversation."

"The point," Mr. Gaines cried, "is that you've left out important facts! *How* did you know about Curtain's plot, Benedict? How did you know about his spies? How did you know he was at the prison? And, for the last time, *what happened to the Whisperer?*"

"You seem to have something in mind already," said Mr. Benedict. "Tell me, Mr. Gaines, what do *you* think happened to the Whisperer?"

Mr. Gaines leaped to his feet. "I'll tell you what I think! I think you sabotaged it, Benedict! It didn't simply 'malfunction,' as your report states — you purposely sabotaged it!"

"But Mr. Gaines, if I had sabotaged the Whisperer, wouldn't I have done so while it was still in my possession? Yet it was obviously functioning when my brother stole it. Otherwise he wouldn't have arranged to bring your advisers to the prison. He couldn't possibly hope to get away with his plan without using the Whisperer, now could he?"

Mr. Gaines stomped his foot. "You're playing tricks, Benedict! You keep evading my questions! Did you or did you not —"

"Excuse me," said Mr. Benedict, for just then a telephone rang. The ring was muffled, but it clearly came from somewhere in the study. Mr. Benedict lifted a stack of papers and looked beneath it, then opened the top drawer of his desk. He frowned.

"I think it's in the bottom drawer," Rhonda murmured.

"Thank you," said Mr. Benedict, retrieving the telephone. (He lifted a finger to indicate he would be with Mr. Gaines in a moment.) "Hello, this is Nicholas Benedict. Yes . . . certainly . . . oh no, not at all . . . yes, he's here with me now." Mr. Benedict held out the telephone. "For you, Mr. Gaines. It seems you're being removed from your post."

Mr. Gaines blanched, opened and closed his mouth a few times, then reluctantly took the telephone. After listening a moment, he sat down again. And for some time he continued to listen, occasionally muttering dejected replies.

Meanwhile Mr. Benedict laced his fingers together and turned to address Ms. Argent, who seemed uncertain what to do. "Never fear, Ms. Argent. The official reason for Mr. Gaines's dismissal is his filing of an erroneous report, the one concerning the smoldering wreckage my brother's men deposited in this house. That report wrongly suggested, as you know, that the Whisperer had been destroyed, and that I was somehow responsible. The evidence has since repudiated this suggestion, and supports your own report, in which you expressed a conviction that I was telling the truth. Thank you for that confidence, by the way. Also, allow me to offer you my congratulations — you're about to be promoted."

Ms. Argent's eyebrows shot up. "Promoted?"

"Indeed. Apparently you're being given full responsibility for this case."

By the time Mr. Gaines finished his telephone conversation, Ms. Argent was sitting up straight in her seat, her shoulders squared with new confidence and a determined, eager look in her eyes. Mr. Gaines handed her the telephone without quite looking at her.

"I've been told to leave at once," Mr. Gaines mumbled, staring at his feet.

"Well, if you must," Mr. Benedict said. "Rhonda will see you out. Would you like an aspirin or glass of water first? You look unwell."

"No . . . thank you," muttered Mr. Gaines with a faint nod, and with Rhonda gripping his elbow he shuffled out the door.

"Dismissal seems to suit him," Number Two observed. "He's milder and more polite, at any rate."

Ms. Argent spoke on the telephone only for a minute, and was in Mr. Benedict's study only a few minutes more. She was closing the case immediately, she said; any relevant paperwork would be delivered to Mr. Benedict to sign at his convenience. "I'll draw the papers up myself," she concluded. "I don't believe you'll find anything objectionable in them."

"Thank you, Ms. Argent," said Mr. Benedict, shaking her hand. "And now for more joyful matters. Our friend Moocho has prepared tea and cookies for a small celebration, if you'd care to join us."

"I'd be delighted!" Ms. Argent exclaimed, and for the first time anyone could remember, she smiled. "What is the celebration for?"

Mr. Benedict pursed his lips. "That's a reasonable question, Ms. Argent, but I'm afraid . . . Now, which is it today, Number Two? We've had so many lately, I forget. Last week we celebrated the Whisperer's demise, and yesterday we celebrated Milligan's retirement from secret agent work — he means to spend more time with his daughter, Ms. Argent, and to do so in one piece. But what is the occasion *today*, Number Two, do you remember?"

"For shame, Mr. Benedict!" scolded Number Two in a shocked tone. "We're celebrating the discovery of the papers!"

"I was only joking," said Mr. Benedict, laughing. (Number Two blinked at him, obviously baffled.) "You see, Ms. Argent, we've finally located the documents that will allow me to officially adopt Constance. It's truly a wonderful occasion!"

"Why, that's marvelous, Mr. Benedict! Allow *me* to congratulate *you*!"

"Thank you, thank you," said Mr. Benedict warmly, once again shaking her hand. "You know your way to the dining room, don't you? Number Two and I will be along in a moment."

As soon as Ms. Argent had gone out, Mr. Benedict turned toward the wall behind him and said, "I thought we agreed there would be no more eavesdropping, children."

Number Two gasped indignantly and rapped on the wall with her knuckles. "Honestly, children! How rude!"

After a brief silence, three muffled, contrite voices said they were sorry.

"I never agreed to any such thing!" protested a fourth. "Also, Mr. Benedict, I know perfectly well you made that joke just to get my goat."

"Well," said Mr. Benedict with a chuckle. "Perhaps I did."

~:~

Some weeks after the incidents at Third Island Prison, and some days after the eavesdropping incident in Mr. Benedict's house, the young members of the Mysterious Benedict Society paid their first visit to Ledroptha Curtain. They were accompanied by Mr. Benedict, Rhonda Kazembe, and Number Two, but even so they went reluctantly and with no small amount of misgivings. Only afterward, as they were riding away from the special high-security prison in which Mr. Curtain now resided, did they begin to feel good at all about the trip.

"You were right, Mr. Benedict," Kate said from the back seat of the station wagon. "Things are much more pleasant when you stop being angry. I wonder if Mr. Curtain will ever figure that out."

Mr. Benedict turned to smile at her. "I'm curious myself, Kate. I do hope to find out eventually. Perhaps after ten or fifteen years of weekly visits, Ledroptha will turn the corner. Who knows? He may even be persuaded to use his talents for good. It would be far more rewarding than using them for nothing."

"I hope you aren't expecting *me* to go along on those visits," Constance grumbled. "He didn't even accept the cookies! He threw them on the floor! And they were perfectly good cookies!"

"You can decide for yourself whether to accompany me," Mr. Benedict said. "You certainly needn't feel obligated. He isn't *your* brother, after all — though it's true he'll soon be your uncle. In any case, you'll be welcome to join me whenever you wish. That's true for all of you, I should add."

"Well, it *was* good to see S.Q. again," Reynie said. "And I suppose he'll be there often. Did you hear him say he's been visiting every day, and that yesterday Mr. Curtain looked at him once without growling?"

"That's progress, I guess," said Sticky, blinking exaggeratedly. He had just been prescribed contact lenses and was still getting used to them. His eyes constantly felt as if they had something in them (which, of course, they did) and without his glasses, his face felt as bald as his head.

For a while they talked about the Ten Men, Mr. Pressius, and Mr. Bane, and all the other figures involved with Mr. Curtain who had been taken into custody at last. And then, as they skirted Stonetown Harbor, they discussed Mr. Benedict's new project — he was studying his brother's tidal turbines with the aim of replicating them for the benefit of other cities. It was one of many projects he had planned now that Mr. Curtain and the Whisperer no longer occupied all his time and energy.

"Speaking of time and energy," Constance said. "I've been wondering something, Mr. Benedict. Why didn't you just disable the Whisperer right away? I mean, once you learned it was going to be taken from you, why did you spend all that time in the basement programming it to go kaput *later*?"

Mr. Benedict hesitated a split second before saying, "To protect myself, Constance. Mr. Bane had private orders to check up on me — and on the Whisperer in particular — every day until the hour appointed for its removal. If he discovered it was no longer functioning . . . well, the situation at that time was delicate, and I might have been arrested for destroying government property."

These remarks were followed by an uncomfortable silence. At least, it was uncomfortable for Reynie, who sensed that some things had gone unspoken, and that the adults were in secret conflict over it. He detected Number Two's look of disapproval (though she tried to conceal it) as well as Rhonda's impulse, barely checked, to add to what Mr. Benedict had said.

"You did it for *me*!" Constance cried suddenly. "But why would you try to hide that?"

"Oh, there was no reason to go into it," Mr. Benedict said breezily. "It's true I didn't wish to disable the Whisperer until we'd had a chance to recover your memories. And then again, if I had been arrested, all the questions surrounding your adoption would only have grown more complicated. But

Constance, my dear," he went on quickly when she began to ask another question, "you really must stop reading our minds without permission. Not only is it impolite, it is unwise. Think of all the surprise parties you'll ruin."

"I wasn't trying to!" Constance protested. "Sometimes it just happens."

"It would happen less if you practiced," Number Two said irritably. (She had shared her snack with S.Q. Pedalian and was suffering from it now.) "Every day we sit down with you to work on it, and every day you refuse . . ."

"You're one to talk about refusing!" Constance snipped. "After all this time, you still won't tell us your real name!"

This comment, which seemed to have come out of nowhere, prompted curious glances from the other children. Constance's eyes were squeezed tightly closed. Number Two had just begun to chide her for changing the subject when Constance's eyes popped open with a look of delight.

"Pencilla!" she exclaimed triumphantly. "That's your name — Pencilla!"

The other children gasped. So did Number Two.

"You . . . you set me up!" cried Number Two, flustered and indignant. "You mentioned my name just so I'd think of it!"

"That was extremely inappropriate, Constance," said Rhonda, frowning at her in the rearview mirror. But to Number Two she murmured, "Still, it *was* about time they knew your given name."

"Oh, I suppose, but it's just . . ." Number Two blushed and put a hand to her head. "It just doesn't *feel* right. It never has."

"I think Pencilla is a perfectly lovely name," Kate declared. "Don't you, boys?"

"I love it, Number Two," Reynie said. "Really, it's a great name."

Sticky nodded. "Me, too. I think it suits you."

"Suits me? How do you mean?" said Number Two, knitting her brow.

There was a tense pause. Reynie whispered into Sticky's ear.

"Because it's pretty!" Sticky said, and everyone immediately, emphatically agreed.

⌣∴∼

That night, Mr. Benedict was sitting on the floor of his study, as was his habit when working alone, when there came a knock on his door. He contemplated the door before answering — in fact he almost didn't, which was *not* his habit — but then he lowered his papers and said, "Come in, all of you."

The children filed into the study. Reynie closed the door, and everyone sat on the floor around Mr. Benedict. Their expressions were serious.

"I see we have something to discuss," Mr. Benedict said.

"More than that," Kate said. "We have something to do."

Constance pointed her finger at him. "I know why you didn't want to talk about the Whisperer today. You didn't want me to find out how close you were to finding a cure for your narcolepsy!"

Mr. Benedict considered a moment before replying. "Forgive me, my dear, but I was a bit embarrassed. I hope you can understand. With such urgent problems afoot, it seems selfish to have spent time working on what was, at bottom, a personal matter. But you're right; I was closer than I let on. I am sorry for keeping it from you."

"How close were you?" Constance demanded. "*Exactly* how close?"

Mr. Benedict had looked apologetic; now he looked resigned. "I see you already know the answer." He waved his hand carelessly. "It's really of no consequence, Constance. I'm more than used to living with my condition, and —"

"You put it off!" Constance cried. "You were only a few hours away! *Hours*! But you didn't go through with it — because of me!"

"It's more complicated than —"

"Don't try to explain it away! I've already gotten the whole truth from Rhonda and Number Two."

"Not exactly with their permission," Sticky put in, with a significant look.

Constance pressed on. "You thought it might exhaust you to try it, and so you didn't. You wanted to be alert and strong enough to deal with Mr. Pressius, and to help me recover my memories! You knew you were risking your opportunity — you knew you might lose it, but you put it off anyway, because of me! You gave up your chance for my sake, and *that's* what you didn't want me to know about, because you didn't want me to feel bad about it!"

Mr. Benedict pursed his lips and said nothing for several moments. But at last, as all the children were staring at him with the clear expectation of a truthful answer, he smiled somewhat ruefully and tapped his nose.

Suddenly Constance was all business. "That's all right," she said in a matter-of-fact tone. "I'll forgive you on one condition." She paused dramatically. "You let me try to fix your problem."

"That's what I meant when I said we have something to do," Kate said.

"I gathered as much," Mr. Benedict said, and with a wondering expression he looked from face to face. "And I see you are all determined that this should happen. But Constance, you know I cannot possibly allow it. I am deeply touched, you must know that, but —"

"You don't think I can do it?" Constance snapped.

"I . . ." Mr. Benedict frowned. "I . . ."

"You're not sure how to answer," Reynie said, "because she has you trapped. If you do say that she can do it, she'll insist on trying. If you say that she can't, you'll be lying. She already knows you think she can do it. We've been talking about this all evening, Mr. Benedict."

Mr. Benedict gave Reynie a helpless, ironic smile. "Thank you, Reynie, for clearing that up."

"We know you don't want her to try it," Kate said, "because of how sick you think it will make her, and how if it doesn't work she'll have gone through all that misery for nothing. But she doesn't care, Mr. Benedict. She wants to try it anyway — and we want you to let her!"

"That's why we're here," Sticky said. "For moral support. And we've agreed to take turns sitting with her all night, to keep her company while she's so miserable."

"I want to do this," Constance insisted. "*Please* let me try!"

"Please," Reynie said.

"Pretty please," Kate said.

"Beautiful please," Sticky said, then winced a little, for it had seemed wittier when he thought it than when he spoke it aloud.

All of the children clasped their hands together pleadingly.

Mr. Benedict looked at them, his bright green eyes shining. Then he fell asleep. When he woke up, there they were, still clasping their hands together and widening their eyes with exaggerated, puppy-dog looks, and this time he laughed. He fell asleep twice more. And when he awoke the last time, he agreed to let Constance try.

"You'll tell me exactly what to think," Constance said. "Right? With your mind, I mean."

"Yes, my dear. And the thoughts will be fairly simple, but you will need to think them with as much intensity as you can manage."

"That's what I figured," Constance said. "I'm ready to try." She swallowed dryly, thinking of the misery that would soon be upon her. But she did not flinch.

"I think it will be best," Mr. Benedict said quietly, "if you stare directly at me. Do not close your eyes."

Constance nodded and began to stare. "Let's go."

Mr. Benedict took a deep breath, relaxed his shoulders, and fixedly returned Constance's gaze. For five minutes and more the two of them stared and stared. The others were reminded of a contest in which each person tries to get the other to laugh. But never had any of them seen two people gazing with such intensity. It was disconcerting — so much so they were tempted to look away. But they held still, afraid of causing distraction, until at last a look of frustration passed over Constance's face, and she broke off the stare with an irritated grunt.

"I don't feel like it's working!" She thumped her fists against her knees. "It's . . . somehow it doesn't feel strong enough. It isn't like it was the other times."

"Never fret," Mr. Benedict said gently. He seemed a bit relieved. "Perhaps someday, when —"

But Reynie, thinking back, felt a sudden flash of inspiration. "Try getting angry!" he suggested.

Mr. Benedict lifted an eyebrow and glanced sidelong at Reynie. His lips twitched as if he were suppressing a smile.

"Angry at Mr. Benedict?" said Constance with a helpless look. "But I don't . . . I don't think I can . . ."

"At the problem," Reynie said. "Try getting angry at *that*."

"Angry," Constance repeated thoughtfully. She gave a tight, resolute nod. "Okay," she said. "I can do that. Let's try again, Mr. Benedict."

Mr. Benedict's eyes twinkled (whether with amusement or anticipation it was impossible to say — perhaps it was both), and taking another deep breath he folded his hands together and said, "By all means, my dear. Let us try again."

They locked eyes as they had done before. This time, however, Constance's face began to darken. She furrowed her brow, her lips pressed together, and her jaw began to clench and unclench. In moments her face was the exact hue of a pomegranate. She was visibly trembling now — she looked not just angry but furious. Indeed, had the others not known better, they would have thought she was ready to fly at Mr. Benedict and try to pull his hair out.

And then, abruptly, she stopped scowling and fell back. "There!" she gasped. "That time I felt it." Putting a hand to her head, she looked hopefully at Mr. Benedict. "Well?"

Mr. Benedict nodded and smiled. He reached forward and squeezed her hand. "I am enormously proud of your courage and selflessness, Constance. Thank you, my dear — thank you from the bottom of my heart."

"I know you're *proud* of me," Constance said in an exasperated tone. "But —" She shuddered. The color had begun to drain from her face. "Oh no . . . oh no, here it comes! Tell me quick, Mr. Benedict — did it work?"

"I'm afraid I can't say, Constance. Not yet. But we'll know soon enough. Right now you should —"

"No! I want to know *now*! Reynie, give him the poem! Quick!"

Reynie was already unfolding a sheet of paper. He thrust it at Mr. Benedict. "Constance wrote you a funny poem," he explained. "She hoped you might use it as a sort of test."

Constance groaned, crossed her arms tightly, and sank over onto her side.

Mr. Benedict gazed at her with concern. Then he looked at the poem and read the title aloud: *"Why I Find Green Plaid So Annoying, And What I Intend to Do About It: An Explanation of My Heroic Actions."*

Mr. Benedict's lips jerked upward. He coughed into his hand, looked round at the older children (all of whom were grinning expectantly), and continued reading aloud from the first stanza:

For one thing, plaid's hideous, a pattern
cooked up
By dimwit designers who must have been mad.
It's also perfidious (a word I looked up —
It means lots of different things, all of them
bad).

Mr. Benedict chuckled, then laughed outright. And as he
went on reading the poem he laughed again, and then again,
until finally he was laughing so hard his shoulders were
shaking and he could hardly hold the paper still enough to
read from it. The children began to giggle. Even normal
laughter is contagious, and Mr. Benedict's high-pitched,
chattering squeals — so very much like dolphin speech —
were not only contagious but funny in themselves. Even
Constance, shivering and pale, managed to snicker through
her moans.

The giggles turned into laughter; and Mr. Benedict's
laughs turned into guffaws and strange, coyote-like yelps;
and soon the laughter grew so uproarious it drew others to
the study, so that eventually the room was packed with family and friends, with everyone laughing (though only a few
knew why) and looking at everyone else with giddy, wondering expressions. Indeed, the laughter was so boisterous that
it took awhile for the newcomers to notice that Constance
was not only laughing but crying, too, and that in fact she
looked terribly ill, and that despite this she kept gazing happily at Mr. Benedict, who had never laughed with such gusto
for so long.

The More Things Change

The time had almost come. The bags were packed, the early-morning sunlight was growing stronger, and the children were gathered in Constance's room, eating doughnuts Kate had smuggled up from the kitchen. She had tapped on the boys' door as she passed, and a minute later they had come trudging groggily down the hall in their pajamas and slippers. Constance hadn't even risen but sat munching her jelly roll in bed, heedless of the crumbs and jelly dropping onto her covers. It was a bittersweet moment. Everyone was excited, yet never again would it be so easy to convene a meeting of the Mysterious Benedict Society.

"I can't quite get over it," Kate was saying. "When I see Mr. Benedict walking around by himself, without Number Two or Rhonda hovering nearby — well, it's strange, isn't it? It's as if he didn't cast a shadow anymore."

"Number Two is having a hard time with it," Reynie said. "Every time he stands up, she does too, then sits down again looking kind of disoriented."

"It isn't just that," said Sticky, licking his fingers. "When I saw him in that blue blazer yesterday, with his hair so neatly combed, I had to do a double take. I thought he was someone else."

"I don't like any of this as much as I thought I would," said Constance. "I really did hate that green plaid suit, but it's weird seeing him in other clothes. And Sticky used to drive me crazy polishing his spectacles, but now I hate the way he's always wincing and squinting and running to the mirror to fix his contact lenses. And I couldn't *wait* for Kate to move out, but now that the day is here the whole thing makes me grumpy." She frowned and wiped jelly from her chin with her pillow.

"You're a sweetheart, Constance," said Kate, shaking her head.

Reynie smiled and handed another doughnut to Sticky, who was glowering at Constance resentfully. "At least now we know what's making her grumpy — I used to think it was just how she was."

"That isn't all of it," Constance whined. "I'm having writer's block, too. I've been trying to write a poem about all of this — the whole adventure, I mean, from the moment we met up to the very end. But I can't find the right words."

"I imagine it would be hard to come up with a rhyme for 'Whisperer,'" Kate said absently. She was contemplating the empty space in her bucket. At the prison she had recovered only a few of her lost items, and since then she'd been considering what should be replaced and what should be bidden farewell. Now seemed like the right time. There was only so much room in the bucket, after all, and her needs might well be changing. Everything else was, wasn't it?

"Rhyming isn't the problem," Constance protested. "It's the *feeling*. After all this time, after all we've been through and all we've accomplished — well, we should be thrilled, shouldn't we? We should be on top of the world! Mr. Curtain isn't a threat anymore, just a horrible old bore I may have to visit sometimes. And the Whisperer's out of commission forever. It's all incredibly important, and yet . . ."

"And yet it isn't that simple," Sticky finished for her, and everyone nodded, because everyone understood.

"I do wish things had worked out a bit differently," Kate said. "When I think of all the good Mr. Benedict could have done with the Whisperer, all the people he might have helped if only there hadn't been these other, nastier people trying to get their hands on it for their own greedy purposes —"

"But the Whisperer wouldn't even have existed if not for a nasty person with greedy purposes," Sticky pointed out. "It's kind of disconcerting, isn't it?"

"Exactly!" Kate said. "I keep thinking about how every good thing in this whole business has been completely tangled up with some *bad* thing. I mean if not for Mr. Curtain and the Whisperer, we never would have met each other, much less become friends! And if not for Mr. Benedict, we might never have considered the good the Whisperer could do, so we wouldn't have been the least bit troubled to see it go."

"It's true," Sticky said. "Everything has been bittersweet."

"Maybe we should acquire a taste for bittersweet," said Reynie with a grin. "Then everything would feel wonderful."

"That's stupid," Constance snipped. "If it felt wonderful, then it wouldn't be bittersweet, would it?"

Reynie only shrugged. He wasn't at all sure about that.

Kate had wandered over to the window. "Uh-oh," she said. "Looks like it's starting."

Constance humphed and covered her head with her sheets, but the boys joined Kate looking out. The courtyard was filled with adults. Mrs. Washington in her wheelchair was turning this way and that, directing traffic, and Mrs. Perumal was holding open the iron gate; everyone else toted bags, boxes, furniture, and odd-shaped bundles. Mr. Benedict, wearing an unfortunate, huge-collared shirt that Number Two had made for him, was carrying an ugly lamp that resembled a stork. Miss Perumal and Number Two were at opposite ends of a trunk, chatting and laughing, and behind them came Moocho Brazos carrying a desk, two suitcases, and a bookshelf. Rhonda and Mr. Washington were out at the curb, adjusting a makeshift ramp for Mrs. Washington's wheelchair. And calling out encouragement from the bench beneath the elm tree was Milligan, both legs and one arm still in casts.

Reynie's gaze lingered on poor Milligan. Not for the first time, he reflected upon his role in the events that led to those injuries. It was Reynie, after all, who had suggested they go to the roof, and not long ago he would have felt terribly burdened by that. And yet, to his relief, he'd found that somehow his sympathy for Milligan was only that — sympathy, not guilt.

You aren't responsible for all of us, Kate had said in the prison. *We're all responsible for each other, right?*

Evidently her words had taken root in fertile soil, for despite the many problems that had remained to be dealt with — and despite his knowledge that new ones would always crop up — Reynie had never felt quite so light of step. It was an unexpected development, this new feeling, and remarkably pleasant. Indeed, he had felt so grateful for it that, on the day Milligan came home from the hospital, he'd drawn Kate aside to thank her.

"Good grief!" Kate had cried. "Thank *me*? I just said the same stuff you're always saying to us! You should thank yourself!" Then her expression had turned thoughtful. "But you know what? I'm glad you mentioned this, because I've been feeling guilty myself. I did sort of kick Milligan out of that elevator. He keeps reminding me that I was just trying to help him save Moocho and Ms. Plugg, but . . ."

"We were all doing the best we could," Reynie said. "It's McCracken who should feel guilty — though I don't suppose he knows how."

Instantly cheered (it never took much), Kate snorted. "Maybe in prison he'll learn something about guilt and responsibility."

"Maybe," Reynie said. He shrugged. "*I* did, I guess."

Kate looked at him askance, then leaned to whisper in his ear as if telling him a secret. "Yes, but you're smarter than he is, Reynie. Also, you're not *evil*."

They had both laughed — they'd been in high spirits that day, and any little thing had set them tittering — and now, gazing down upon the moving-day hubbub, Reynie smiled at the memory. *How many times had they all laughed together?* he wondered. Before Kate entered his life, before Sticky and Constance and Miss Perumal and all those people he loved down in the courtyard — before them, laughter had been in rather short supply. Reynie marveled to think of those days; they seemed so long ago now. He had had no idea what he was missing.

"They're really hustling out there, aren't they?" Kate said.

"It won't take long at this rate," Sticky sighed.

"No," Kate agreed. "I think it took much longer to coordinate than it will to actually move. Rhonda has it all laid out like clockwork."

"Has what laid out?" asked Constance from her bed.

"The moving plan," Reynie said. "First Sticky's family goes; then Amma, Pati, and me; then Kate, Milligan, and Moocho."

"Don't say *goes*," Constance said, scowling. "I'm starting to get upset."

The others exchanged private looks. For days now Constance had been clamoring for the move, while the rest of

them had spoken of it in more subdued tones. They were all
pleased with the way things had developed, and yet they felt
melancholy, too, for something they had grown used to was
now changing forever. It came as no surprise that Constance
had arrived at the same feeling rather late. Mr. Benedict had
warned them it would happen that way — and had asked
them to shore up their patience.

"Fair enough," Reynie said. "Instead of *goes* I'll say *relo-
cates*. After all, Kate and I are only moving downstairs."

"And I'm just moving across the street," Sticky said,
sounding as if he didn't quite believe it. In fact he almost
didn't — he'd been in a perpetual state of surprise ever since
the adults had announced this new arrangement. His friends
had also been astonished.

"Wait a minute," Reynie had asked. "You really were
working on a project in the house across the street? I thought
that was a cover story for errand day!"

"It was," Mrs. Washington had said, "but it was also tech-
nically true. In addition to the errands, we were renovating
the house."

"And Reynie and I are really staying, too?" Kate asked.

"We're remodeling the bottom two floors," said Mr.
Benedict. "If it suits everyone, the basement will be con-
verted into apartments for you, Milligan, and Moocho,
while the Perumals will continue to occupy their rooms on
the first floor. Reynie will move down the hall from them.
Mr. Washington has some excellent ideas for a common sitting room and —"

"Are you serious?" Sticky interrupted, gazing earnestly
at his parents. "I mean, can we *really*?"

"Really?" Kate and Reynie echoed. "We really, really can?"

The answer had been yes, they really could. After all, Miss Perumal had explained, it was an unusually felicitous arrangement. The adults would all be involved with Mr. Benedict's new projects, and to some extent so would the children — it would be part of their education. The only remaining question was whether the children themselves approved.

"Although, we must confess it wasn't much of a question," Mr. Benedict had laughed as the children danced and shouted.

The euphoria had lasted for days, and it still flashed upon all of them from time to time, though it had been tempered by the knowledge that the boys would no longer be roommates, that Kate would no longer be just down the hall, and that the regular meetings of the Society might never again feel so urgent or important as they had in the past. Certainly it was a relief, but it was also, strangely, a kind of loss, and they all understood what Constance was feeling now.

"Look, Constance," Sticky said in an effort to comfort her. "If you stand here at your window, and I stand at mine across the street, we can send each other Morse code messages."

"But I don't even have a flashlight!" Constance exclaimed, and she began to cry.

"You can have this one," Kate said quickly, reaching into her bucket, which she had banged back into shape. "Okay, Connie girl? Don't cry! You take this one and I'll get a new one."

"Can we still have our meetings here?" Constance asked, sniffling. And she peeked over at them out of the corners of her eyes.

The others looked at one another. They knew that within a day or two Constance's bedroom would be a horrific mess; they also knew that Constance's request was partly due to laziness. But no one cared to risk a tantrum right now.

"We'll rotate," Reynie suggested. "Tonight's meeting can be here, and next time we can meet in Kate's new room, and so on."

"But what will we even have to talk about?" Constance wailed. "There aren't any problems anymore!"

"Oh, I'll bet we can find *something* to talk about," said Kate, grinning at the boys. "Don't you?"

"Like what? The stupid weather?" Constance grumbled. She was no longer truly upset, but simply complaining out of habit.

"Why not?" Reynie said, and he chuckled to himself, for just then he was feeling as happy as he ever had. "It's going to be a beautiful day, Constance. It's springtime!"

And indeed, out along Mr. Benedict's fence, the roses were blooming.

KEEP READING

for a sneak peek at

THE SECRET KEEPERS

TRENTON LEE STEWART

AUTHOR OF THE *NEW YORK TIMES* BESTSELLER THE MYSTERIOUS BENEDICT SOCIETY

COMING SEPTEMBER 2016

AVAILABLE WHEREVER BOOKS ARE SOLD

WALKING BACKWARD INTO THE SKY

That summer morning in the Lower Downs began as usual for Reuben Pedley. He rose early to have breakfast with his mom before she left for work, a quiet breakfast because they were both still sleepy. Afterward, also as usual, he cleaned up their tiny kitchen while his mom moved faster and faster in her race against the clock (whose numerals she seemed quite unable to read before she'd had coffee and a shower). Then his mom was hugging him good-bye at the apartment door, where Reuben told her he loved her, which was true—and that she had no reason to worry about him, which was not.

His mom had not even reached the bus stop before Reuben had brushed his teeth, yanked on his sneakers (a fitting term, he thought, being a sneaker himself), and climbed onto the kitchen counter to retrieve his wallet. He kept it among the mousetraps on top of the cupboard. The traps were never sprung; Reuben never baited them, and so far no thieves had reached up there to see what they might find. Not that the wallet contained much, but for Reuben "not much" was still everything he had.

Next he went into his bedroom and removed the putty from the little hole in the wall behind his bed. He took his key from the hole and smooshed the putty back into place. Then, locking the apartment door behind him, he headed out in search of new places to hide.

Reuben lived in the city of New Umbra, a metropolis that was nonetheless as gloomy and rundown as a city could be. Though it had once enjoyed infinitely hopeful prospects (people used to say that it was born under a promising star), New Umbra had long since ceased to be prosperous and was not generally well kept. Some might have said the same of Reuben Pedley, who used to have two fine and loving parents, but only briefly, when he was a baby, and who in elementary school had been considered an excellent student but in middle school had faded into the walls.

Eleven years had passed since the factory accident that left Reuben without a father and his mother a young widow scrambling for work—eleven years, in other words, since his own promising star had begun to fall. And though in reality he was as loved and cared for as any child could hope to be, anyone who followed him through his days might well have believed otherwise. Especially on a day like today.

Reuben exited his shabby high-rise apartment building in the usual manner: He bypassed the elevator and stole down the rarely used stairwell, descending unseen all the way past the lobby to the basement, where he slipped out of a storage-room window. The young building manager kept that window slightly ajar to accommodate the comings and goings of a certain alley cat she hoped to tame, enticing it with bowls of food and water. She wasn't supposed to be doing that, but no one knew about it except Reuben, and he certainly wasn't going to tell anyone. He wasn't supposed to be in the storage room in the first place. Besides, he liked the building manager and secretly wished her luck with the cat, though only in his mind, for she didn't know that he knew about it. She barely even knew he existed.

From his hidden vantage point in the window well, which was slightly below street level and encircled by an iron railing, Reuben confirmed that the alley behind the building was empty. With practiced ease, he climbed out of the window well, monkeyed up the railing, grabbed the lower rungs of the building's rusty fire escape, and swung out over empty space. He hit the ground at a trot. Today he wanted to strike out into new territory, and there was no time to waste. When they'd lived in the northern part of the Lower Downs,

Reuben had known the surrounding blocks as well as his own bedroom, but then they'd had to move south, and despite having lived here a year, his mental map remained incomplete.

Of all the city's depressed and depressing neighborhoods, the Lower Downs was considered the worst. Many of its old buildings were abandoned; others seemed permanently under repair. Its backstreets and alleys were marked by missing shutters, tilted light poles, broken gates and railings, fences with gaps in them. The Lower Downs, in other words, was perfect for any boy who wanted to explore and to hide.

Reuben was just such a boy. In fact, exploring and hiding were almost all he ever did. He shinned up the tilted light poles and dropped behind fences; he slipped behind the busted shutters and through the broken windows; he found his way into cramped spaces and high places, into spots where no one would ever think to look. This was how he spent his solitary days.

It never occurred to him to be afraid. Even here in the Lower Downs, there was very little crime on the streets of New Umbra, at least not the sort you could easily see. Vandals and pickpockets were rare, muggers and car thieves unheard of. Everyone knew that. The Directions took care of all that business. Nobody crossed the Directions, not even the police.

Because the Directions worked for The Smoke.

Reuben headed south, moving from alley to alley, keeping close to the buildings and ducking beneath windows. He paused at every corner, first listening, then peering around it.

He was only a few blocks off the neighborhood's main thoroughfare and could hear some early-morning traffic there, but the alleys and backstreets were dead.

About ten blocks south, Reuben ventured into new territory. He was already well beyond his bounds: His mom had given him permission to walk to the community center and the branch library—both within a few blocks of their apartment—but that was all. And so he kept these wanderings of his a secret.

Despite her excessive caution, his mom was something else, and Reuben knew it. He wouldn't have traded her for half a dozen moms with better jobs and more money, and in fact had told her exactly that just the week before.

"Oh my goodness, Reuben, that is so sweet," she'd said, pretending to wipe tears from her eyes. "I hope you know that I probably wouldn't trade you, either. Not for half a dozen boys or even a whole dozen."

"*Probably?*"

"Almost certainly," she'd said, squeezing his hand as if to reassure him.

That was what his mom was like. Their conversations were usually the best part of his day.

Crossing an empty street, Reuben made his habitual rapid inventory of potential hiding places: a shady corner between a building's front steps and street-facing wall; a pile of broken furniture that someone had hauled to the curb; a window well with no protective railing. But none of these places was within easy reach, when, just as he attained the far curb, a door opened in a building down the block.

Reuben abruptly sat on the curb and watched the door. He held perfectly still as an old man in pajamas stepped outside and checked the sky, sniffing with evident satisfaction and glancing up and down the street before going back in. The old man never saw the small brown-haired boy watching him from the curb.

Reuben rose and moved on, quietly triumphant. He preferred bona fide hiding places when he could find them, but there was nothing quite like hiding in plain sight. Sometimes people saw you and then instantly forgot you, because you were just a random kid, doing nothing. As long as you didn't look lost, anxious, or interesting, you might as well be a trash can or a stunted tree, part of the city landscape. Reuben considered such encounters successes, too. But to go completely unnoticed on an otherwise empty street was almost impossible, and therefore superior. He was reliving the moment in his mind, exulting in the memory of the old man's eyes passing right over him without registering his presence—not once but twice!—when he came upon the narrowest alley he'd ever seen, and made his big mistake.

It was the narrowness that tempted him. The brick walls of the abandoned buildings were so close to each other, Reuben saw at once how he might scale them. By leaning forward and pressing his palms against one, then lifting his feet behind him and pressing them against the other, he could hold himself up, suspended above the alley floor. Then, by moving one hand higher, then the other, then doing the same with his feet, he could work his way upward. It would be like walking backward into the sky.

No sooner had he imagined it than Reuben knew he had to try it. Glancing around to ensure he was unobserved, he moved deeper into the alley. He could see a ledge high above him—probably too high to reach, but it gave him something to shoot for, at any rate.

He started out slowly, then gained momentum as he found his rhythm. Hand over hand, foot over foot, smoothly and steadily. Now he was fifteen feet up, now twenty, and still he climbed. Craning his head around, Reuben saw the ledge not too far above him. Unfortunately, he also saw how difficult it would be to climb onto it—his position was all wrong. He frowned. What had he been thinking? He didn't dare try such a risky maneuver, not at that height. He'd be a fool to chance it.

That was when Reuben felt his arms begin to tremble and realized, with horror, that he had made a terrible mistake.

He hadn't anticipated how drastically his arms would tire, nor how abruptly. It seemed to happen all at once, without warning. Now, looking at the alley floor far below him, Reuben became sickeningly aware of how high he had actually climbed. At least thirty feet, maybe more. The way his arms felt, there was no way he'd make it back to the ground safely. He probably couldn't even get back down to twenty feet.

Thus the action he'd just rejected as being foolishly dangerous suddenly became the only choice left to him, the only hope he had. He had to make the ledge, and by some miracle he had to get himself onto it.

With a whimper of panic, Reuben resumed his climbing. The trembling in his arms grew worse. He could no longer see the grimy, broken pavement of the alley floor below. His vision was blurred by sweat, which had trickled into his eyes and couldn't be wiped away. He was burning up on the inside but weirdly cold on the outside, like a furnace encased in ice; the alley's quirky cross breezes were cooling his sweat-slick skin. Beads of perspiration dripped from his nose and blew away.

In desperate silence he pressed upward. He heard the wind fluttering in his ears, the scrape of his shoe soles against brick, his own labored breath, and that was all. He was so high up, and so quietly intent on climbing, that had any passersby glanced down that narrow alley they'd have noticed nothing unusual. Certainly none would have guessed that an eleven-year-old boy was stretched out high above them, fearing for his life.

As it happened, there were no passersby to see Reuben finally come to the ledge, or to note the terrible moment when he made his fateful lunge, or to watch him struggle for an agonizingly long time to heave himself up, his shoes slipping and scraping, his face purple with strain. No one was around to hear Reuben's gasps and sobs of exhaustion and relief when at last he lay on that narrow ledge—heedless, for the moment, of his bruised arms and raw fingertips. If any passersby had been near enough to hear anything, it would have been only the clatter of startled pigeons rising away above the rooftops. But in the city this was no unusual sound, and without a thought they would have gone on with their lives, reflecting upon their own problems and wondering what to do.

Reuben lay with his face pressed against the cement ledge as if kissing it, which indeed he felt like doing. He felt such immense gratitude for its existence, for its solidity beneath him. After his pulse settled and his breath returned, he rose very cautiously into a sitting position, his back against brick, his legs dangling at the knees. With his shirt he dried his eyes as best he could, wincing a little from the smarting in his scraped fingertips. His every movement was calculated and slow. He was still in a dangerous predicament.

The ledge was keeping Reuben safe for the time being, but it was only a ledge, spattered here and there with pigeon droppings.

When Reuben tried to look up, the wind whipped his hair into his eyes; to keep them clear he had to cup his hands like pretend binoculars. The rooftop seemed miles above him, and might as well have been. Beyond it the early-morning sky was blue as a robin's egg. A perfect summer morning to have gotten stuck on a ledge in a deserted alley.

"Well done, Reuben," he muttered. "Brilliant."

He knew he couldn't get back down the same way he'd come up. He would have to edge around to the back of the building and hope for a fire escape. Otherwise his only option was to follow the ledge around to the street side, try to get in through one of the windows there. If he was lucky, perhaps no one would spot him. But if he couldn't get in, he would have to shout for help. Reuben imagined the fire truck's siren, the fierce disapproval on the firefighters' faces, the gathering crowd—all of it terrible to contemplate, and none of it even half as bad as facing his mom would be.

His mom, who thought he was safe at home in their apartment, reading a book or watching TV or maybe even back in bed. His mom, who even now was on her way to slice and weigh fish at the market, her first and least favorite work shift of the day. His mom, who had never remarried, who had no family, no boyfriend, no time to make friends—meaning Reuben was all she had, Reuben the reason she worked two jobs, Reuben the person for whom she did everything in her life.

His mom, who would not be pleased.

"Oh, let there be a fire escape," Reuben breathed. "Oh, please." Swiveling his eyes to his left, he studied the precious, narrow strip of cement keeping him aloft and alive. It appeared sound enough, no obvious deterioration. A brown crust of bread lay nearby (probably some pigeon's breakfast that he'd rudely interrupted), but that was all—no broken glass or other hazards. His path looked clear.

Reuben began shifting himself sideways, moving left, toward the back of the building. He kept his shoulder blades pressed against the brick wall behind him, his eyes fixed straight ahead at the featureless wall of the building opposite him, just a couple of yards away. He tried very hard not to imagine the dizzying drop below him.

He had progressed a few feet when his hand came down on the crust of bread. Without thinking, he attempted to brush it away. It seemed to be stuck. Glancing down now,

Reuben discovered that the bread crust was actually a scrap of leather, and that it was not in fact resting on the ledge but poking out of the bricks just above it. What in the world? Why would this scrap of leather have been mortared into the wall where no one would ever see it? Was it some kind of secret sign?

Reuben pinched the scrap awkwardly between two knuckles and tugged. It yielded slightly, revealing more leather, and through his fingers he felt an unseen shifting of stubborn dirt or debris, like when he pulled weeds from sidewalk cracks. He tugged again, and a few loose bits of broken brick fell onto the ledge, revealing a small hole in the wall. The brick pieces appeared to have been packed into it.

Reuben took a firmer grip on the leather and gave another tug. More bits of brick came loose. The scrap of leather turned out to be the end of a short strap, which in turn was connected to a dusty leather pouch. Carefully he drew the pouch from the hole and up into his lap.

Not a secret sign. A secret *thing*.

He should wait to open it, he knew. It would be far easier, far wiser to do it after he was safely on the ground.

Reuben stared at the pouch in his lap. "Or you could just be extra careful," he whispered.

With slow, deliberate movements, Reuben brushed away some of the brick dust. The pouch was obviously old, its leather worn and scarred. It was fastened with a rusted buckle that came right off in his hand, along with a rotted bit of strap. He set these aside and opened the pouch. Inside was a small, surprisingly heavy object wrapped in a plastic bread sack. It was bundled up in yet another wrapping, this one of stiff canvas. Whatever it was, its owner had taken great pains to keep it safe and dry.

Reuben unbundled the wrappings to reveal a handsome wooden case, dark brown with streaks of black. Its hinged lid was held closed by a gray metal clasp, the sort that could be secured with a little padlock. There was no lock, though; all Reuben had to do was turn it. He hesitated, wondering what he was about to find. Then he turned the clasp and felt something give. The lid opened with a squeak.

Inside the case were two velvet-lined compartments, both shaped to fit exactly the objects they contained. One of the objects was a small, delicate key with an ornate bow; the other appeared to be a simple metal sphere. Both had the dark coppery color of an old penny and yet, at the same time, the bright sheen of a brand-new one. They were made of a metal Reuben had never seen before. Something like copper or brass, but not exactly either.

Reuben very carefully lifted the sphere from its velvet compartment. It felt as heavy as a billiard ball, though it was not quite as large as one. He turned it in his hands, gazing at it in wonder. What was it? He'd expected that the key would be needed to open it, but there was no keyhole. Looking more closely, he noticed a seam, scarcely wider than a line of thread, circling the middle of the sphere like the equator on a globe, dividing it into two hemispheres.

"So you *can* open it," he murmured.

Holding the sphere in his left hand, Reuben tried, gently, to open it with the other. He used the same gesture that he had seen in countless silly old movies he'd watched with his mom, in which hopeful men drop to a knee and open tiny velvet-covered boxes, proposing marriage with a ring. He imagined he felt every bit as hopeful and excited as those men were supposed to be.

The two hemispheres parted easily, smoothly, without a sound, as if their hidden hinge had been carefully oiled not a minute before. The interior of one hemisphere was hollow, like an empty bowl. It served as the cover for the other hemisphere, which contained the face of a clock. What Reuben had found, evidently, was a pocket watch.

And yet it was a pocket watch of a kind he'd never seen, to say nothing of its quality. Its face was made of a lustrous white material, perhaps ivory, and the hour hand and the Roman numerals around the dial all gleamed black. It was missing a minute hand, but otherwise the parts were all in such perfect condition that the watch might have been constructed that very morning, though Reuben felt sure it was an antique. Indeed, the watch seemed so perfect—so perfect, so unusual, so beautiful—that he almost expected it to show the correct time. But the hour hand was frozen at just before twelve, and when he held the watch to his ear, he heard no telltale ticking.

The key! he thought. Reuben's mom had a music box that his father had given her before Reuben was born. You had to wind it up with a key. It must be the same with this watch.

A closer inspection revealed a tiny, star-shaped hole in the center of the watch face. Could that be a keyhole?

A glance confirmed his suspicion. The key lacked the large rectangular teeth of normal old keys, but rather tapered to a narrow, star-shaped end, small enough to insert into the hole. This was the watch's winding key, no question.

Reuben was tempted. He even laid a finger on the key in its snug compartment. But once again a warning voice was sounding in his head, and this time he listened to it. He might fumble the key, drop it, lose it. Better to wait until he was in a safe place. Better, for once, to resist his impulses. This was far too important.

Reluctantly he closed the watch cover and put the watch back inside the case. He was about to close the lid when he noticed an inscription on its interior: *Property of P. Wm. Light.*

"P. William Light," Reuben muttered, gazing at the name. "So this once belonged to you, whoever you were." He closed the lid, fastened the clasp. "*When*ever you were." For whoever P. William Light was, Reuben felt sure that he'd stopped walking the earth long ago.

Reuben rebundled the case and tucked it back inside the pouch, then stuffed the pouch into the waist of his shorts— no small feat in such an awkward, precarious position. Now he was ready to move.

He took a last look at the hole in the wall, wondering how long the watch had been in there, and who had left it behind. He no longer believed it had anything to do with a bricklayer. No, the watch had been put there by someone like him, someone who found places that were secret to others. It could only have been *found* by someone like him, as well, which made its discovery feel very much like fate.

Just don't blow it by falling, Reuben thought. *Boy finds treasure, plummets to his death. Great story.*

It was with exceeding caution, therefore, that he began to inch sideways along the ledge. A wearisome half hour later he reached the back of the building, only to find that there was no fire escape. No windows, either, and no more ledge.

"Seriously?" Reuben muttered. He felt like banging his head against the brick.

His bottom and the backs of his thighs were aching and tingling. Another hour on this ledge and he'd be in agony. Yet it would take at least that long to reach the front of the building, and possibly longer.

There was, however, a rusty old drainpipe plunging down along the building's corner. Reuben eyed it, then grabbed it with his left hand and tried to shake it. The pipe seemed firmly secured to the wall, and there was enough room between metal and brick for him to get his hands behind it. He peered down along the length of the pipe; it seemed to be intact. He had climbed drainpipes before. Never at anywhere near this height, but if he didn't *think* about the height…

It was as if someone else made the decision for him. Suddenly gathering himself, Reuben reached across his body with his right hand, grabbed the pipe, and swung off the ledge. His stomach wanted to stay behind; he felt it climbing up inside him. Now that he'd acted, the fear was back in full force.

Clenching his jaw, breathing fiercely through his nose, Reuben ignored the lurching inside him and got his feet set. Then, hand under hand, step after step, he began his descent. He went as quickly as he could, knowing he would soon tire. The pipe uttered an initial groan of protest against his weight, then fell silent.

Flakes of rust broke off beneath his fingers and scattered in the wind. Sweat trickled into his eyes again, then into his mouth. He blew it from his nose. Every single part of him seemed to hurt. He didn't dare look down. He concentrated on his hands and his feet and nothing else.

And then the heel of his right foot struck something beneath him, and Reuben looked down to discover that it was the ground. Slowly, almost disbelieving, he set his other foot down. He let go of the pipe. His fingers automatically curled up like claws. He flexed them painfully, wiped his face with his shirt, and looked up at the ledge, so high above him. Had he actually climbed all the way up *there*? He felt dazed, as if in a dream.

Reuben withdrew the pouch from the waistband of his shorts and gazed at it. This was no dream. He began to walk stiffly along the narrow alley, heading for the street. One step, three steps, a dozen—and then he felt the thrill begin to surge through him. He'd made it! He was alive! He'd taken a terrible risk, but he'd come back with treasure. It seemed like the end of an adventure, and yet somehow Reuben knew— he just *knew*—that it was only the beginning.